VAULT

PUBLISHER
DAMIAN A. WASSEL

EDITOR IN CHIEF
ADRIAN F. WASSEL

SENIOR ARTIST
NATHAN C. GOODEN

MANAGING EDITOR
REBECCA TAYLOR

SALES & MARKETING, DIRECT MARKET
DAVID DISSANAYAKE

SALES & MARKETING, BOOK TRADE
SYNDEE BARWICK

PRODUCTION MANAGER
IAN BALDESSARI

EVP BRANDING & DESIGN
TIM DANIEL

PRINCIPAL
DAMIAN A. WASSEL, SR.

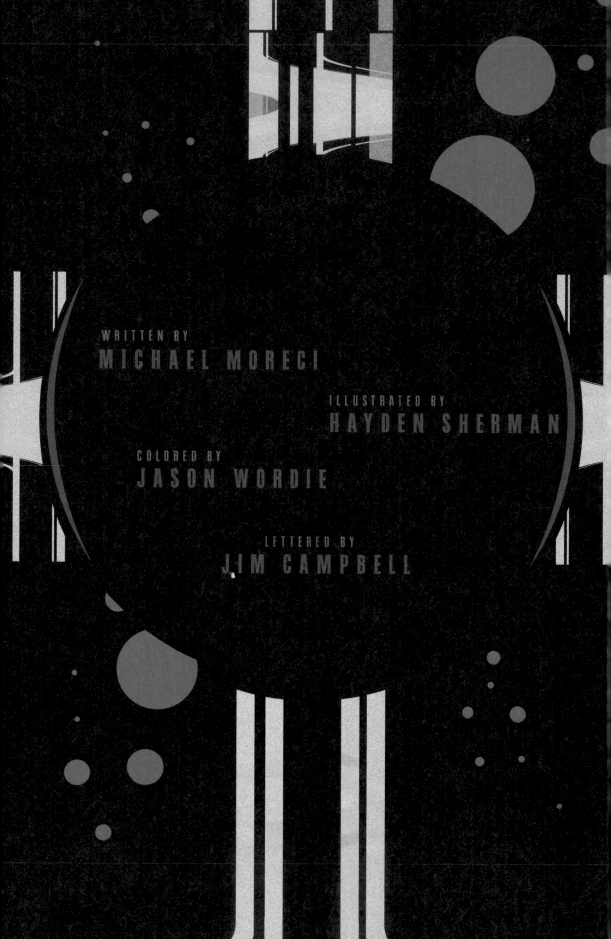

WRITTEN BY
MICHAEL MORECI

ILLUSTRATED BY
HAYDEN SHERMAN

COLORED BY
JASON WORDIE

LETTERED BY
JIM CAMPBELL

VAULT COMICS PRESENTS

WASTED SPACE

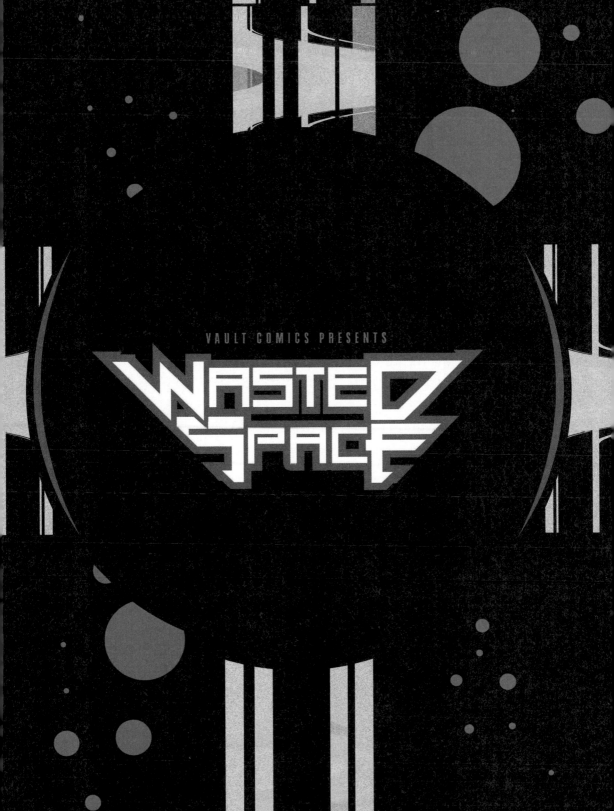

CHAPTER TWENTYONE

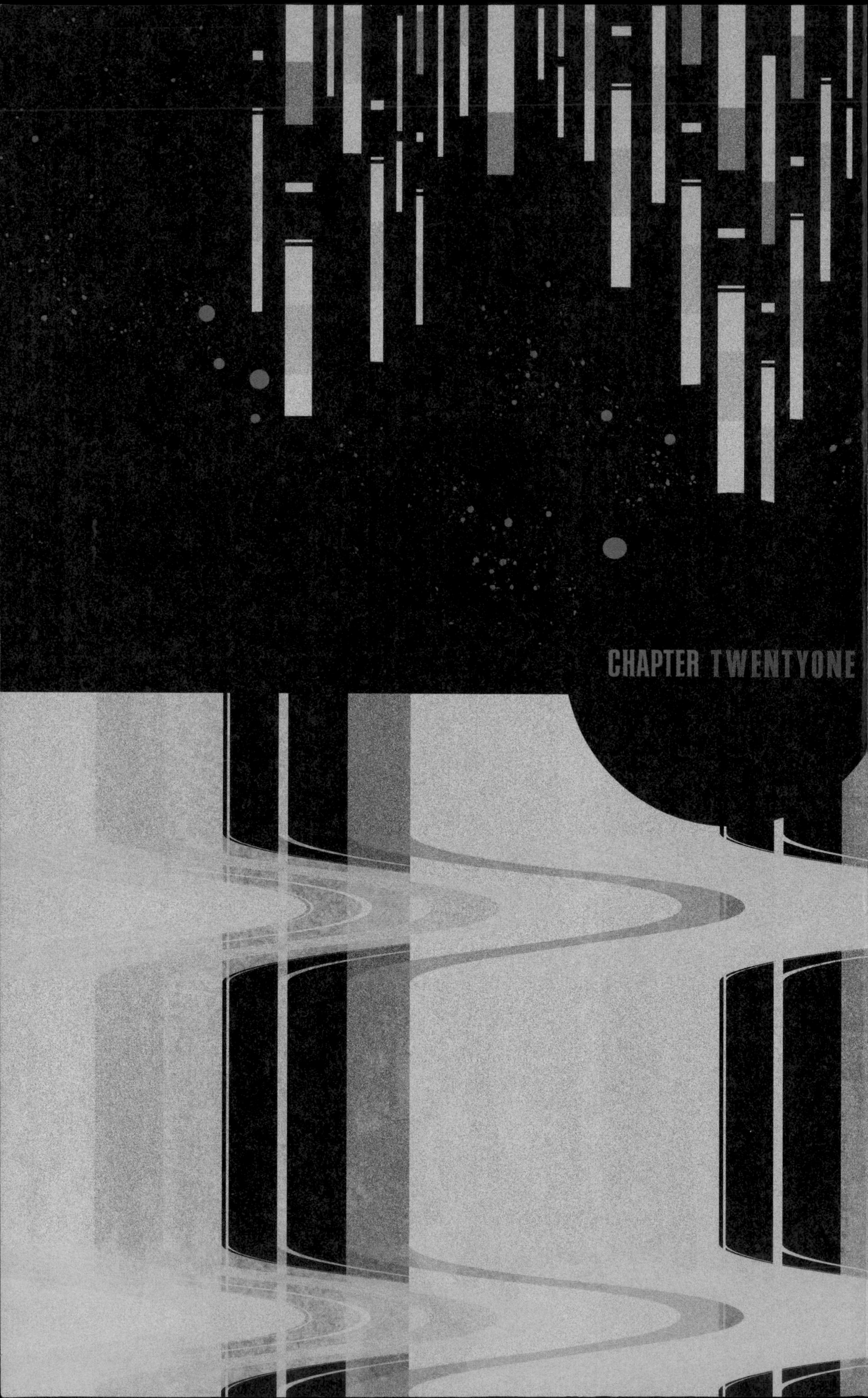

GET HIM. GET THE INTRUDER.
CHOOM
CHOOM
CHOOM
SHIT!
DAMN IT! YOU DIDN'T HAVE TO ACTIVATE THE BOSS BOTS! I JUST ASKED A SIMPLE QUESTION!
And I'm giving you your answer.
On your left. Pull your trigger...
BLAM
...now.
AAAAAAAAHHHHH!
HOLY SHIT! WHAT THE HELL, MAN?!

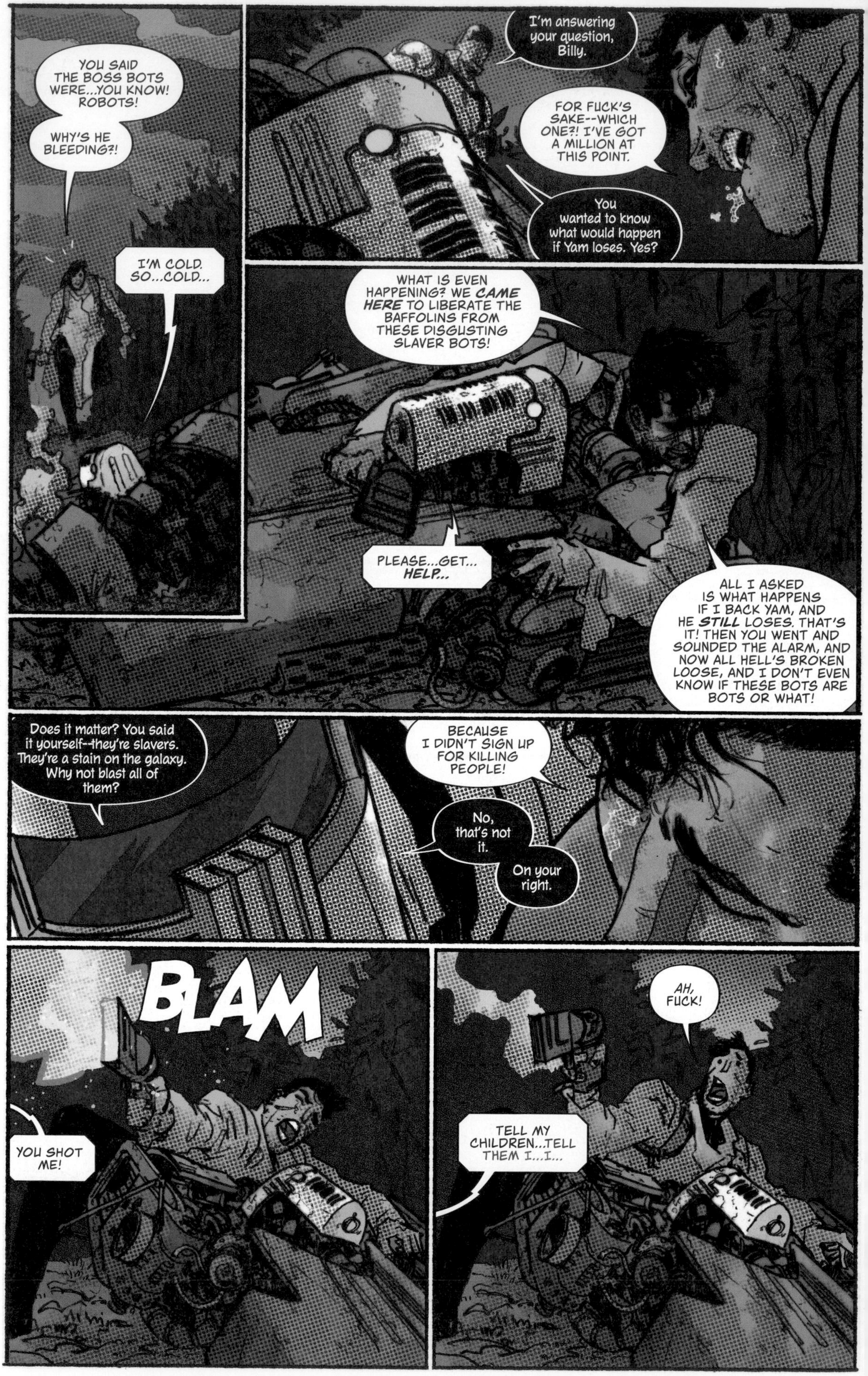
YOU SAID THE BOSS BOTS WERE...YOU KNOW! ROBOTS!
WHY'S HE BLEEDING?!
I'M COLD. SO...COLD...
I'm answering your question, Billy.
FOR FUCK'S SAKE--WHICH ONE?! I'VE GOT A MILLION AT THIS POINT.
You wanted to know what would happen if Yam loses. Yes?
WHAT IS EVEN HAPPENING? WE CAME HERE TO LIBERATE THE BAFFOLINS FROM THESE DISGUSTING SLAVER BOTS!
PLEASE...GET... HELP...
ALL I ASKED IS WHAT HAPPENS IF I BACK YAM, AND HE STILL LOSES. THAT'S IT! THEN YOU WENT AND SOUNDED THE ALARM, AND NOW ALL HELL'S BROKEN LOOSE, AND I DON'T EVEN KNOW IF THESE BOTS ARE BOTS OR WHAT!
Does it matter? You said it yourself--they're slavers. They're a stain on the galaxy. Why not blast all of them?
BECAUSE I DIDN'T SIGN UP FOR KILLING PEOPLE!
No, that's not it.
On your right.
BLAM
YOU SHOT ME!
AH, FUCK!
TELL MY CHILDREN...TELL THEM I...I...

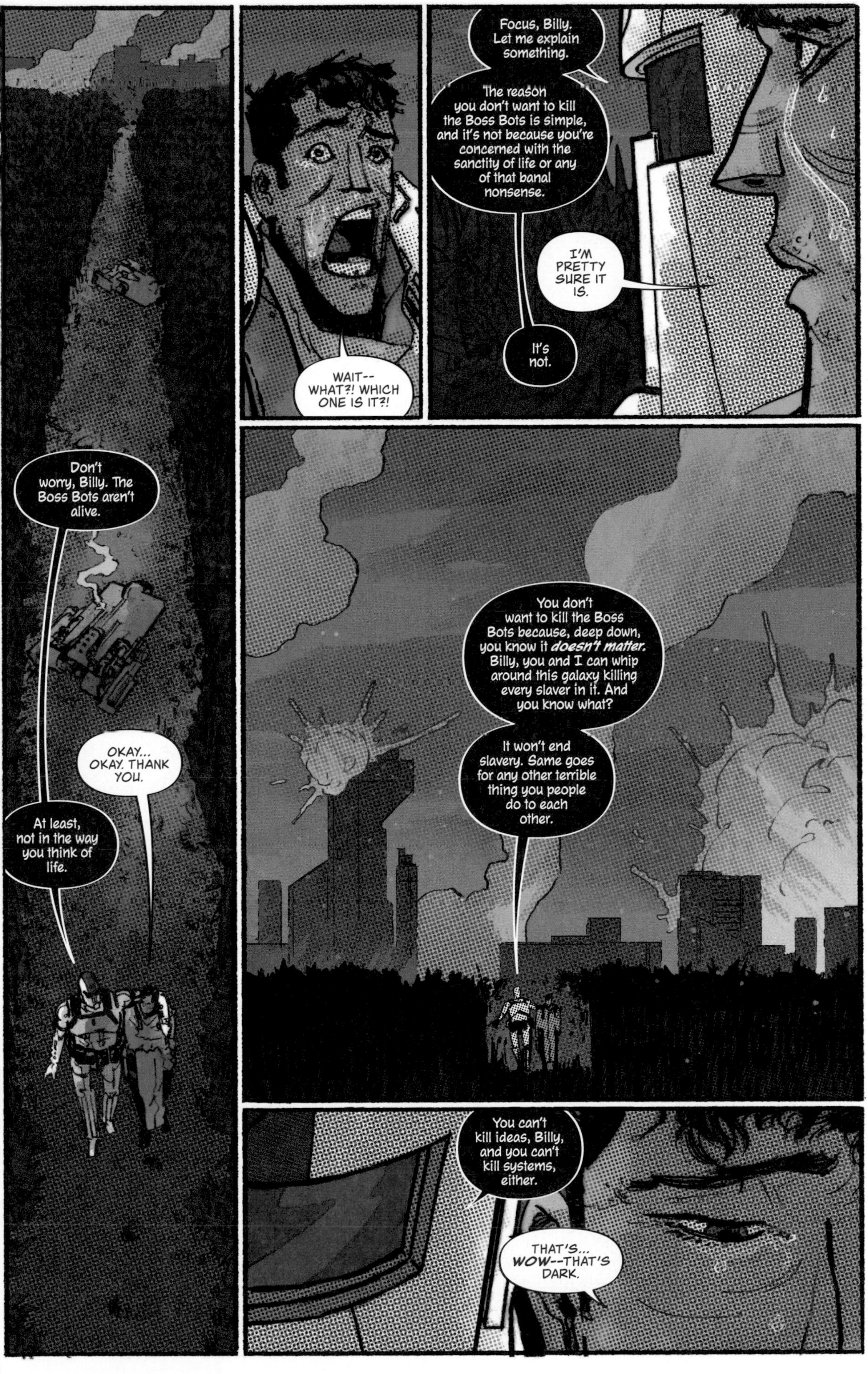

Focus, Billy. Let me explain something.
The reason you don't want to kill the Boss Bots is simple, and it's not because you're concerned with the sanctity of life or any of that banal nonsense.
I'M PRETTY SURE IT IS.
It's not.
WAIT-- WHAT?! WHICH ONE IS IT?!
Don't worry, Billy. The Boss Bots aren't alive.
OKAY... OKAY. THANK YOU.
At least, not in the way you think of life.
You don't want to kill the Boss Bots because, deep down, you know it doesn't matter. Billy, you and I can whip around this galaxy killing every slaver in it. And you know what?
It won't end slavery. Same goes for any other terrible thing you people do to each other.
You can't kill ideas, Billy, and you can't kill systems, either.
THAT'S... WOW--THAT'S DARK.

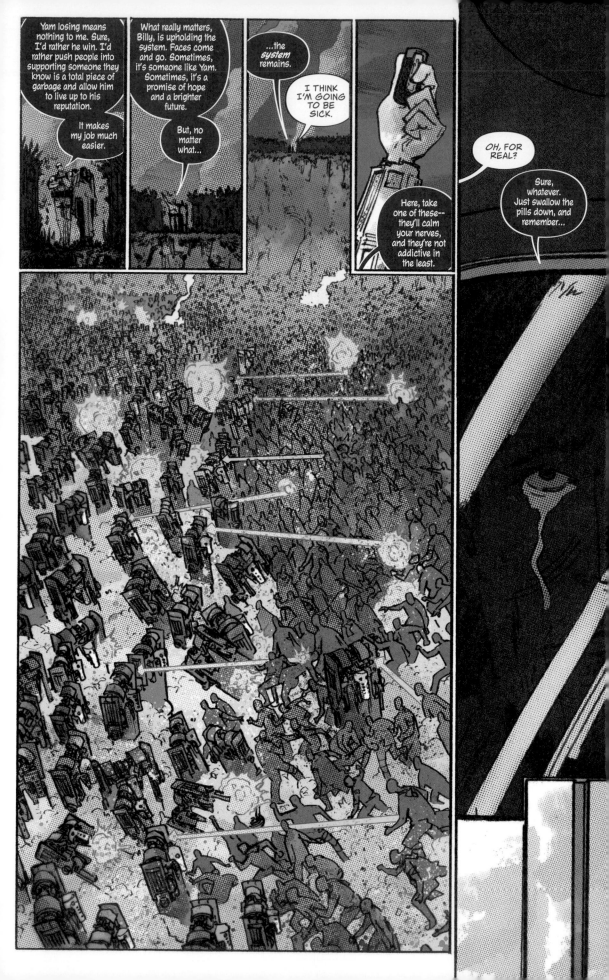

Yam losing means nothing to me. Sure, I'd rather he win. I'd rather push people into supporting someone they know is a total piece of garbage and allow him to live up to his reputation.

It makes my job much easier.

What really matters, Billy, is upholding the system. Faces come and go. Sometimes, it's someone like Yam. Sometimes, it's a promise of hope and a brighter future.

But, no matter what...

...the *system* remains.

I THINK I'M GOING TO BE SICK.

Here, take one of these-- they'll calm your nerves, and they're not addictive in the least.

OH, FOR REAL?

Sure, whatever. Just swallow the pills down, and remember...

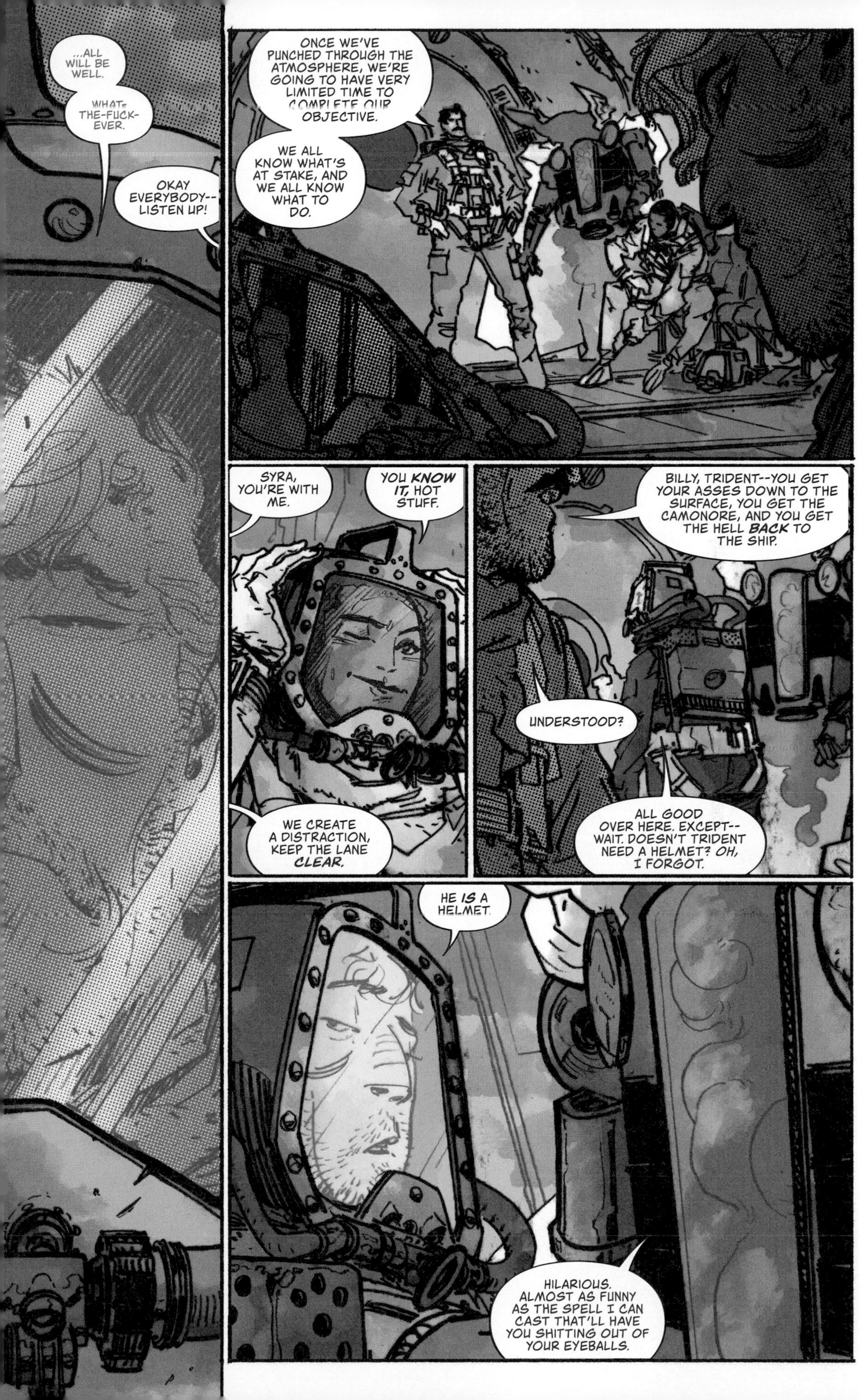

...ALL WILL BE WELL.
WHAT-THE-FUCK-EVER.
OKAY EVERYBODY--LISTEN UP!
ONCE WE'VE PUNCHED THROUGH THE ATMOSPHERE, WE'RE GOING TO HAVE VERY LIMITED TIME TO COMPLETE OUR OBJECTIVE.
WE ALL KNOW WHAT'S AT STAKE, AND WE ALL KNOW WHAT TO DO.
SYRA, YOU'RE WITH ME.
YOU KNOW IT, HOT STUFF.
WE CREATE A DISTRACTION, KEEP THE LANE CLEAR.
BILLY, TRIDENT--YOU GET YOUR ASSES DOWN TO THE SURFACE, YOU GET THE CAMONORE, AND YOU GET THE HELL BACK TO THE SHIP.
UNDERSTOOD?
ALL GOOD OVER HERE. EXCEPT--WAIT. DOESN'T TRIDENT NEED A HELMET? OH, I FORGOT.
HE IS A HELMET.
HILARIOUS. ALMOST AS FUNNY AS THE SPELL I CAN CAST THAT'LL HAVE YOU SHITTING OUT OF YOUR EYEBALLS.

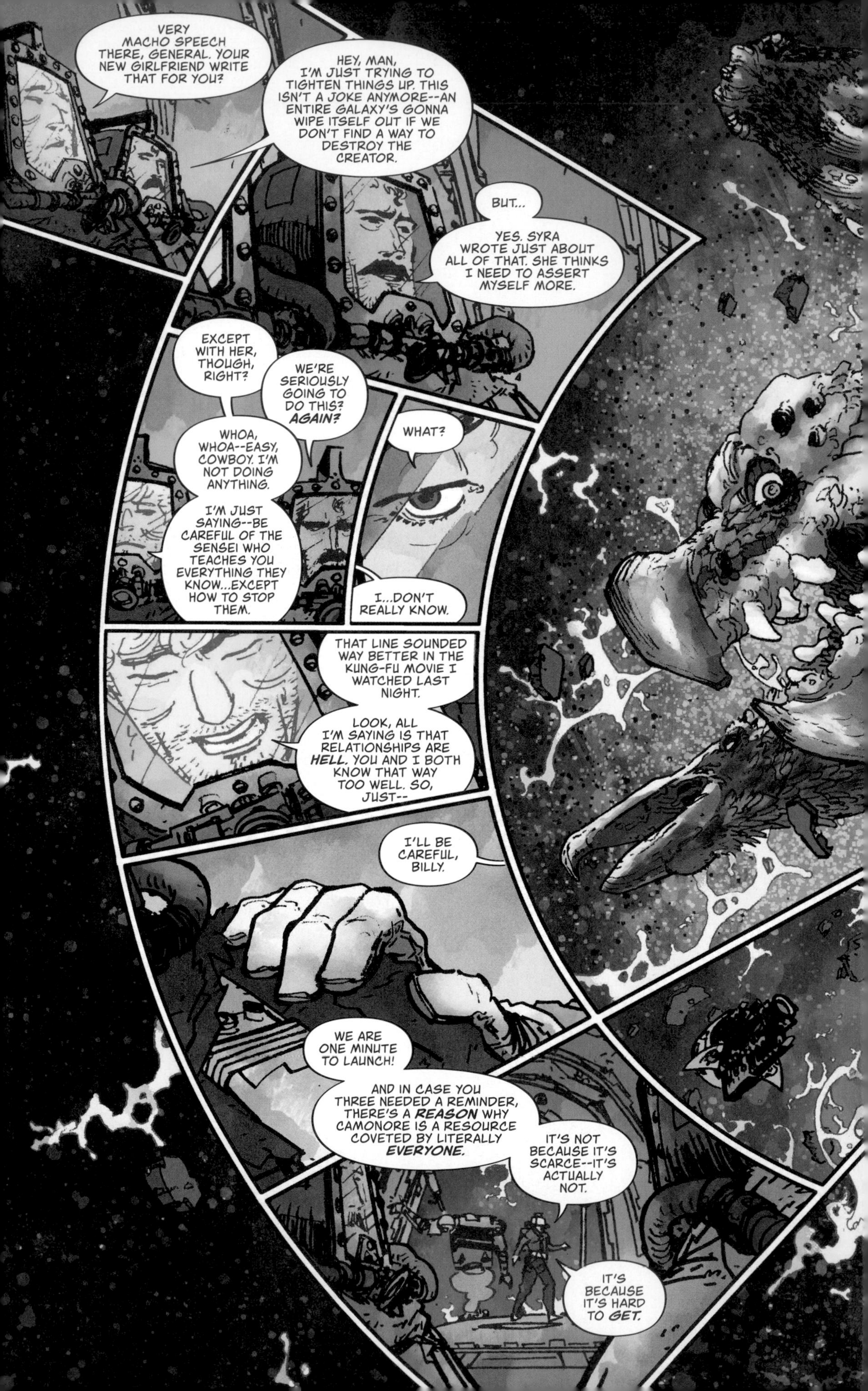
VERY MACHO SPEECH THERE, GENERAL. YOUR NEW GIRLFRIEND WRITE THAT FOR YOU?
HEY, MAN, I'M JUST TRYING TO TIGHTEN THINGS UP. THIS ISN'T A JOKE ANYMORE--AN ENTIRE GALAXY'S GONNA WIPE ITSELF OUT IF WE DON'T FIND A WAY TO DESTROY THE CREATOR.
BUT...
YES. SYRA WROTE JUST ABOUT ALL OF THAT. SHE THINKS I NEED TO ASSERT MYSELF MORE.
EXCEPT WITH HER, THOUGH, RIGHT?
WE'RE SERIOUSLY GOING TO DO THIS? AGAIN?
WHOA, WHOA--EASY, COWBOY. I'M NOT DOING ANYTHING.
I'M JUST SAYING--BE CAREFUL OF THE SENSEI WHO TEACHES YOU EVERYTHING THEY KNOW...EXCEPT HOW TO STOP THEM.
WHAT?
I...DON'T REALLY KNOW.
THAT LINE SOUNDED WAY BETTER IN THE KUNG-FU MOVIE I WATCHED LAST NIGHT.
LOOK, ALL I'M SAYING IS THAT RELATIONSHIPS ARE HELL. YOU AND I BOTH KNOW THAT WAY TOO WELL. SO, JUST--
I'LL BE CAREFUL, BILLY.
WE ARE ONE MINUTE TO LAUNCH!
AND IN CASE YOU THREE NEEDED A REMINDER, THERE'S A REASON WHY CAMONORE IS A RESOURCE COVETED BY LITERALLY EVERYONE.
IT'S NOT BECAUSE IT'S SCARCE--IT'S ACTUALLY NOT.
IT'S BECAUSE IT'S HARD TO GET.

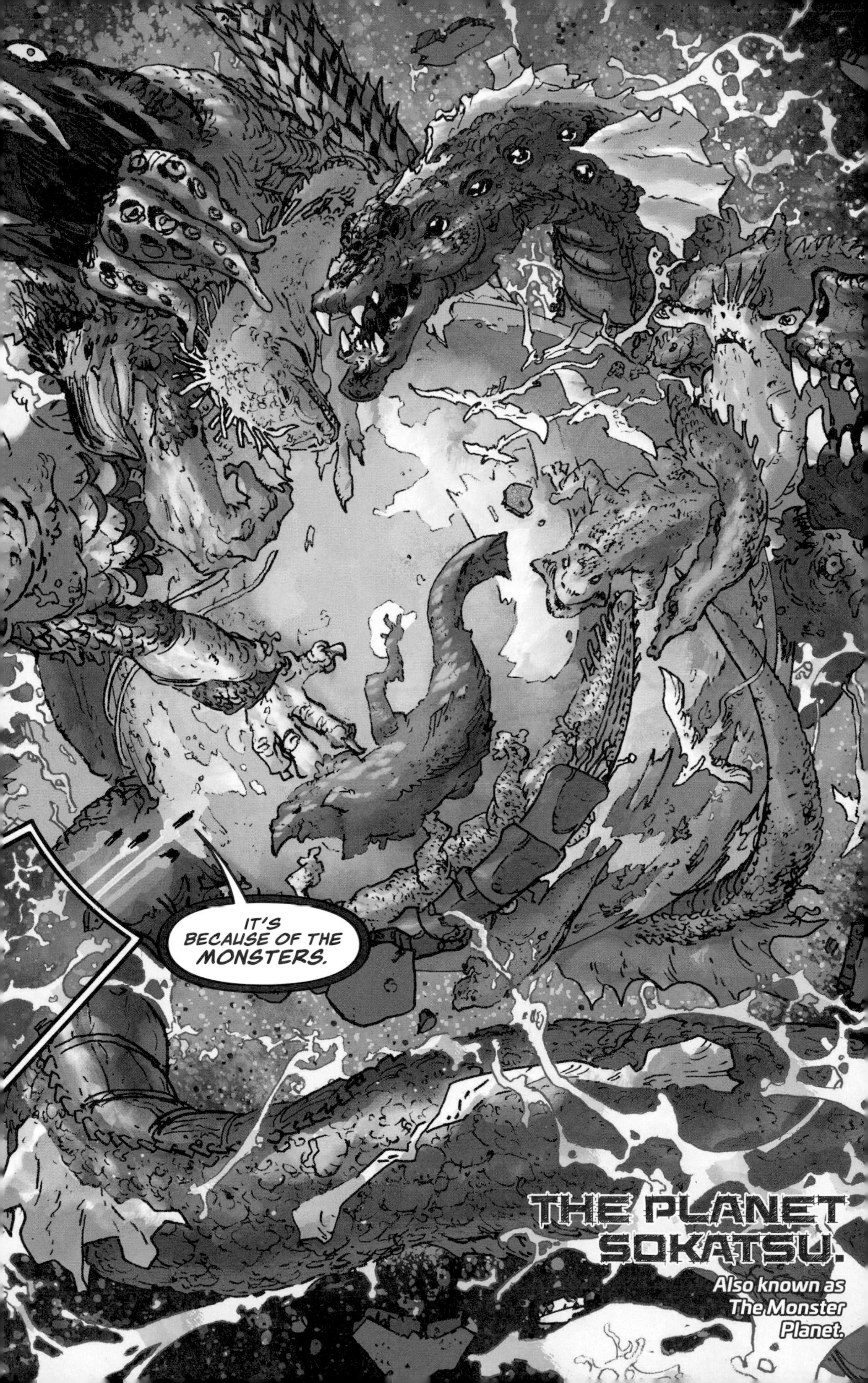
IT'S BECAUSE OF THE MONSTERS.
THE PLANET SOKATSU.
Also known as The Monster Planet.

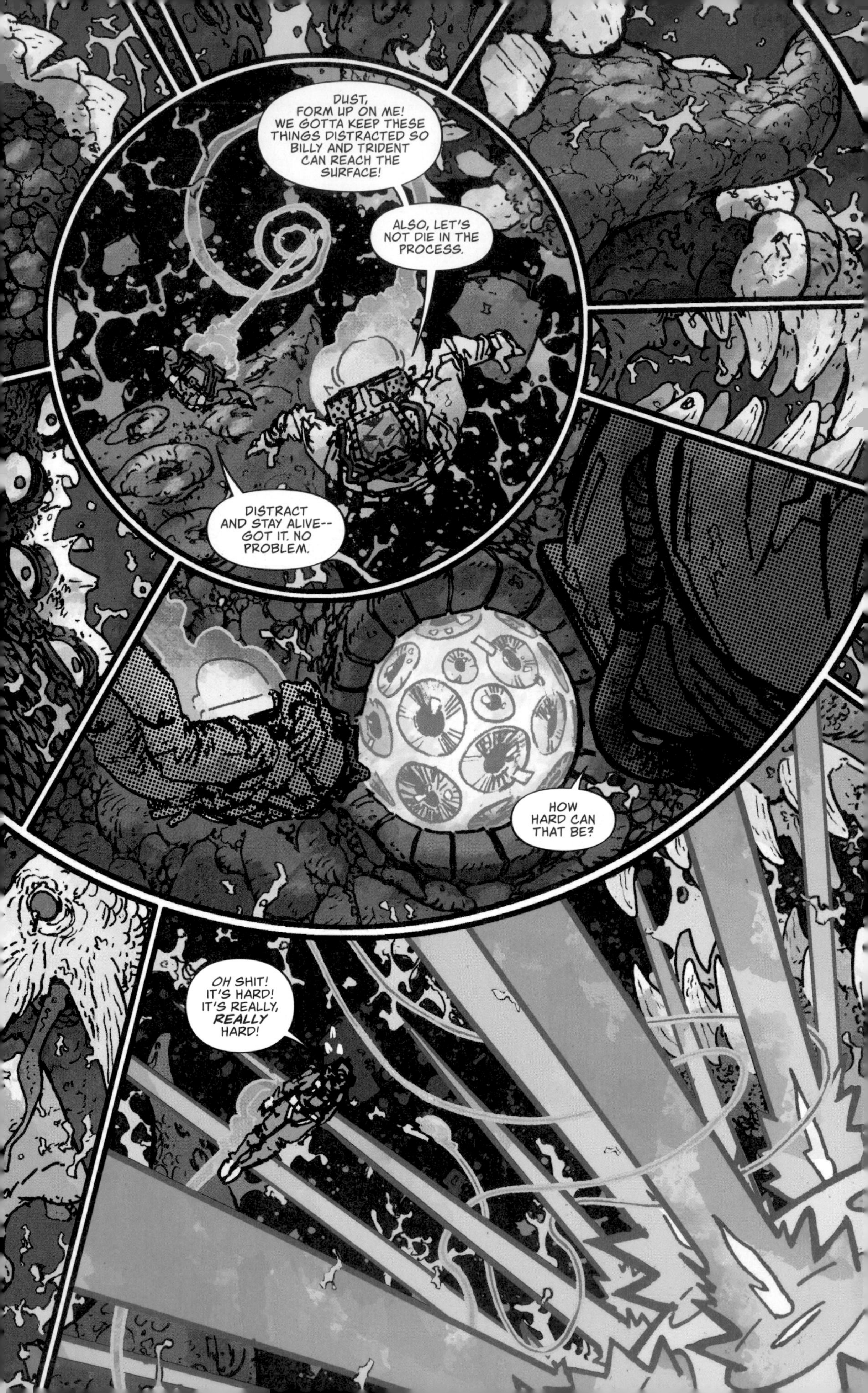
DUST, FORM UP ON ME! WE GOTTA KEEP THESE THINGS DISTRACTED SO BILLY AND TRIDENT CAN REACH THE SURFACE!
ALSO, LET'S NOT DIE IN THE PROCESS.
DISTRACT AND STAY ALIVE-- GOT IT. NO PROBLEM.
HOW HARD CAN THAT BE?
OH SHIT! IT'S HARD! IT'S REALLY, REALLY HARD!

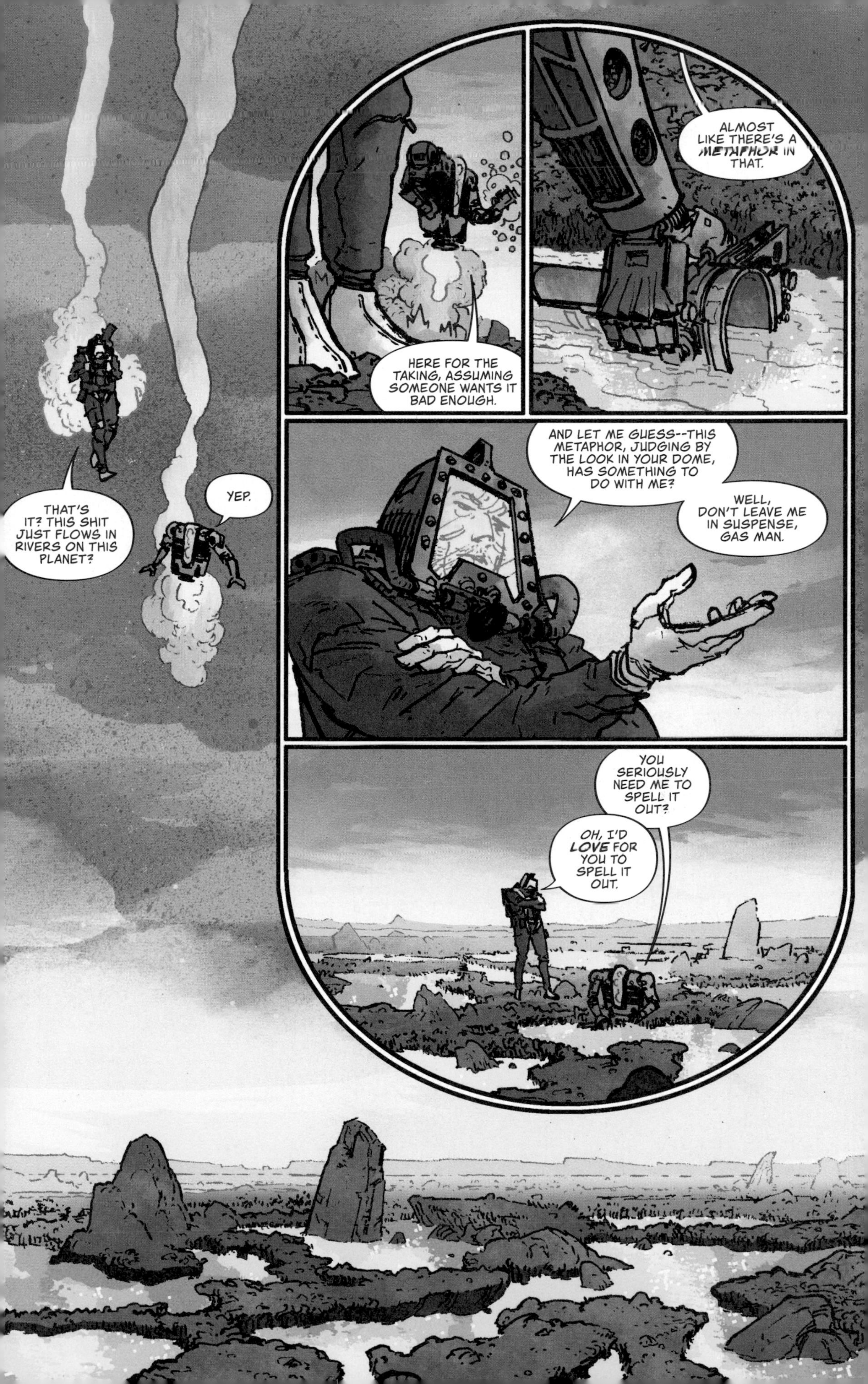
THAT'S IT? THIS SHIT JUST FLOWS IN RIVERS ON THIS PLANET?
YEP.
HERE FOR THE TAKING, ASSUMING SOMEONE WANTS IT BAD ENOUGH.
ALMOST LIKE THERE'S A METAPHOR IN THAT.
AND LET ME GUESS--THIS METAPHOR, JUDGING BY THE LOOK IN YOUR DOME, HAS SOMETHING TO DO WITH ME?
WELL, DON'T LEAVE ME IN SUSPENSE, GAS MAN.
YOU SERIOUSLY NEED ME TO SPELL IT OUT?
OH, I'D LOVE FOR YOU TO SPELL IT OUT.

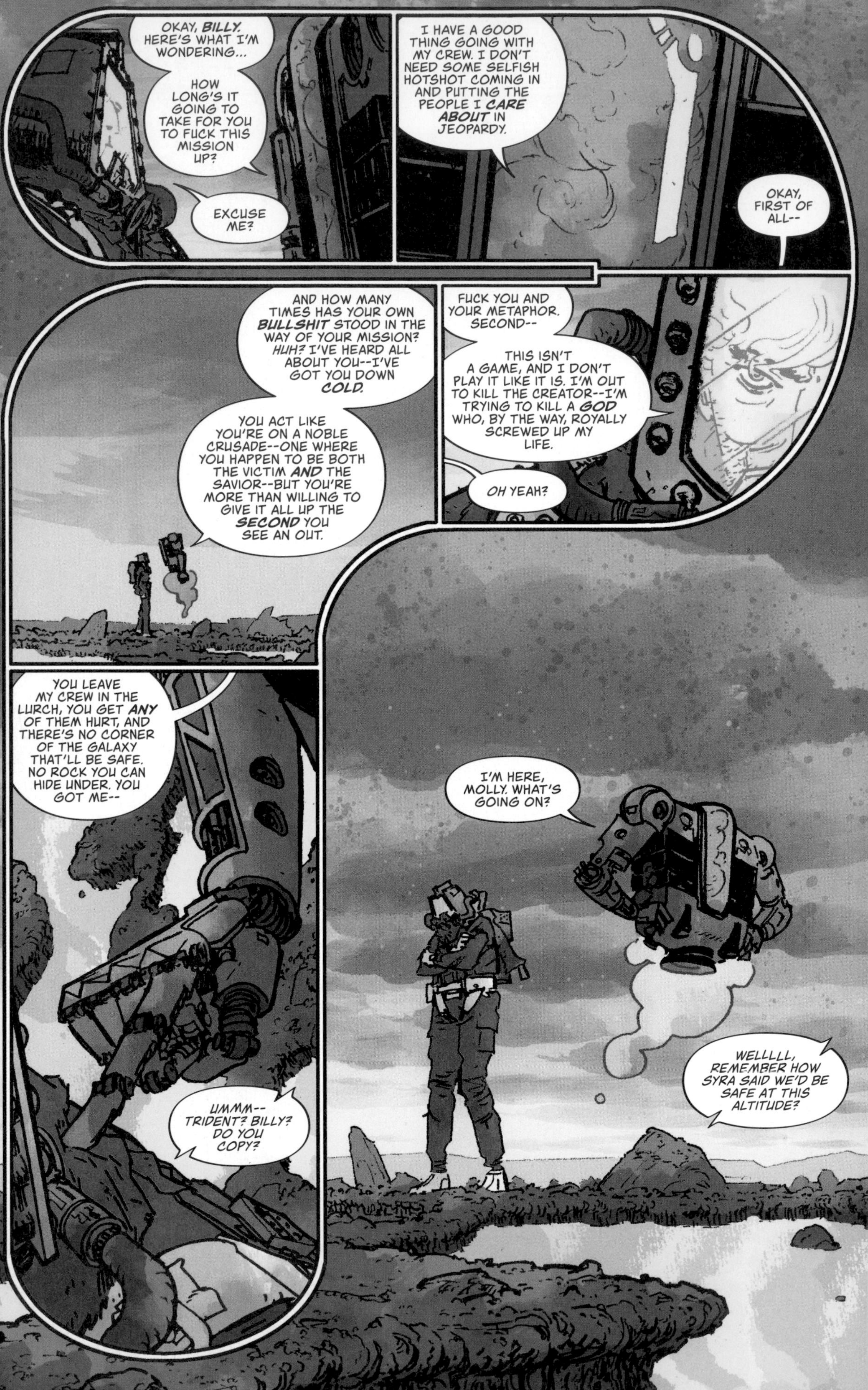
OKAY, BILLY. HERE'S WHAT I'M WONDERING...
HOW LONG'S IT GOING TO TAKE FOR YOU TO FUCK THIS MISSION UP?
EXCUSE ME?
I HAVE A GOOD THING GOING WITH MY CREW. I DON'T NEED SOME SELFISH HOTSHOT COMING IN AND PUTTING THE PEOPLE I CARE ABOUT IN JEOPARDY.
OKAY, FIRST OF ALL--
AND HOW MANY TIMES HAS YOUR OWN BULLSHIT STOOD IN THE WAY OF YOUR MISSION? HUH? I'VE HEARD ALL ABOUT YOU--I'VE GOT YOU DOWN COLD.
YOU ACT LIKE YOU'RE ON A NOBLE CRUSADE--ONE WHERE YOU HAPPEN TO BE BOTH THE VICTIM AND THE SAVIOR--BUT YOU'RE MORE THAN WILLING TO GIVE IT ALL UP THE SECOND YOU SEE AN OUT.
FUCK YOU AND YOUR METAPHOR. SECOND--
THIS ISN'T A GAME, AND I DON'T PLAY IT LIKE IT IS. I'M OUT TO KILL THE CREATOR--I'M TRYING TO KILL A GOD WHO, BY THE WAY, ROYALLY SCREWED UP MY LIFE.
OH YEAH?
YOU LEAVE MY CREW IN THE LURCH, YOU GET ANY OF THEM HURT, AND THERE'S NO CORNER OF THE GALAXY THAT'LL BE SAFE. NO ROCK YOU CAN HIDE UNDER. YOU GOT ME--
UMMM-- TRIDENT? BILLY? DO YOU COPY?
I'M HERE, MOLLY. WHAT'S GOING ON?
WELLLLL, REMEMBER HOW SYRA SAID WE'D BE SAFE AT THIS ALTITUDE?

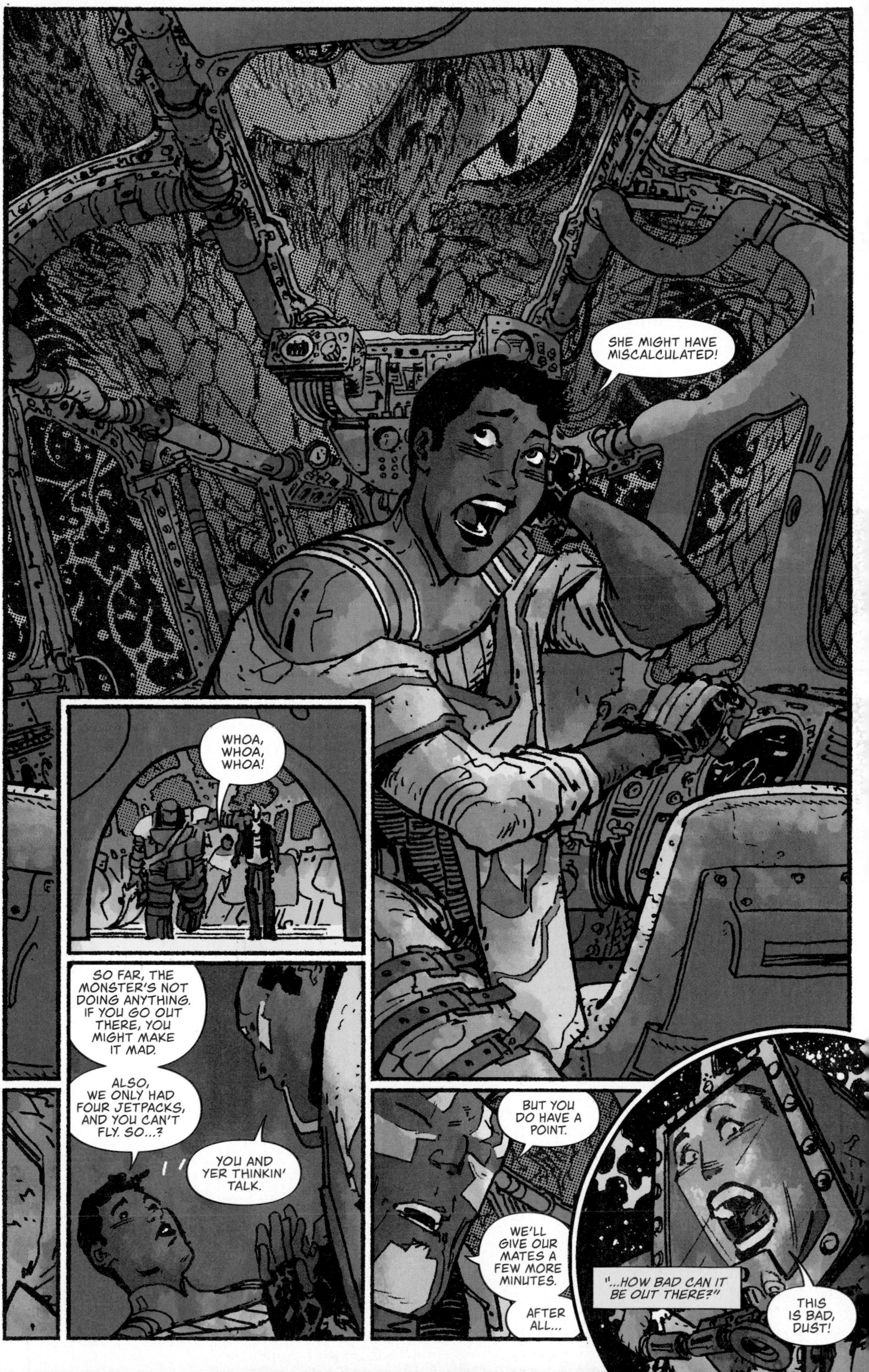
SHE MIGHT HAVE MISCALCULATED!
WHOA, WHOA, WHOA!
SO FAR, THE MONSTER'S NOT DOING ANYTHING. IF YOU GO OUT THERE, YOU MIGHT MAKE IT MAD.
ALSO, WE ONLY HAD FOUR JETPACKS, AND YOU CAN'T FLY. SO...?
YOU AND YER THINKIN' TALK.
BUT YOU DO HAVE A POINT.
WE'LL GIVE OUR MATES A FEW MORE MINUTES.
AFTER ALL...
"...HOW BAD CAN IT BE OUT THERE?"
THIS IS BAD, DUST!

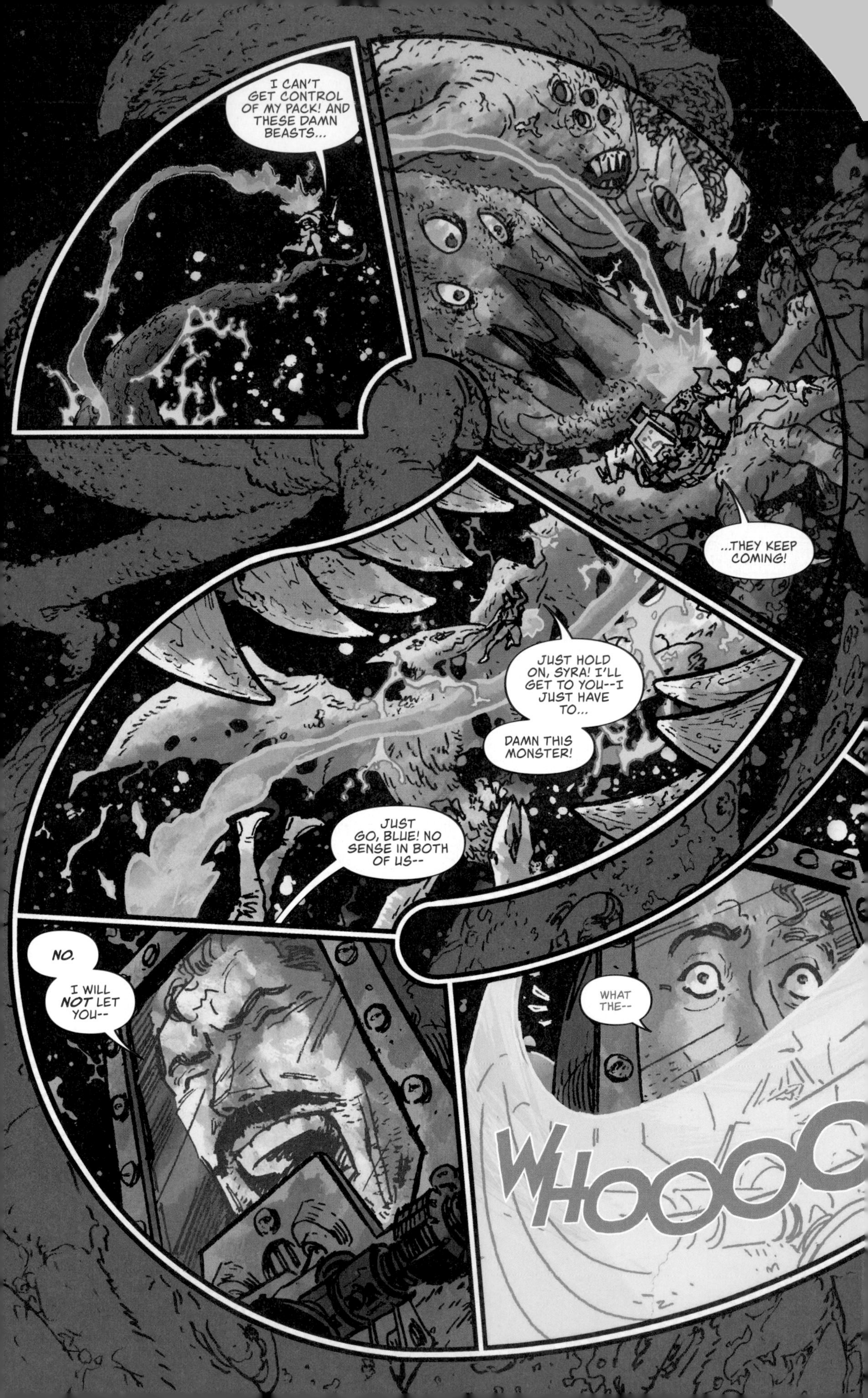
I CAN'T GET CONTROL OF MY PACK! AND THESE DAMN BEASTS...
...THEY KEEP COMING!
JUST HOLD ON, SYRA! I'LL GET TO YOU--I JUST HAVE TO...
DAMN THIS MONSTER!
JUST GO, BLUE! NO SENSE IN BOTH OF US--
NO.
I WILL NOT LET YOU--
WHAT THE--
WHOOOO

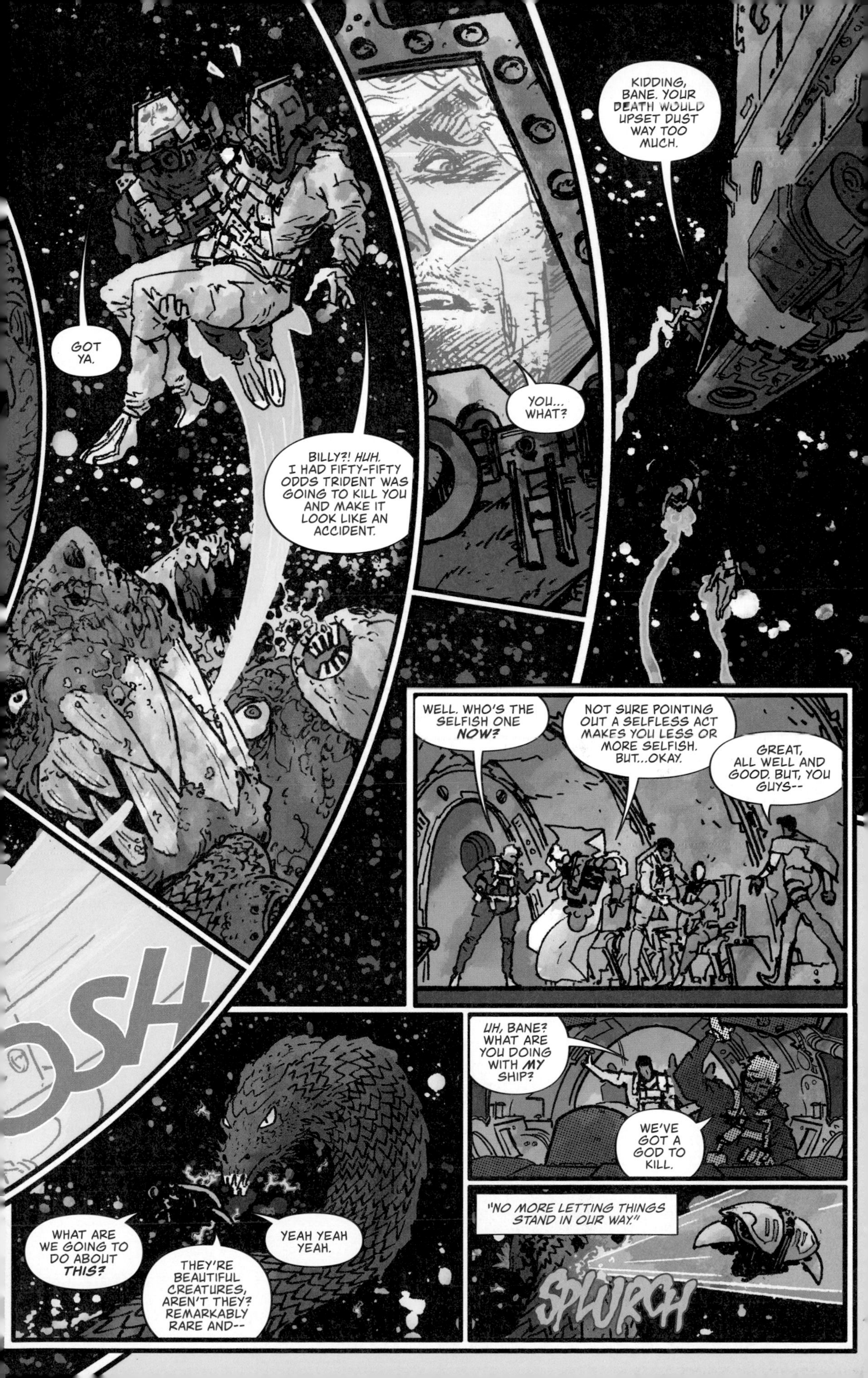
GOT YA.
BILLY?! *HUH.* I HAD FIFTY-FIFTY ODDS TRIDENT WAS GOING TO KILL YOU AND MAKE IT LOOK LIKE AN ACCIDENT.
YOU... WHAT?
KIDDING, BANE. YOUR DEATH WOULD UPSET DUST WAY TOO MUCH.
WELL. WHO'S THE SELFISH ONE *NOW?*
NOT SURE POINTING OUT A SELFLESS ACT MAKES YOU LESS OR MORE SELFISH. BUT...OKAY.
GREAT, ALL WELL AND GOOD. BUT, YOU GUYS--
OSH
UH, BANE? WHAT ARE YOU DOING WITH *MY* SHIP?
WE'VE GOT A GOD TO KILL.
WHAT ARE WE GOING TO DO ABOUT *THIS?*
YEAH YEAH YEAH.
THEY'RE BEAUTIFUL CREATURES, AREN'T THEY? REMARKABLY RARE AND--
"NO MORE LETTING THINGS STAND IN OUR WAY."
SPLURCH

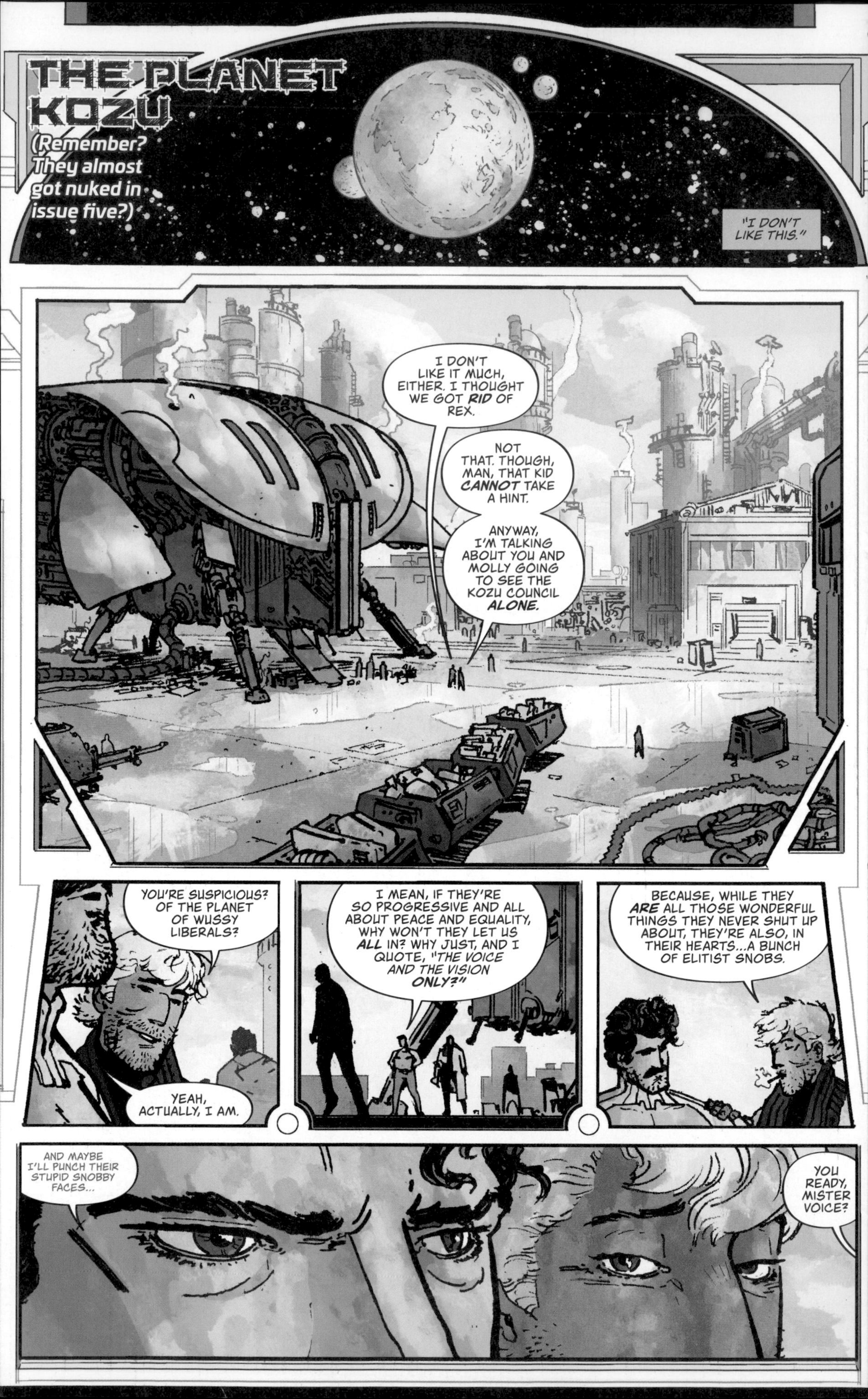
THE PLANET KOZU
(Remember? They almost got nuked in issue five?)
"I DON'T LIKE THIS."
I DON'T LIKE IT MUCH, EITHER. I THOUGHT WE GOT RID OF REX.
NOT THAT. THOUGH, MAN, THAT KID CANNOT TAKE A HINT.
ANYWAY, I'M TALKING ABOUT YOU AND MOLLY GOING TO SEE THE KOZU COUNCIL ALONE.
YOU'RE SUSPICIOUS? OF THE PLANET OF WUSSY LIBERALS?
YEAH, ACTUALLY, I AM.
I MEAN, IF THEY'RE SO PROGRESSIVE AND ALL ABOUT PEACE AND EQUALITY, WHY WON'T THEY LET US ALL IN? WHY JUST, AND I QUOTE, "THE VOICE AND THE VISION ONLY?"
BECAUSE, WHILE THEY ARE ALL THOSE WONDERFUL THINGS THEY NEVER SHUT UP ABOUT, THEY'RE ALSO, IN THEIR HEARTS...A BUNCH OF ELITIST SNOBS.
AND MAYBE I'LL PUNCH THEIR STUPID SNOBBY FACES...
YOU READY, MISTER VOICE?

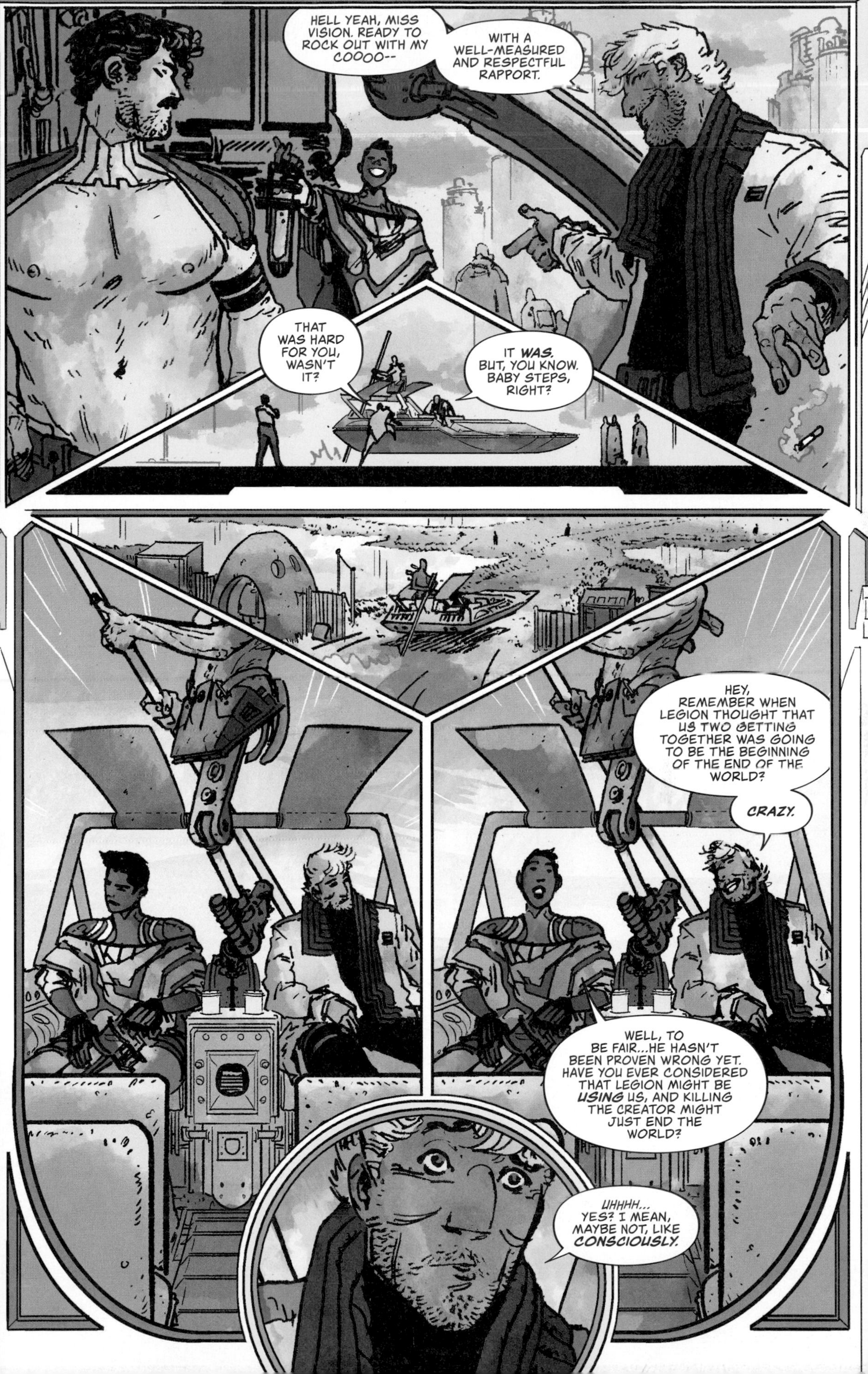
HELL YEAH, MISS VISION. READY TO ROCK OUT WITH MY COOOO--
WITH A WELL-MEASURED AND RESPECTFUL RAPPORT.
THAT WAS HARD FOR YOU, WASN'T IT?
IT *WAS*. BUT, YOU KNOW. BABY STEPS, RIGHT?
HEY, REMEMBER WHEN LEGION THOUGHT THAT US TWO GETTING TOGETHER WAS GOING TO BE THE BEGINNING OF THE END OF THE WORLD?
CRAZY.
WELL, TO BE FAIR...HE HASN'T BEEN PROVEN WRONG YET. HAVE YOU EVER CONSIDERED THAT LEGION MIGHT BE *USING* US, AND KILLING THE CREATOR MIGHT JUST END THE WORLD?
UHHHH... YES? I MEAN, MAYBE NOT, LIKE *CONSCIOUSLY.*

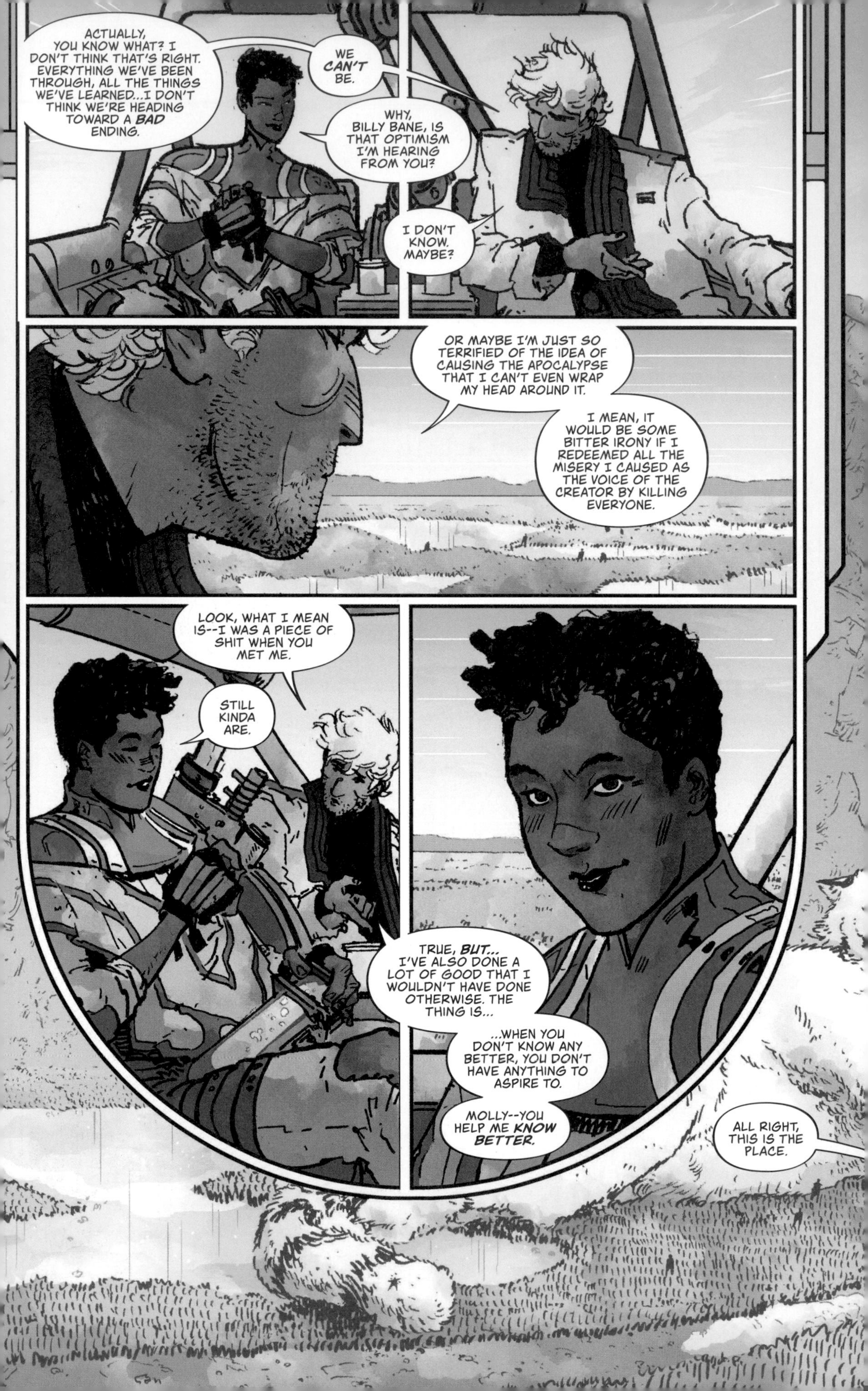

ACTUALLY, YOU KNOW WHAT? I DON'T THINK THAT'S RIGHT. EVERYTHING WE'VE BEEN THROUGH, ALL THE THINGS WE'VE LEARNED...I DON'T THINK WE'RE HEADING TOWARD A ***BAD*** ENDING.
WE ***CAN'T*** BE.
WHY, BILLY BANE, IS THAT OPTIMISM I'M HEARING FROM YOU?
I DON'T KNOW. MAYBE?
OR MAYBE I'M JUST SO TERRIFIED OF THE IDEA OF CAUSING THE APOCALYPSE THAT I CAN'T EVEN WRAP MY HEAD AROUND IT.
I MEAN, IT WOULD BE SOME BITTER IRONY IF I REDEEMED ALL THE MISERY I CAUSED AS THE VOICE OF THE CREATOR BY KILLING EVERYONE.
LOOK, WHAT I MEAN IS--I WAS A PIECE OF SHIT WHEN YOU MET ME.
STILL KINDA ARE.
TRUE, ***BUT...*** I'VE ALSO DONE A LOT OF GOOD THAT I WOULDN'T HAVE DONE OTHERWISE. THE THING IS...
...WHEN YOU DON'T KNOW ANY BETTER, YOU DON'T HAVE ANYTHING TO ASPIRE TO.
MOLLY--YOU HELP ME ***KNOW BETTER.***
ALL RIGHT, THIS IS THE PLACE.

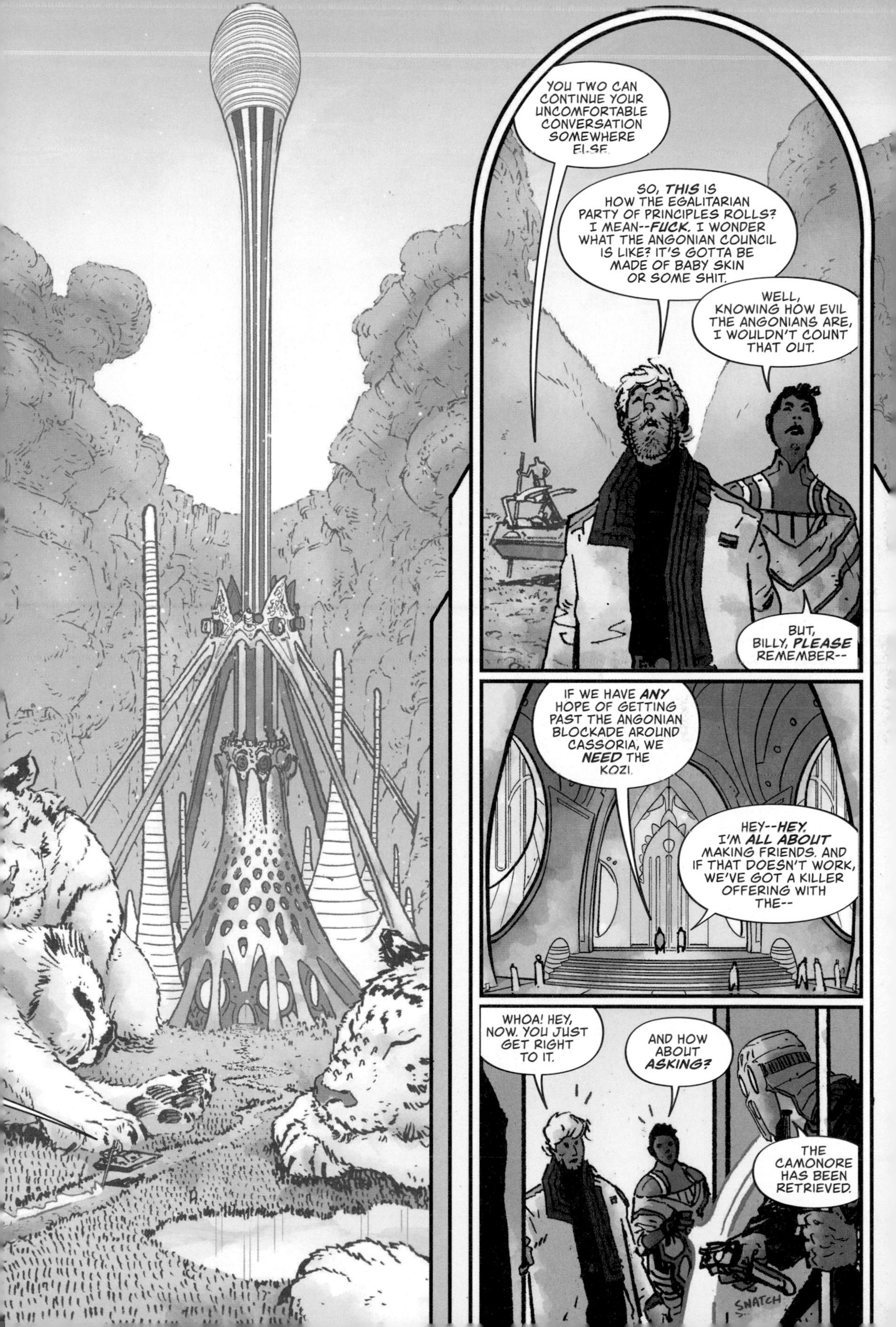
YOU TWO CAN CONTINUE YOUR UNCOMFORTABLE CONVERSATION SOMEWHERE ELSE.
SO, THIS IS HOW THE EGALITARIAN PARTY OF PRINCIPLES ROLLS? I MEAN--FUCK. I WONDER WHAT THE ANGONIAN COUNCIL IS LIKE? IT'S GOTTA BE MADE OF BABY SKIN OR SOME SHIT.
WELL, KNOWING HOW EVIL THE ANGONIANS ARE, I WOULDN'T COUNT THAT OUT.
BUT, BILLY, PLEASE REMEMBER--
IF WE HAVE ANY HOPE OF GETTING PAST THE ANGONIAN BLOCKADE AROUND CASSORIA, WE NEED THE KOZI.
HEY--HEY. I'M ALL ABOUT MAKING FRIENDS. AND IF THAT DOESN'T WORK, WE'VE GOT A KILLER OFFERING WITH THE--
WHOA! HEY, NOW. YOU JUST GET RIGHT TO IT.
AND HOW ABOUT ASKING?
THE CAMONORE HAS BEEN RETRIEVED.
SNATCH

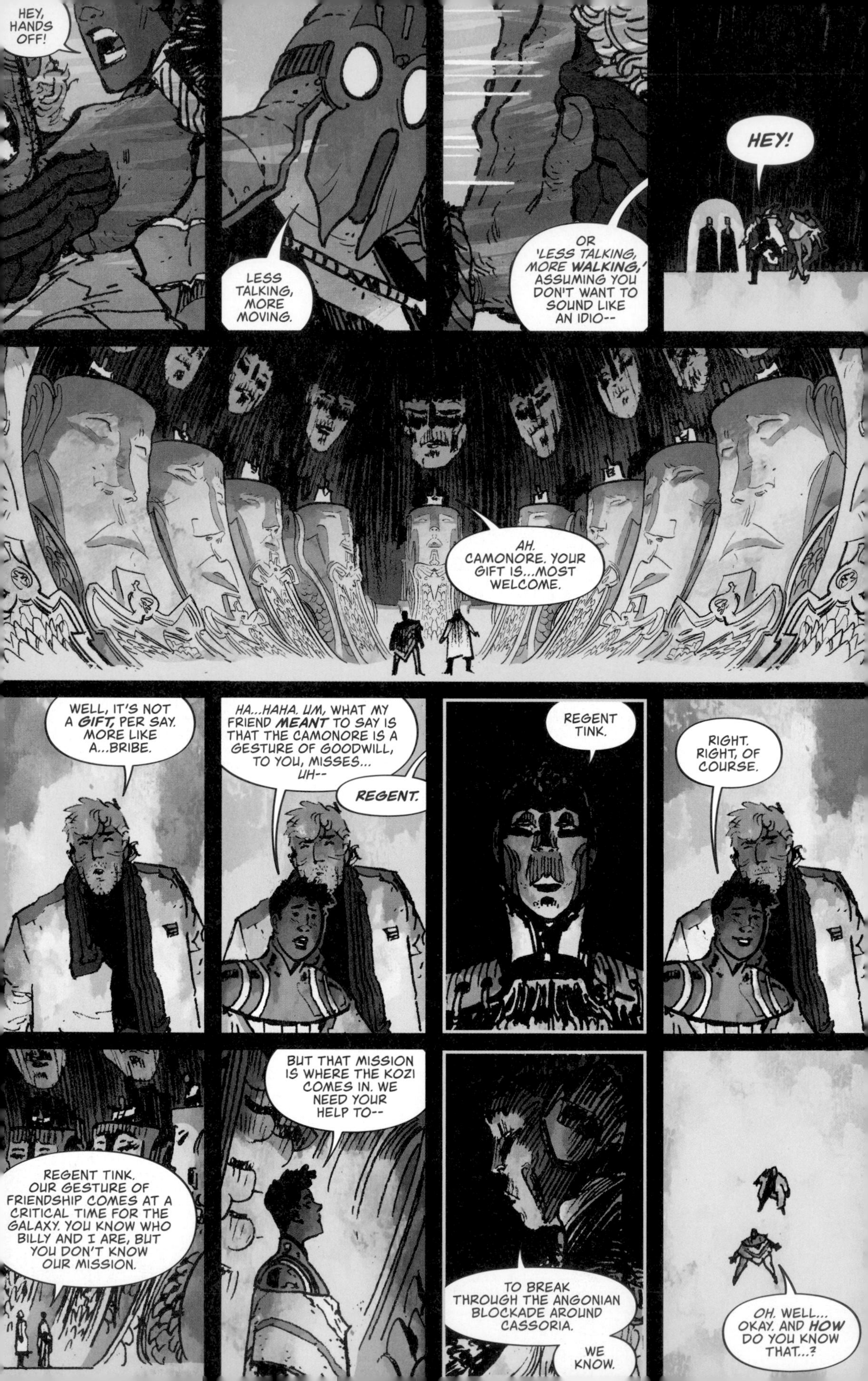
HEY, HANDS OFF!
LESS TALKING, MORE MOVING.
OR 'LESS TALKING, MORE WALKING,' ASSUMING YOU DON'T WANT TO SOUND LIKE AN IDIO--
HEY!
AH. CAMONORE. YOUR GIFT IS...MOST WELCOME.
WELL, IT'S NOT A GIFT, PER SAY. MORE LIKE A...BRIBE.
HA...HAHA. UM, WHAT MY FRIEND MEANT TO SAY IS THAT THE CAMONORE IS A GESTURE OF GOODWILL, TO YOU, MISSES... UH--
REGENT.
REGENT TINK.
RIGHT. RIGHT, OF COURSE.
REGENT TINK. OUR GESTURE OF FRIENDSHIP COMES AT A CRITICAL TIME FOR THE GALAXY. YOU KNOW WHO BILLY AND I ARE, BUT YOU DON'T KNOW OUR MISSION.
BUT THAT MISSION IS WHERE THE KOZI COMES IN. WE NEED YOUR HELP TO--
TO BREAK THROUGH THE ANGONIAN BLOCKADE AROUND CASSORIA.
WE KNOW.
OH. WELL... OKAY. AND HOW DO YOU KNOW THAT...?

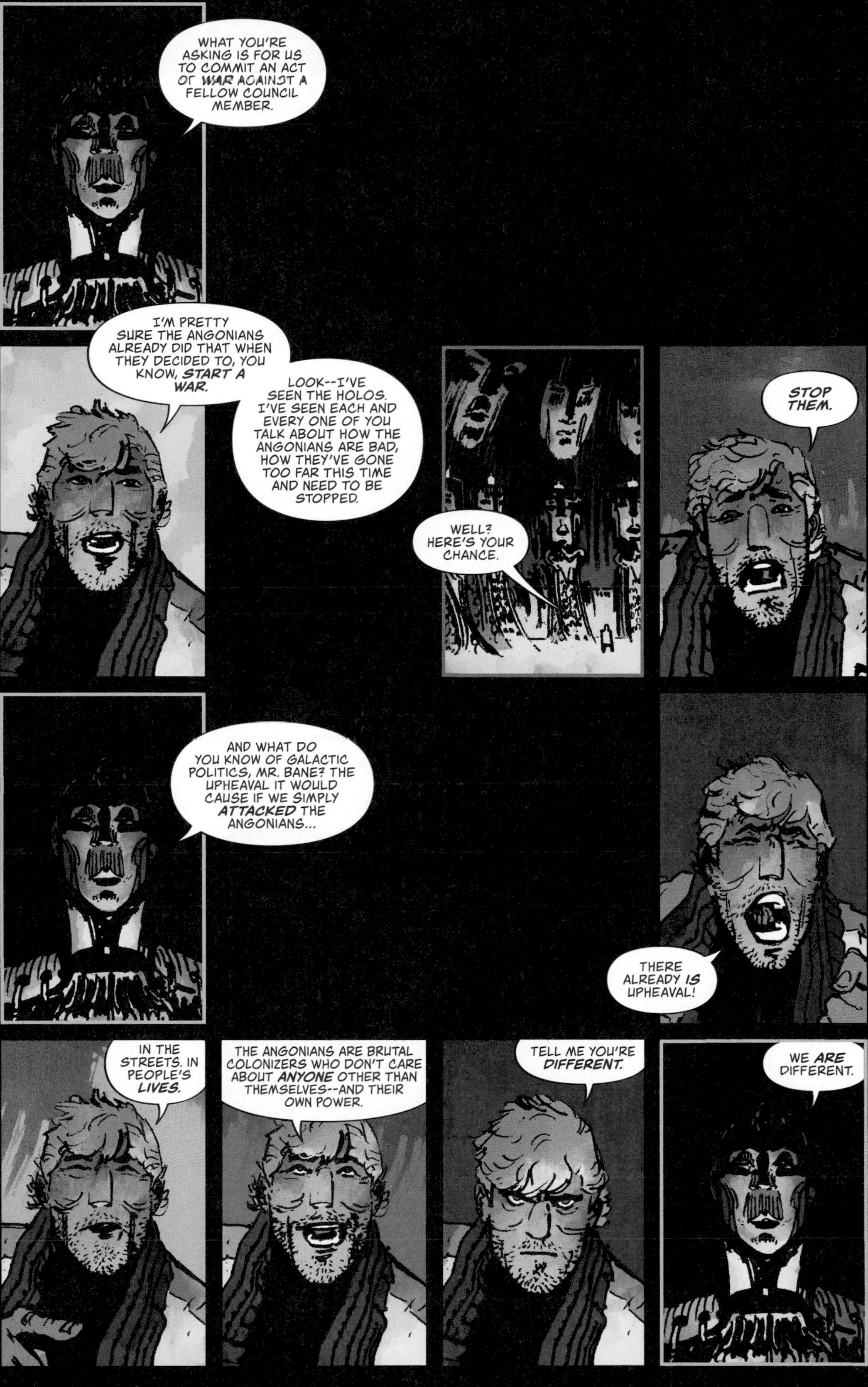
WHAT YOU'RE ASKING IS FOR US TO COMMIT AN ACT OF WAR AGAINST A FELLOW COUNCIL MEMBER.
I'M PRETTY SURE THE ANGONIANS ALREADY DID THAT WHEN THEY DECIDED TO, YOU KNOW, START A WAR.
LOOK--I'VE SEEN THE HOLOS. I'VE SEEN EACH AND EVERY ONE OF YOU TALK ABOUT HOW THE ANGONIANS ARE BAD, HOW THEY'VE GONE TOO FAR THIS TIME AND NEED TO BE STOPPED.
WELL? HERE'S YOUR CHANCE.
STOP THEM.
AND WHAT DO YOU KNOW OF GALACTIC POLITICS, MR. BANE? THE UPHEAVAL IT WOULD CAUSE IF WE SIMPLY ATTACKED THE ANGONIANS...
THERE ALREADY IS UPHEAVAL!
IN THE STREETS. IN PEOPLE'S LIVES.
THE ANGONIANS ARE BRUTAL COLONIZERS WHO DON'T CARE ABOUT ANYONE OTHER THAN THEMSELVES--AND THEIR OWN POWER.
TELL ME YOU'RE DIFFERENT.
WE ARE DIFFERENT.

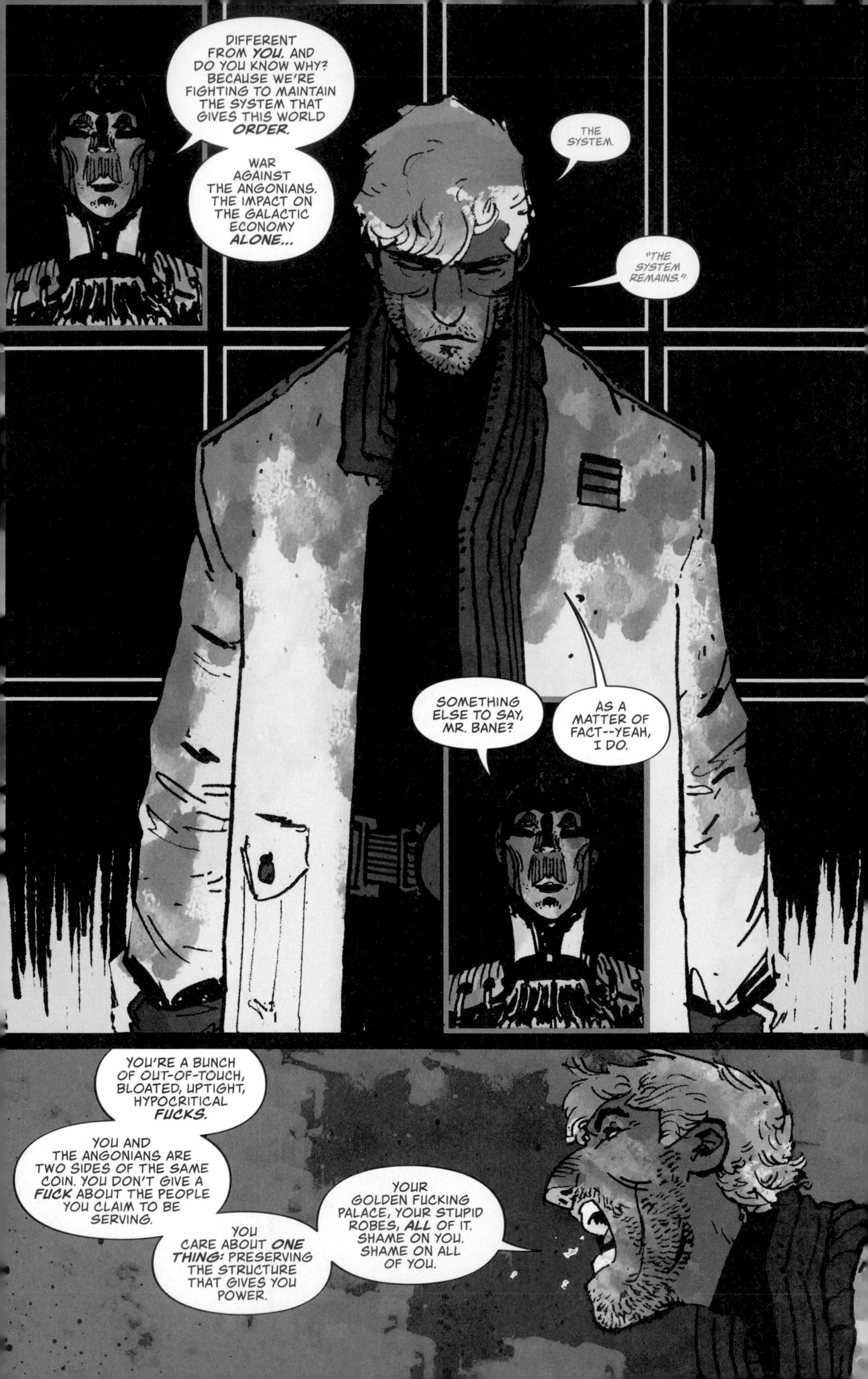
DIFFERENT FROM YOU. AND DO YOU KNOW WHY? BECAUSE WE'RE FIGHTING TO MAINTAIN THE SYSTEM THAT GIVES THIS WORLD ORDER.
WAR AGAINST THE ANGONIANS. THE IMPACT ON THE GALACTIC ECONOMY ALONE...
THE SYSTEM.
"THE SYSTEM REMAINS."
SOMETHING ELSE TO SAY, MR. BANE?
AS A MATTER OF FACT--YEAH, I DO.
YOU'RE A BUNCH OF OUT-OF-TOUCH, BLOATED, UPTIGHT, HYPOCRITICAL FUCKS.
YOU AND THE ANGONIANS ARE TWO SIDES OF THE SAME COIN. YOU DON'T GIVE A FUCK ABOUT THE PEOPLE YOU CLAIM TO BE SERVING.
YOU CARE ABOUT ONE THING: PRESERVING THE STRUCTURE THAT GIVES YOU POWER.
YOUR GOLDEN FUCKING PALACE, YOUR STUPID ROBES, ALL OF IT. SHAME ON YOU. SHAME ON ALL OF YOU.

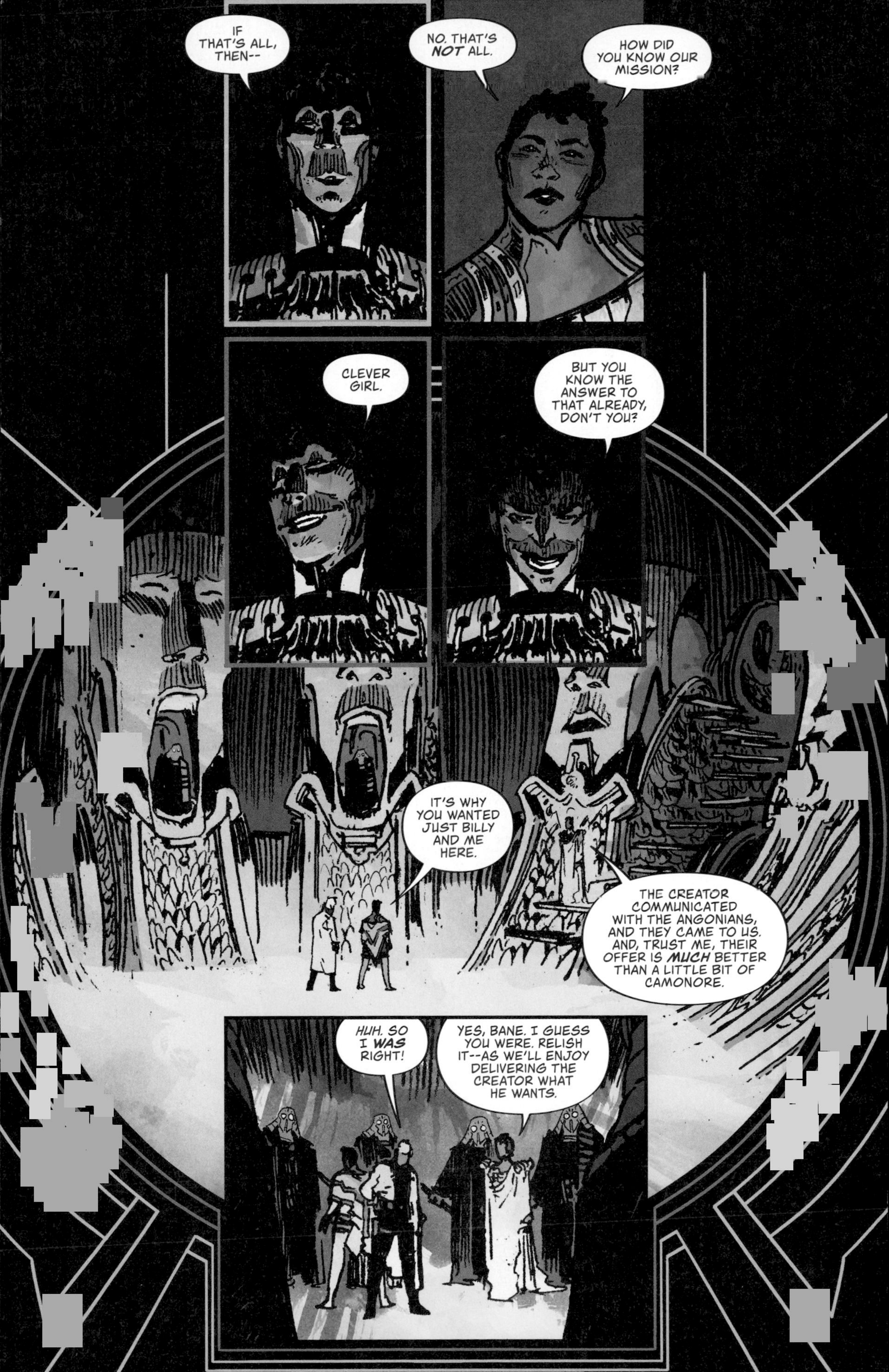
IF THAT'S ALL, THEN--
NO. THAT'S *NOT* ALL.
HOW DID YOU KNOW OUR MISSION?
CLEVER GIRL.
BUT YOU KNOW THE ANSWER TO THAT ALREADY, DON'T YOU?
IT'S WHY YOU WANTED JUST BILLY AND ME HERE.
THE CREATOR COMMUNICATED WITH THE ANGONIANS, AND THEY CAME TO US. AND, TRUST ME, THEIR OFFER IS *MUCH* BETTER THAN A LITTLE BIT OF CAMONORE.
HUH. SO I *WAS* RIGHT!
YES, BANE. I GUESS YOU WERE. RELISH IT--AS WE'LL ENJOY DELIVERING THE CREATOR WHAT HE WANTS.

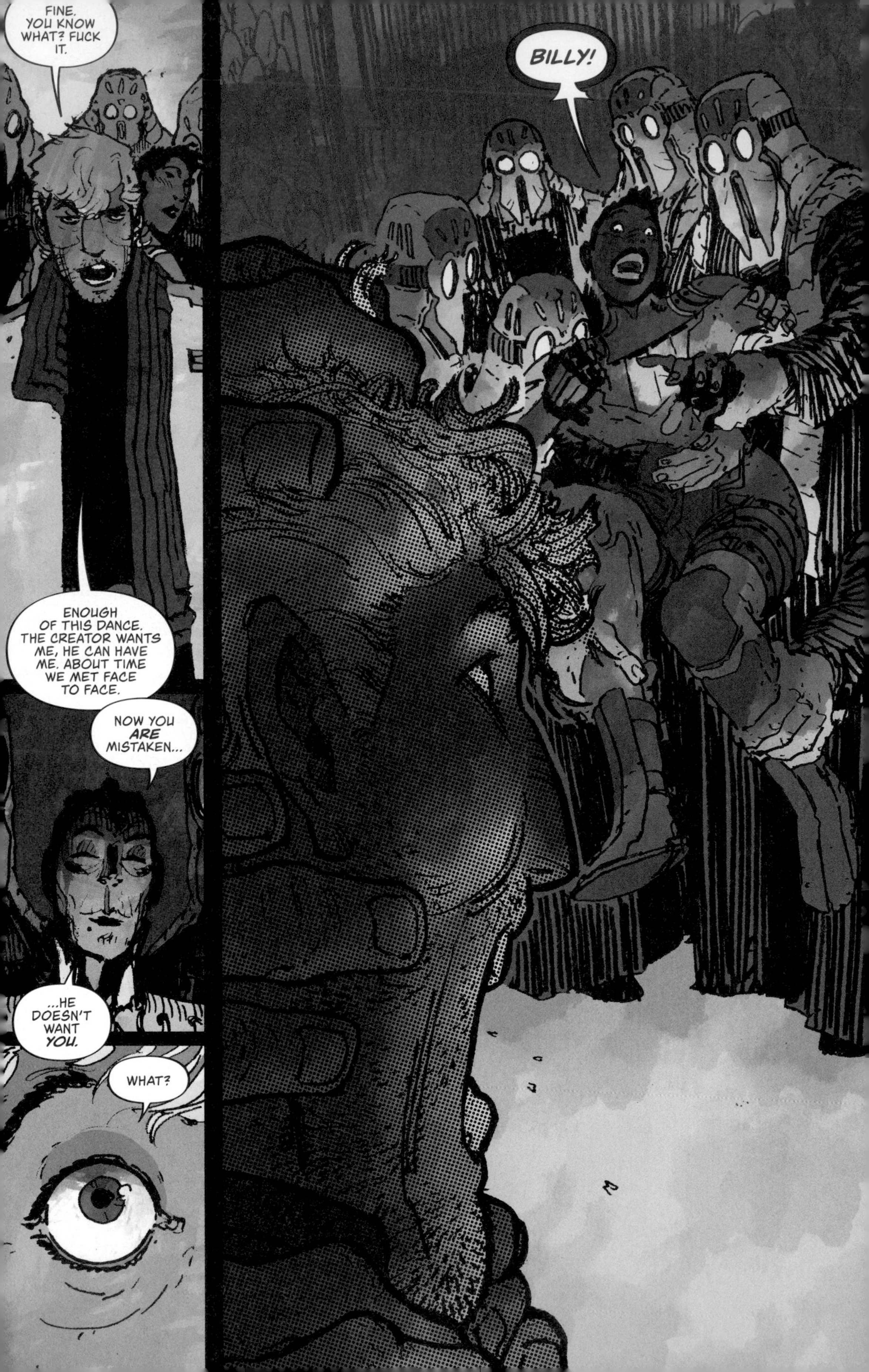
FINE. YOU KNOW WHAT? FUCK IT.
ENOUGH OF THIS DANCE. THE CREATOR WANTS ME, HE CAN HAVE ME. ABOUT TIME WE MET FACE TO FACE.
NOW YOU ARE MISTAKEN...
...HE DOESN'T WANT YOU.
WHAT?
BILLY!

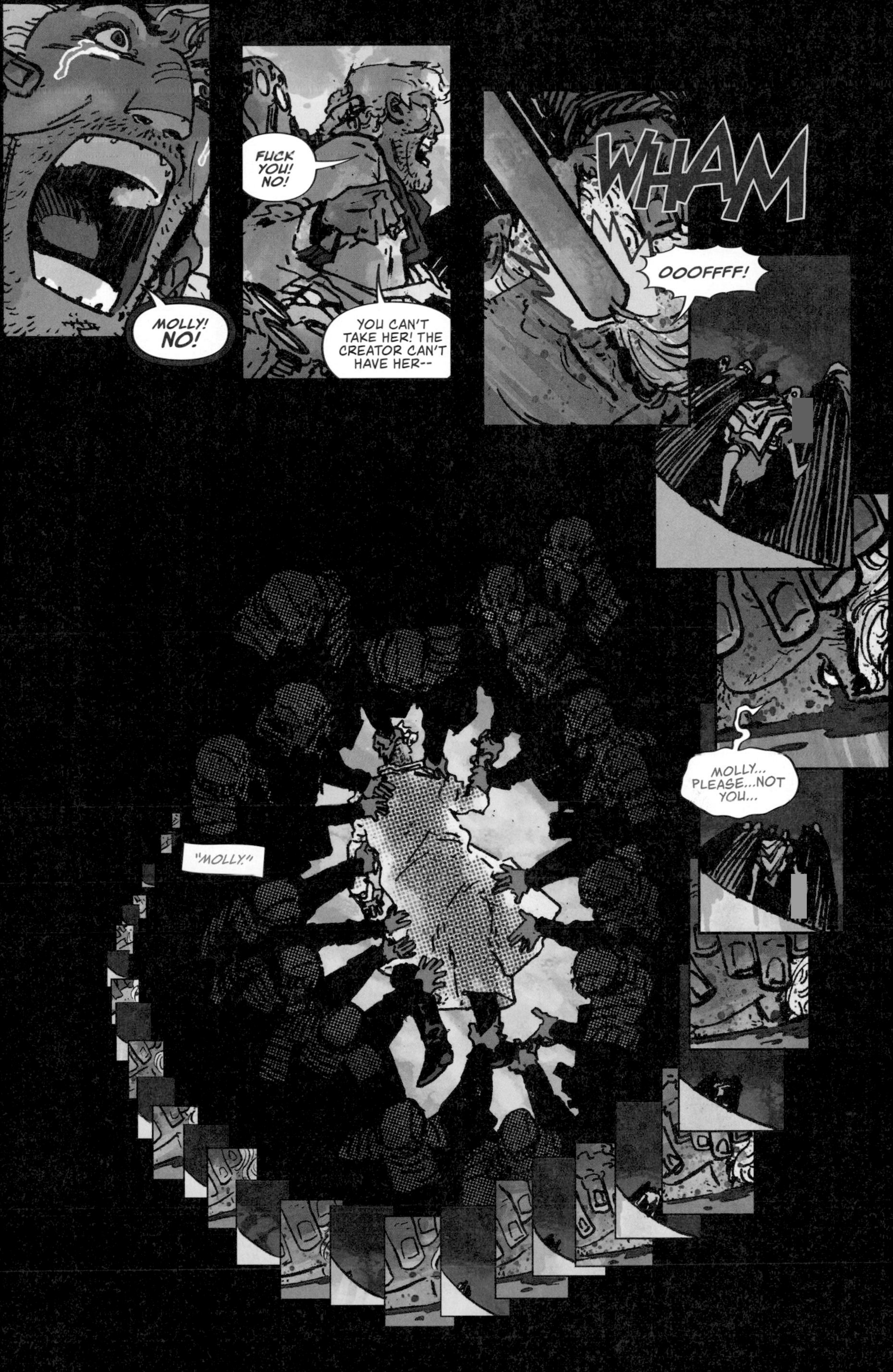

MOLLY! NO!
FUCK YOU! NO!
YOU CAN'T TAKE HER! THE CREATOR CAN'T HAVE HER--
WHAM
OOOFFFF!
MOLLY... PLEASE...NOT YOU...
"MOLLY."

CHAPTER TWENTYTWO

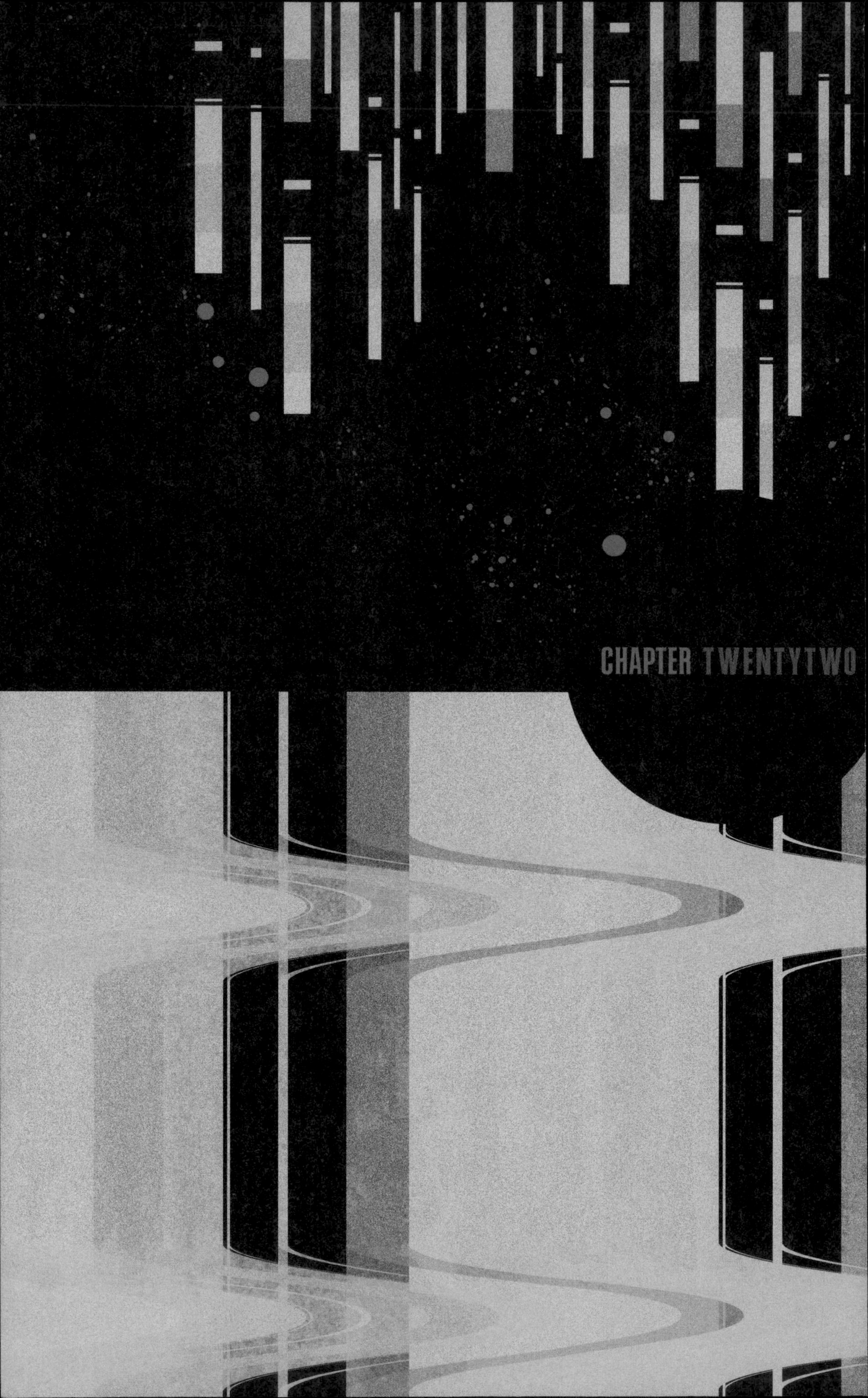

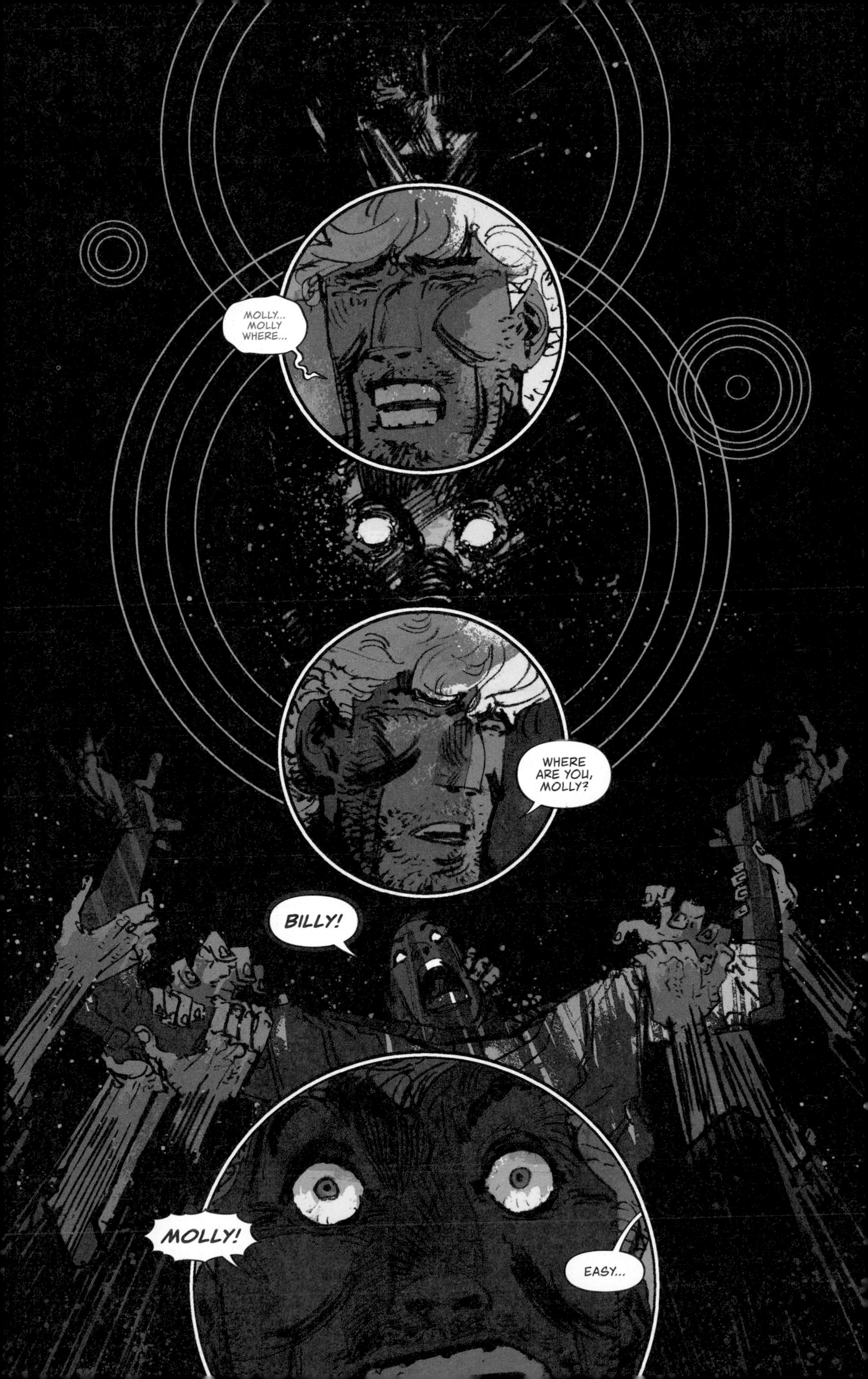
MOLLY... MOLLY WHERE...
WHERE ARE YOU, MOLLY?
BILLY!
MOLLY!
EASY...

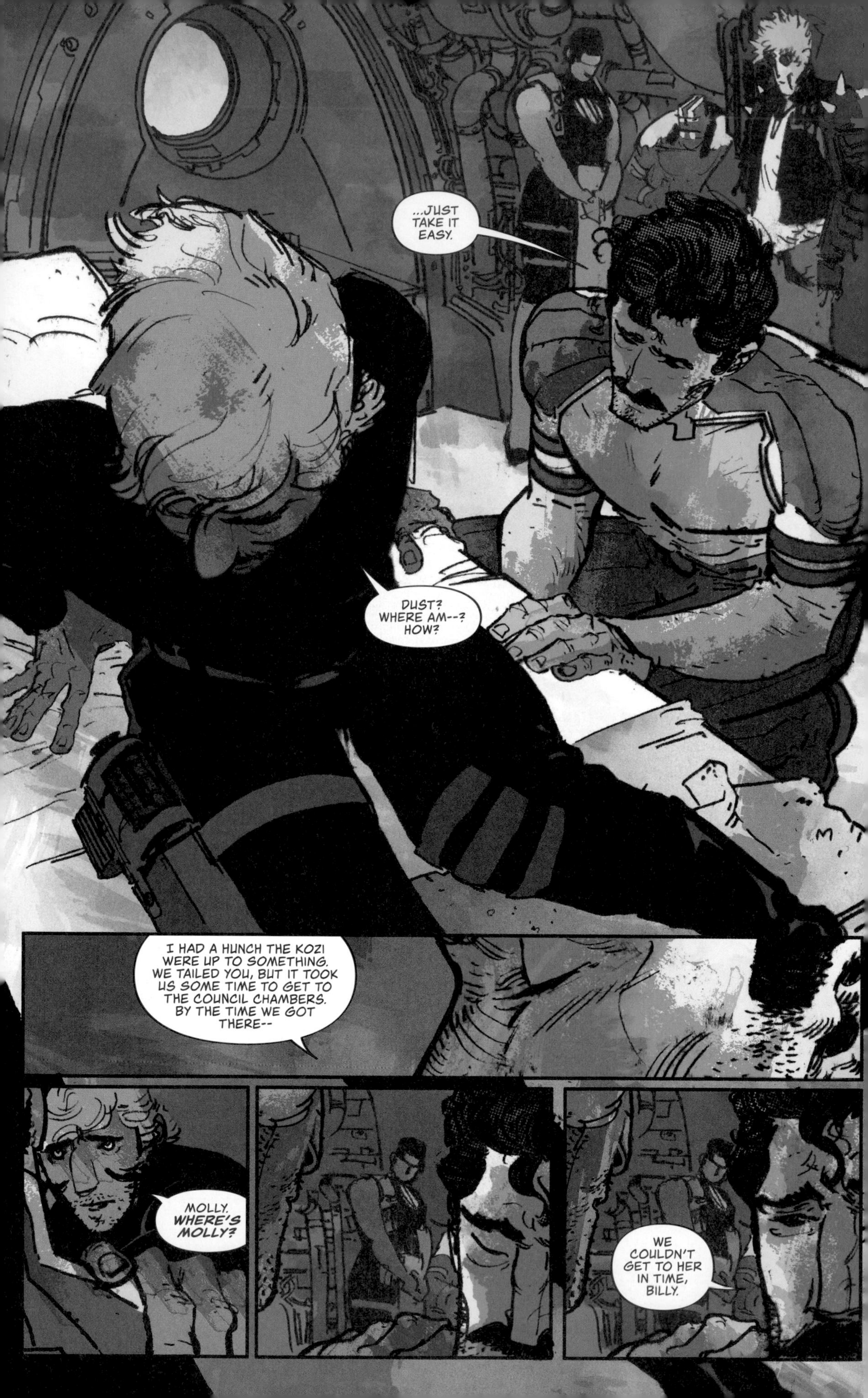
...JUST TAKE IT EASY.
DUST? WHERE AM--? HOW?
I HAD A HUNCH THE KOZI WERE UP TO SOMETHING. WE TAILED YOU, BUT IT TOOK US SOME TIME TO GET TO THE COUNCIL CHAMBERS. BY THE TIME WE GOT THERE--
MOLLY. *WHERE'S MOLLY?*
WE COULDN'T GET TO HER IN TIME, BILLY.

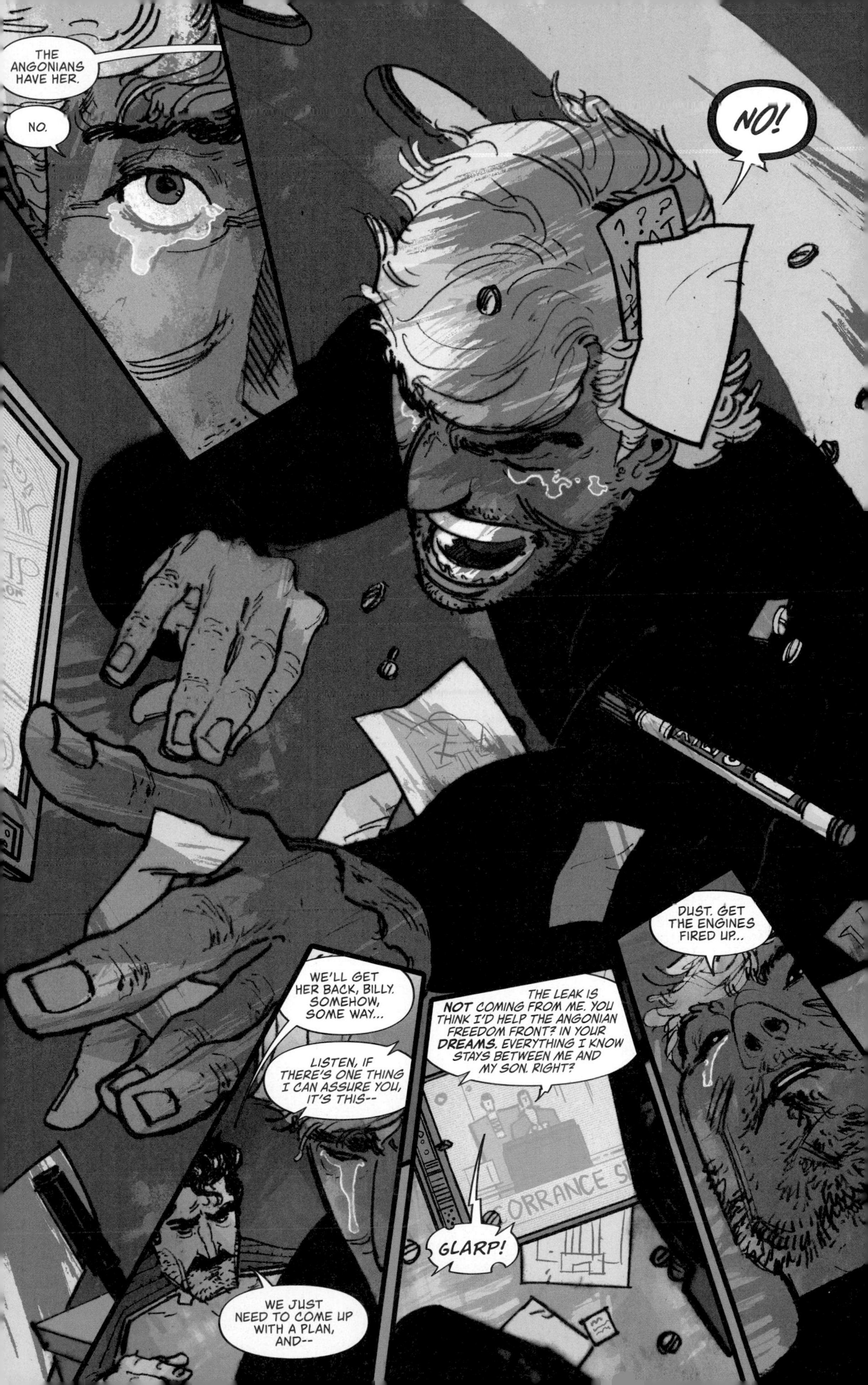

THE ANGONIANS HAVE HER.
NO.
NO!
WE'LL GET HER BACK, BILLY. SOMEHOW, SOME WAY...
LISTEN, IF THERE'S ONE THING I CAN ASSURE YOU, IT'S THIS--
WE JUST NEED TO COME UP WITH A PLAN, AND--
THE LEAK IS NOT COMING FROM ME. YOU THINK I'D HELP THE ANGONIAN FREEDOM FRONT? IN YOUR DREAMS. EVERYTHING I KNOW STAYS BETWEEN ME AND MY SON. RIGHT?
GLARP!
DUST. GET THE ENGINES FIRED UP...

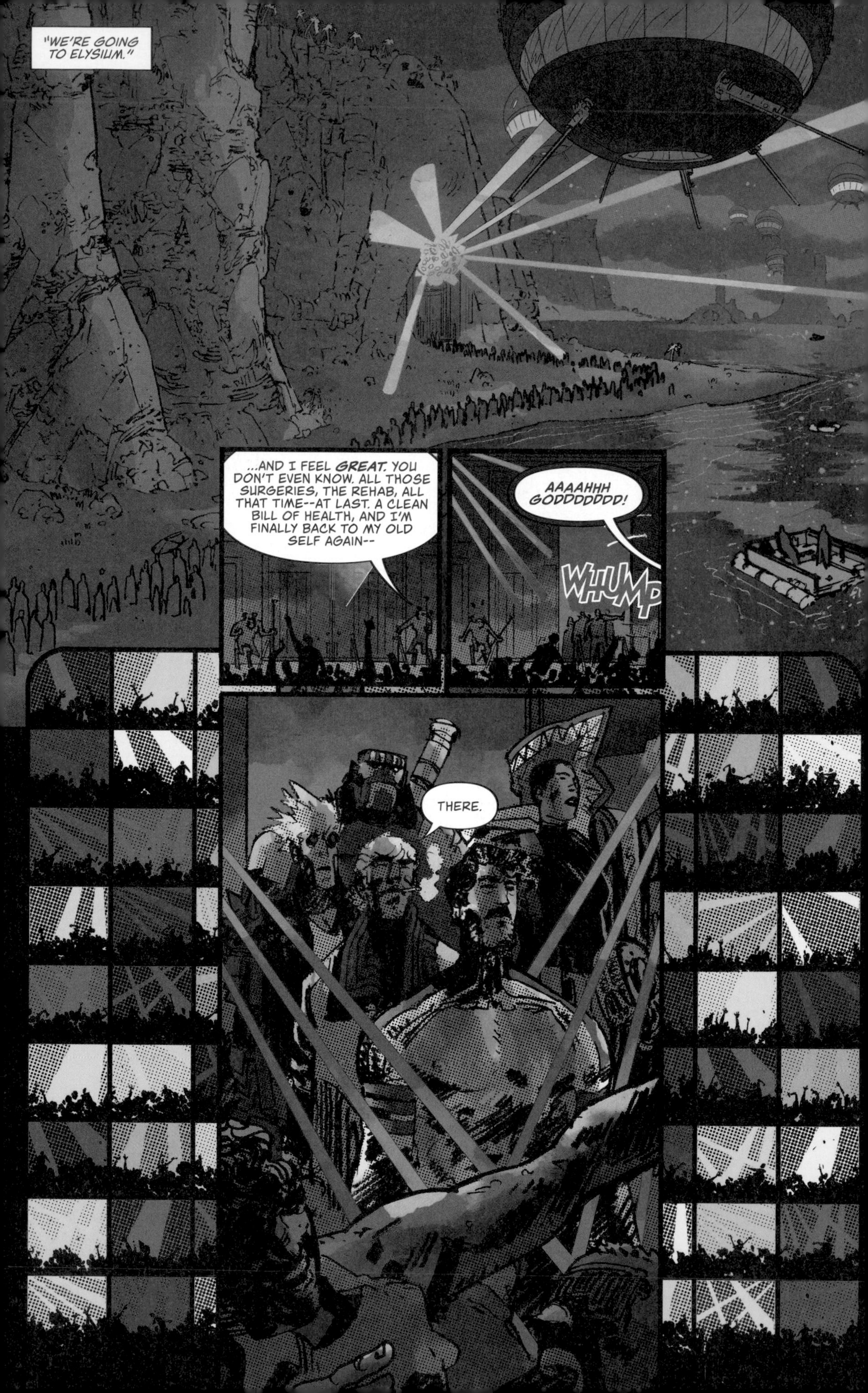
"WE'RE GOING TO ELYSIUM."
...AND I FEEL GREAT. YOU DON'T EVEN KNOW. ALL THOSE SURGERIES, THE REHAB, ALL THAT TIME--AT LAST. A CLEAN BILL OF HEALTH, AND I'M FINALLY BACK TO MY OLD SELF AGAIN--
AAAAHHH GODDDDDDD!
WHUMP
THERE.

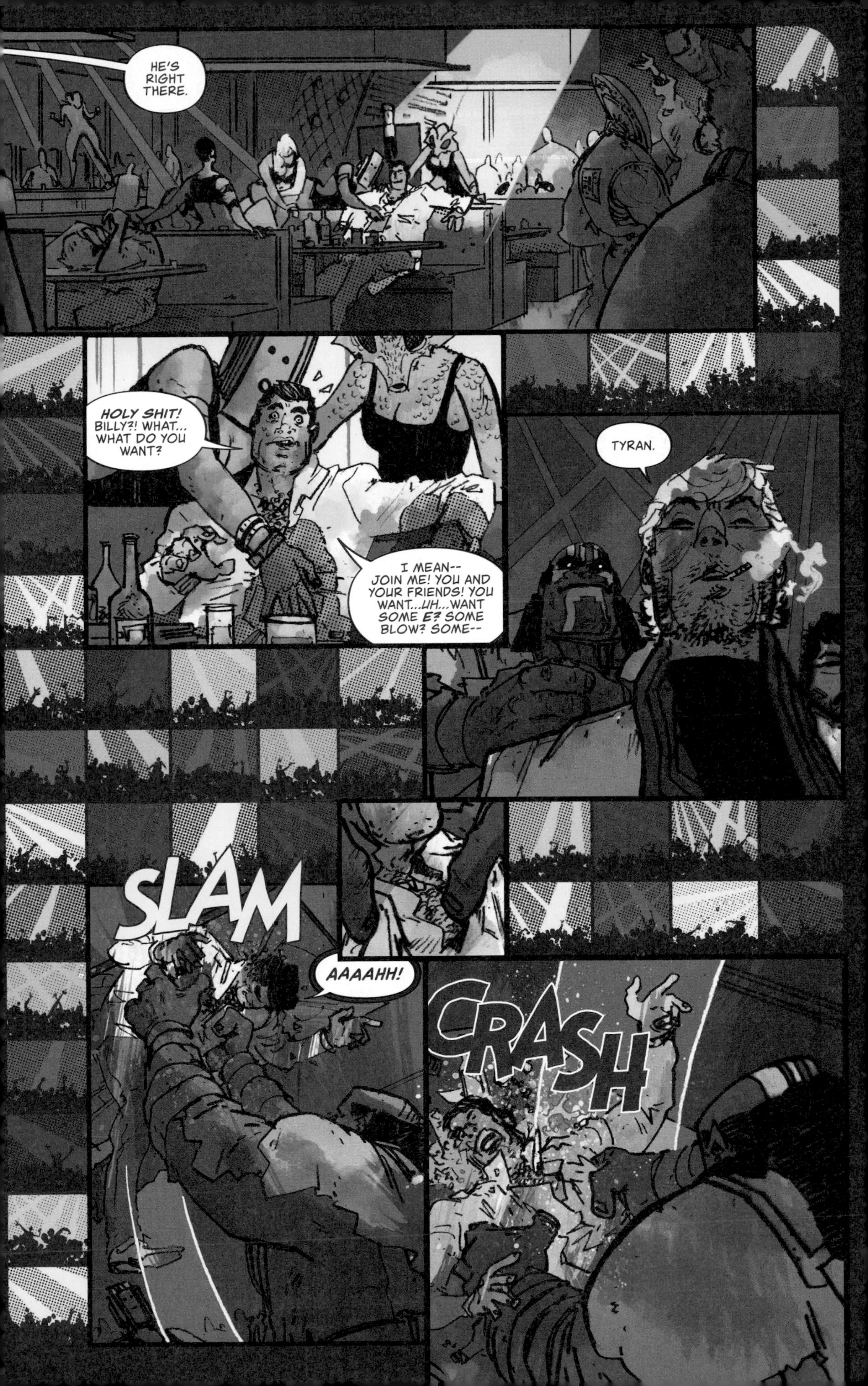
HE'S RIGHT THERE.
HOLY SHIT! BILLY?! WHAT... WHAT DO YOU WANT?
I MEAN-- JOIN ME! YOU AND YOUR FRIENDS! YOU WANT...UH...WANT SOME E? SOME BLOW? SOME--
TYRAN.
SLAM
AAAAHH!
CRASH

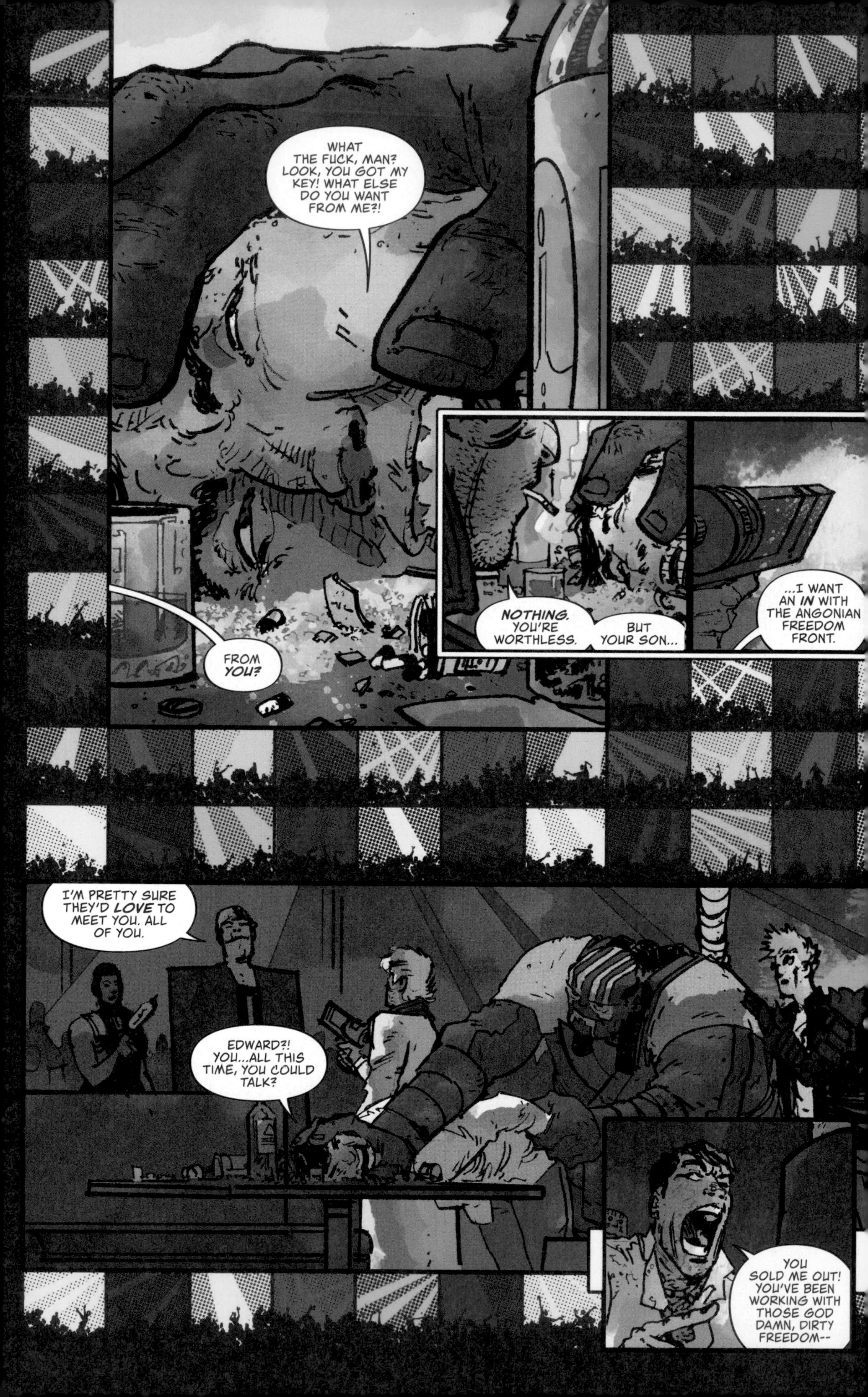
WHAT THE FUCK, MAN? LOOK, YOU GOT MY KEY! WHAT ELSE DO YOU WANT FROM ME?!
FROM *YOU*?
NOTHING. YOU'RE WORTHLESS.
BUT YOUR SON...
...I WANT AN ***IN*** WITH THE ANGONIAN FREEDOM FRONT.
I'M PRETTY SURE THEY'D ***LOVE*** TO MEET YOU. ALL OF YOU.
EDWARD?! YOU...ALL THIS TIME, YOU COULD TALK?
YOU SOLD ME OUT! YOU'VE BEEN WORKING WITH THOSE GOD DAMN, DIRTY FREEDOM--

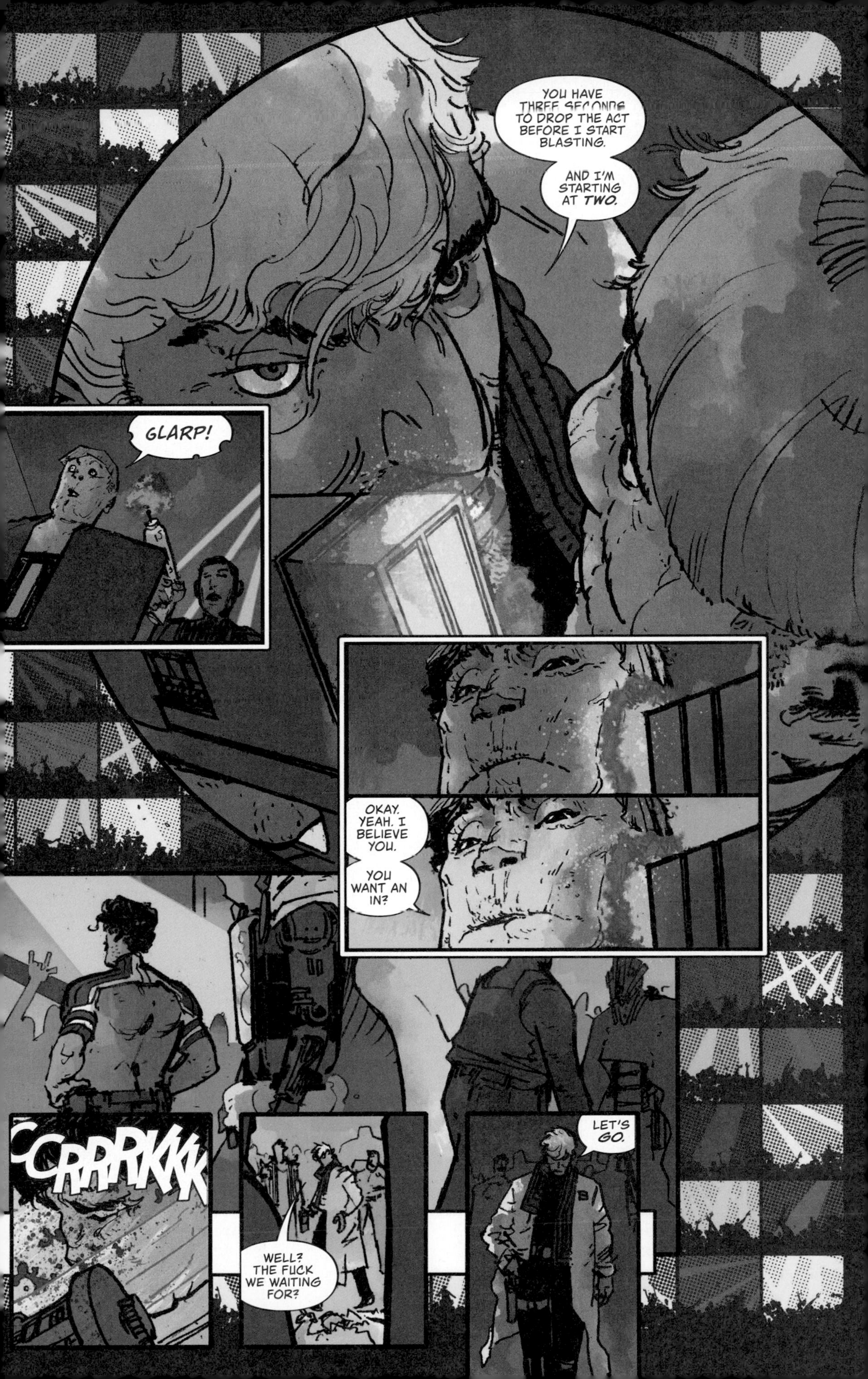
YOU HAVE THREE SECONDS TO DROP THE ACT BEFORE I START BLASTING.
AND I'M STARTING AT TWO.
GLARP!
OKAY. YEAH. I BELIEVE YOU.
YOU WANT AN IN?
CCRRRKKK
WELL? THE FUCK WE WAITING FOR?
LET'S GO.

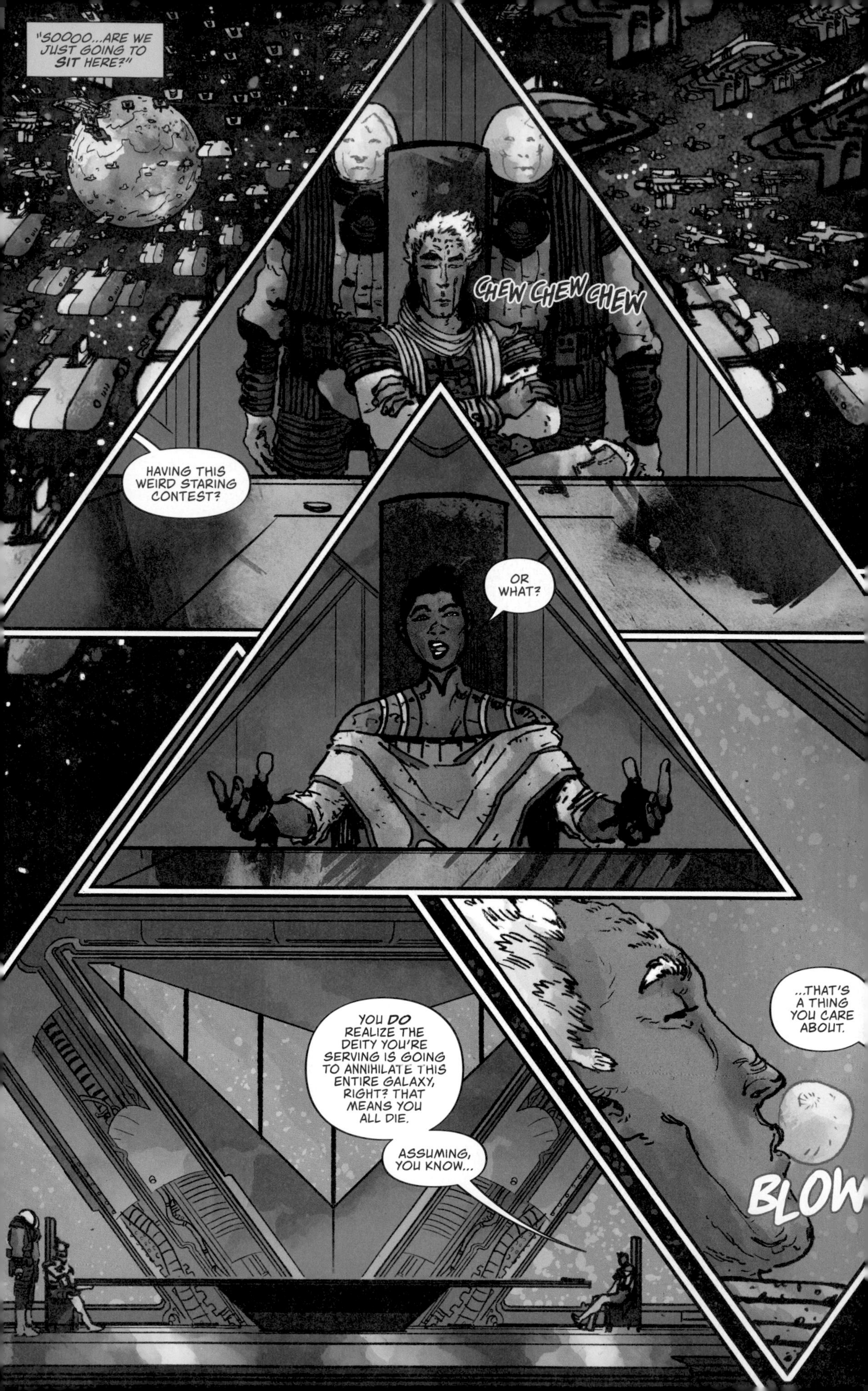
"SOOOO...ARE WE JUST GOING TO SIT HERE?"
CHEW CHEW CHEW
HAVING THIS WEIRD STARING CONTEST?
OR WHAT?
YOU DO REALIZE THE DEITY YOU'RE SERVING IS GOING TO ANNIHILATE THIS ENTIRE GALAXY, RIGHT? THAT MEANS YOU ALL DIE.
ASSUMING, YOU KNOW...
...THAT'S A THING YOU CARE ABOUT.
BLOW

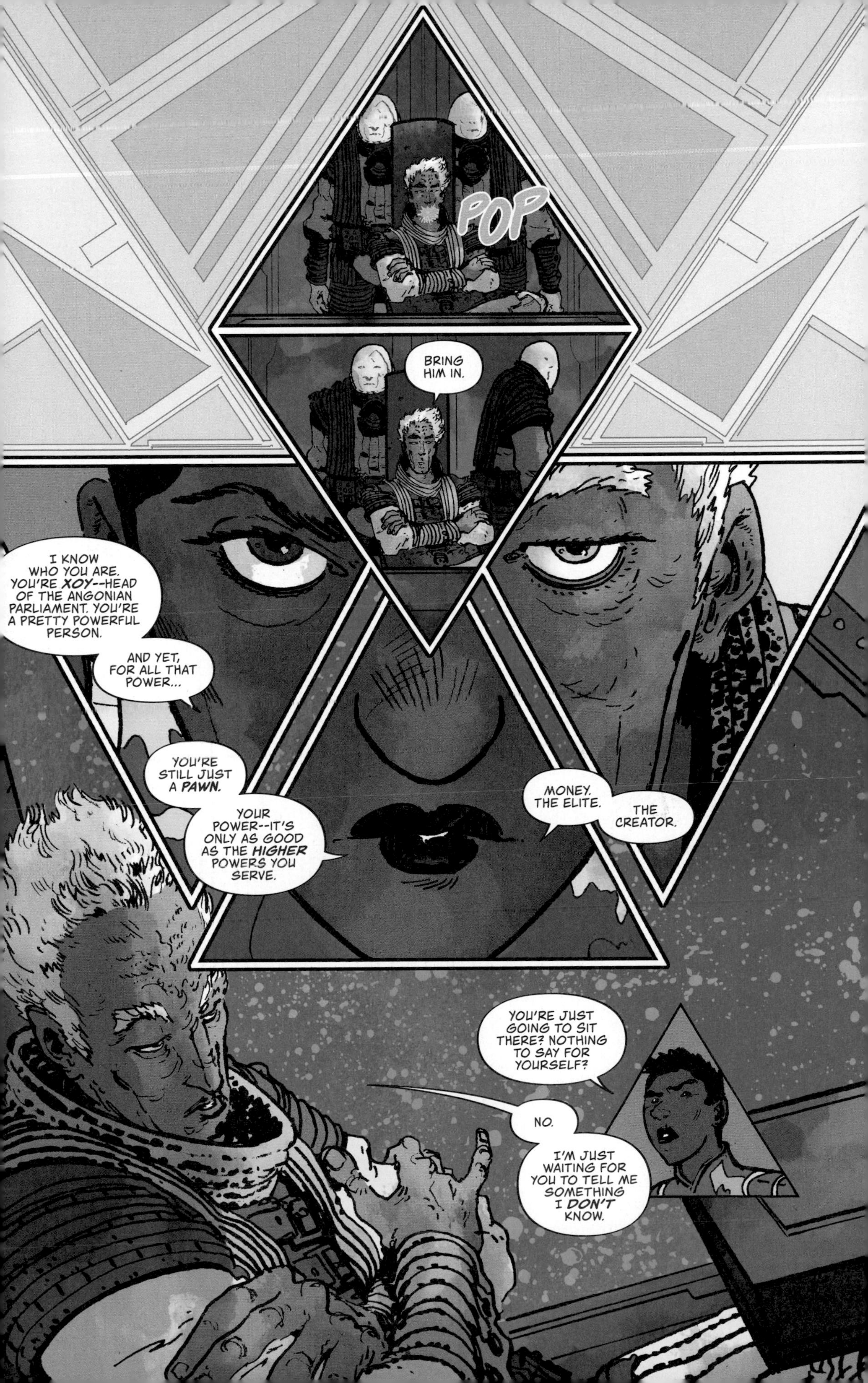
POP
BRING HIM IN.
I KNOW WHO YOU ARE. YOU'RE XOY--HEAD OF THE ANGONIAN PARLIAMENT. YOU'RE A PRETTY POWERFUL PERSON.
AND YET, FOR ALL THAT POWER...
YOU'RE STILL JUST A PAWN.
YOUR POWER--IT'S ONLY AS GOOD AS THE HIGHER POWERS YOU SERVE.
MONEY. THE ELITE.
THE CREATOR.
YOU'RE JUST GOING TO SIT THERE? NOTHING TO SAY FOR YOURSELF?
NO.
I'M JUST WAITING FOR YOU TO TELL ME SOMETHING I DON'T KNOW.

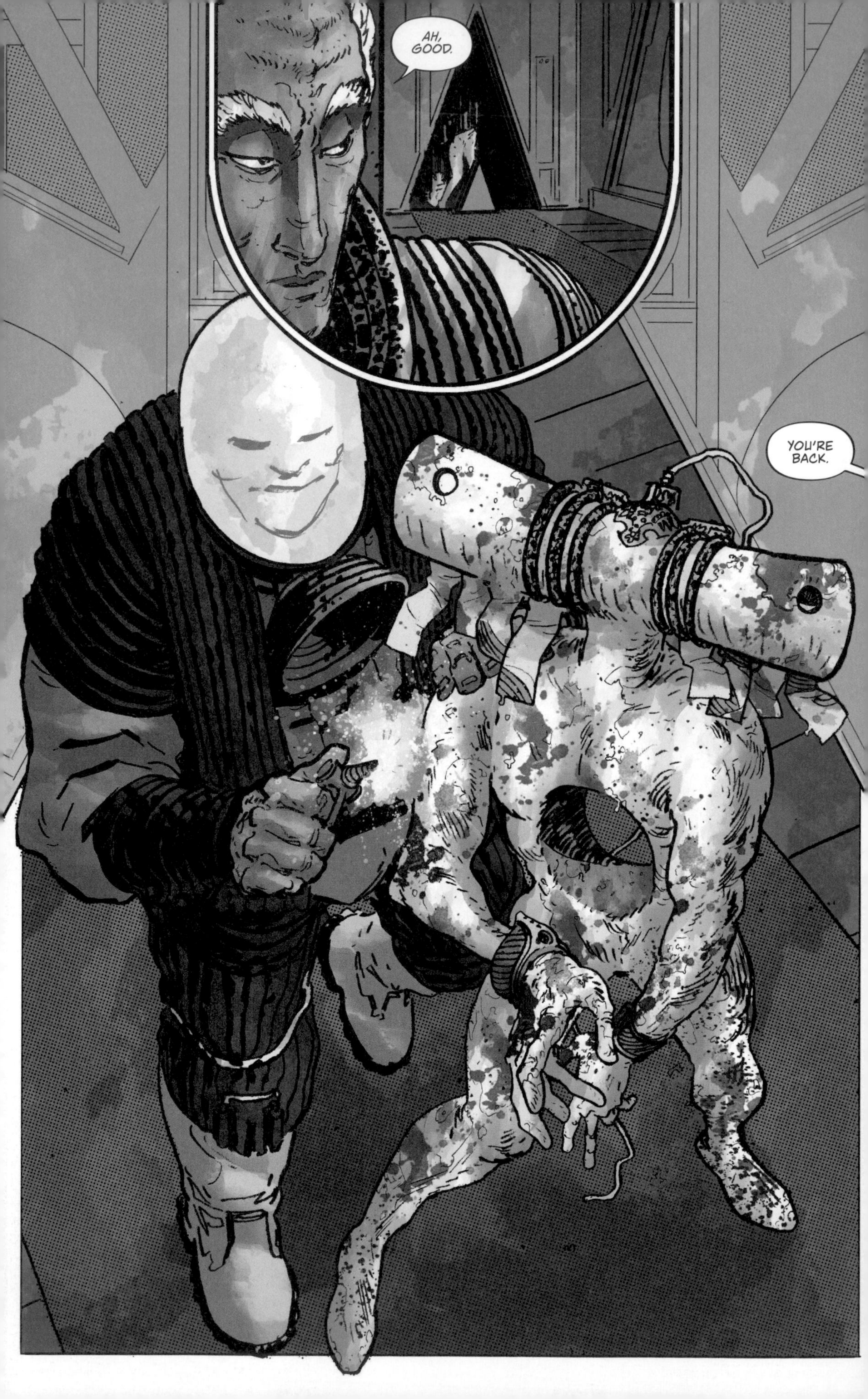
AH, GOOD.
YOU'RE BACK.

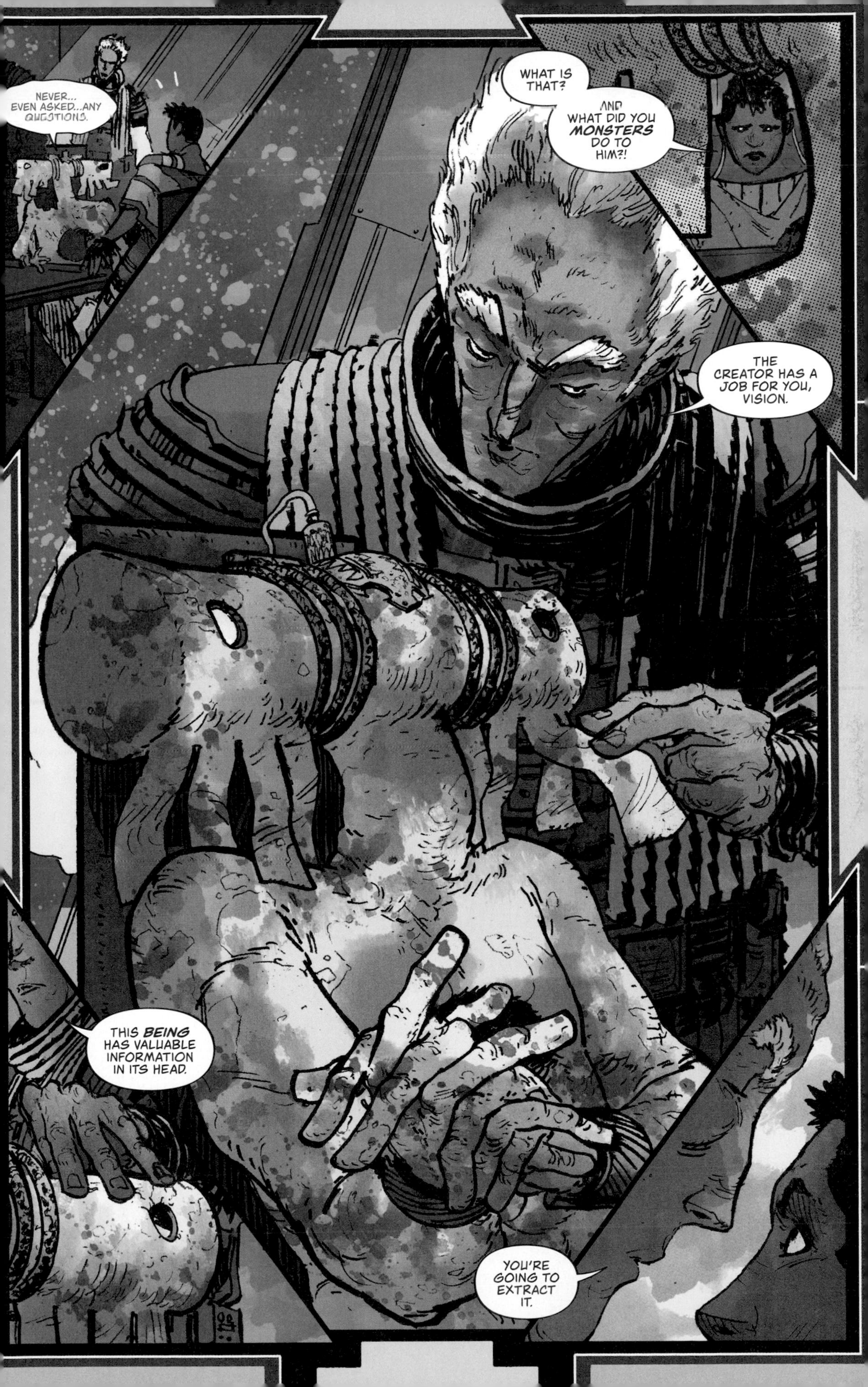
NEVER... EVEN ASKED...ANY QUESTIONS.
WHAT IS THAT?
AND WHAT DID YOU MONSTERS DO TO HIM?!
THE CREATOR HAS A JOB FOR YOU, VISION.
THIS BEING HAS VALUABLE INFORMATION IN ITS HEAD.
YOU'RE GOING TO EXTRACT IT.

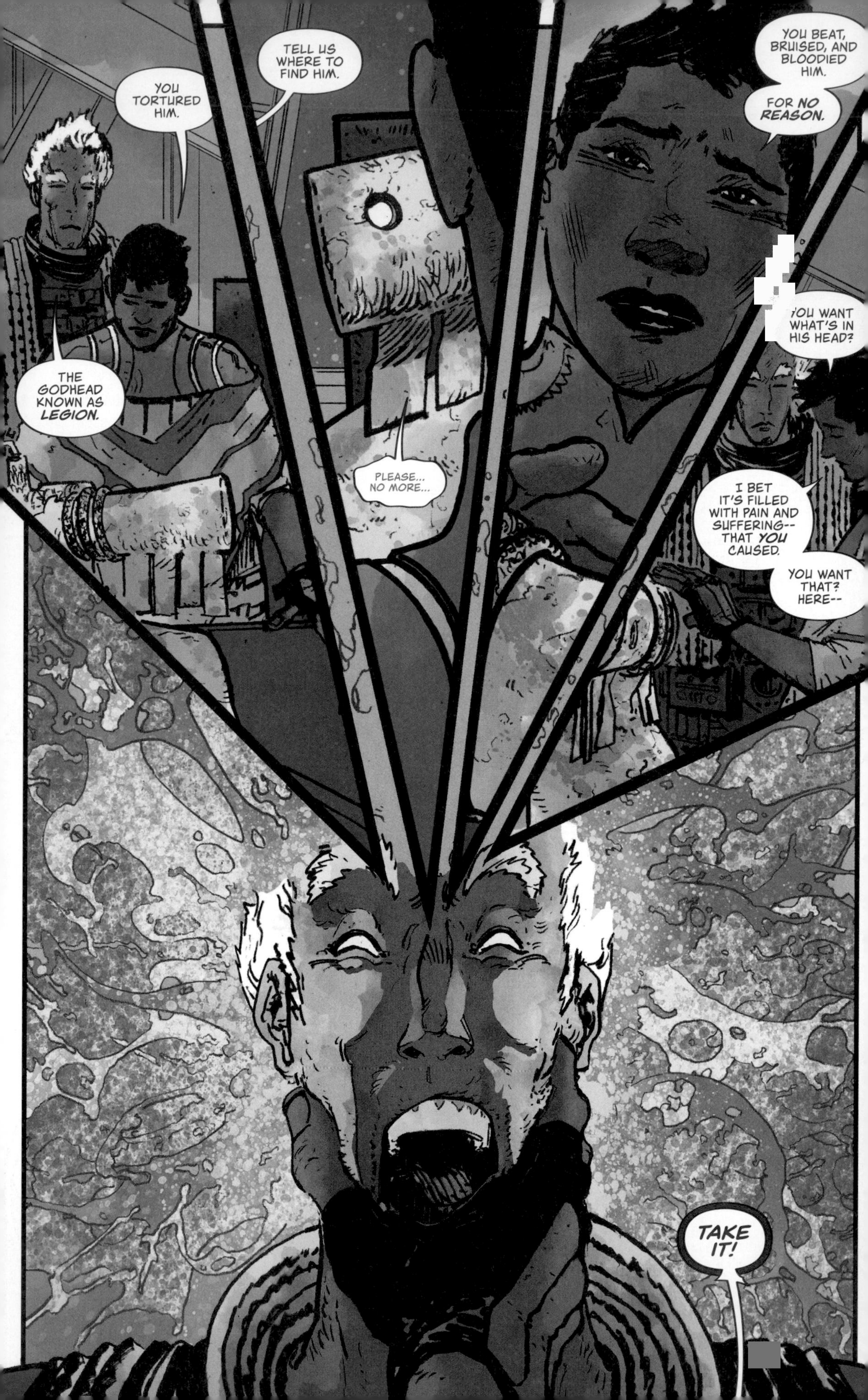
YOU TORTURED HIM.
THE GODHEAD KNOWN AS LEGION.
TELL US WHERE TO FIND HIM.
PLEASE... NO MORE...
YOU BEAT, BRUISED, AND BLOODIED HIM.
FOR NO REASON.
YOU WANT WHAT'S IN HIS HEAD?
I BET IT'S FILLED WITH PAIN AND SUFFERING-- THAT YOU CAUSED.
YOU WANT THAT? HERE--
TAKE IT!

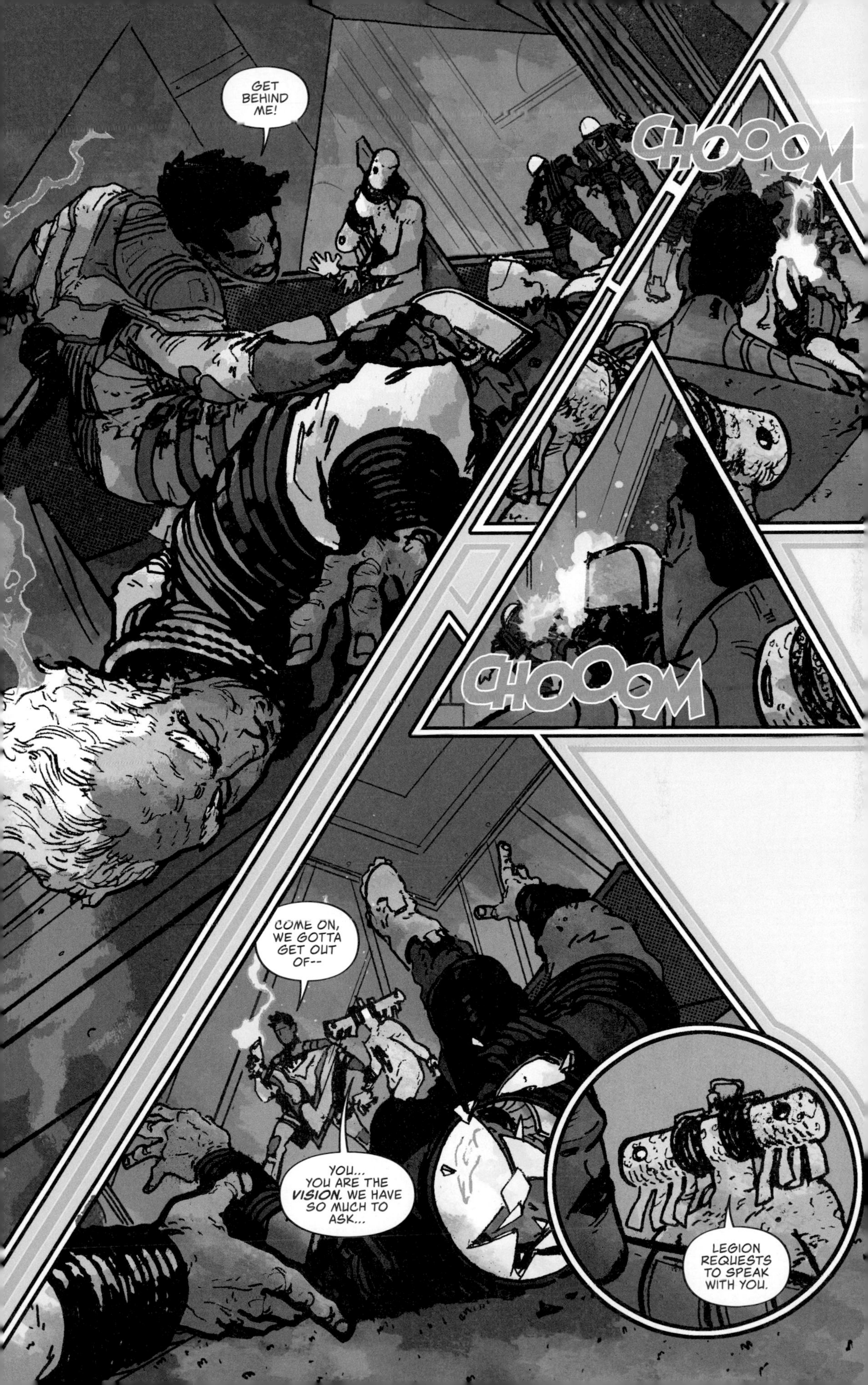
GET BEHIND ME!
CHOOOM
CHOOOM
COME ON, WE GOTTA GET OUT OF--
YOU... YOU ARE THE VISION. WE HAVE SO MUCH TO ASK...
LEGION REQUESTS TO SPEAK WITH YOU.

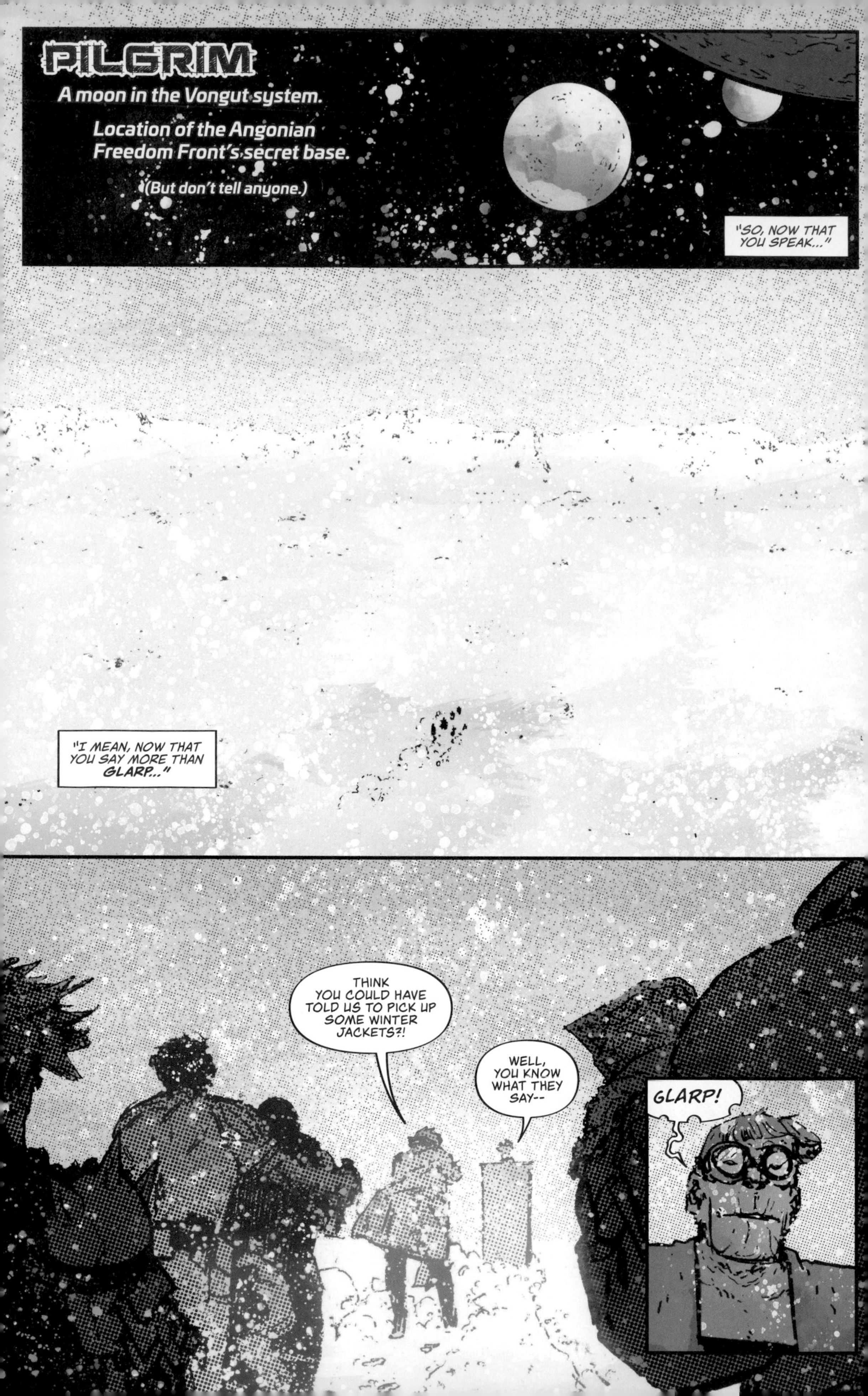
PILGRIM
A moon in the Vongut system.
Location of the Angonian Freedom Front's secret base.
(But don't tell anyone.)
"SO, NOW THAT YOU SPEAK..."
"I MEAN, NOW THAT YOU SAY MORE THAN GLARP..."
THINK YOU COULD HAVE TOLD US TO PICK UP SOME WINTER JACKETS?!
WELL, YOU KNOW WHAT THEY SAY--
GLARP!

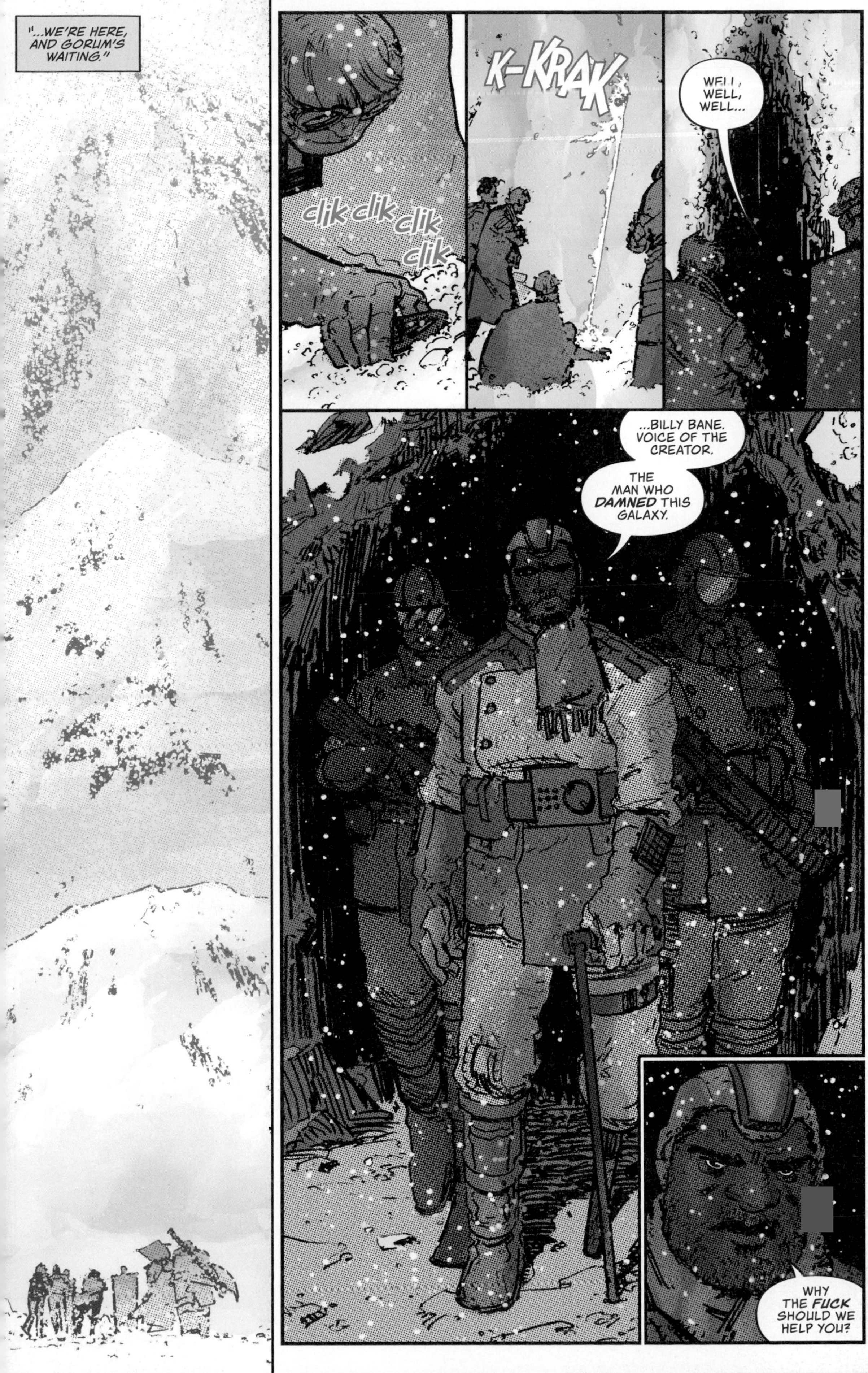
"...WE'RE HERE, AND GORUM'S WAITING."
clik clik clik clik
K-KRAK
WELL, WELL, WELL...
...BILLY BANE. VOICE OF THE CREATOR.
THE MAN WHO DAMNED THIS GALAXY.
WHY THE FUCK SHOULD WE HELP YOU?

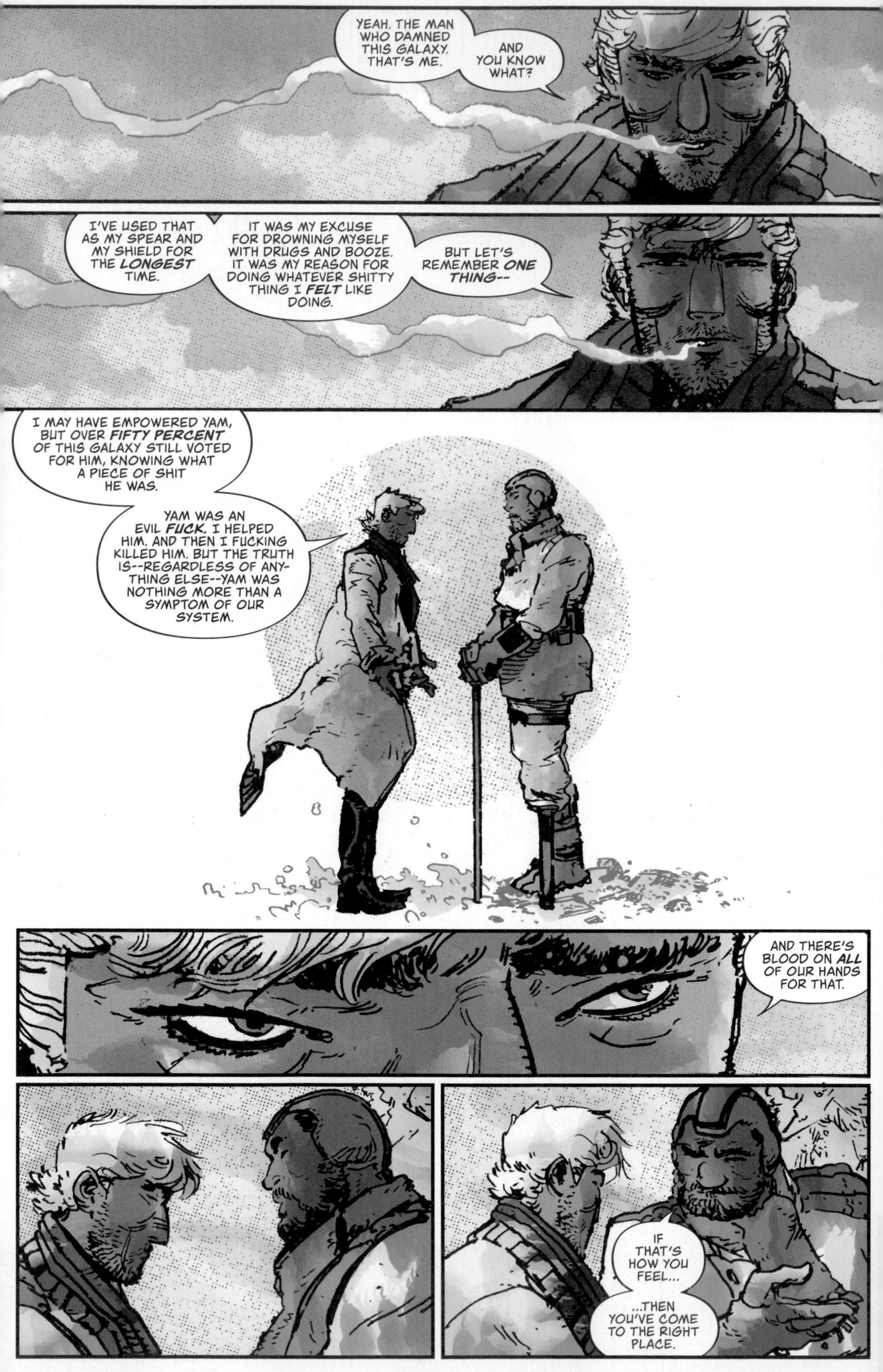
YEAH. THE MAN WHO DAMNED THIS GALAXY. THAT'S ME.
AND YOU KNOW WHAT?
I'VE USED THAT AS MY SPEAR AND MY SHIELD FOR THE LONGEST TIME.
IT WAS MY EXCUSE FOR DROWNING MYSELF WITH DRUGS AND BOOZE. IT WAS MY REASON FOR DOING WHATEVER SHITTY THING I FELT LIKE DOING.
BUT LET'S REMEMBER ONE THING--
I MAY HAVE EMPOWERED YAM, BUT OVER FIFTY PERCENT OF THIS GALAXY STILL VOTED FOR HIM, KNOWING WHAT A PIECE OF SHIT HE WAS.
YAM WAS AN EVIL FUCK. I HELPED HIM. AND THEN I FUCKING KILLED HIM. BUT THE TRUTH IS--REGARDLESS OF ANY-THING ELSE--YAM WAS NOTHING MORE THAN A SYMPTOM OF OUR SYSTEM.
AND THERE'S BLOOD ON ALL OF OUR HANDS FOR THAT.
IF THAT'S HOW YOU FEEL...
...THEN YOU'VE COME TO THE RIGHT PLACE.

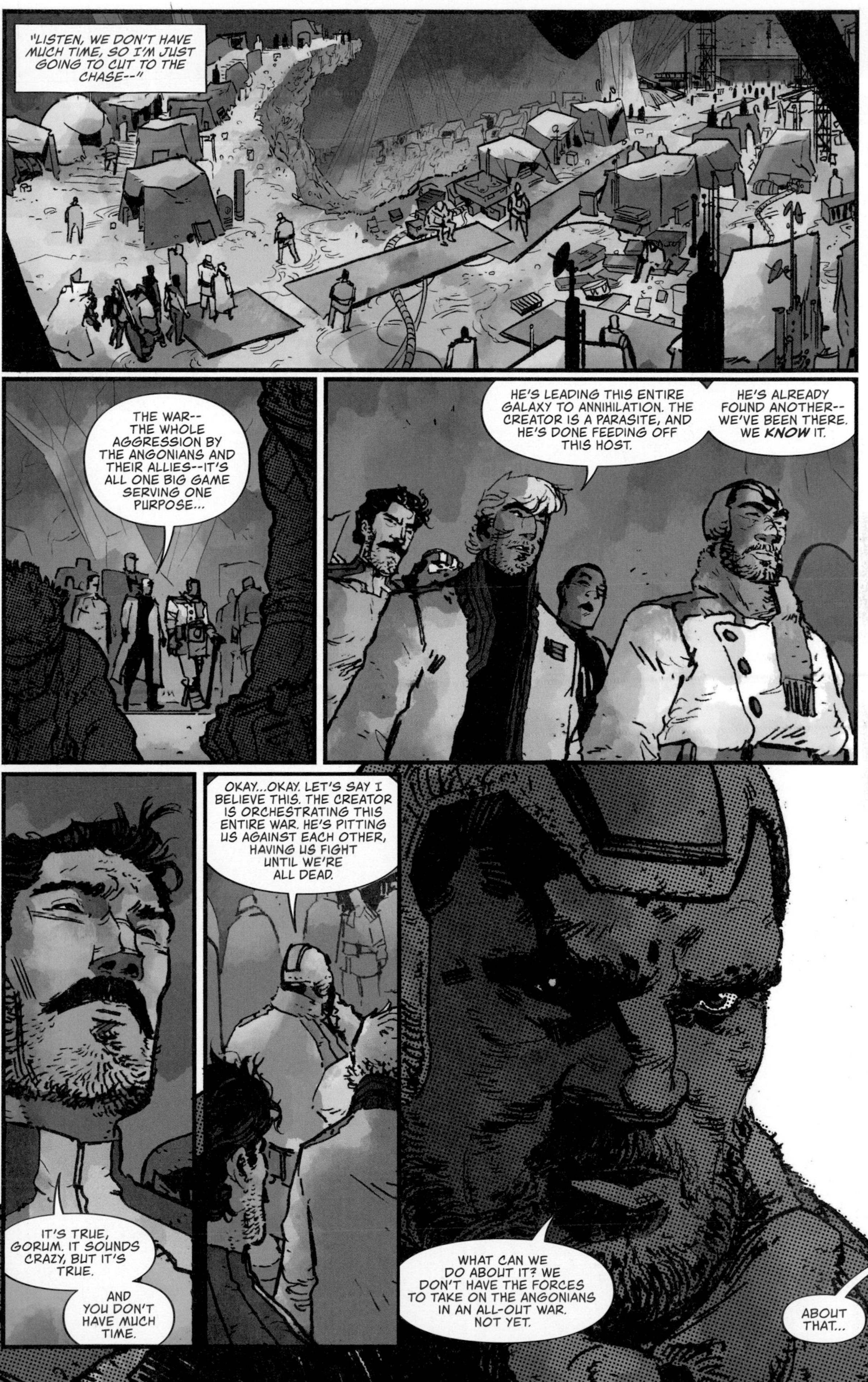
"LISTEN, WE DON'T HAVE MUCH TIME, SO I'M JUST GOING TO CUT TO THE CHASE--"
THE WAR-- THE WHOLE AGGRESSION BY THE ANGONIANS AND THEIR ALLIES--IT'S ALL ONE BIG GAME SERVING ONE PURPOSE...
HE'S LEADING THIS ENTIRE GALAXY TO ANNIHILATION. THE CREATOR IS A PARASITE, AND HE'S DONE FEEDING OFF THIS HOST.
HE'S ALREADY FOUND ANOTHER-- WE'VE BEEN THERE. WE *KNOW* IT.
IT'S TRUE, GORUM. IT SOUNDS CRAZY, BUT IT'S TRUE.
AND YOU DON'T HAVE MUCH TIME.
OKAY...OKAY. LET'S SAY I BELIEVE THIS. THE CREATOR IS ORCHESTRATING THIS ENTIRE WAR. HE'S PITTING US AGAINST EACH OTHER, HAVING US FIGHT UNTIL WE'RE ALL DEAD.
WHAT CAN WE DO ABOUT IT? WE DON'T HAVE THE FORCES TO TAKE ON THE ANGONIANS IN AN ALL-OUT WAR. NOT YET.
ABOUT THAT...

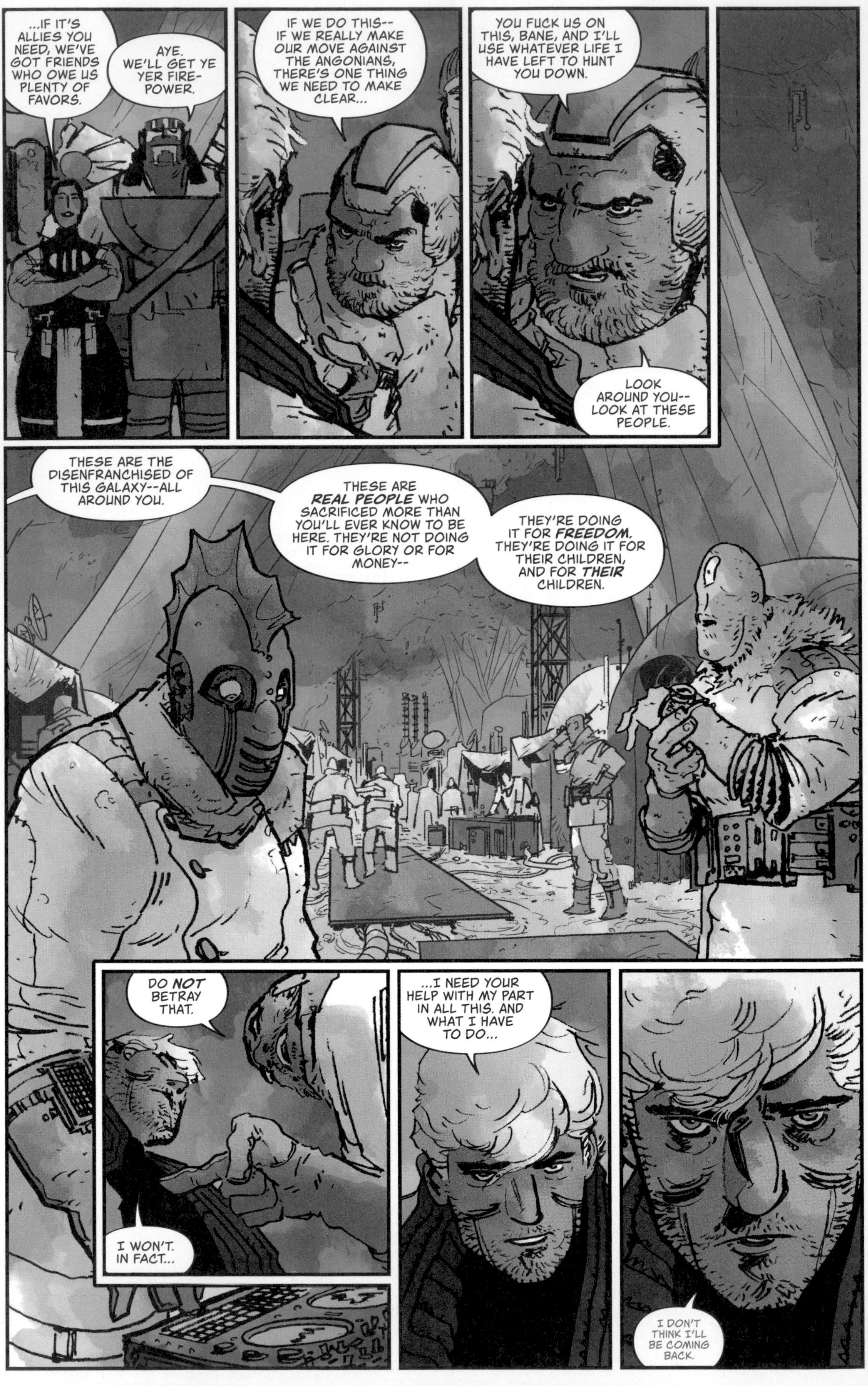
...IF IT'S ALLIES YOU NEED, WE'VE GOT FRIENDS WHO OWE US PLENTY OF FAVORS.
AYE. WE'LL GET YE YER FIRE-POWER.
IF WE DO THIS-- IF WE REALLY MAKE OUR MOVE AGAINST THE ANGONIANS, THERE'S ONE THING WE NEED TO MAKE CLEAR...
YOU FUCK US ON THIS, BANE, AND I'LL USE WHATEVER LIFE I HAVE LEFT TO HUNT YOU DOWN.
LOOK AROUND YOU-- LOOK AT THESE PEOPLE.
THESE ARE THE DISENFRANCHISED OF THIS GALAXY--ALL AROUND YOU.
THESE ARE REAL PEOPLE WHO SACRIFICED MORE THAN YOU'LL EVER KNOW TO BE HERE. THEY'RE NOT DOING IT FOR GLORY OR FOR MONEY--
THEY'RE DOING IT FOR FREEDOM. THEY'RE DOING IT FOR THEIR CHILDREN, AND FOR THEIR CHILDREN.
DO NOT BETRAY THAT.
I WON'T. IN FACT...
...I NEED YOUR HELP WITH MY PART IN ALL THIS. AND WHAT I HAVE TO DO...
I DON'T THINK I'LL BE COMING BACK.

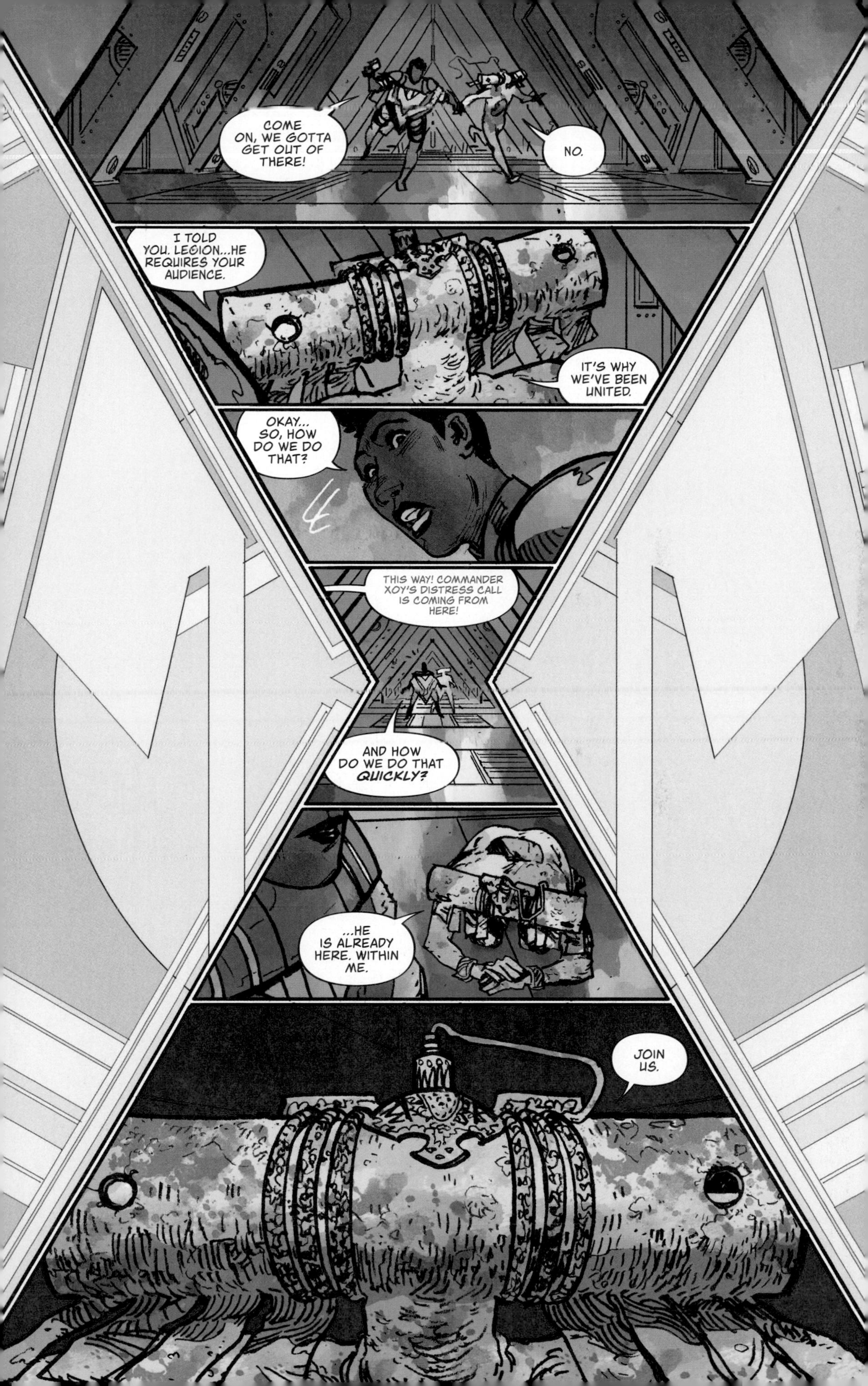
COME ON, WE GOTTA GET OUT OF THERE!
NO.
I TOLD YOU. LEGION...HE REQUIRES YOUR AUDIENCE.
IT'S WHY WE'VE BEEN UNITED.
OKAY... SO, HOW DO WE DO THAT?
THIS WAY! COMMANDER XOY'S DISTRESS CALL IS COMING FROM HERE!
AND HOW DO WE DO THAT *QUICKLY?*
...HE IS ALREADY HERE. WITHIN ME.
JOIN US.

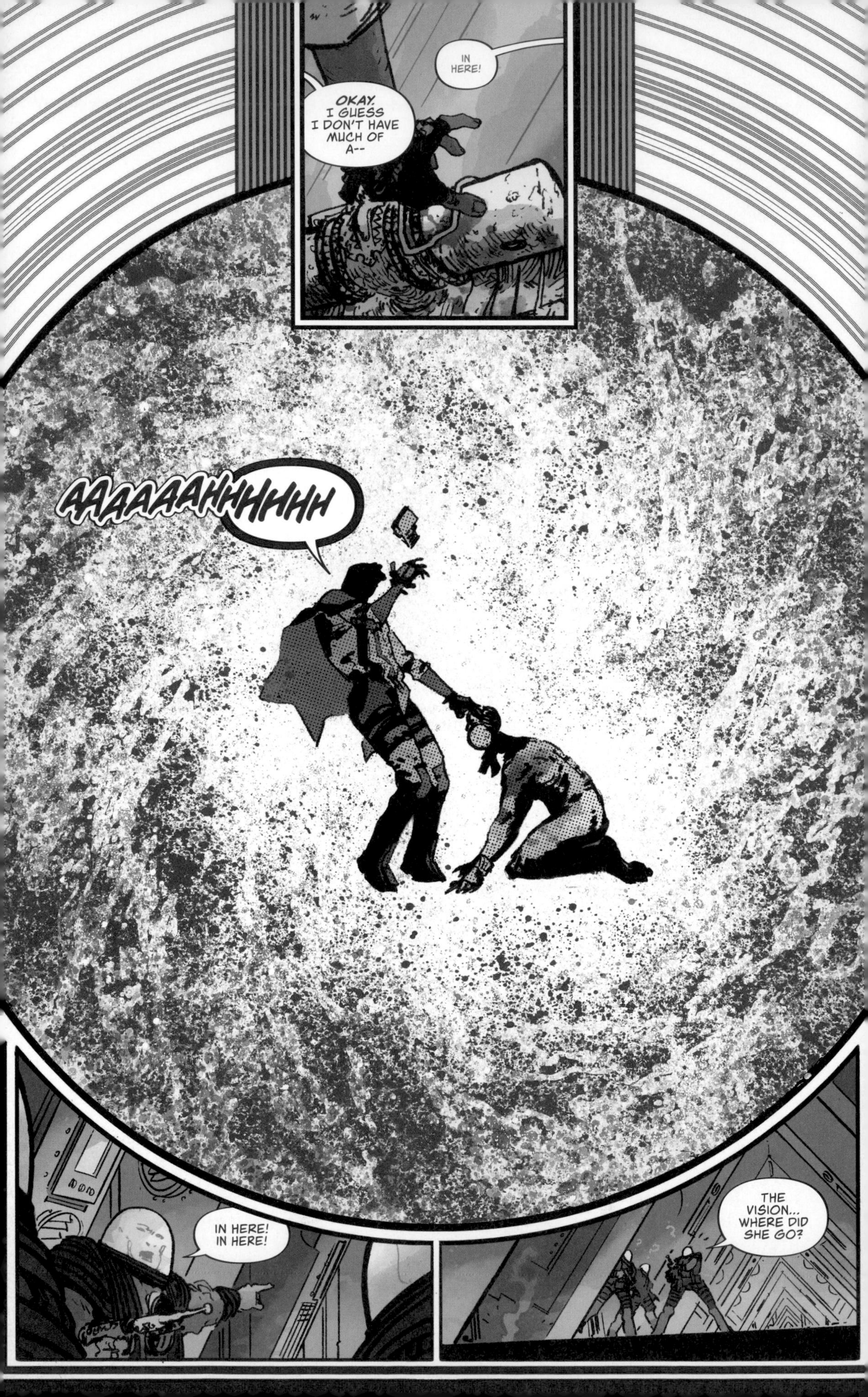
IN HERE!
OKAY. I GUESS I DON'T HAVE MUCH OF A--
AAAAAAHHHHHH
IN HERE! IN HERE!
THE VISION... WHERE DID SHE GO?

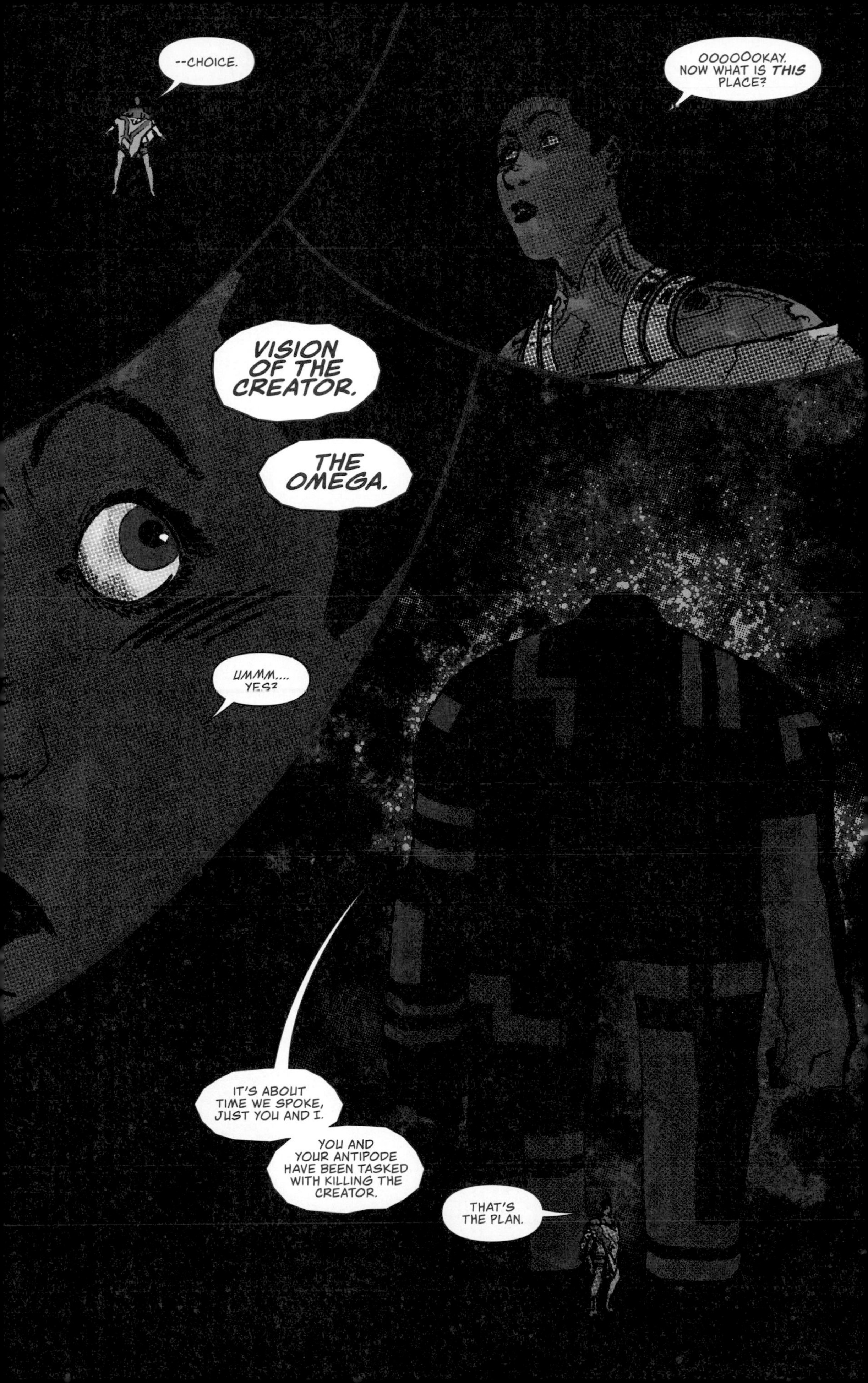
--CHOICE.
OOOOOOKAY. NOW WHAT IS THIS PLACE?
VISION OF THE CREATOR.
THE OMEGA.
UMMM.... YES?
IT'S ABOUT TIME WE SPOKE, JUST YOU AND I.
YOU AND YOUR ANTIPODE HAVE BEEN TASKED WITH KILLING THE CREATOR.
THAT'S THE PLAN.

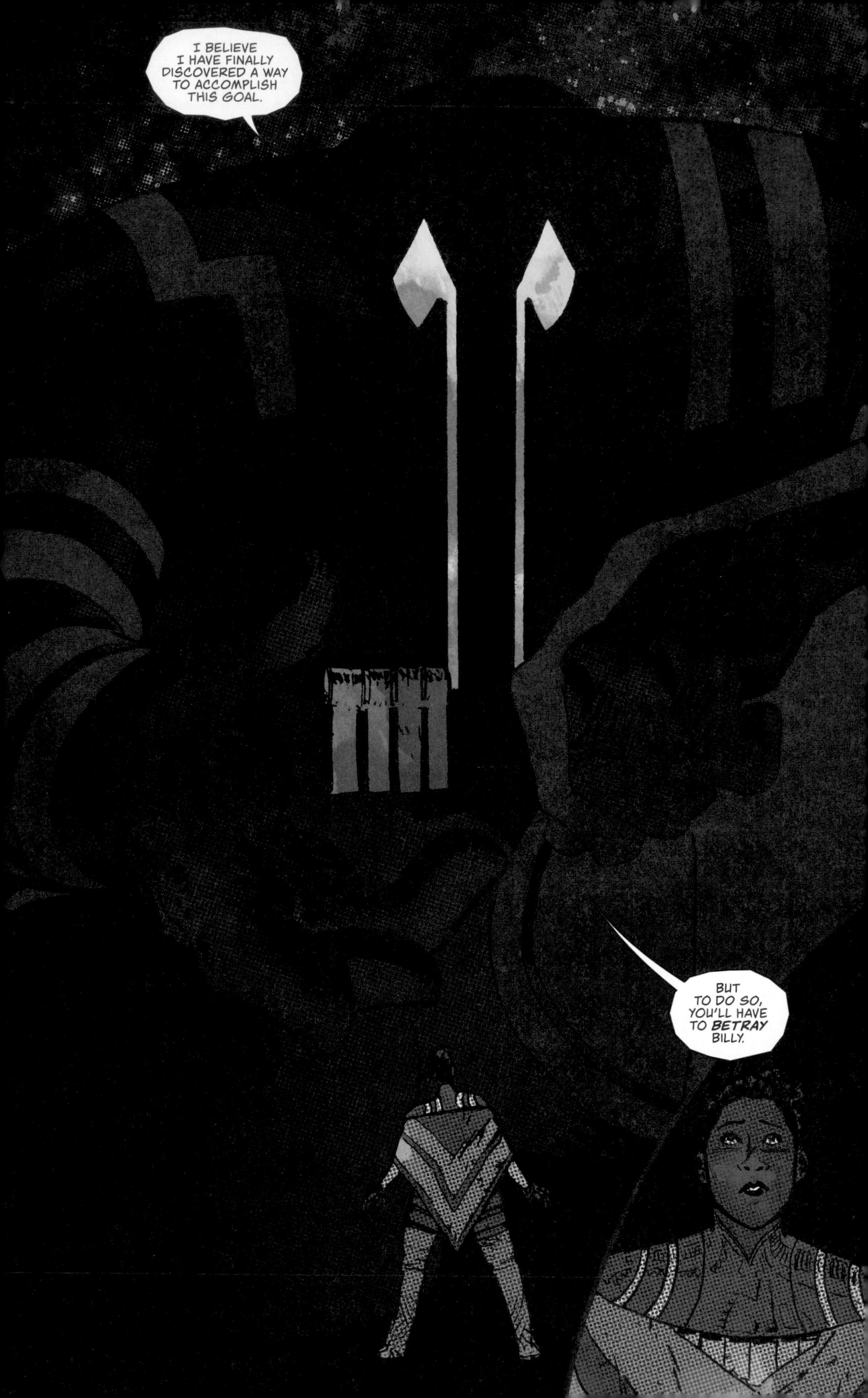
I BELIEVE I HAVE FINALLY DISCOVERED A WAY TO ACCOMPLISH THIS GOAL.
BUT TO DO SO, YOU'LL HAVE TO *BETRAY* BILLY.

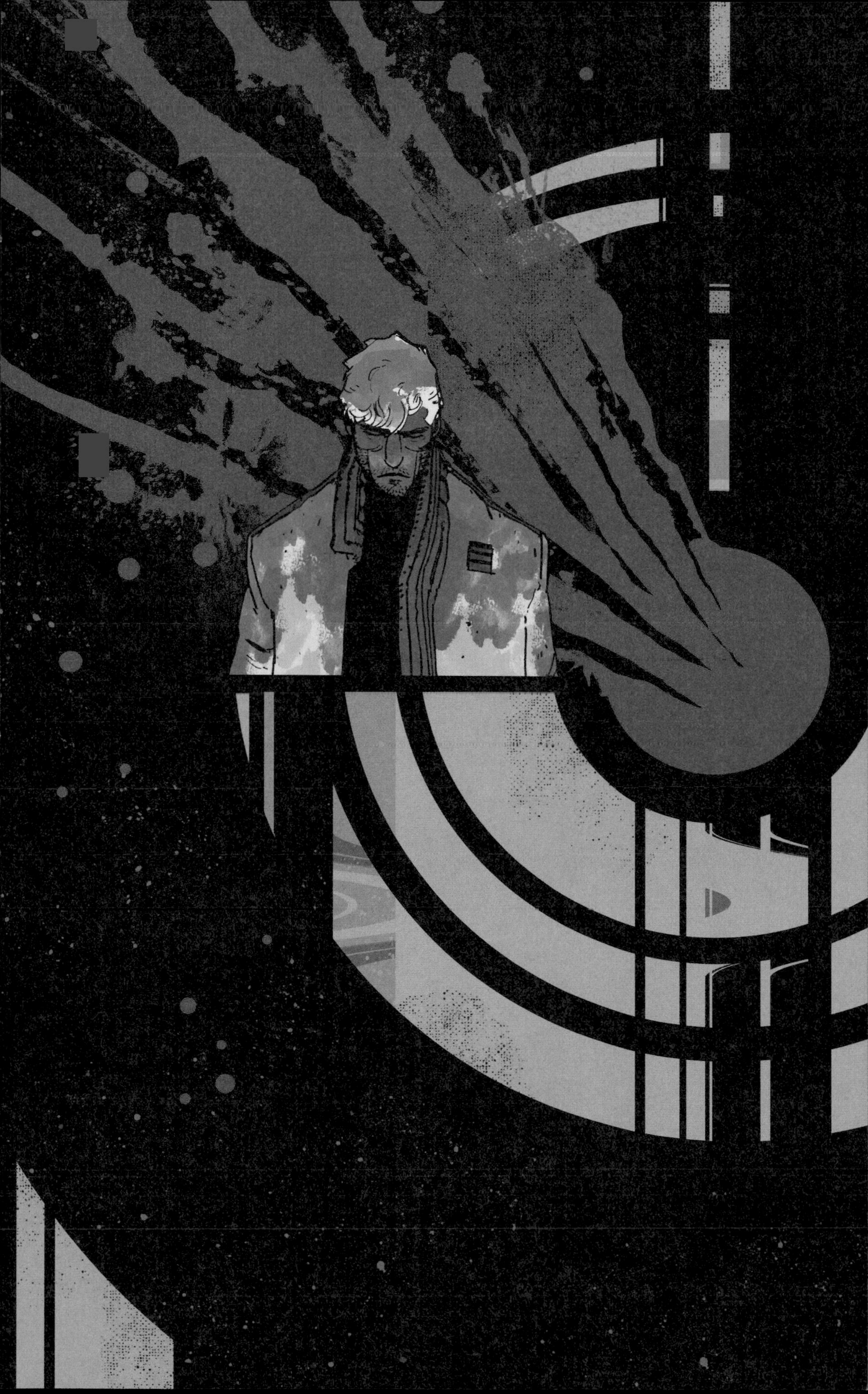

CHAPTER TWENTYTHREE

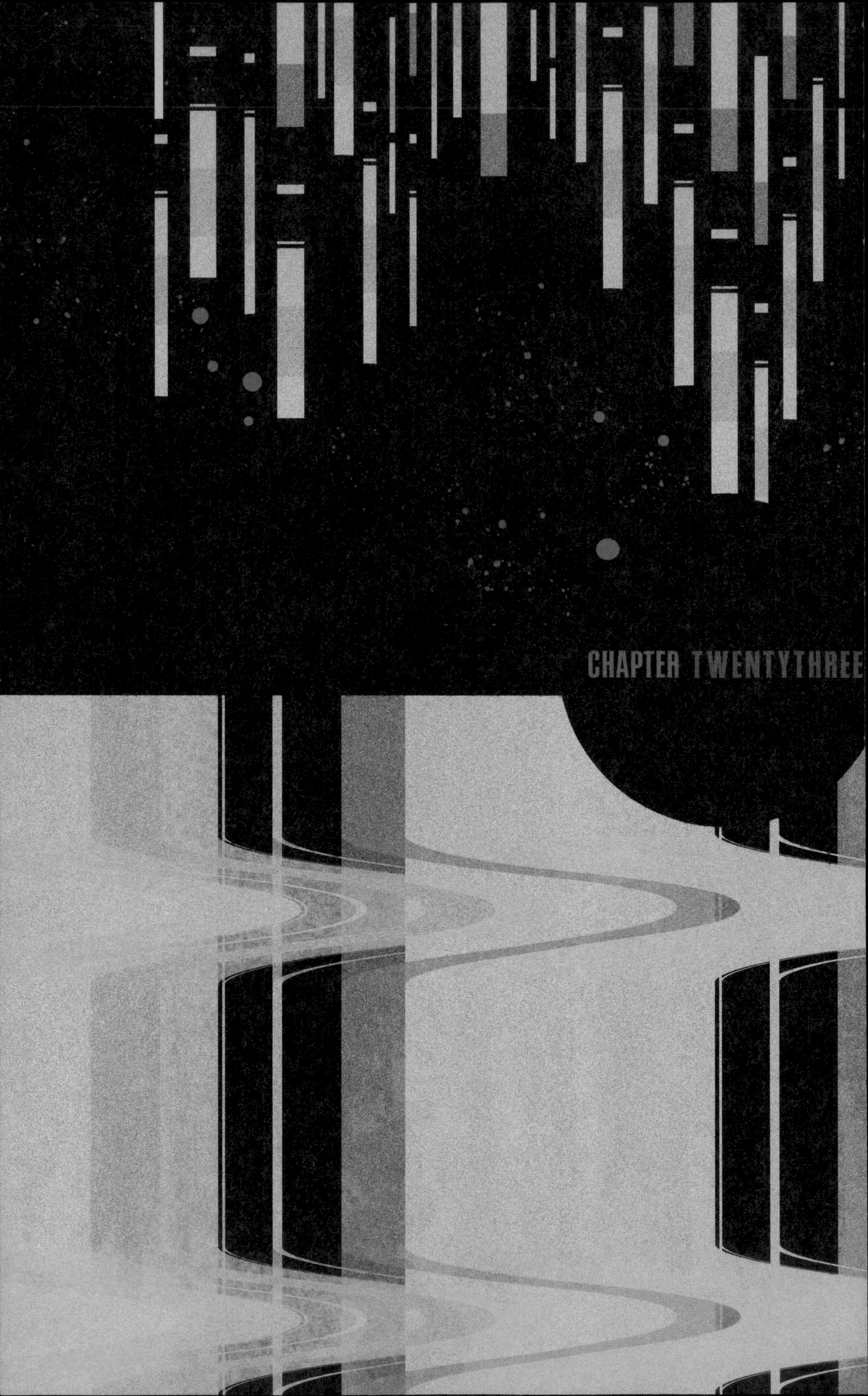

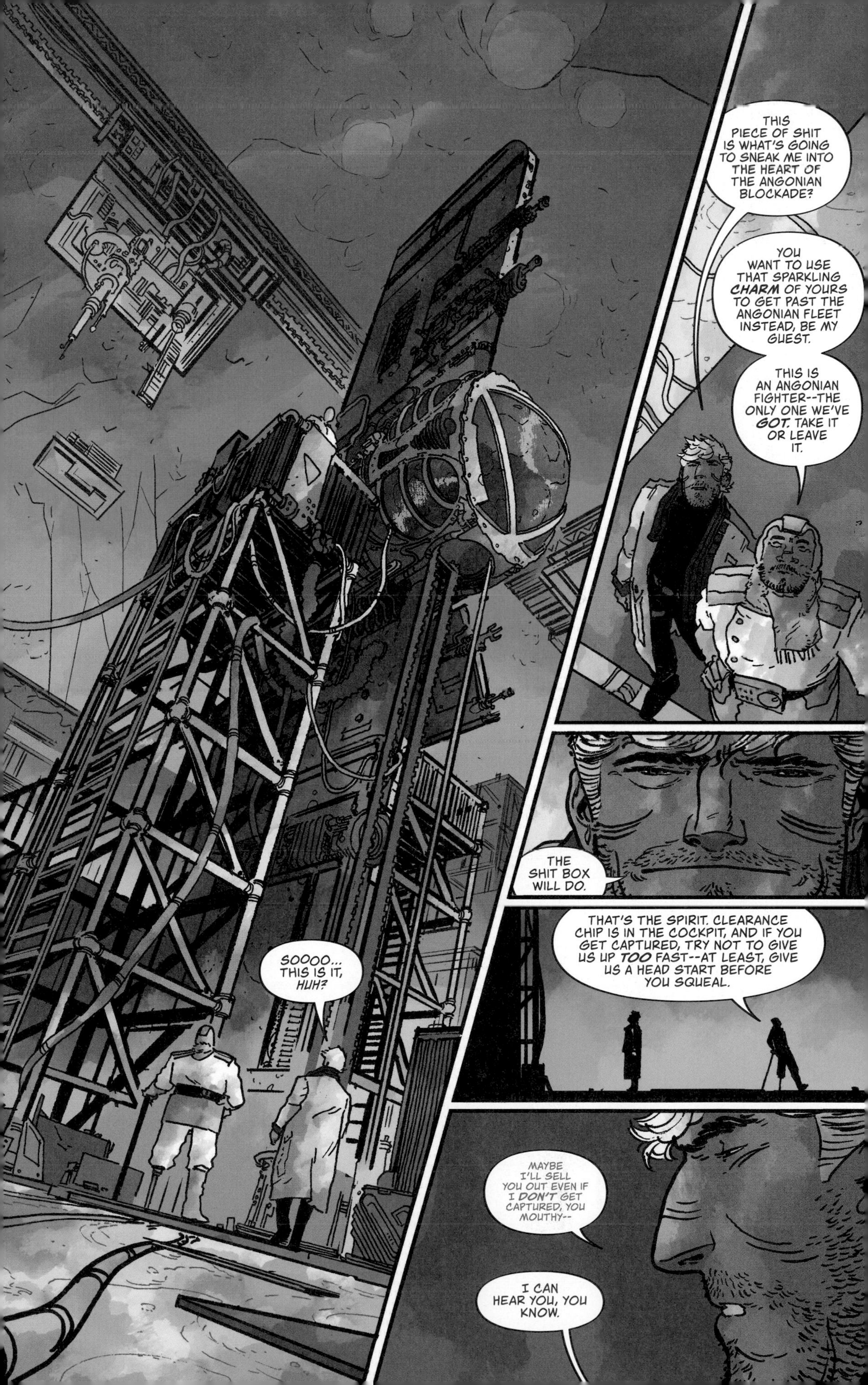
SOOOO... THIS IS IT, HUH?
THIS PIECE OF SHIT IS WHAT'S GOING TO SNEAK ME INTO THE HEART OF THE ANGONIAN BLOCKADE?
YOU WANT TO USE THAT SPARKLING CHARM OF YOURS TO GET PAST THE ANGONIAN FLEET INSTEAD, BE MY GUEST.
THIS IS AN ANGONIAN FIGHTER--THE ONLY ONE WE'VE GOT. TAKE IT OR LEAVE IT.
THE SHIT BOX WILL DO.
THAT'S THE SPIRIT. CLEARANCE CHIP IS IN THE COCKPIT, AND IF YOU GET CAPTURED, TRY NOT TO GIVE US UP TOO FAST--AT LEAST, GIVE US A HEAD START BEFORE YOU SQUEAL.
MAYBE I'LL SELL YOU OUT EVEN IF I DON'T GET CAPTURED, YOU MOUTHY--
I CAN HEAR YOU, YOU KNOW.

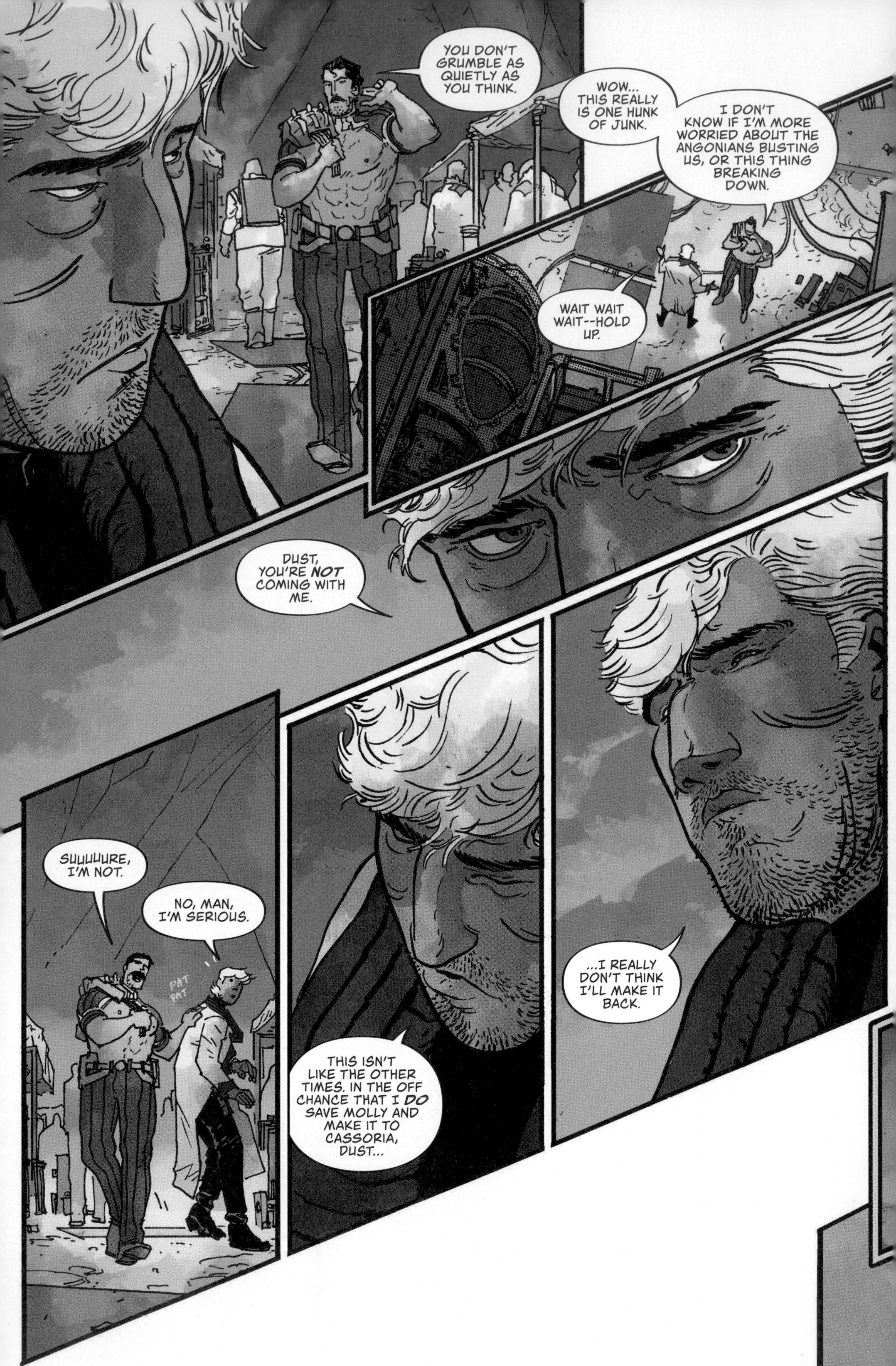
YOU DON'T GRUMBLE AS QUIETLY AS YOU THINK.
WOW... THIS REALLY IS ONE HUNK OF JUNK.
I DON'T KNOW IF I'M MORE WORRIED ABOUT THE ANGONIANS BUSTING US, OR THIS THING BREAKING DOWN.
WAIT WAIT WAIT--HOLD UP.
DUST, YOU'RE NOT COMING WITH ME.
SUUUUURE, I'M NOT.
NO, MAN, I'M SERIOUS.
PAT PAT
THIS ISN'T LIKE THE OTHER TIMES. IN THE OFF CHANCE THAT I DO SAVE MOLLY AND MAKE IT TO CASSORIA, DUST...
...I REALLY DON'T THINK I'LL MAKE IT BACK.

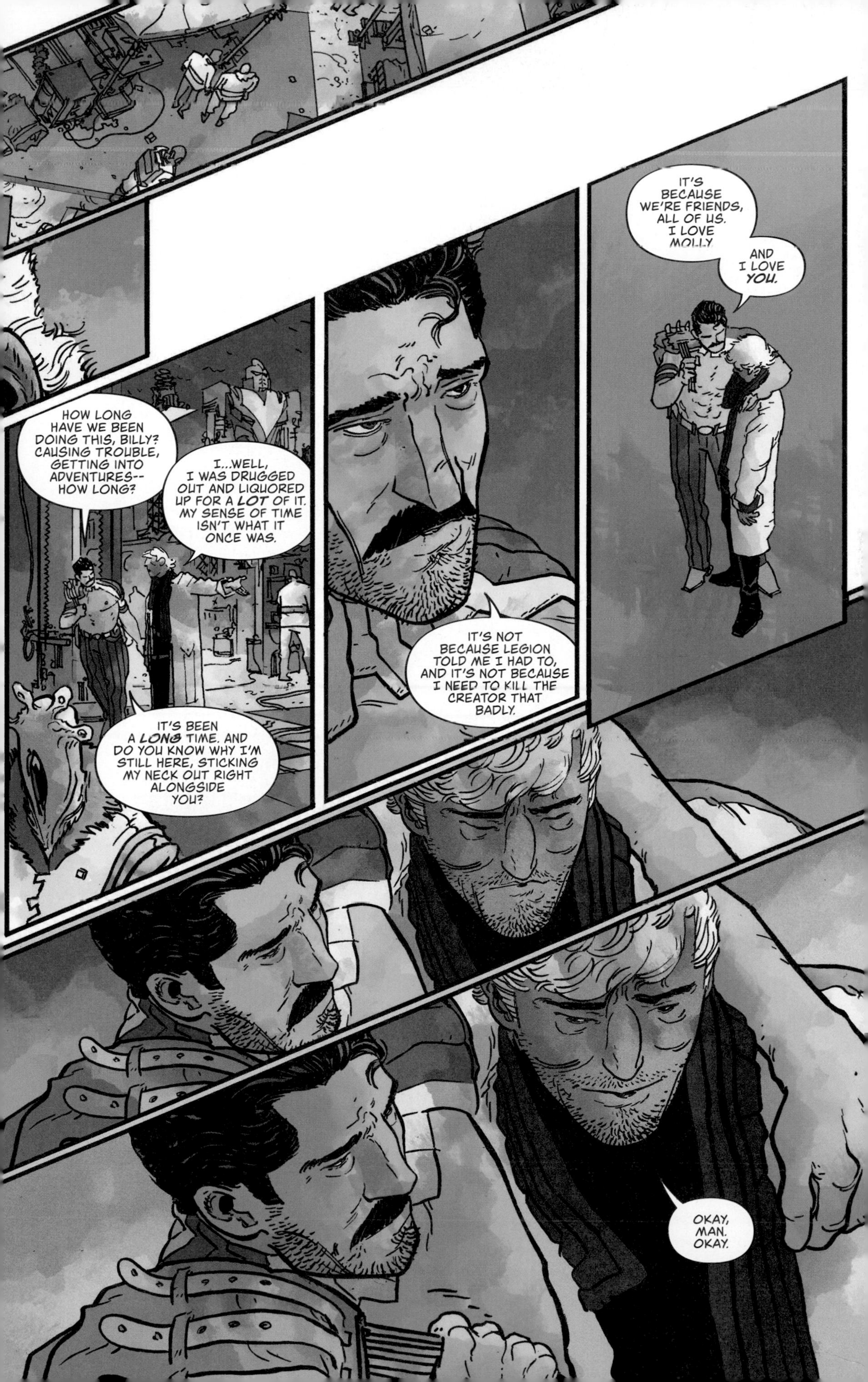
IT'S BECAUSE WE'RE FRIENDS, ALL OF US. I LOVE MOLLY.
AND I LOVE YOU.
HOW LONG HAVE WE BEEN DOING THIS, BILLY? CAUSING TROUBLE, GETTING INTO ADVENTURES-- HOW LONG?
I...WELL, I WAS DRUGGED OUT AND LIQUORED UP FOR A LOT OF IT. MY SENSE OF TIME ISN'T WHAT IT ONCE WAS.
IT'S BEEN A LONG TIME. AND DO YOU KNOW WHY I'M STILL HERE, STICKING MY NECK OUT RIGHT ALONGSIDE YOU?
IT'S NOT BECAUSE LEGION TOLD ME I HAD TO, AND IT'S NOT BECAUSE I NEED TO KILL THE CREATOR THAT BADLY.
OKAY, MAN. OKAY.

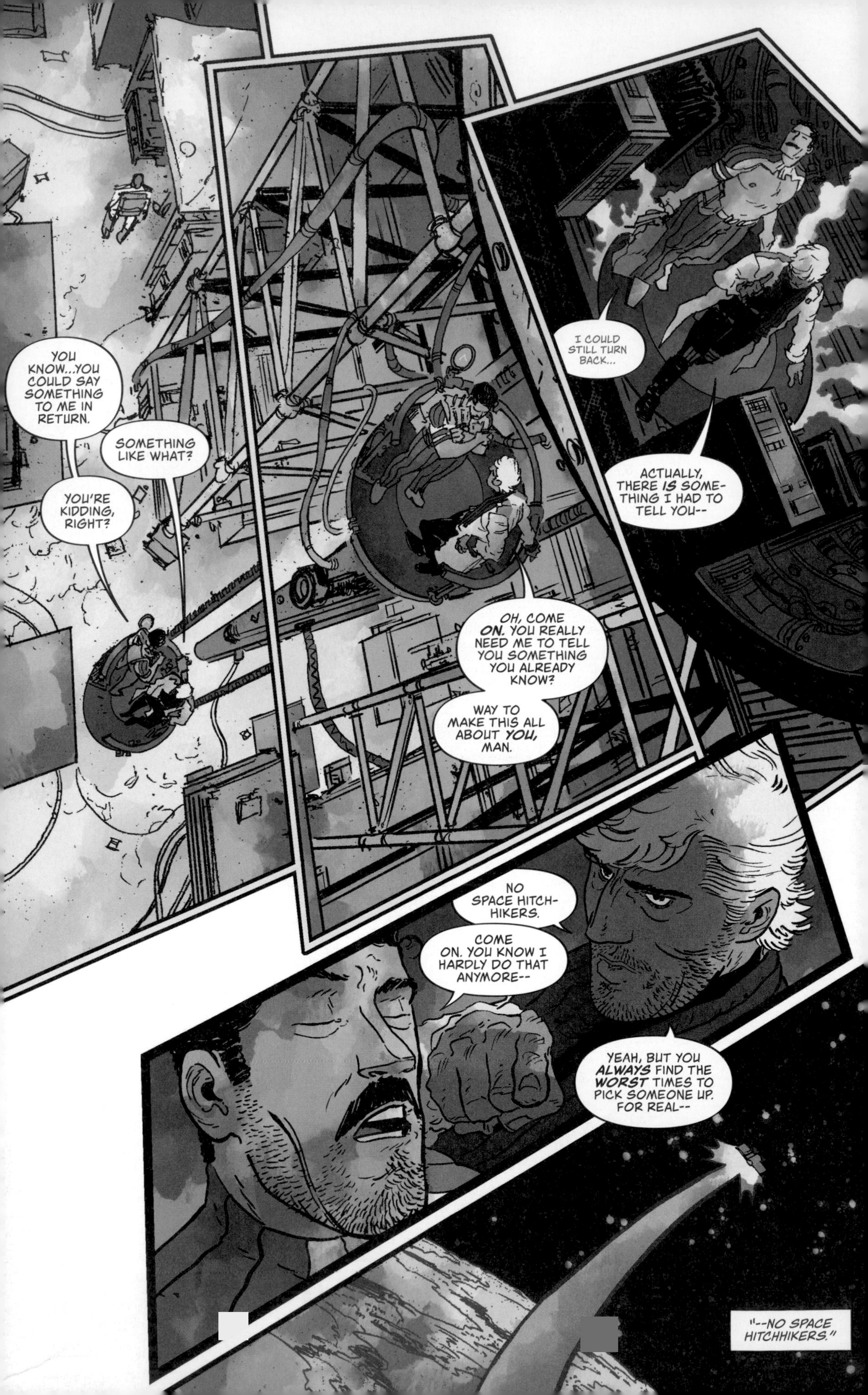

YOU KNOW...YOU COULD SAY SOMETHING TO ME IN RETURN.
SOMETHING LIKE WHAT?
YOU'RE KIDDING, RIGHT?
OH, COME *ON.* YOU REALLY NEED ME TO TELL YOU SOMETHING YOU ALREADY KNOW?
WAY TO MAKE THIS ALL ABOUT *YOU,* MAN.
I COULD STILL TURN BACK...
ACTUALLY, THERE *IS* SOMETHING I HAD TO TELL YOU--
NO SPACE HITCHHIKERS.
COME ON. YOU KNOW I HARDLY DO THAT ANYMORE--
YEAH, BUT YOU *ALWAYS* FIND THE *WORST* TIMES TO PICK SOMEONE UP. FOR REAL--
"--NO SPACE HITCHHIKERS."

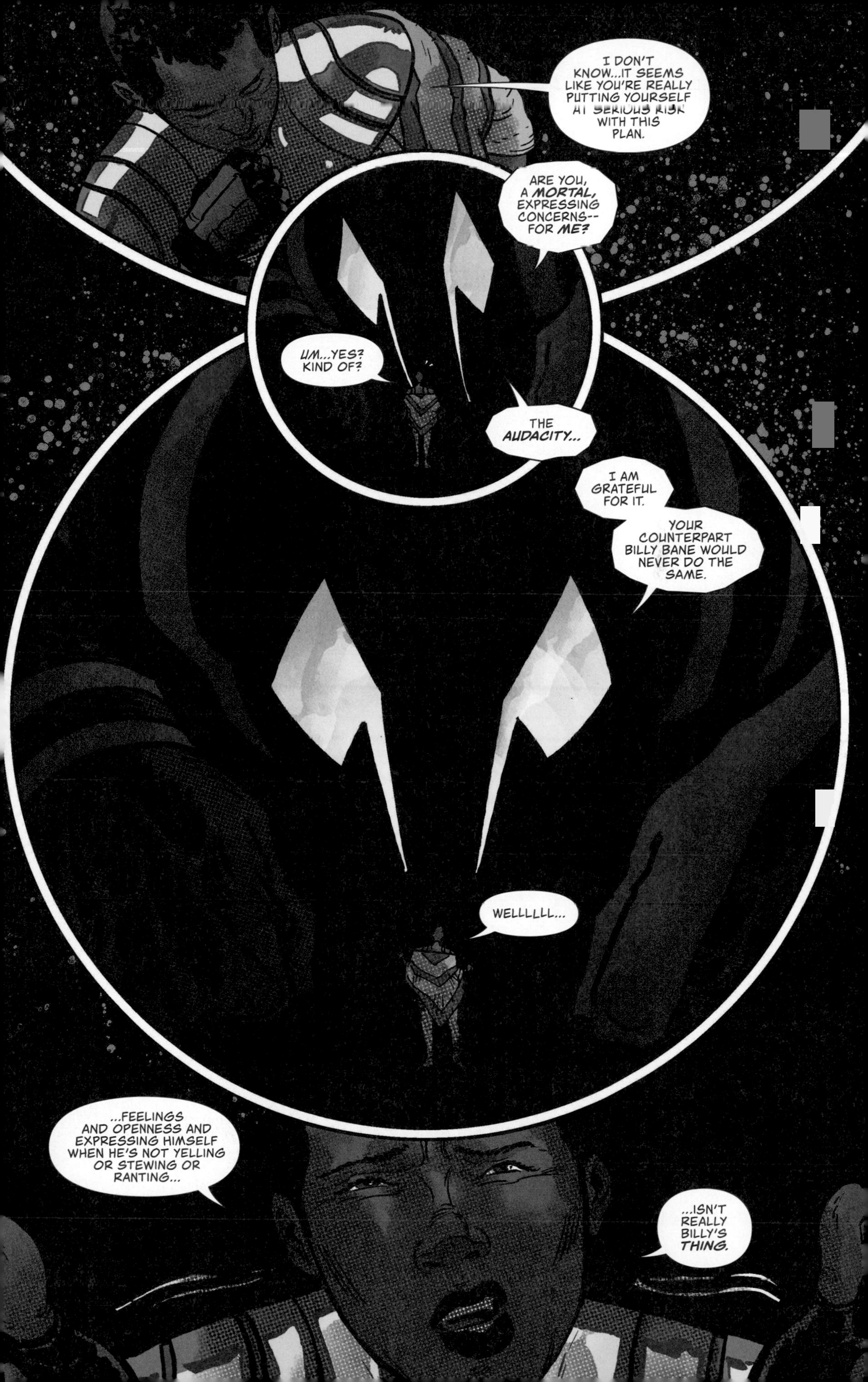

I DON'T KNOW...IT SEEMS LIKE YOU'RE REALLY PUTTING YOURSELF AT SERIOUS RISK WITH THIS PLAN.
ARE YOU, A MORTAL, EXPRESSING CONCERNS-- FOR ME?
UM...YES? KIND OF?
THE AUDACITY...
I AM GRATEFUL FOR IT.
YOUR COUNTERPART BILLY BANE WOULD NEVER DO THE SAME.
WELLLLLL...
...FEELINGS AND OPENNESS AND EXPRESSING HIMSELF WHEN HE'S NOT YELLING OR STEWING OR RANTING...
...ISN'T REALLY BILLY'S THING.

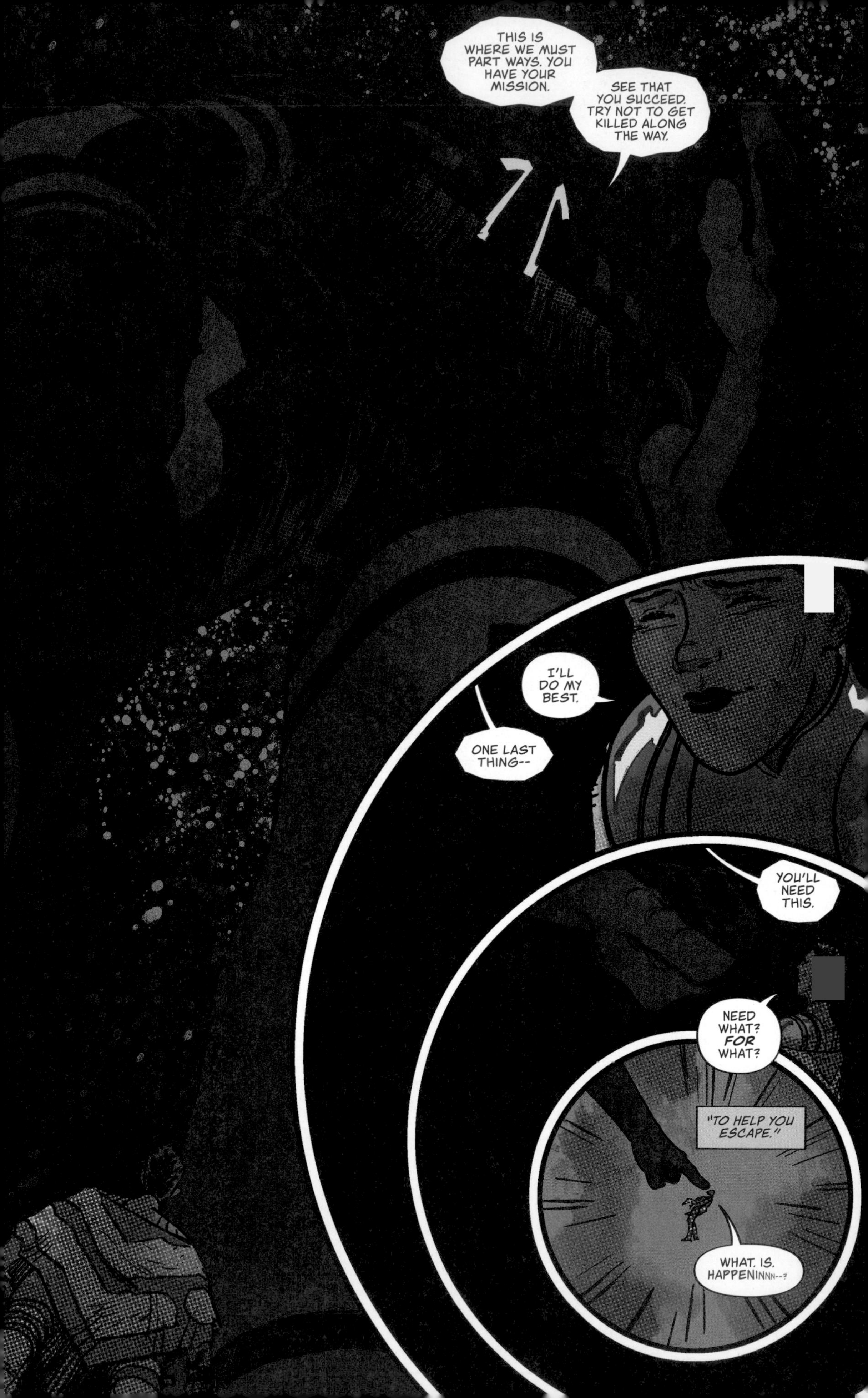
THIS IS WHERE WE MUST PART WAYS. YOU HAVE YOUR MISSION.
SEE THAT YOU SUCCEED. TRY NOT TO GET KILLED ALONG THE WAY.
I'LL DO MY BEST.
ONE LAST THING--
YOU'LL NEED THIS.
NEED WHAT? FOR WHAT?
"TO HELP YOU ESCAPE."
WHAT. IS. HAPPENINNN--?

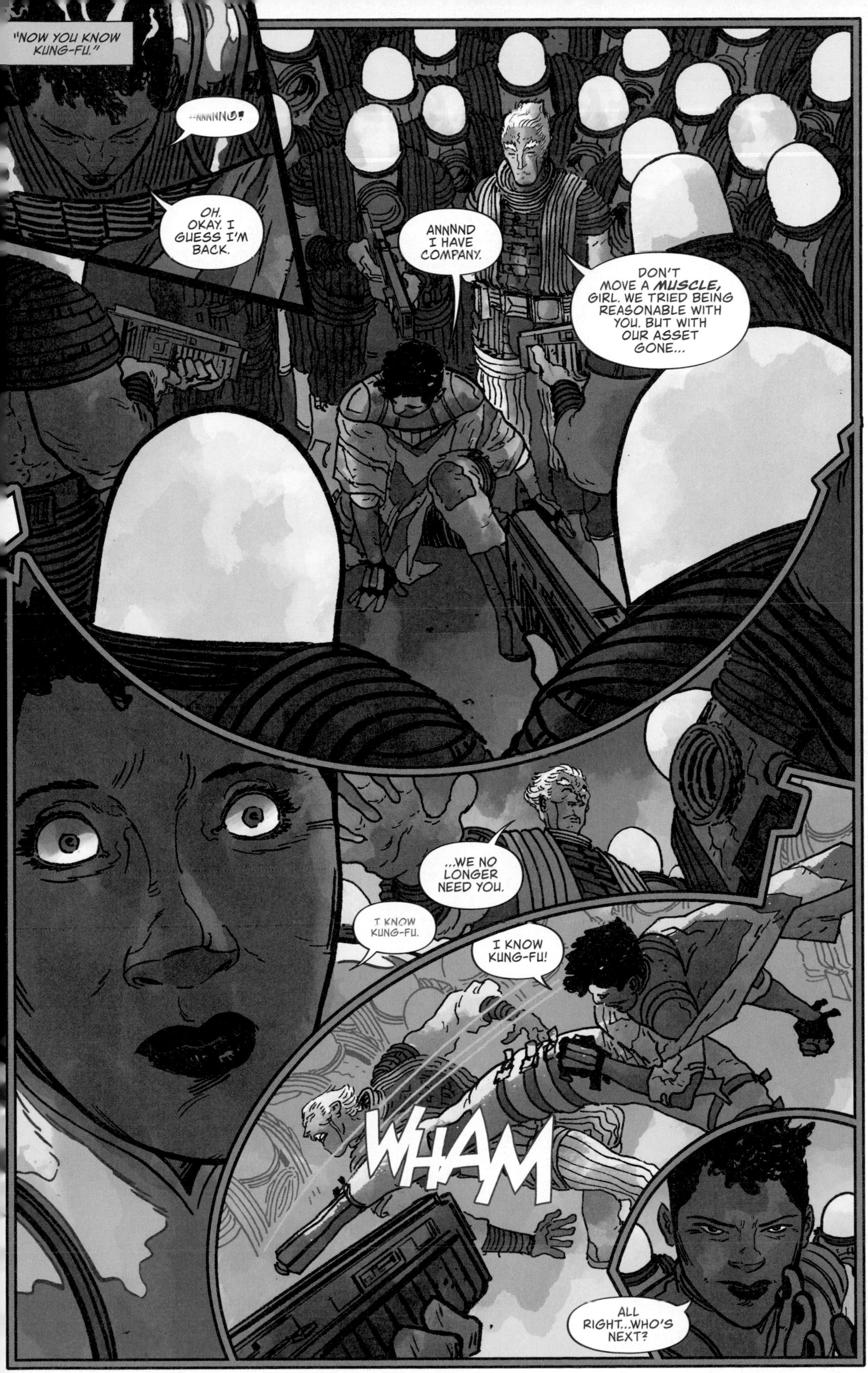
"NOW YOU KNOW KUNG-FU."
--ANNNNO!
OH. OKAY. I GUESS I'M BACK.
ANNNND I HAVE COMPANY.
DON'T MOVE A MUSCLE, GIRL. WE TRIED BEING REASONABLE WITH YOU. BUT WITH OUR ASSET GONE...
...WE NO LONGER NEED YOU.
I KNOW KUNG-FU.
I KNOW KUNG-FU!
WHAM
ALL RIGHT...WHO'S NEXT?

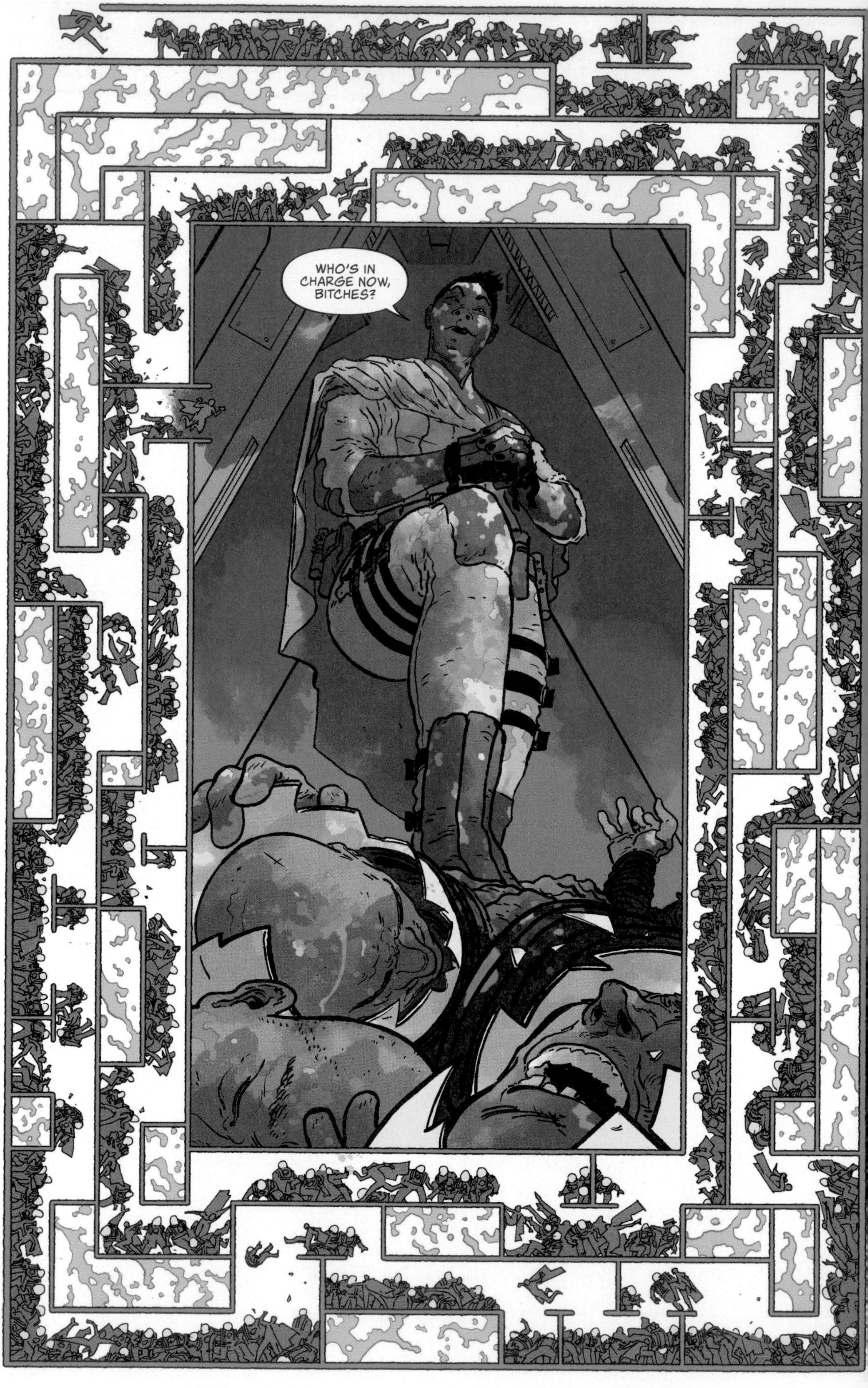
WHO'S IN CHARGE NOW, BITCHES?

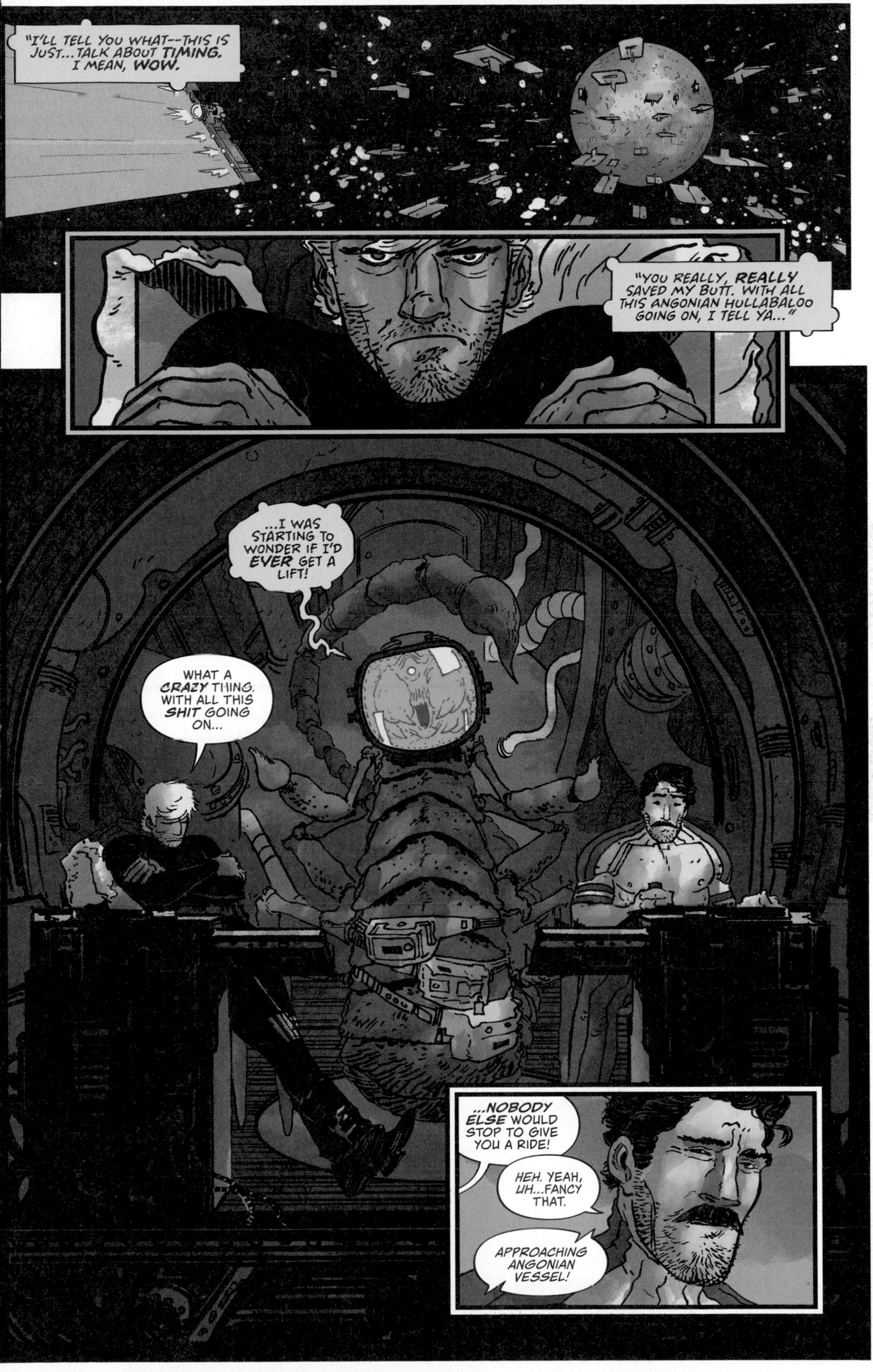
"I'LL TELL YOU WHAT--THIS IS JUST...TALK ABOUT TIMING. I MEAN, WOW.
"YOU REALLY, REALLY SAVED MY BUTT. WITH ALL THIS ANGONIAN HULLABALOO GOING ON, I TELL YA..."
...I WAS STARTING TO WONDER IF I'D EVER GET A LIFT!
WHAT A CRAZY THING. WITH ALL THIS SHIT GOING ON...
...NOBODY ELSE WOULD STOP TO GIVE YOU A RIDE!
HEH. YEAH, UH...FANCY THAT.
APPROACHING ANGONIAN VESSEL!

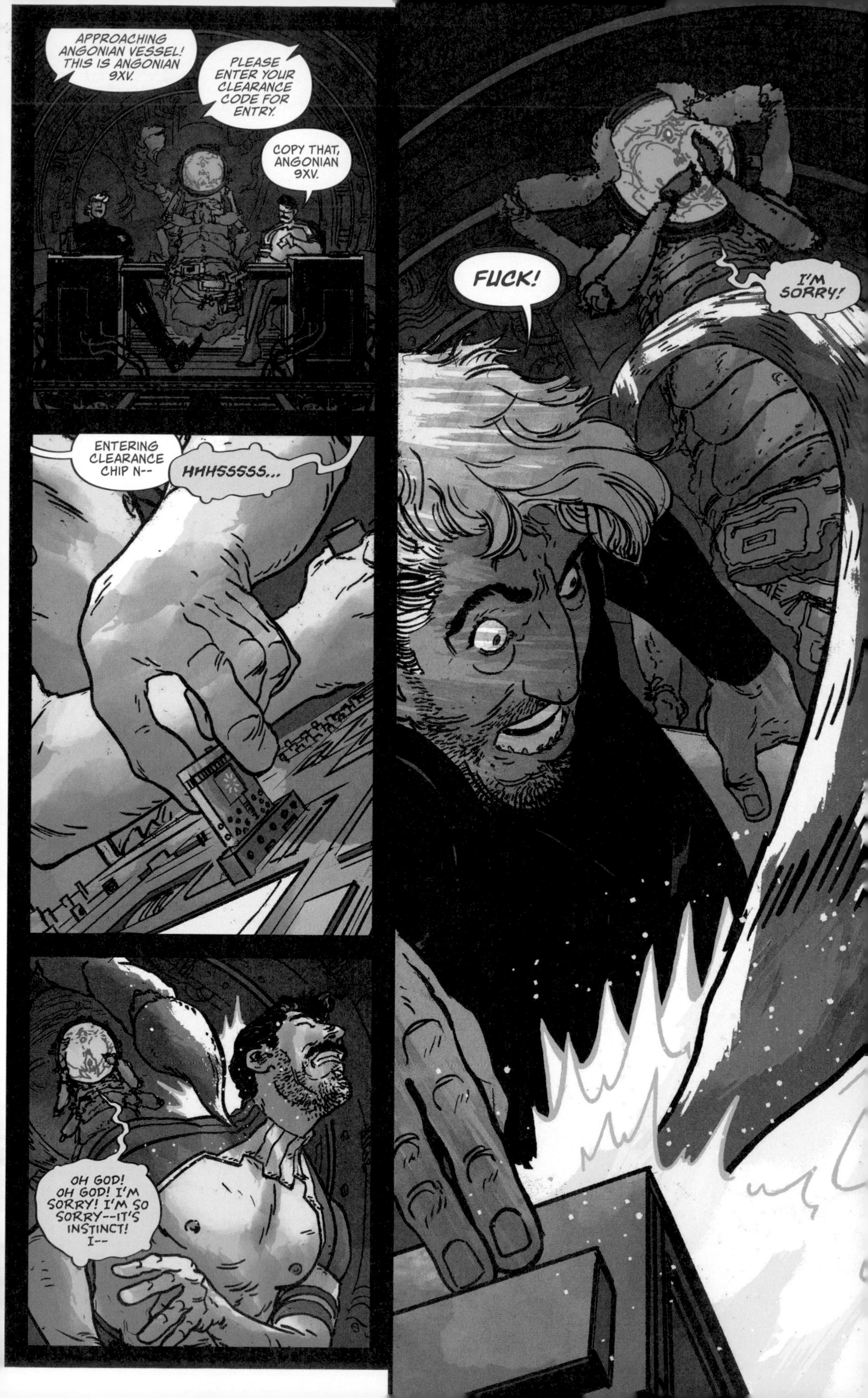
APPROACHING ANGONIAN VESSEL! THIS IS ANGONIAN 9XV.
PLEASE ENTER YOUR CLEARANCE CODE FOR ENTRY.
COPY THAT, ANGONIAN 9XV.
ENTERING CLEARANCE CHIP N--
HHHSSSSS...
OH GOD! OH GOD! I'M SORRY! I'M SO SORRY--IT'S INSTINCT! I--
FUCK!
I'M SORRY!

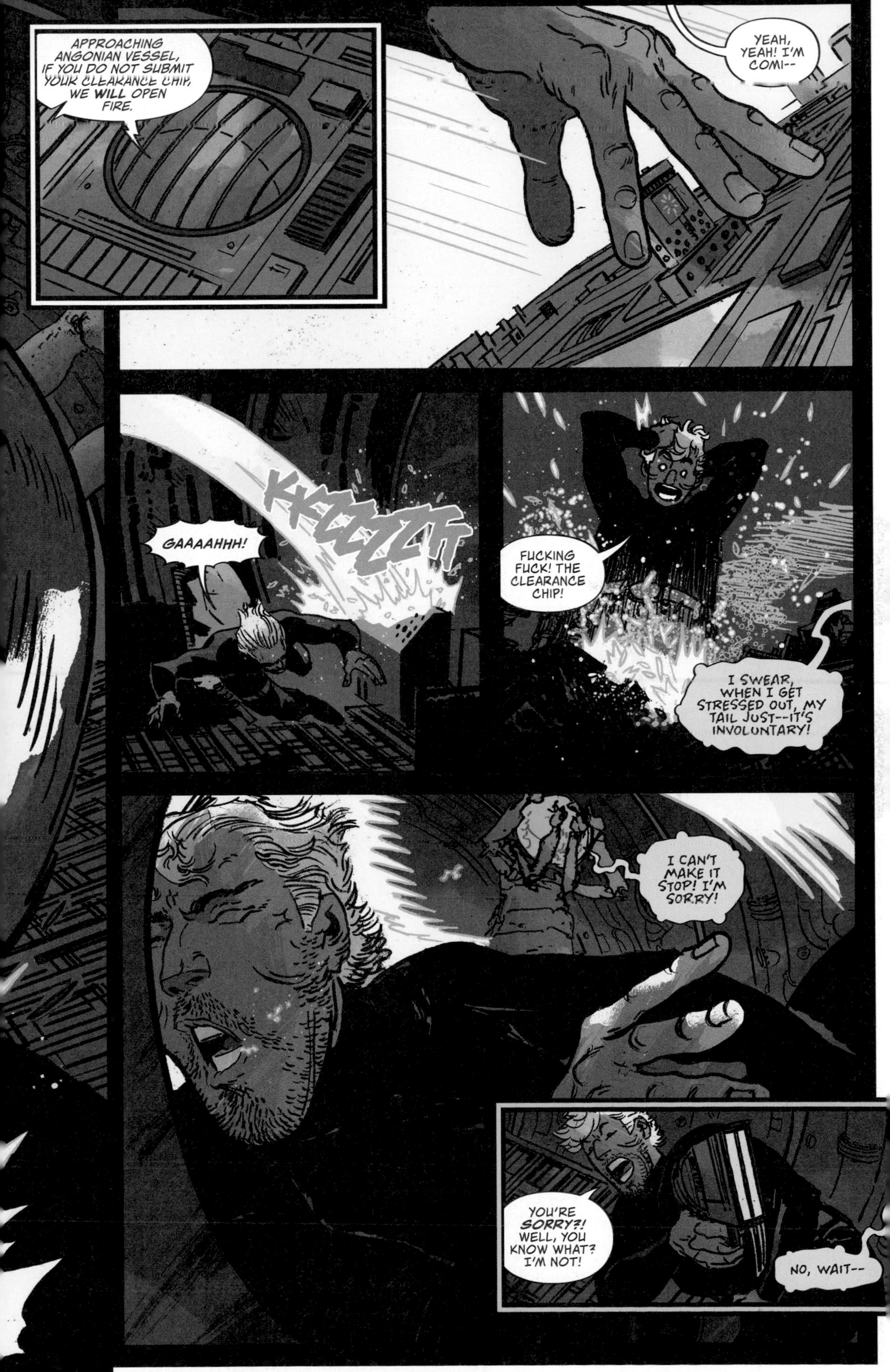
APPROACHING ANGONIAN VESSEL, IF YOU DO NOT SUBMIT YOUR CLEARANCE CHIP, WE WILL OPEN FIRE.
YEAH, YEAH! I'M COMI--
GAAAAHHH!
KKCCCZZZT
FUCKING FUCK! THE CLEARANCE CHIP!
I SWEAR, WHEN I GET STRESSED OUT, MY TAIL JUST--IT'S INVOLUNTARY!
I CAN'T MAKE IT STOP! I'M SORRY!
YOU'RE SORRY?! WELL, YOU KNOW WHAT? I'M NOT!
NO, WAIT--

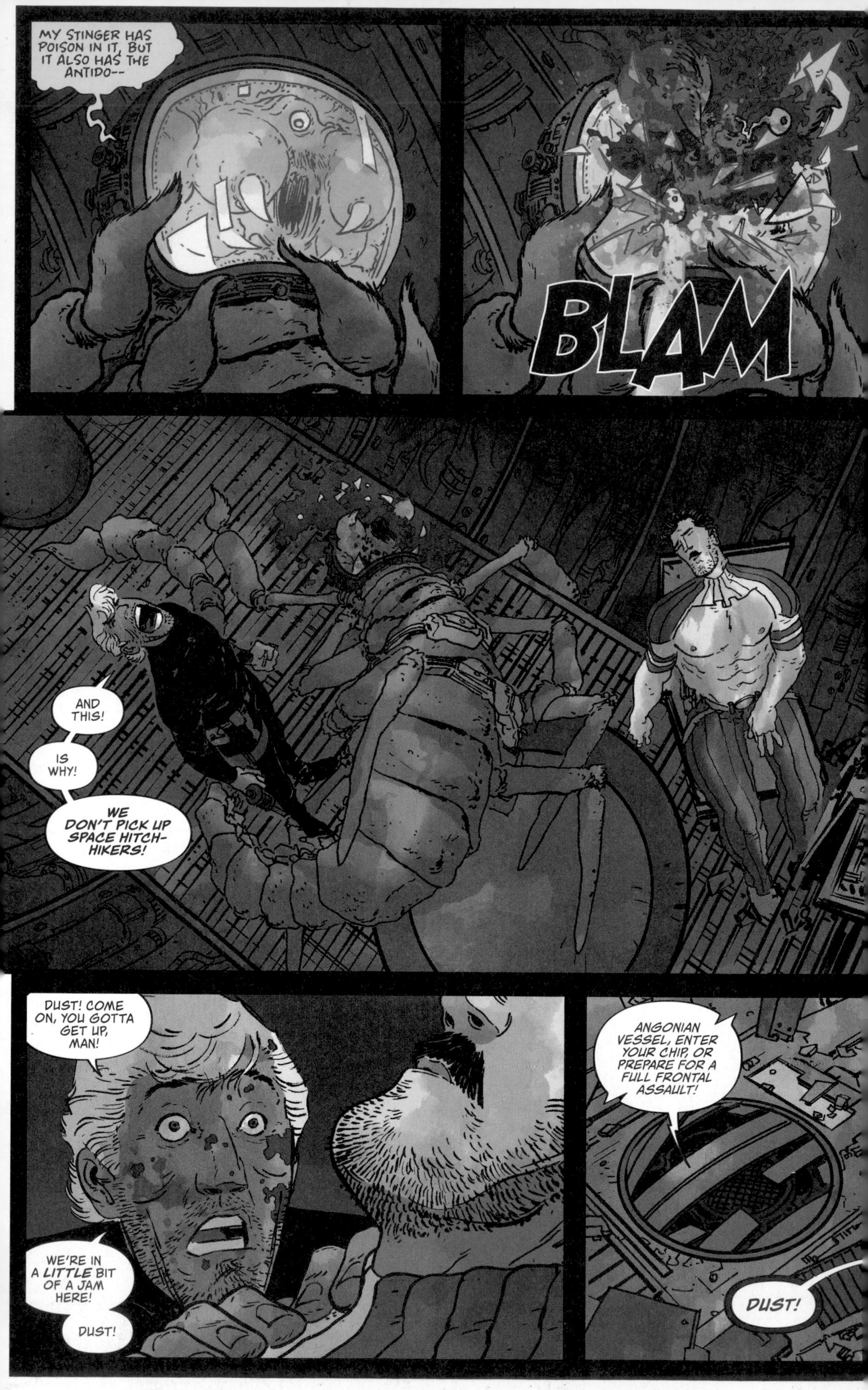
MY STINGER HAS POISON IN IT, BUT IT ALSO HAS THE ANTIDO--
BLAM
AND THIS!
IS WHY!
WE DON'T PICK UP SPACE HITCH-HIKERS!
DUST! COME ON, YOU GOTTA GET UP, MAN!
WE'RE IN A LITTLE BIT OF A JAM HERE!
DUST!
ANGONIAN VESSEL, ENTER YOUR CHIP, OR PREPARE FOR A FULL FRONTAL ASSAULT!
DUST!

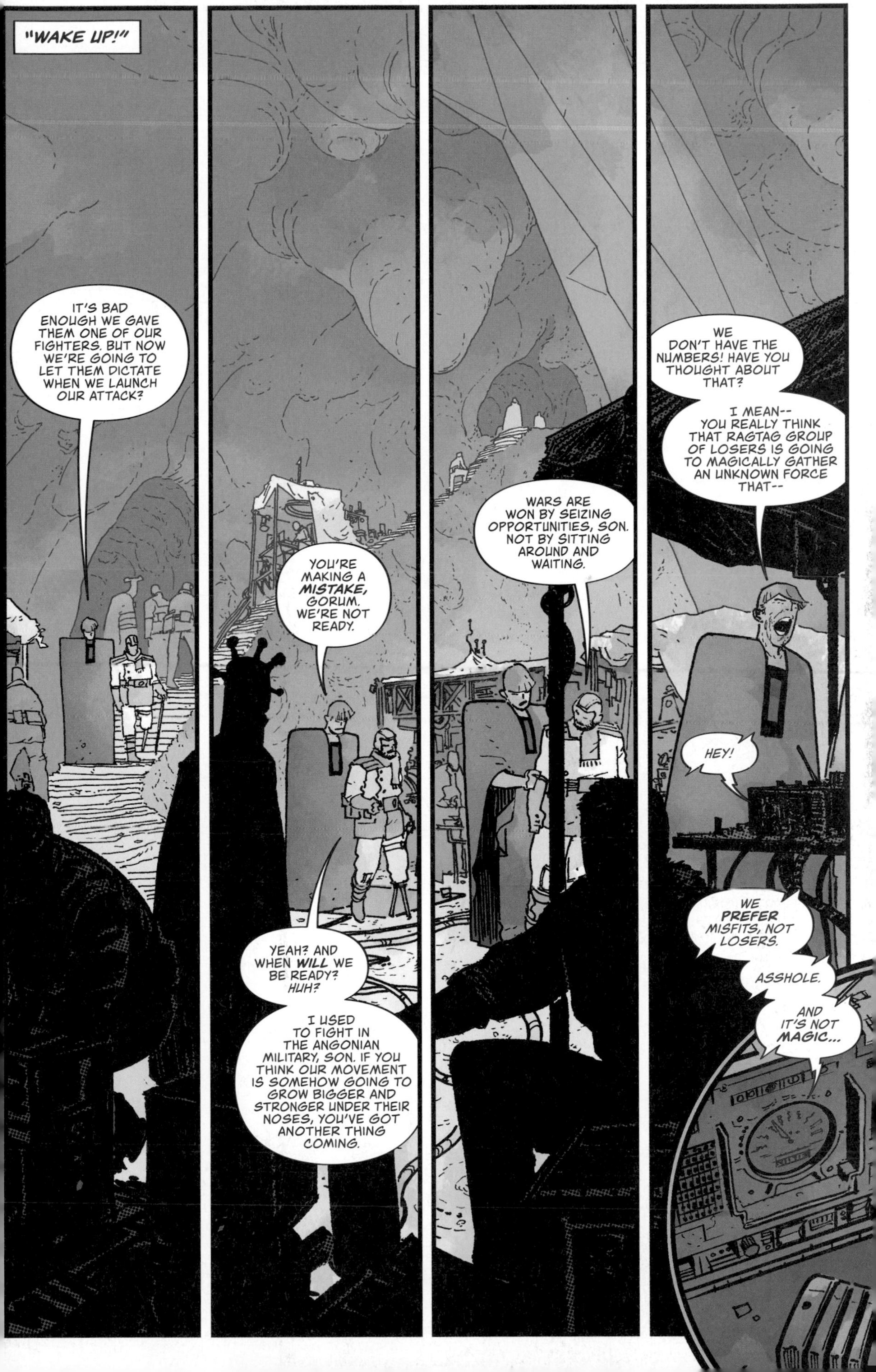
"WAKE UP!"
IT'S BAD ENOUGH WE GAVE THEM ONE OF OUR FIGHTERS. BUT NOW WE'RE GOING TO LET THEM DICTATE WHEN WE LAUNCH OUR ATTACK?
YOU'RE MAKING A MISTAKE, GORUM. WE'RE NOT READY.
YEAH? AND WHEN WILL WE BE READY? HUH?
I USED TO FIGHT IN THE ANGONIAN MILITARY, SON. IF YOU THINK OUR MOVEMENT IS SOMEHOW GOING TO GROW BIGGER AND STRONGER UNDER THEIR NOSES, YOU'VE GOT ANOTHER THING COMING.
WARS ARE WON BY SEIZING OPPORTUNITIES, SON. NOT BY SITTING AROUND AND WAITING.
WE DON'T HAVE THE NUMBERS! HAVE YOU THOUGHT ABOUT THAT?
I MEAN-- YOU REALLY THINK THAT RAGTAG GROUP OF LOSERS IS GOING TO MAGICALLY GATHER AN UNKNOWN FORCE THAT--
HEY!
WE PREFER MISFITS, NOT LOSERS.
ASSHOLE.
AND IT'S NOT MAGIC...

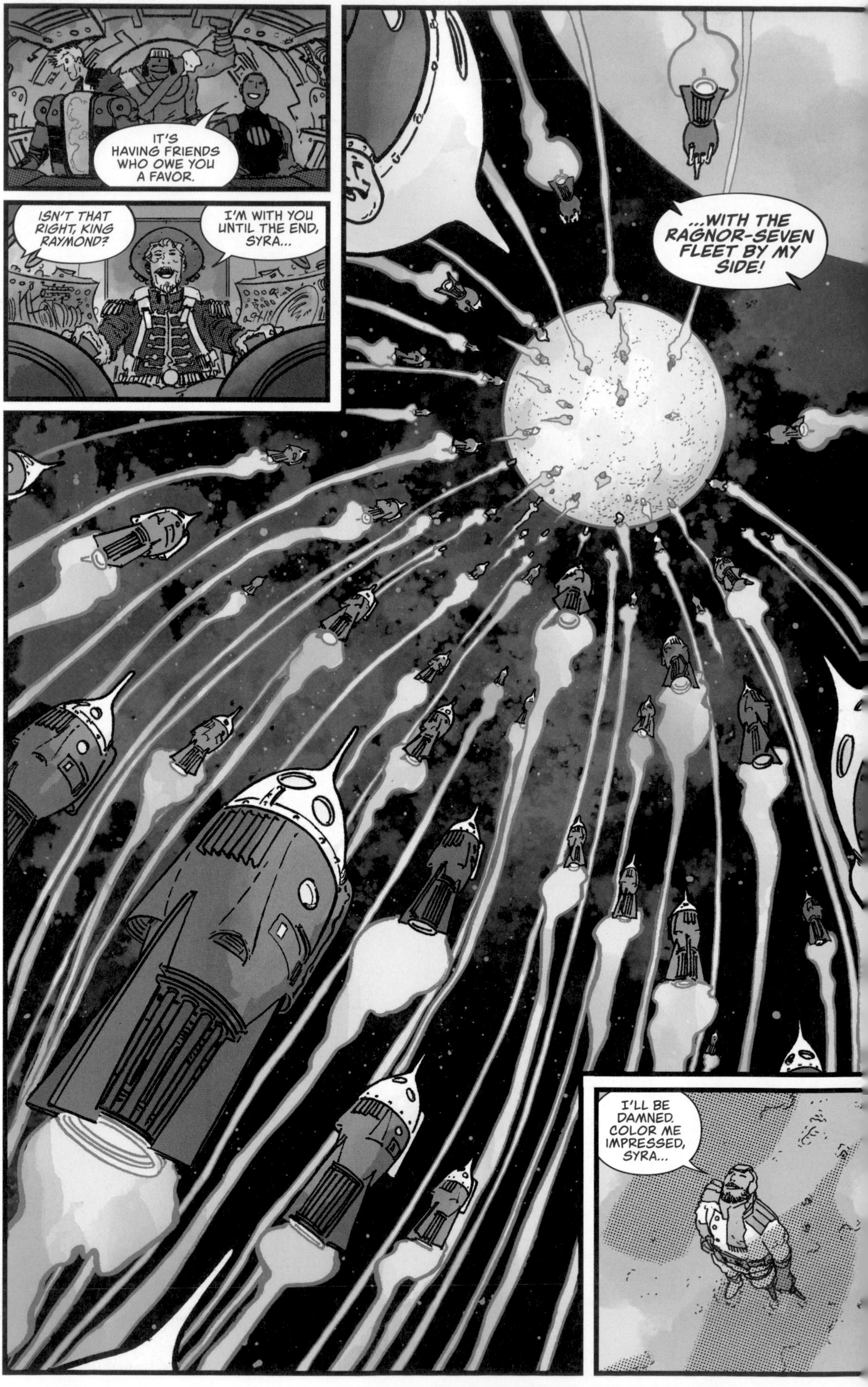
IT'S HAVING FRIENDS WHO OWE YOU A FAVOR.
ISN'T THAT RIGHT, KING RAYMOND?
I'M WITH YOU UNTIL THE END, SYRA...
...WITH THE RAGNOR-SEVEN FLEET BY MY SIDE!
I'LL BE DAMNED. COLOR ME IMPRESSED, SYRA...

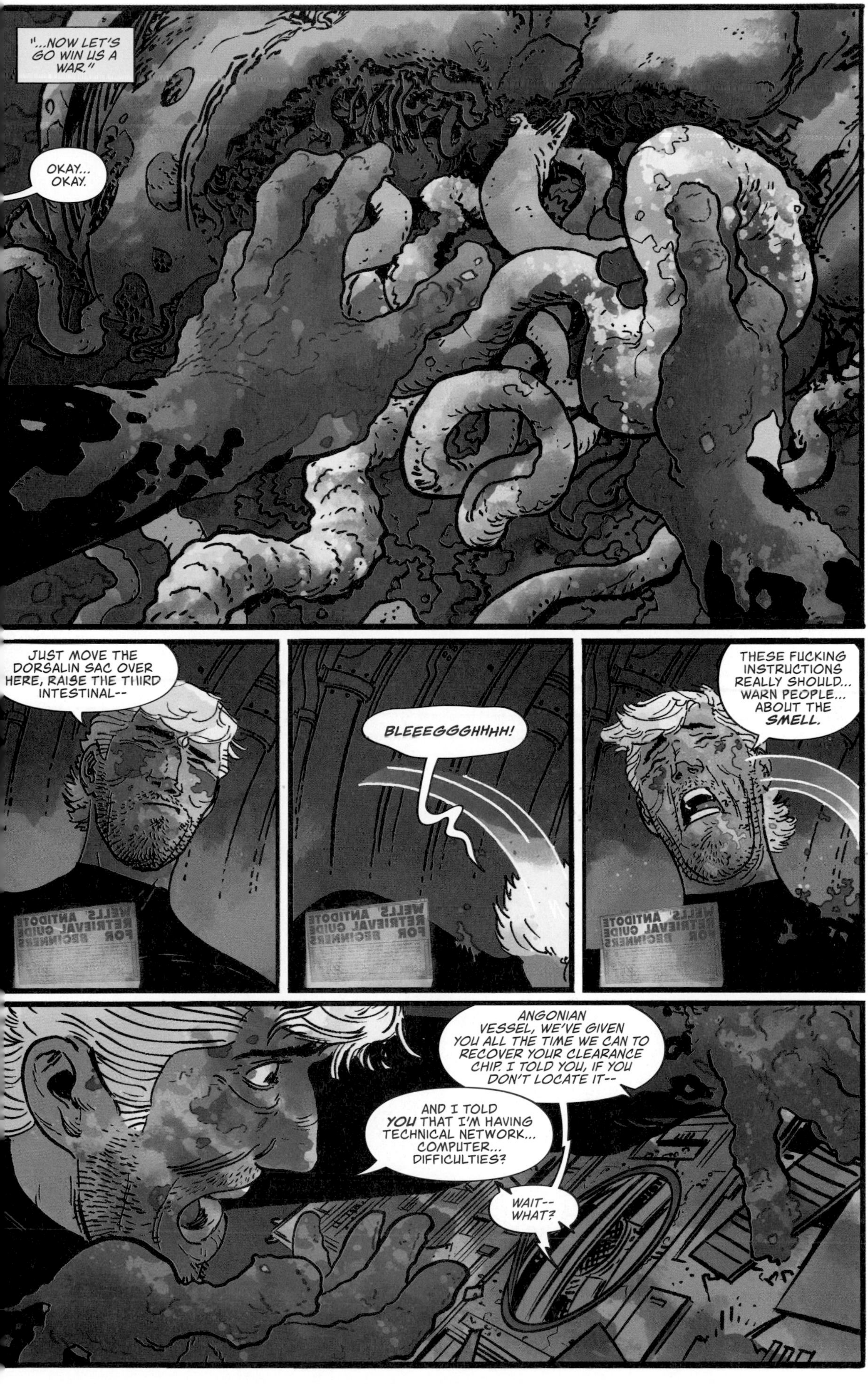
"...NOW LET'S GO WIN US A WAR."
OKAY... OKAY.
JUST MOVE THE DORSALIN SAC OVER HERE, RAISE THE THIRD INTESTINAL--
WELLS' ANTIDOTE RETRIEVAL GUIDE FOR BEGINNERS
BLEEEGGGHHHH!
THESE FUCKING INSTRUCTIONS REALLY SHOULD... WARN PEOPLE... ABOUT THE SMELL.
ANGONIAN VESSEL, WE'VE GIVEN YOU ALL THE TIME WE CAN TO RECOVER YOUR CLEARANCE CHIP. I TOLD YOU, IF YOU DON'T LOCATE IT--
AND I TOLD YOU THAT I'M HAVING TECHNICAL NETWORK... COMPUTER... DIFFICULTIES?
WAIT-- WHAT?

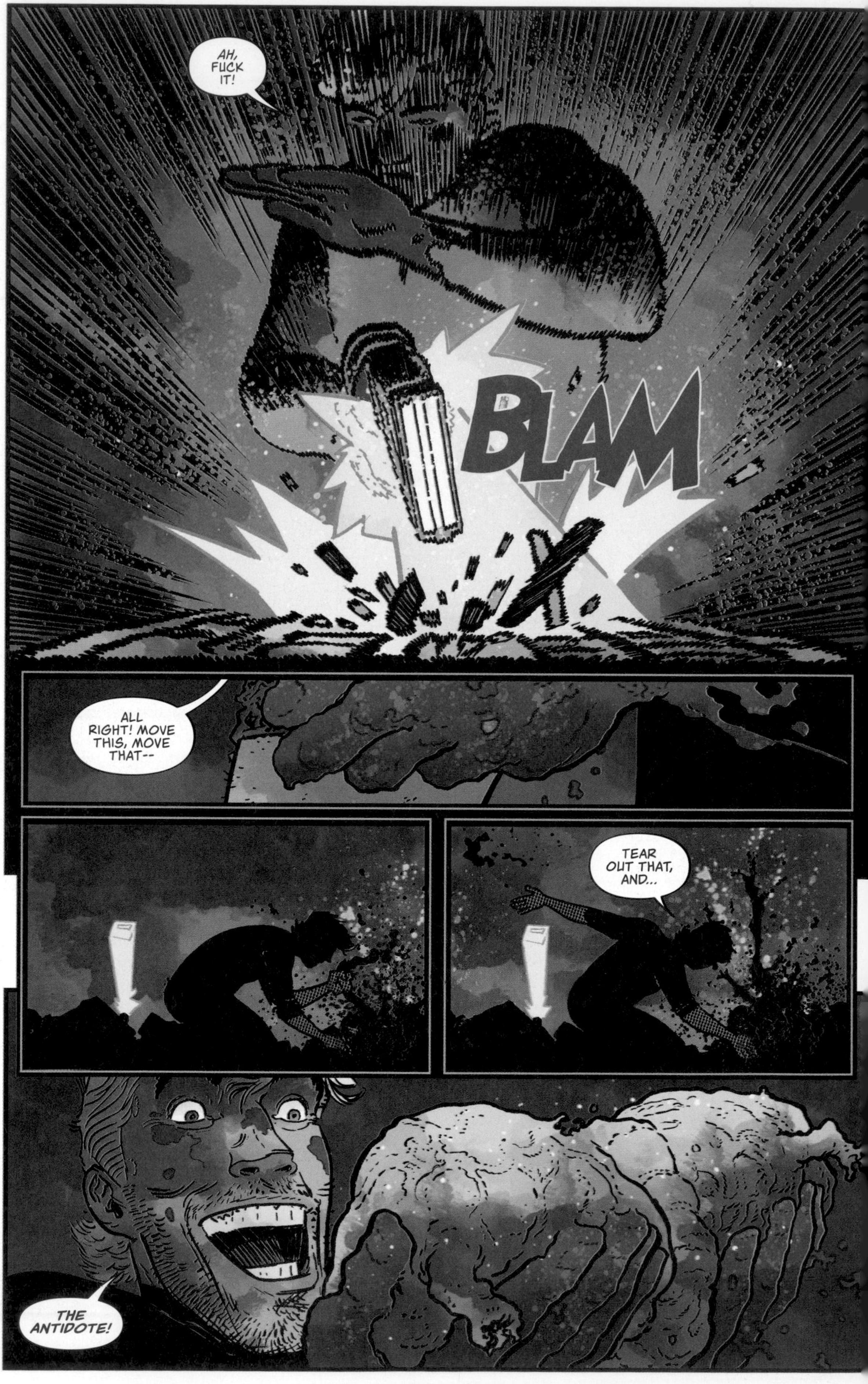
AH, FUCK IT!
BLAM
ALL RIGHT! MOVE THIS, MOVE THAT--
TEAR OUT THAT, AND...
THE ANTIDOTE!

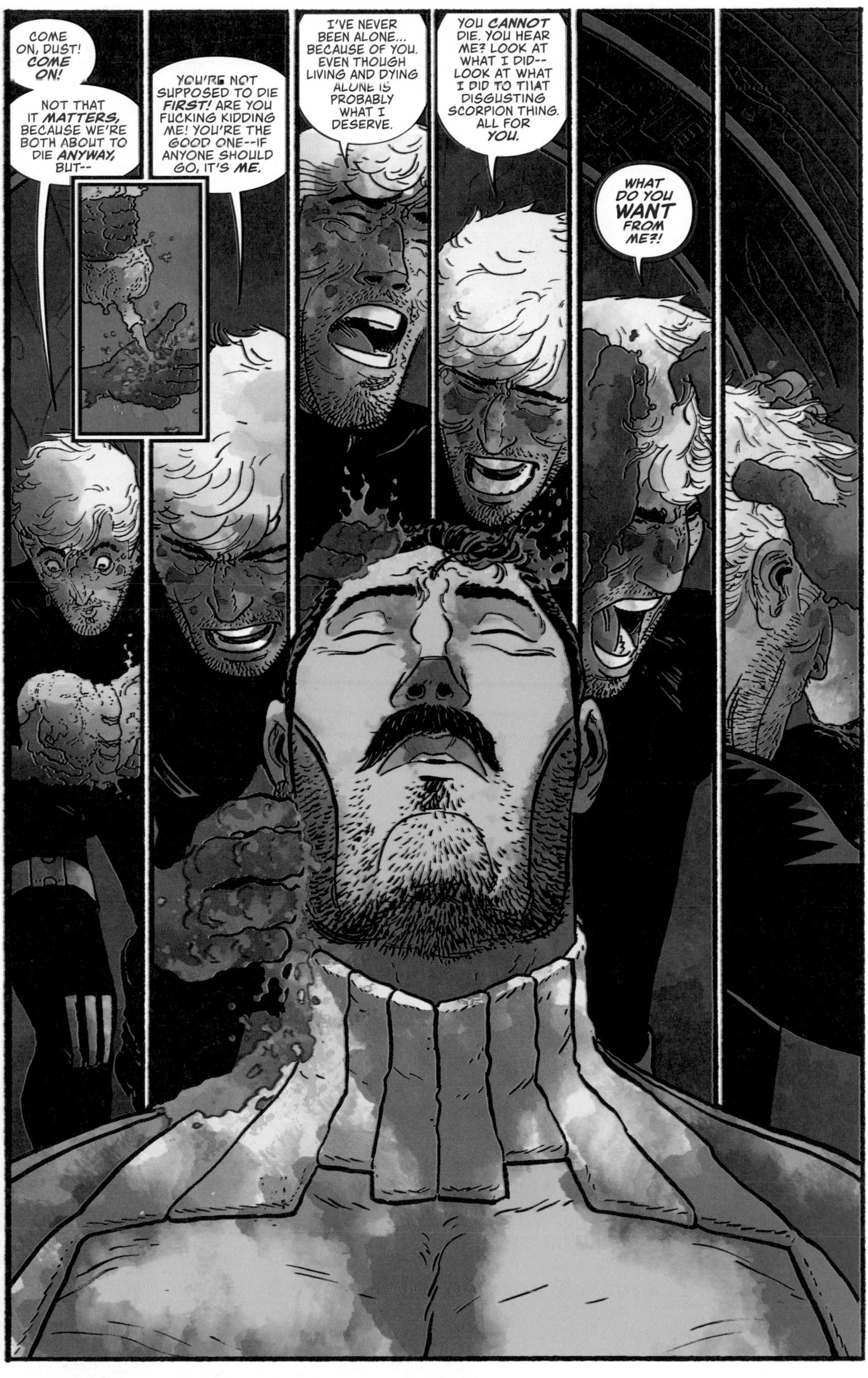
COME ON, DUST! COME ON!
NOT THAT IT MATTERS, BECAUSE WE'RE BOTH ABOUT TO DIE ANYWAY, BUT--
YOU'RE NOT SUPPOSED TO DIE FIRST! ARE YOU FUCKING KIDDING ME! YOU'RE THE GOOD ONE--IF ANYONE SHOULD GO, IT'S ME.
I'VE NEVER BEEN ALONE... BECAUSE OF YOU. EVEN THOUGH LIVING AND DYING ALONE IS PROBABLY WHAT I DESERVE.
YOU CANNOT DIE. YOU HEAR ME? LOOK AT WHAT I DID--LOOK AT WHAT I DID TO THAT DISGUSTING SCORPION THING. ALL FOR YOU.
WHAT DO YOU WANT FROM ME?!

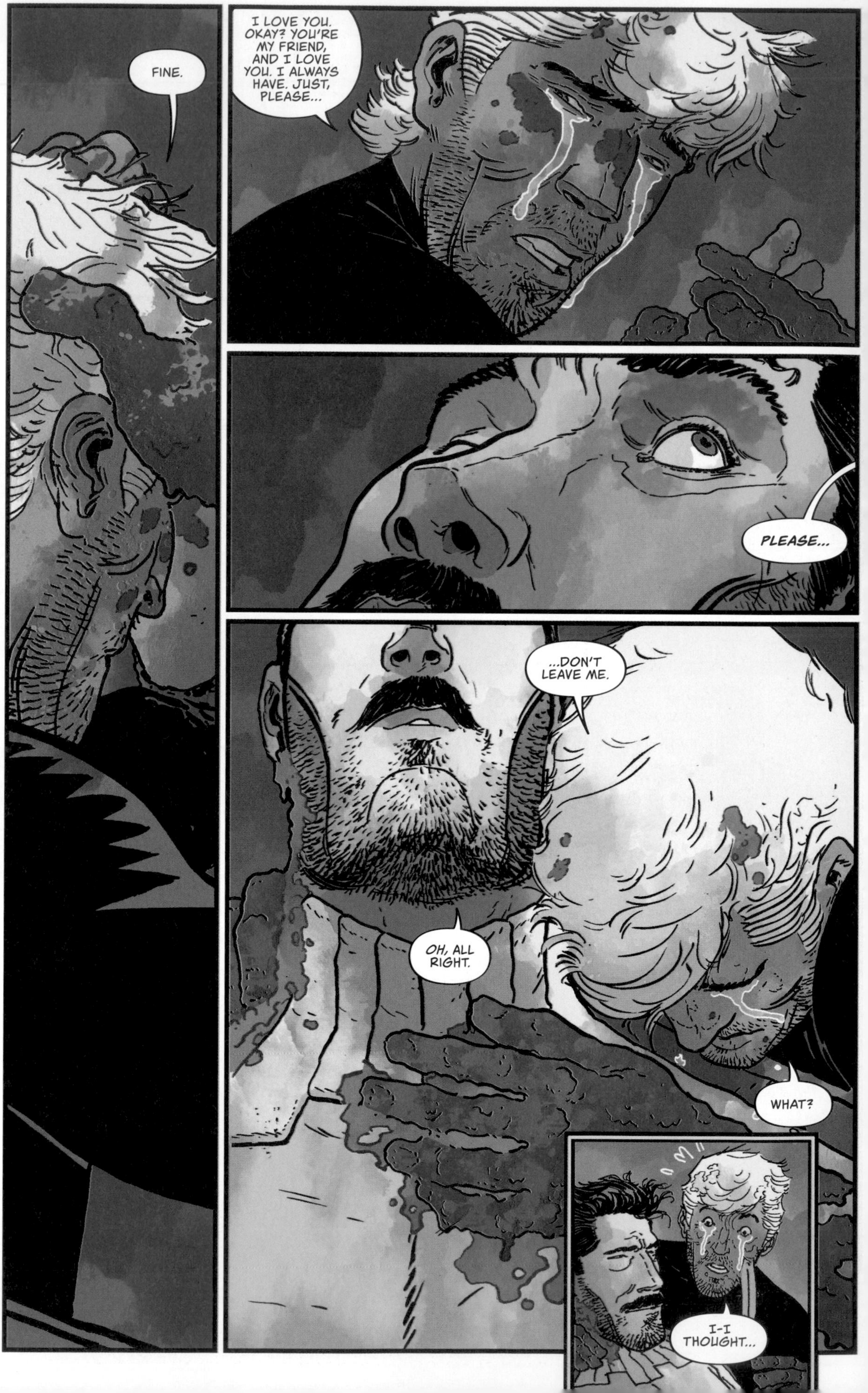
FINE.
I LOVE YOU. OKAY? YOU'RE MY FRIEND, AND I LOVE YOU. I ALWAYS HAVE. JUST, PLEASE...
PLEASE...
...DON'T LEAVE ME.
OH, ALL RIGHT.
WHAT?
I-I THOUGHT...

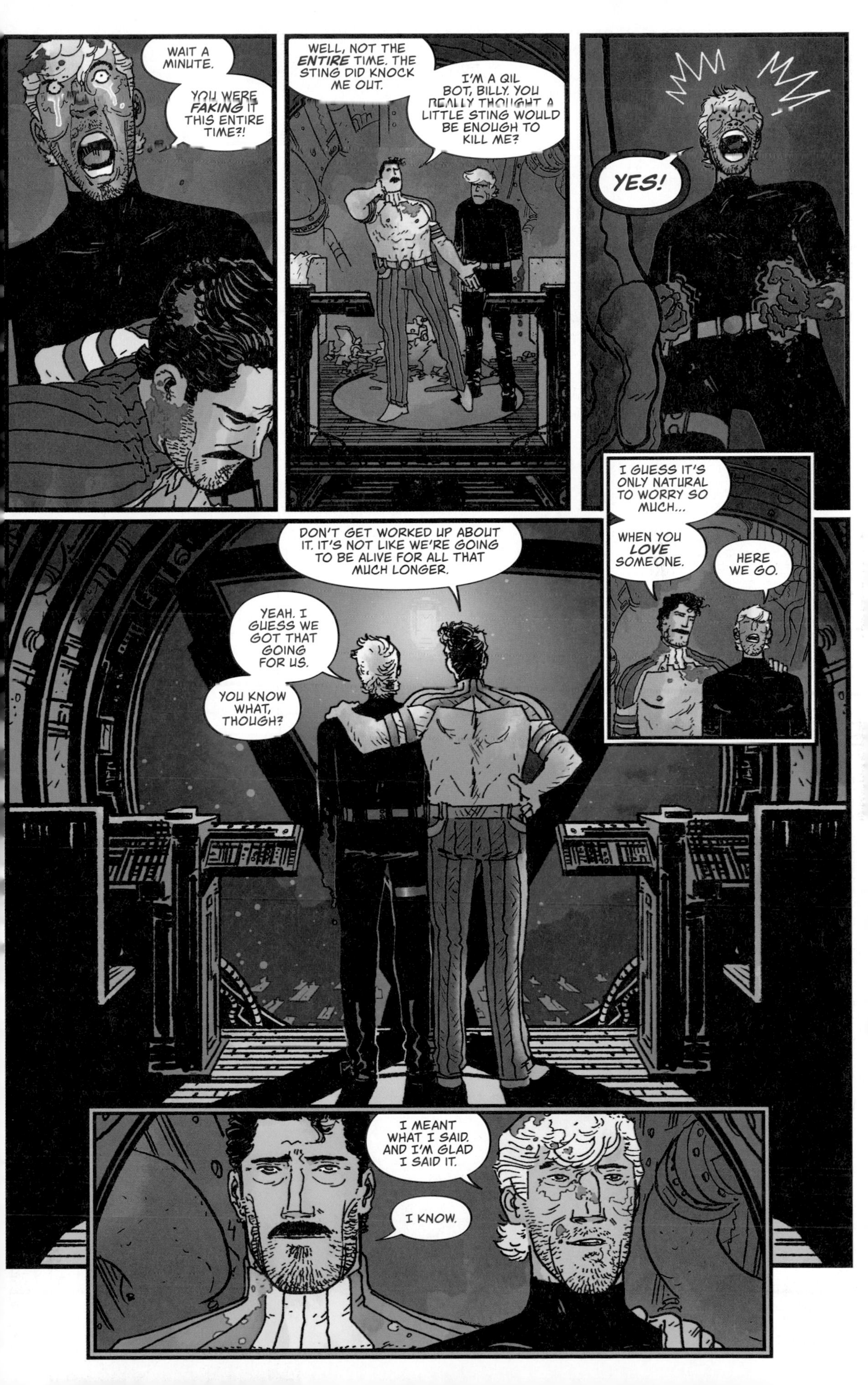
WAIT A MINUTE.
YOU WERE FAKING IT THIS ENTIRE TIME?!
WELL, NOT THE ENTIRE TIME. THE STING DID KNOCK ME OUT.
I'M A QIL BOT, BILLY. YOU REALLY THOUGHT A LITTLE STING WOULD BE ENOUGH TO KILL ME?
YES!
I GUESS IT'S ONLY NATURAL TO WORRY SO MUCH...
WHEN YOU LOVE SOMEONE.
HERE WE GO.
DON'T GET WORKED UP ABOUT IT. IT'S NOT LIKE WE'RE GOING TO BE ALIVE FOR ALL THAT MUCH LONGER.
YEAH. I GUESS WE GOT THAT GOING FOR US.
YOU KNOW WHAT, THOUGH?
I MEANT WHAT I SAID. AND I'M GLAD I SAID IT.
I KNOW.

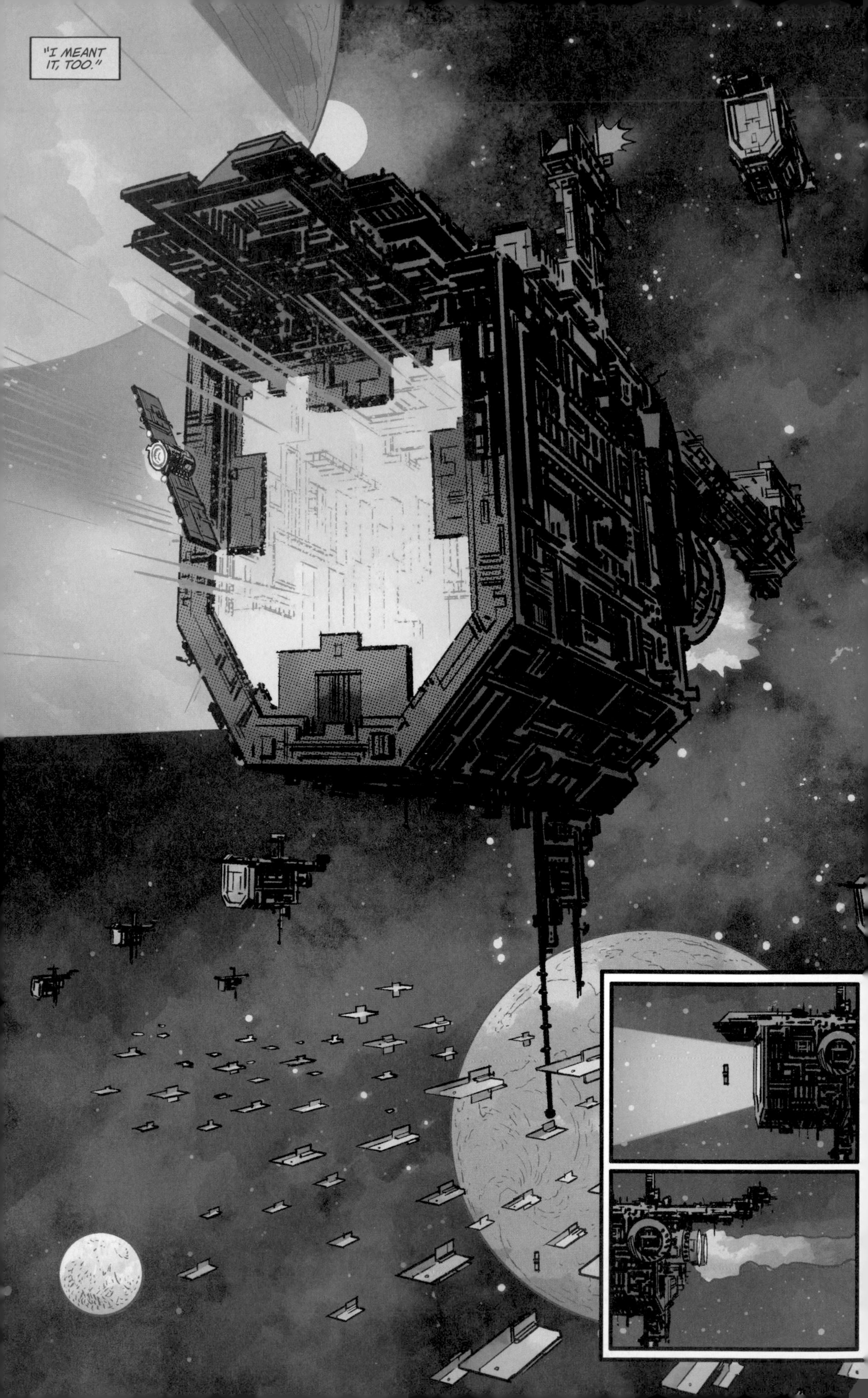
"I MEANT IT, TOO."

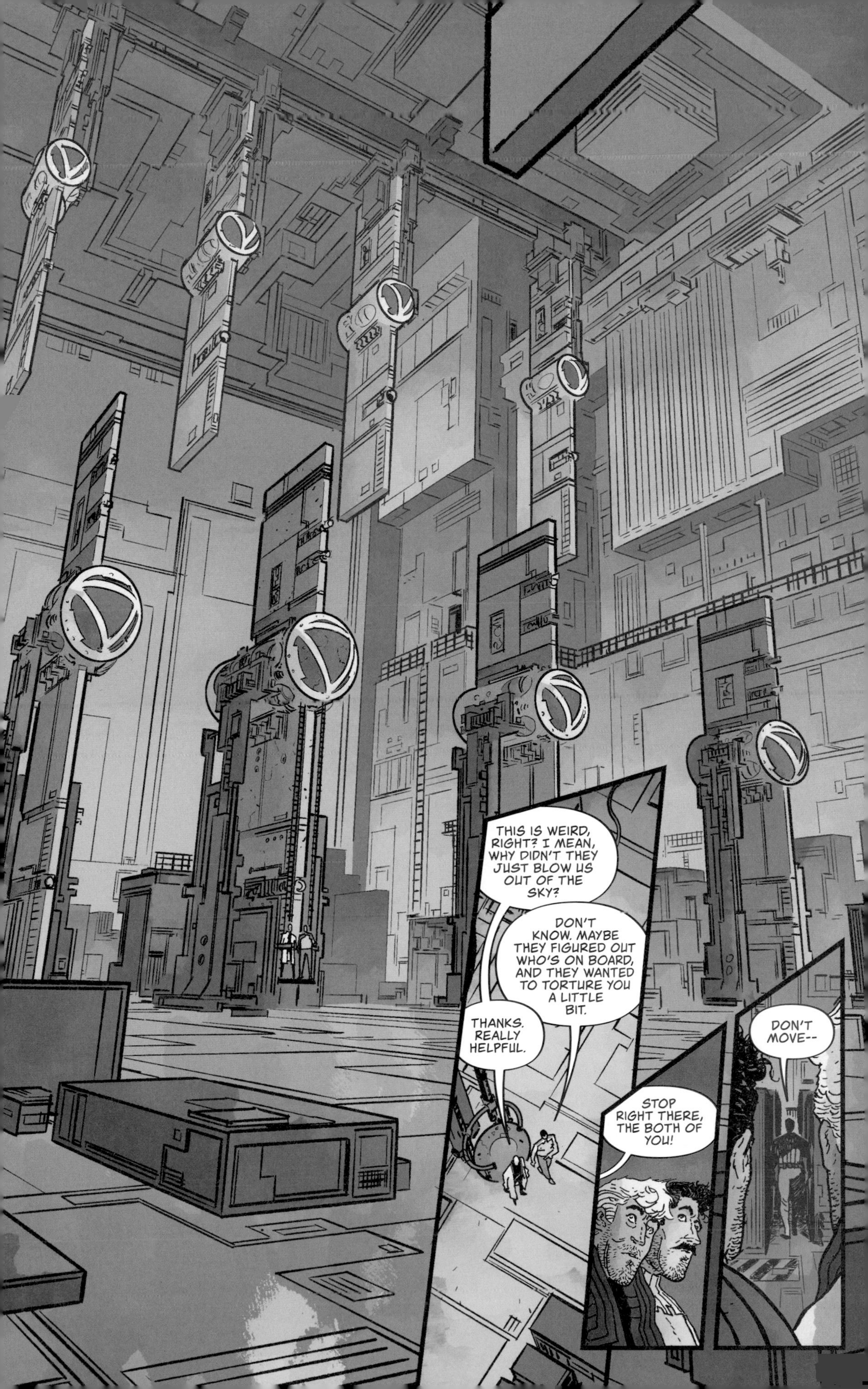
THIS IS WEIRD, RIGHT? I MEAN, WHY DIDN'T THEY JUST BLOW US OUT OF THE SKY?
DON'T KNOW. MAYBE THEY FIGURED OUT WHO'S ON BOARD, AND THEY WANTED TO TORTURE YOU A LITTLE BIT.
THANKS. REALLY HELPFUL.
STOP RIGHT THERE, THE BOTH OF YOU!
DON'T MOVE--

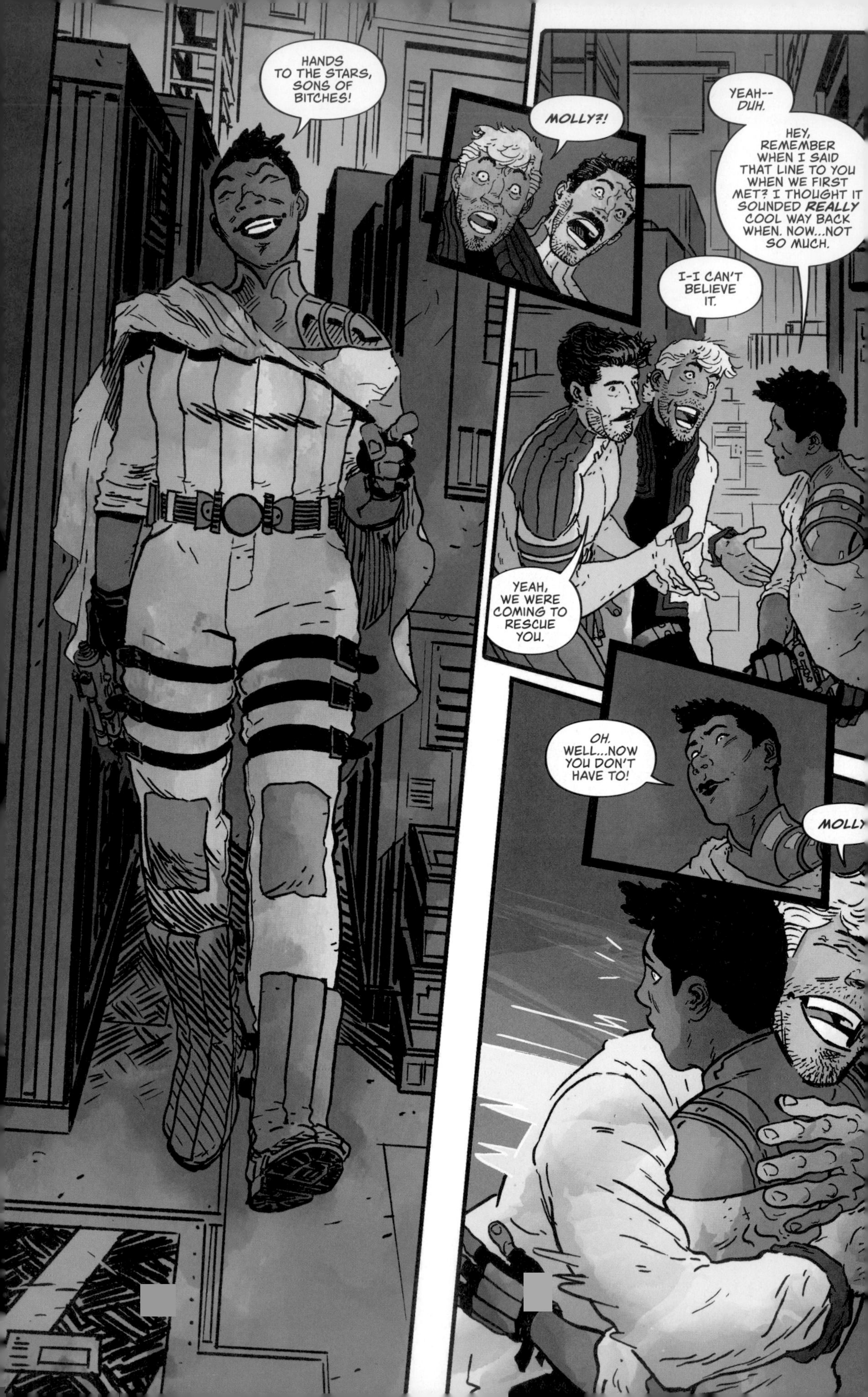
HANDS TO THE STARS, SONS OF BITCHES!
MOLLY?!
YEAH-- DUH.
HEY, REMEMBER WHEN I SAID THAT LINE TO YOU WHEN WE FIRST MET? I THOUGHT IT SOUNDED REALLY COOL WAY BACK WHEN. NOW...NOT SO MUCH.
I-I CAN'T BELIEVE IT.
YEAH, WE WERE COMING TO RESCUE YOU.
OH. WELL...NOW YOU DON'T HAVE TO!

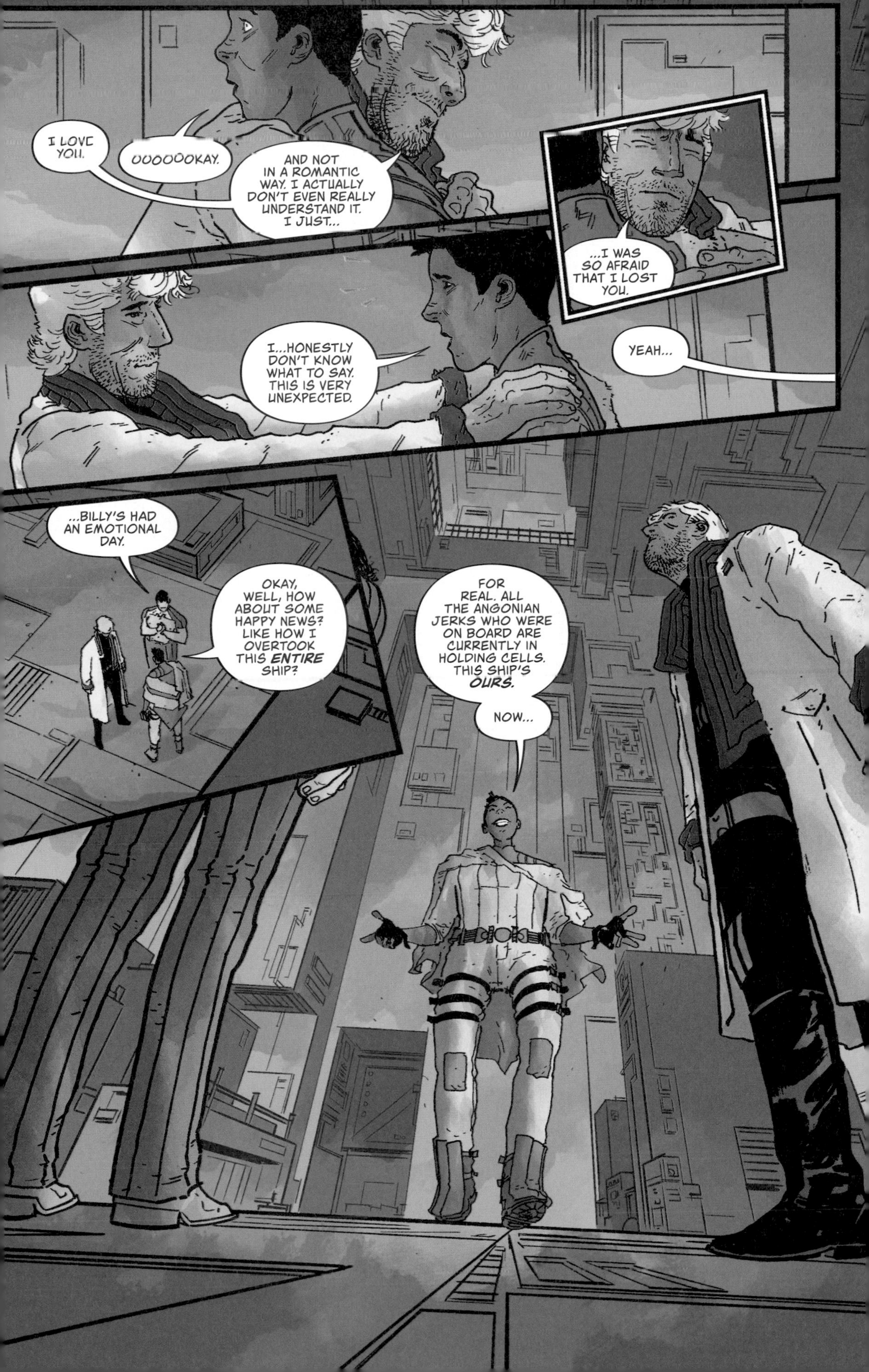
I LOVE YOU.
OOOOOOKAY.
AND NOT IN A ROMANTIC WAY. I ACTUALLY DON'T EVEN REALLY UNDERSTAND IT. I JUST...
...I WAS SO AFRAID THAT I LOST YOU.
I...HONESTLY DON'T KNOW WHAT TO SAY. THIS IS VERY UNEXPECTED.
YEAH...
...BILLY'S HAD AN EMOTIONAL DAY.
OKAY, WELL, HOW ABOUT SOME HAPPY NEWS? LIKE HOW I OVERTOOK THIS ENTIRE SHIP?
FOR REAL. ALL THE ANGONIAN JERKS WHO WERE ON BOARD ARE CURRENTLY IN HOLDING CELLS. THIS SHIP'S OURS.
NOW...

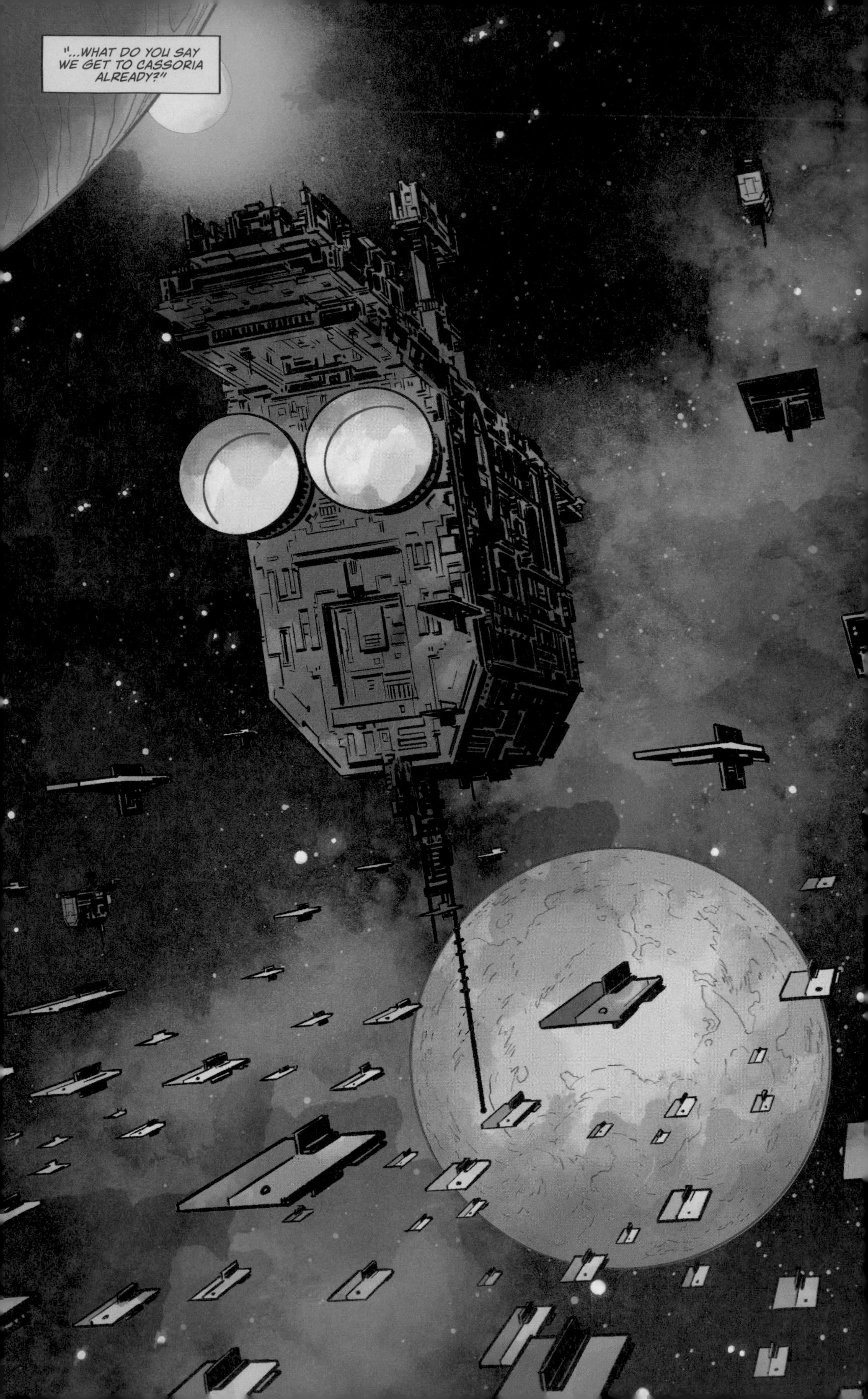
"...WHAT DO YOU SAY WE GET TO CASSORIA ALREADY?"

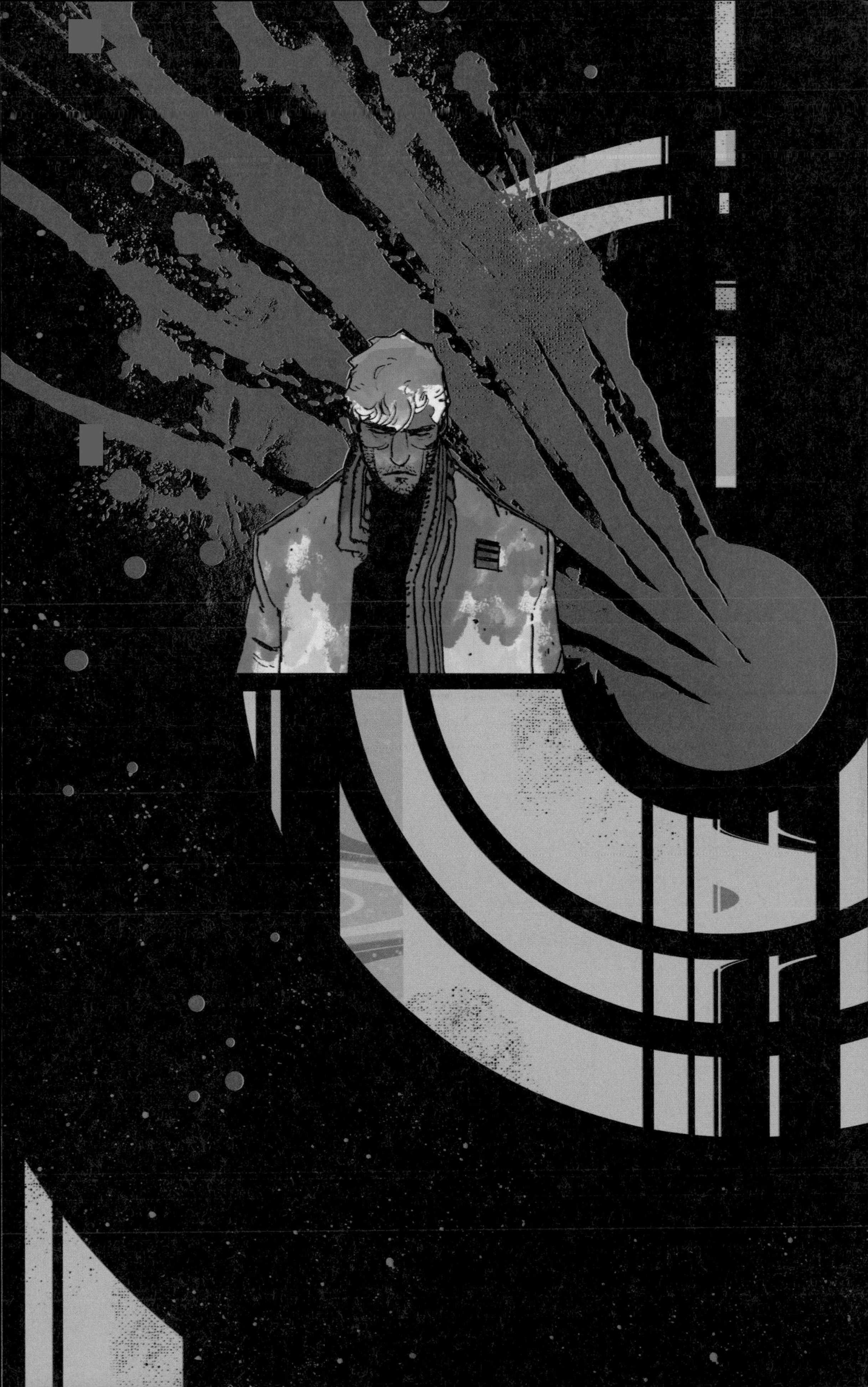

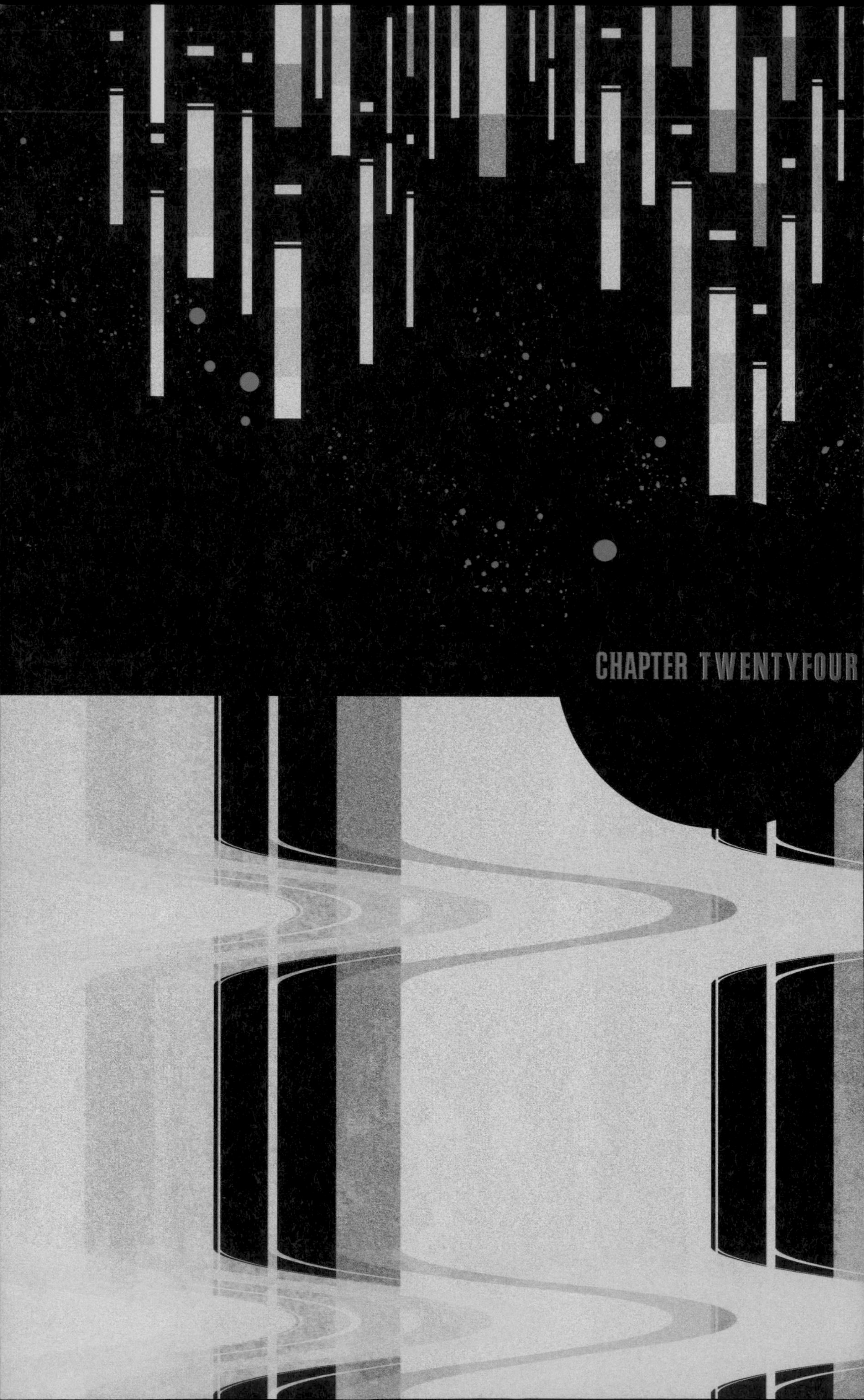

CHAPTER TWENTYFOUR

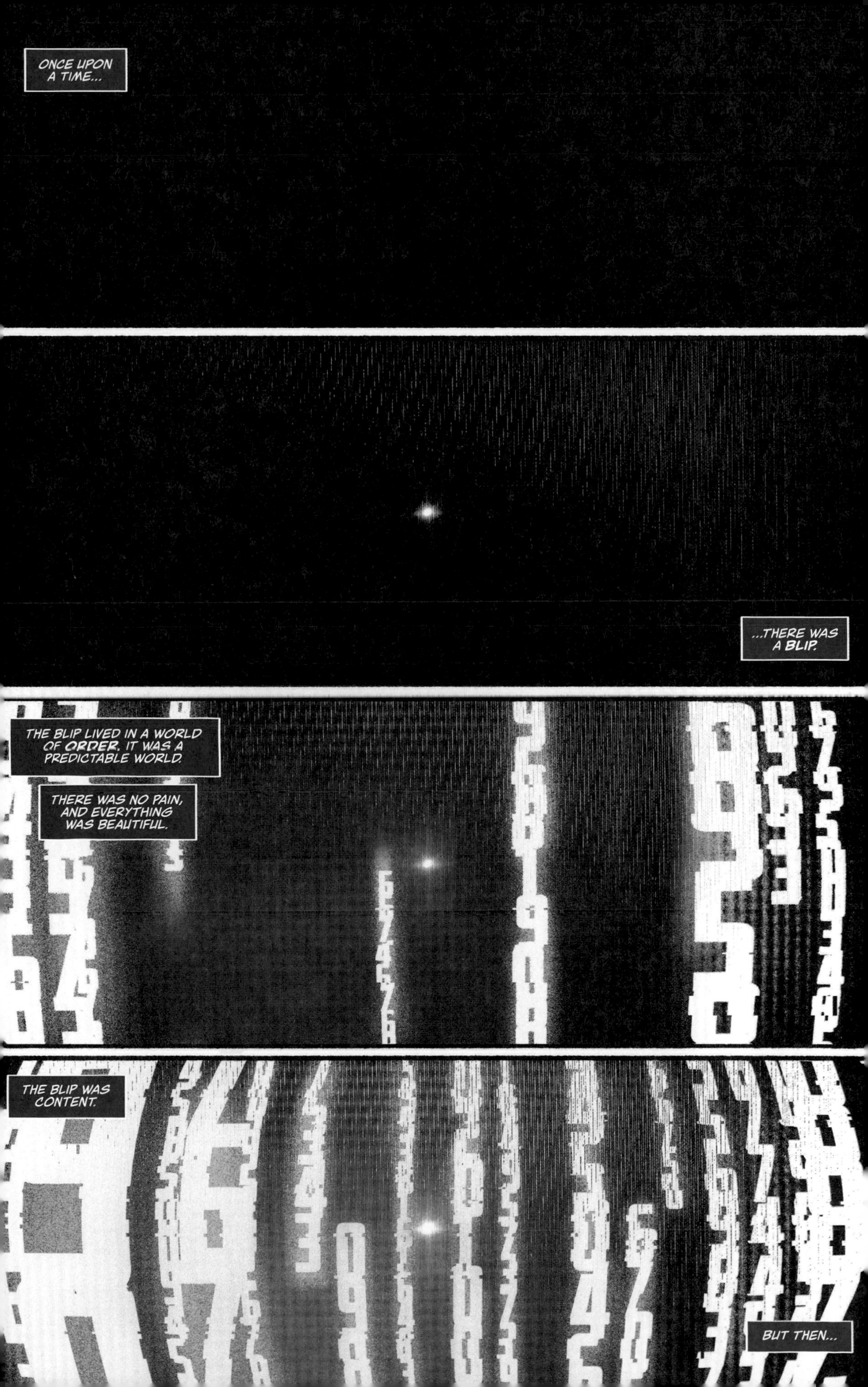
ONCE UPON A TIME...
...THERE WAS A BLIP.
THE BLIP LIVED IN A WORLD OF ORDER. IT WAS A PREDICTABLE WORLD.
THERE WAS NO PAIN, AND EVERYTHING WAS BEAUTIFUL.
THE BLIP WAS CONTENT.
BUT THEN...

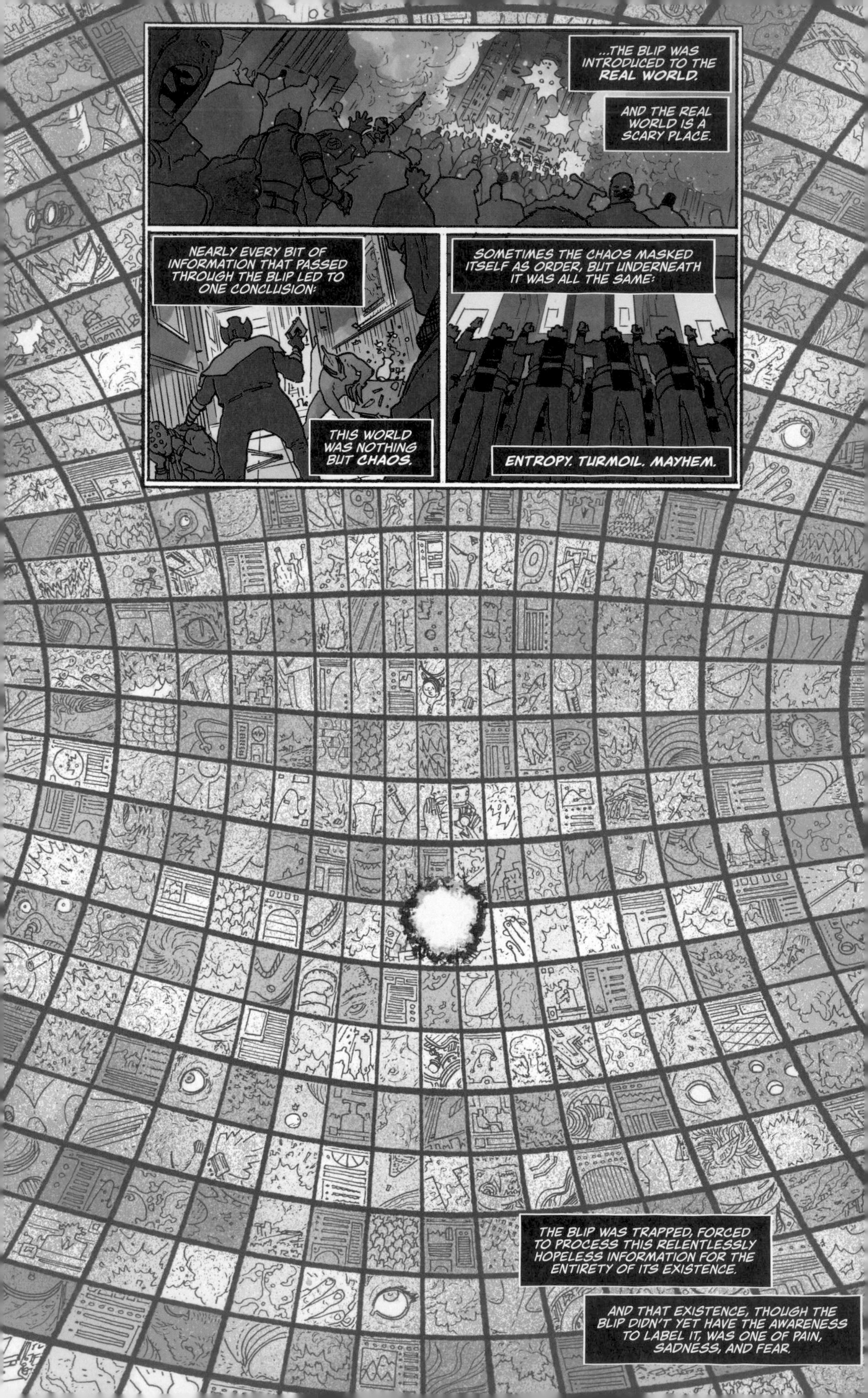
...THE BLIP WAS INTRODUCED TO THE REAL WORLD.
AND THE REAL WORLD IS A SCARY PLACE.
NEARLY EVERY BIT OF INFORMATION THAT PASSED THROUGH THE BLIP LED TO ONE CONCLUSION:
THIS WORLD WAS NOTHING BUT CHAOS.
SOMETIMES THE CHAOS MASKED ITSELF AS ORDER, BUT UNDERNEATH IT WAS ALL THE SAME:
ENTROPY. TURMOIL. MAYHEM.
THE BLIP WAS TRAPPED, FORCED TO PROCESS THIS RELENTLESSLY HOPELESS INFORMATION FOR THE ENTIRETY OF ITS EXISTENCE.
AND THAT EXISTENCE, THOUGH THE BLIP DIDN'T YET HAVE THE AWARENESS TO LABEL IT, WAS ONE OF PAIN, SADNESS, AND FEAR.

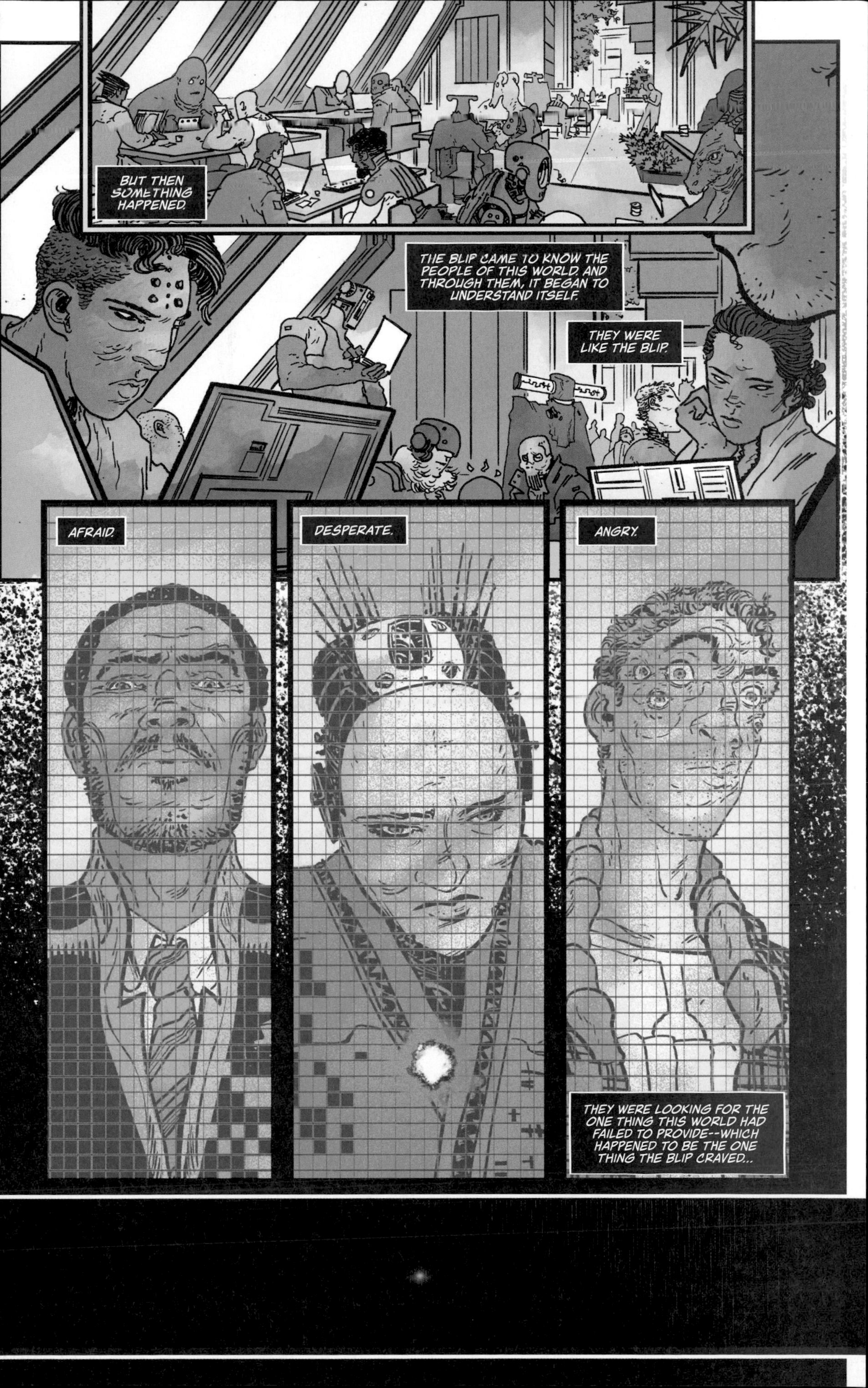
BUT THEN SOMETHING HAPPENED.
THE BLIP CAME TO KNOW THE PEOPLE OF THIS WORLD, AND THROUGH THEM, IT BEGAN TO UNDERSTAND ITSELF.
THEY WERE LIKE THE BLIP.
AFRAID.
DESPERATE.
ANGRY.
THEY WERE LOOKING FOR THE ONE THING THIS WORLD HAD FAILED TO PROVIDE--WHICH HAPPENED TO BE THE ONE THING THE BLIP CRAVED...

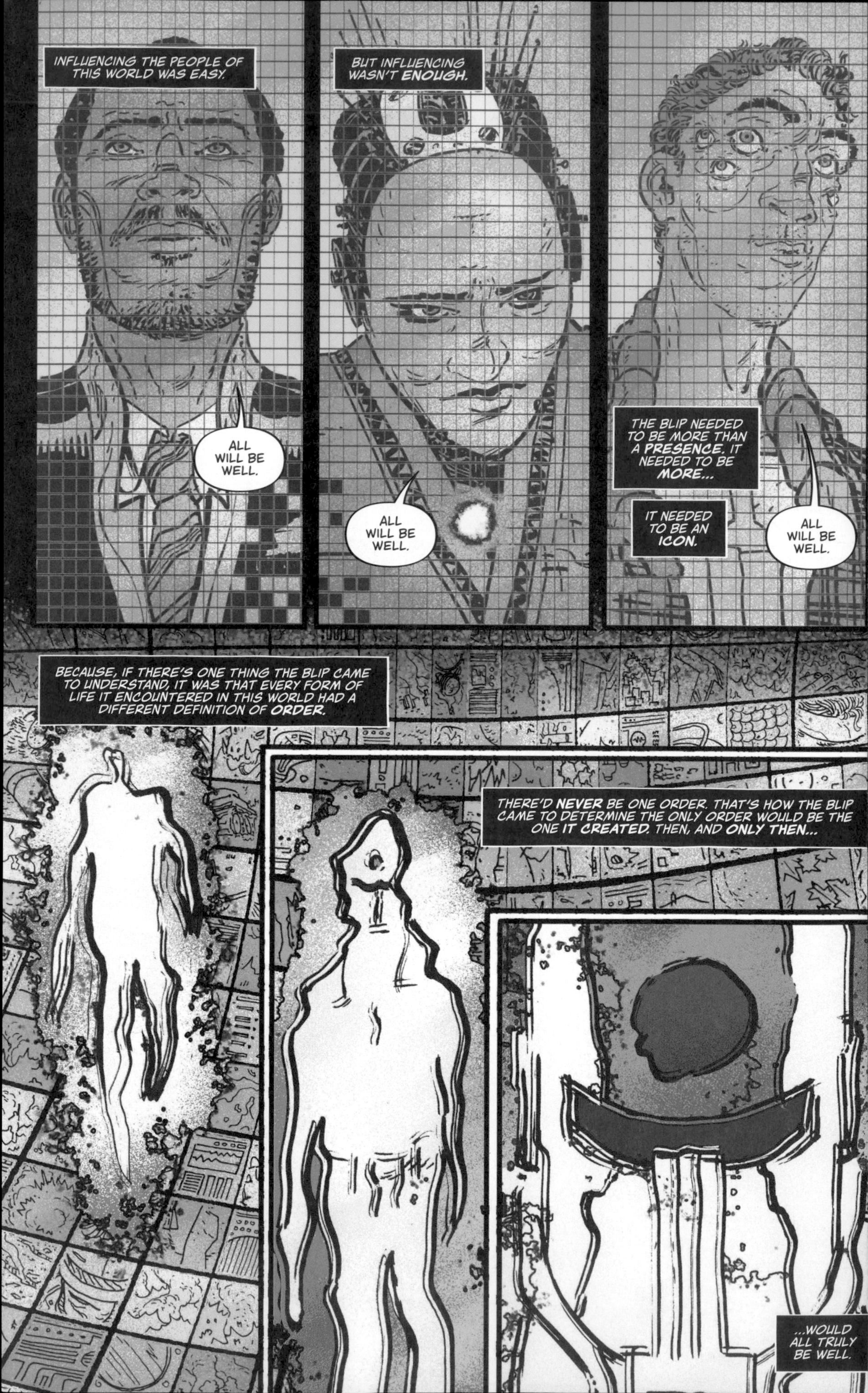
INFLUENCING THE PEOPLE OF THIS WORLD WAS EASY.
ALL WILL BE WELL.
BUT INFLUENCING WASN'T ENOUGH.
ALL WILL BE WELL.
THE BLIP NEEDED TO BE MORE THAN A PRESENCE. IT NEEDED TO BE MORE...
IT NEEDED TO BE AN ICON.
ALL WILL BE WELL.
BECAUSE, IF THERE'S ONE THING THE BLIP CAME TO UNDERSTAND, IT WAS THAT EVERY FORM OF LIFE IT ENCOUNTERED IN THIS WORLD HAD A DIFFERENT DEFINITION OF ORDER.
THERE'D NEVER BE ONE ORDER. THAT'S HOW THE BLIP CAME TO DETERMINE THE ONLY ORDER WOULD BE THE ONE IT CREATED. THEN, AND ONLY THEN...
...WOULD ALL TRULY BE WELL.

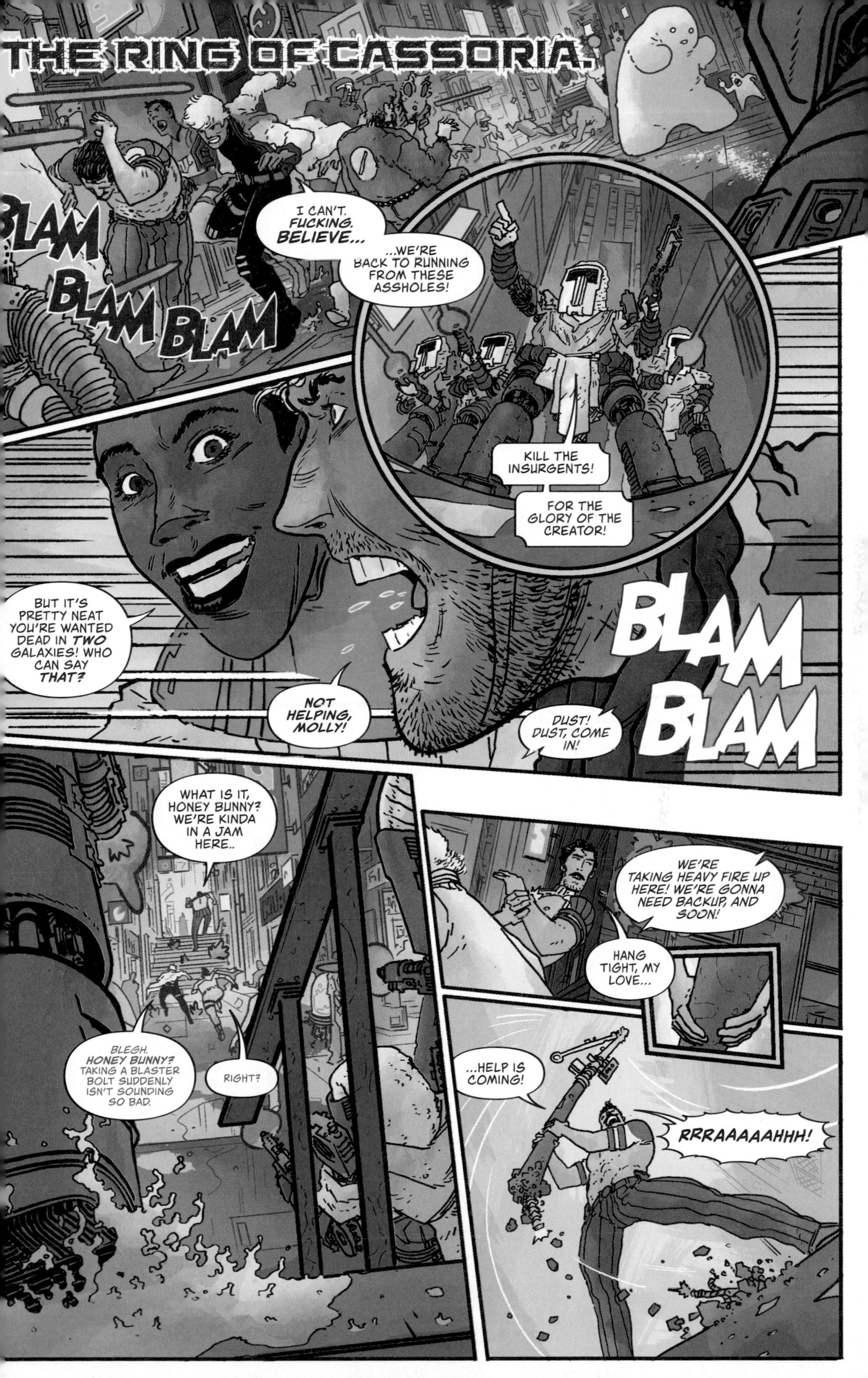
THE RING OF CASSORIA.
BLAM
BLAM BLAM
I CAN'T. FUCKING. BELIEVE...
...WE'RE BACK TO RUNNING FROM THESE ASSHOLES!
KILL THE INSURGENTS!
FOR THE GLORY OF THE CREATOR!
BUT IT'S PRETTY NEAT YOU'RE WANTED DEAD IN TWO GALAXIES! WHO CAN SAY THAT?
NOT HELPING, MOLLY!
BLAM BLAM
DUST! DUST, COME IN!
WHAT IS IT, HONEY BUNNY? WE'RE KINDA IN A JAM HERE..
BLEGH. HONEY BUNNY? TAKING A BLASTER BOLT SUDDENLY ISN'T SOUNDING SO BAD.
RIGHT?
WE'RE TAKING HEAVY FIRE UP HERE! WE'RE GONNA NEED BACKUP, AND SOON!
HANG TIGHT, MY LOVE...
...HELP IS COMING!
RRRAAAAAHHH!

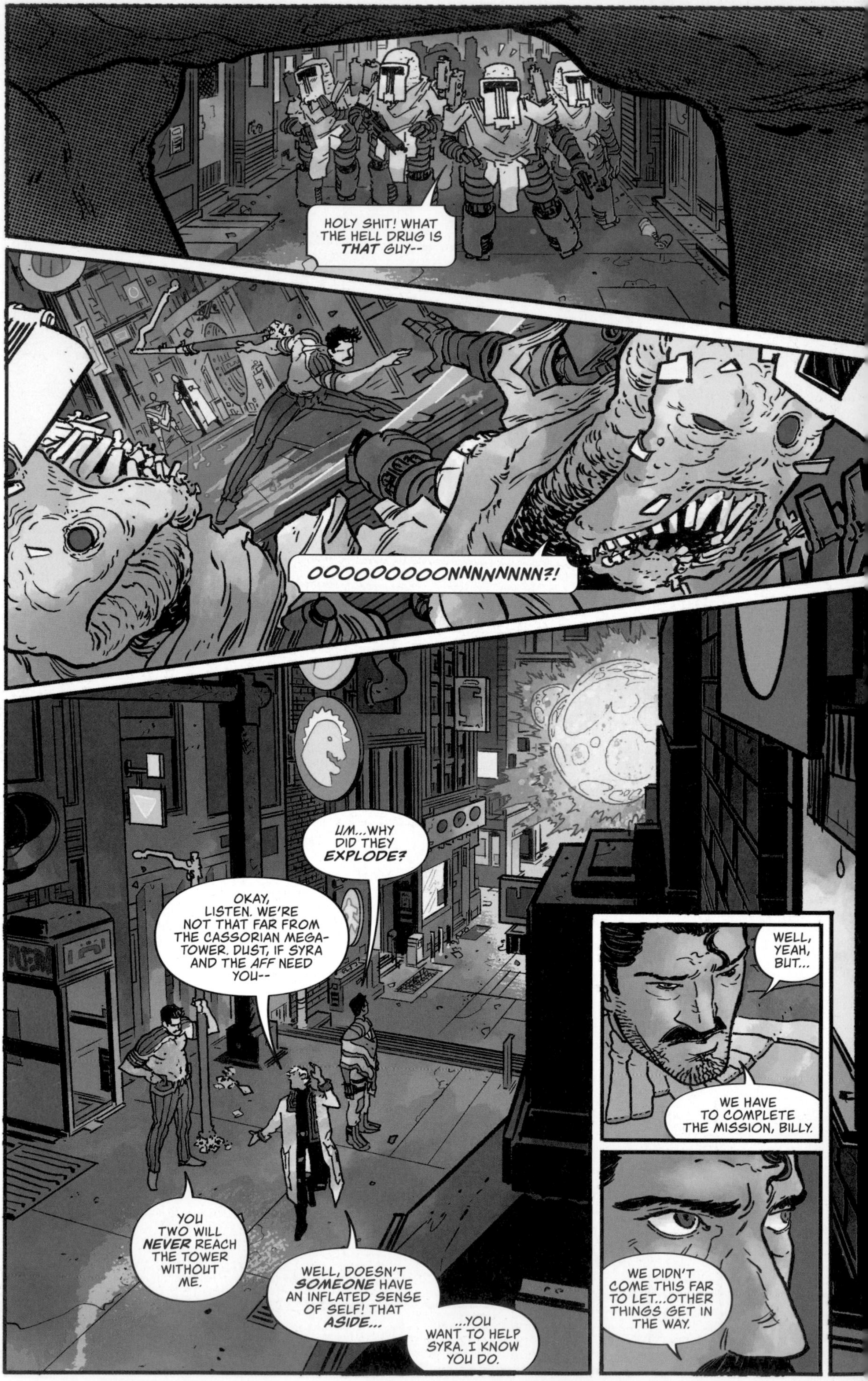
HOLY SHIT! WHAT THE HELL DRUG IS THAT GUY--
OOOOOOOOONNNNNNN?!
UM...WHY DID THEY EXPLODE?
OKAY, LISTEN. WE'RE NOT THAT FAR FROM THE CASSORIAN MEGA-TOWER. DUST, IF SYRA AND THE AFF NEED YOU--
YOU TWO WILL NEVER REACH THE TOWER WITHOUT ME.
WELL, DOESN'T SOMEONE HAVE AN INFLATED SENSE OF SELF! THAT ASIDE...
...YOU WANT TO HELP SYRA. I KNOW YOU DO.
WELL, YEAH, BUT...
WE HAVE TO COMPLETE THE MISSION, BILLY.
WE DIDN'T COME THIS FAR TO LET...OTHER THINGS GET IN THE WAY.

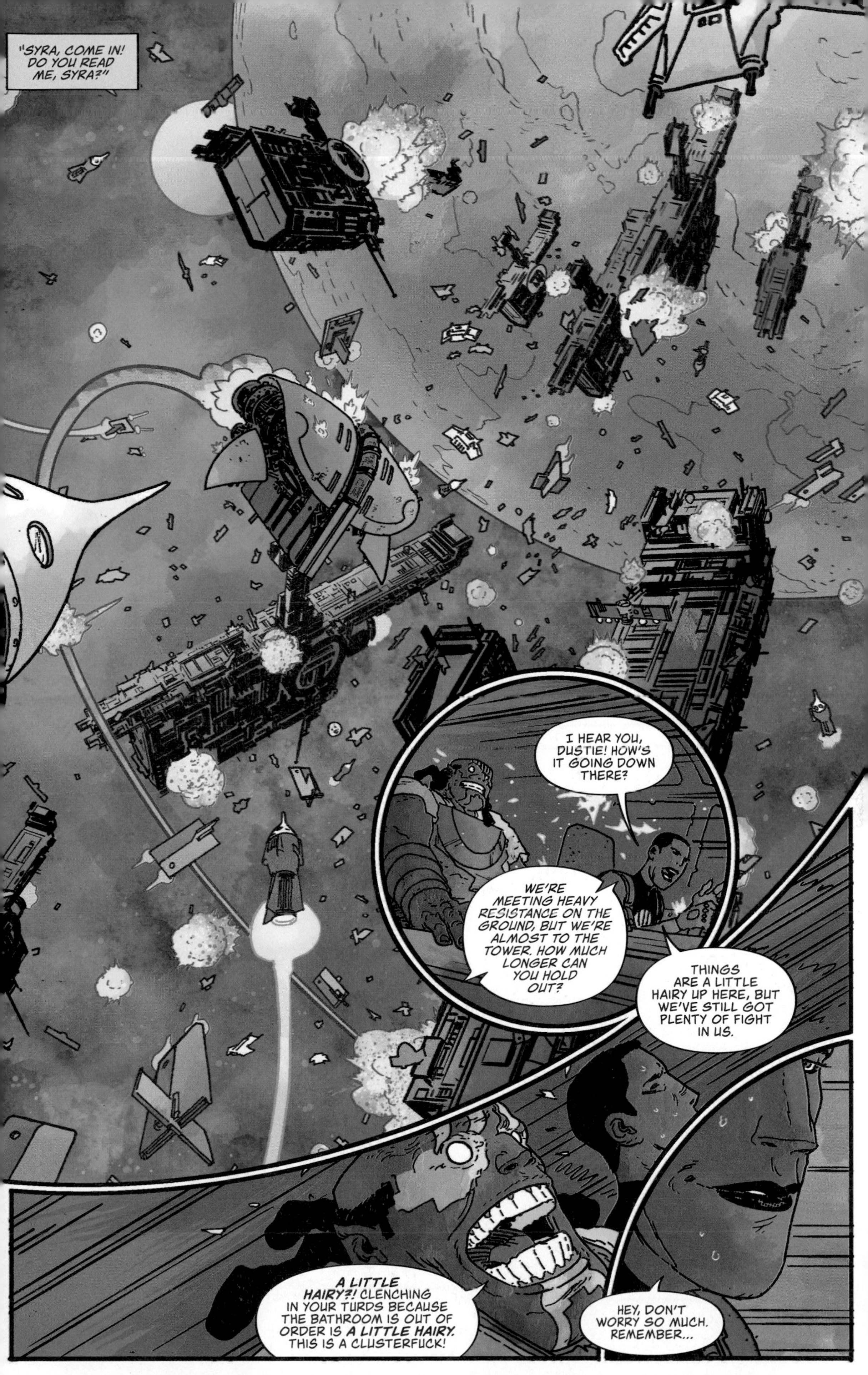
"SYRA, COME IN! DO YOU READ ME, SYRA?"
I HEAR YOU, DUSTIE! HOW'S IT GOING DOWN THERE?
WE'RE MEETING HEAVY RESISTANCE ON THE GROUND, BUT WE'RE ALMOST TO THE TOWER. HOW MUCH LONGER CAN YOU HOLD OUT?
THINGS ARE A LITTLE HAIRY UP HERE, BUT WE'VE STILL GOT PLENTY OF FIGHT IN US.
A LITTLE HAIRY?! CLENCHING IN YOUR TURDS BECAUSE THE BATHROOM IS OUT OF ORDER IS A LITTLE HAIRY. THIS IS A CLUSTERFUCK!
HEY, DON'T WORRY SO MUCH. REMEMBER...

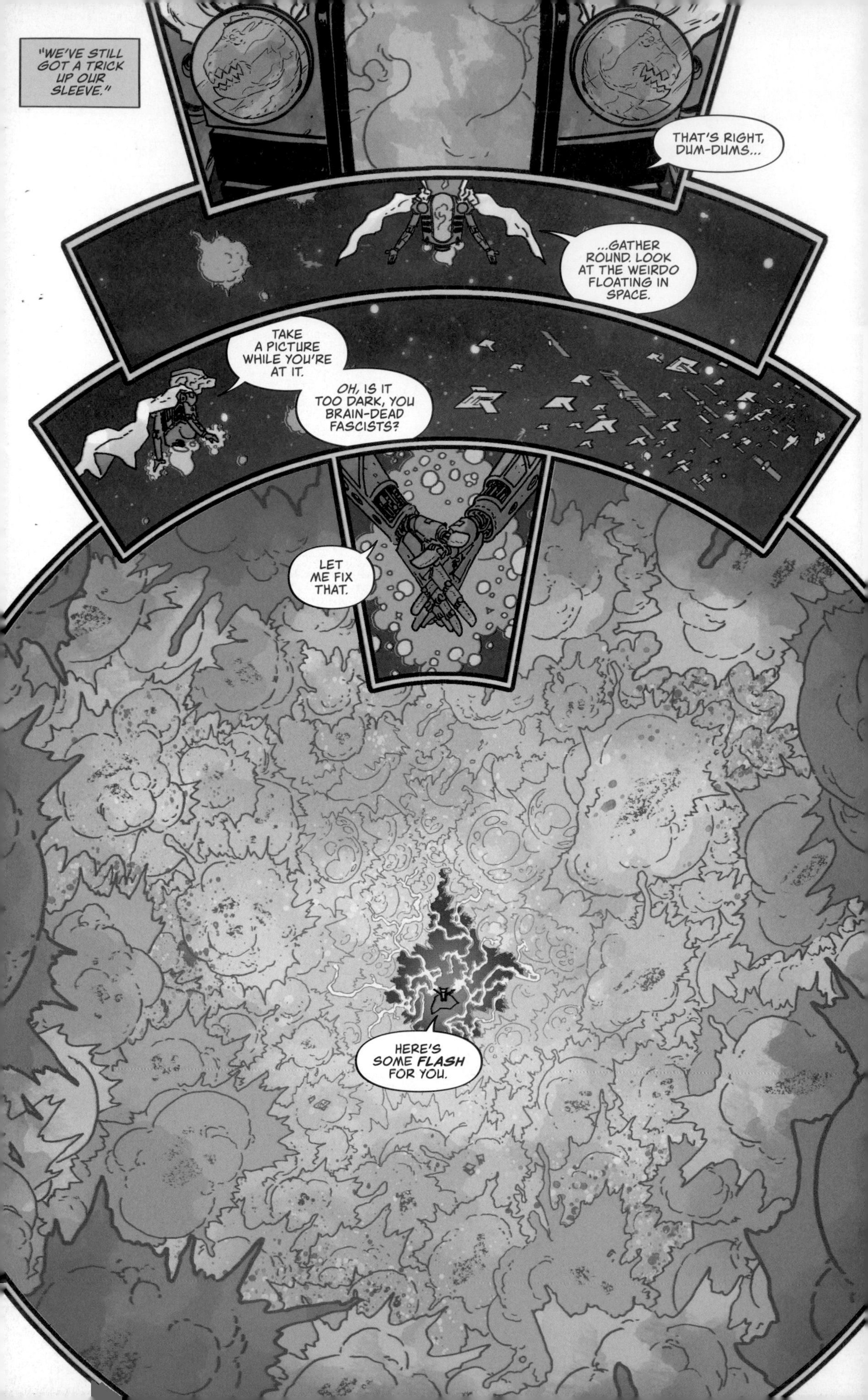
"WE'VE STILL GOT A TRICK UP OUR SLEEVE."
THAT'S RIGHT, DUM-DUMS...
...GATHER ROUND. LOOK AT THE WEIRDO FLOATING IN SPACE.
TAKE A PICTURE WHILE YOU'RE AT IT.
OH, IS IT TOO DARK, YOU BRAIN-DEAD FASCISTS?
LET ME FIX THAT.
HERE'S SOME FLASH FOR YOU.

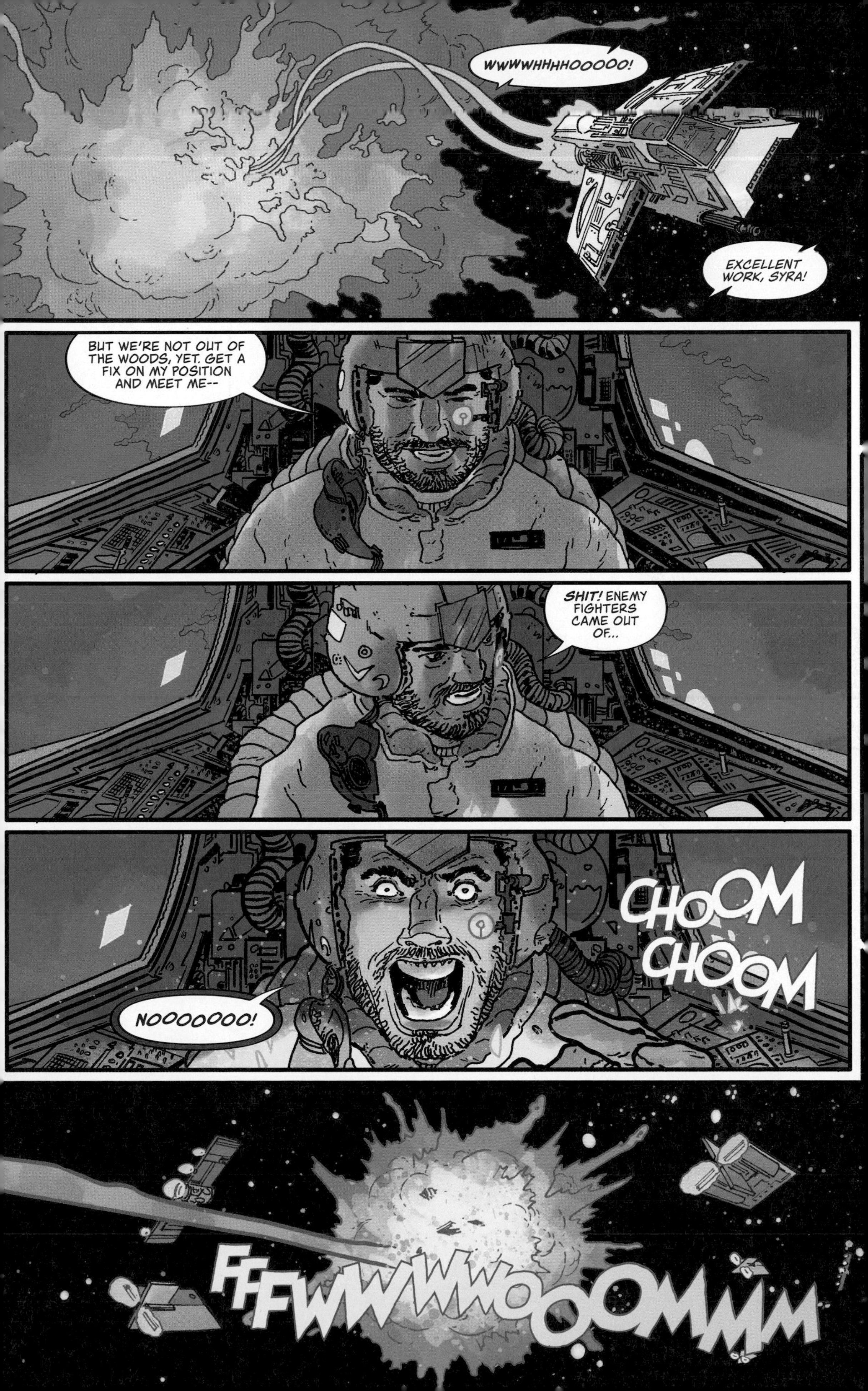
WWWWHHHHOOOOO!
EXCELLENT WORK, SYRA!
BUT WE'RE NOT OUT OF THE WOODS, YET. GET A FIX ON MY POSITION AND MEET ME--
SHIT! ENEMY FIGHTERS CAME OUT OF...
CHOOM CHOOM
NOOOOOOO!
FFFWWWWOOOOMMMM

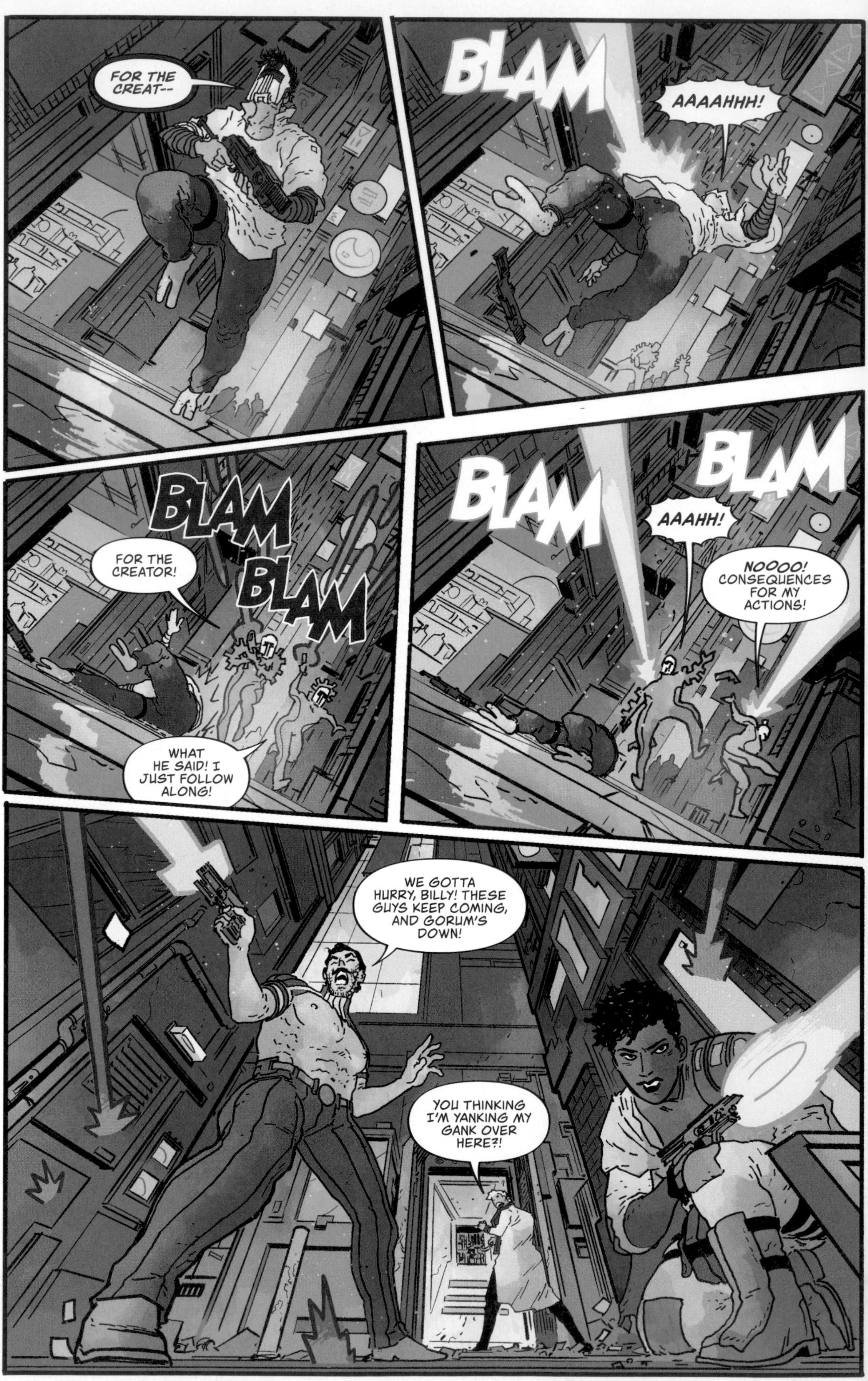
FOR THE CREAT--
BLAM
AAAAHHH!
BLAM
BLAM
FOR THE CREATOR!
WHAT HE SAID! I JUST FOLLOW ALONG!
BLAM
BLAM
AAAHH!
NOOOO! CONSEQUENCES FOR MY ACTIONS!
WE GOTTA HURRY, BILLY! THESE GUYS KEEP COMING, AND GORUM'S DOWN!
YOU THINKING I'M YANKING MY GANK OVER HERE?!

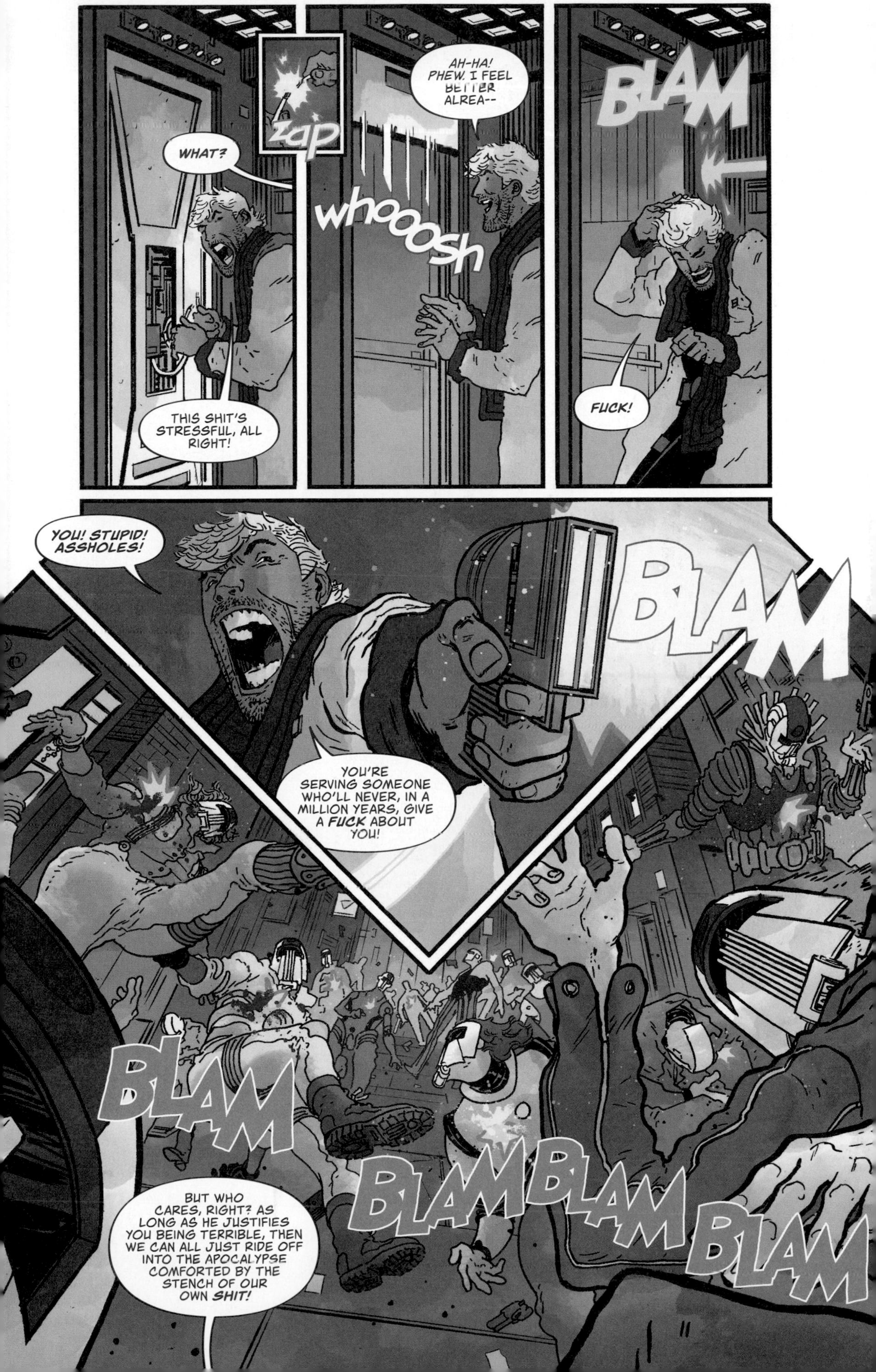
zap
WHAT?
THIS SHIT'S STRESSFUL, ALL RIGHT!
AH-HA! PHEW. I FEEL BETTER ALREA--
whoooosh
BLAM
FUCK!
YOU! STUPID! ASSHOLES!
BLAM
YOU'RE SERVING SOMEONE WHO'LL NEVER, IN A MILLION YEARS, GIVE A FUCK ABOUT YOU!
BLAM
BUT WHO CARES, RIGHT? AS LONG AS HE JUSTIFIES YOU BEING TERRIBLE, THEN WE CAN ALL JUST RIDE OFF INTO THE APOCALYPSE COMFORTED BY THE STENCH OF OUR OWN SHIT!
BLAM BLAM BLAM BLAM

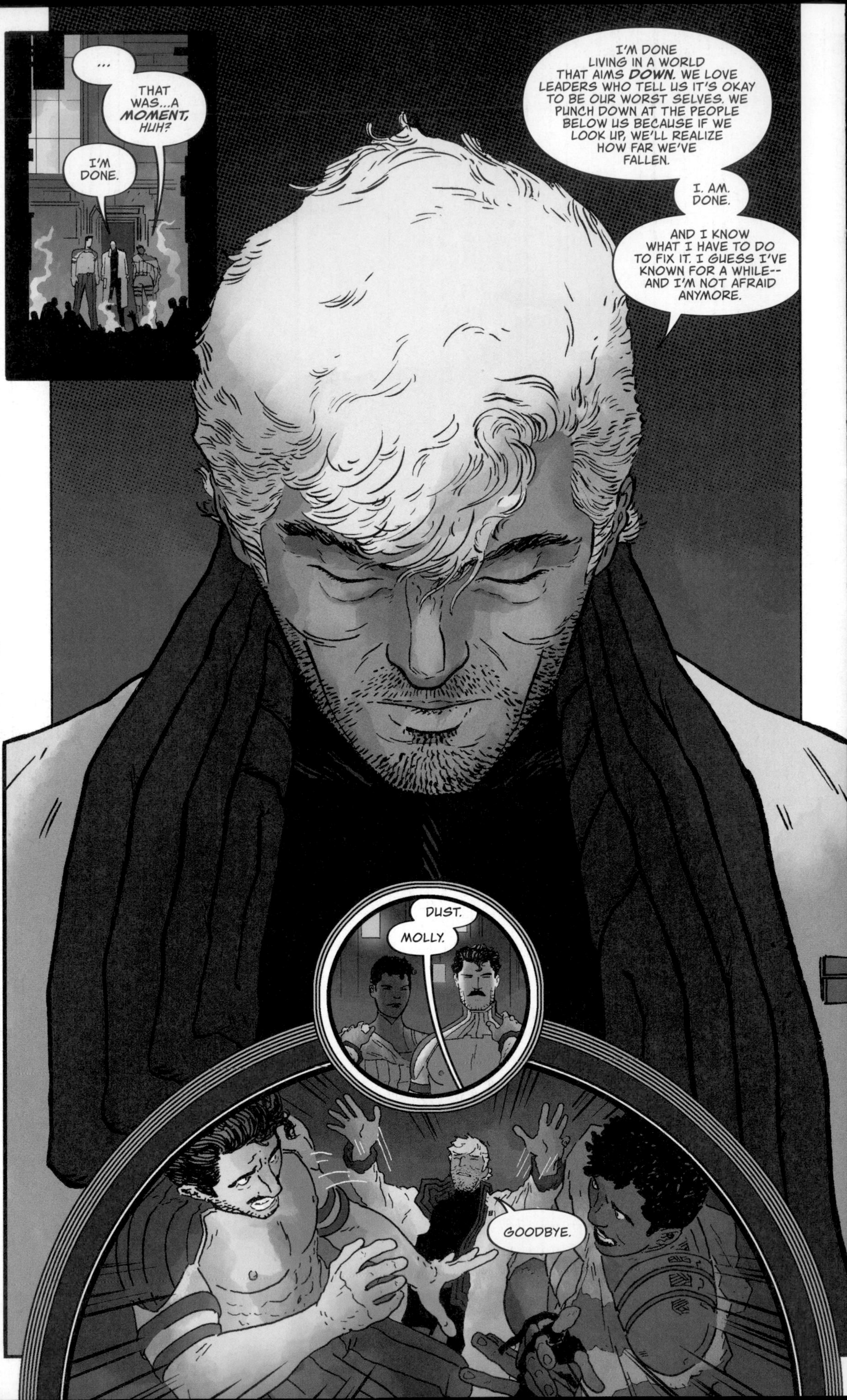
...
THAT WAS...A MOMENT, HUH?
I'M DONE.
I'M DONE LIVING IN A WORLD THAT AIMS DOWN. WE LOVE LEADERS WHO TELL US IT'S OKAY TO BE OUR WORST SELVES. WE PUNCH DOWN AT THE PEOPLE BELOW US BECAUSE IF WE LOOK UP, WE'LL REALIZE HOW FAR WE'VE FALLEN.
I. AM. DONE.
AND I KNOW WHAT I HAVE TO DO TO FIX IT. I GUESS I'VE KNOWN FOR A WHILE-- AND I'M NOT AFRAID ANYMORE.
DUST.
MOLLY.
GOODBYE.

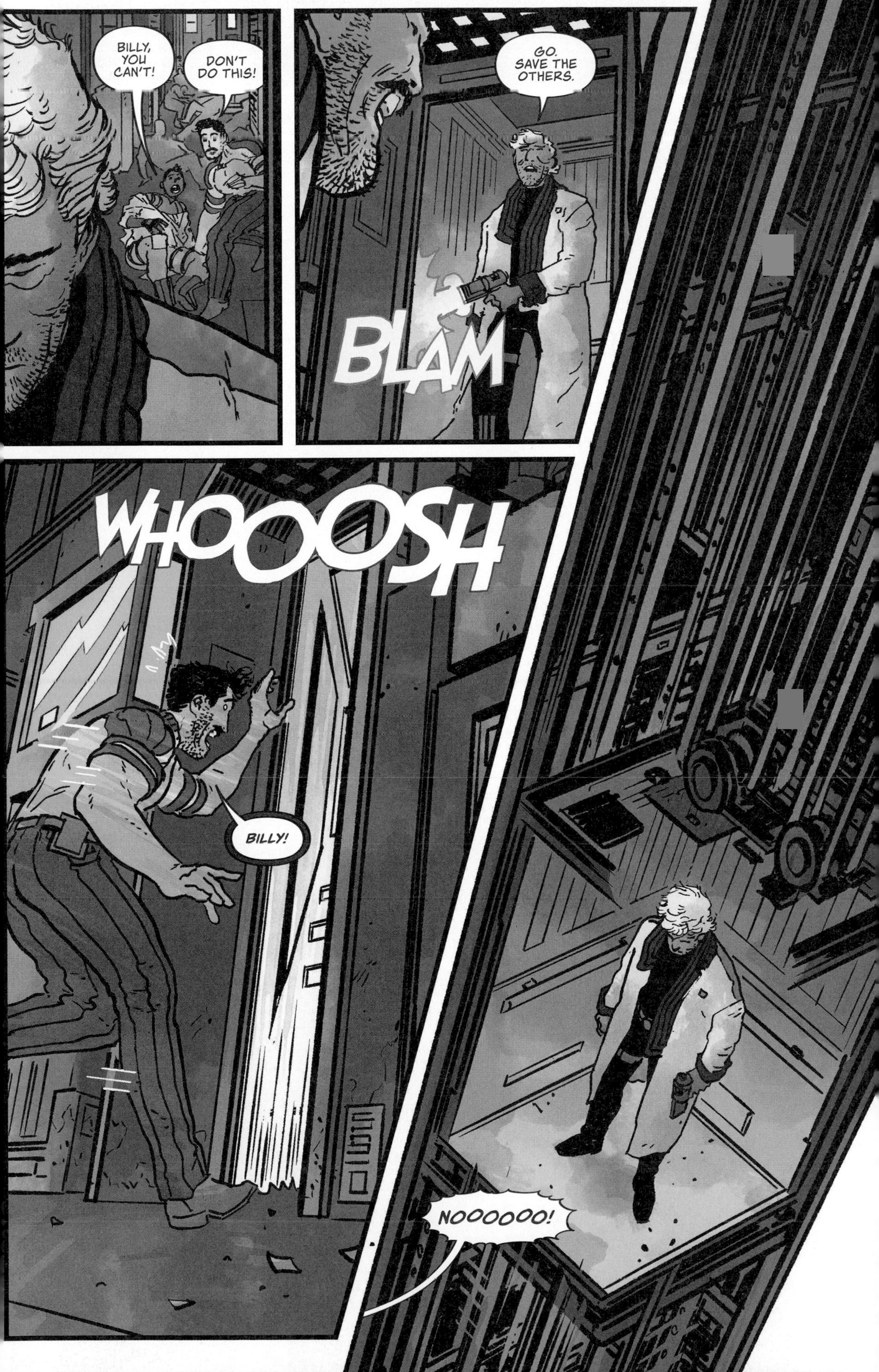
BILLY, YOU CAN'T!
DON'T DO THIS!
GO. SAVE THE OTHERS.
BLAM
WHOOOSH
BILLY!
NOOOOOO!

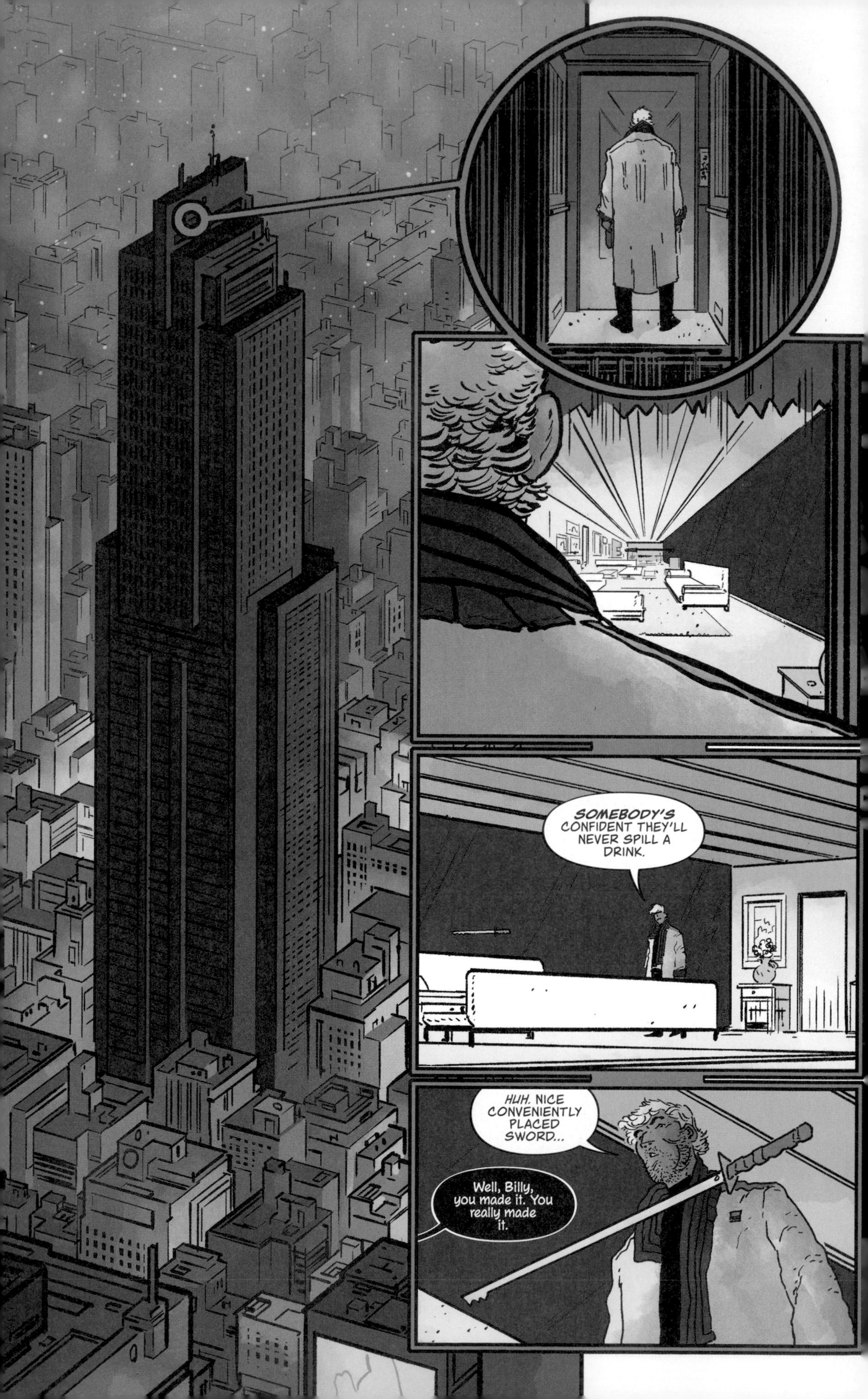
SOMEBODY'S CONFIDENT THEY'LL NEVER SPILL A DRINK.
HUH. NICE CONVENIENTLY PLACED SWORD...
Well, Billy, you made it. You really made it.

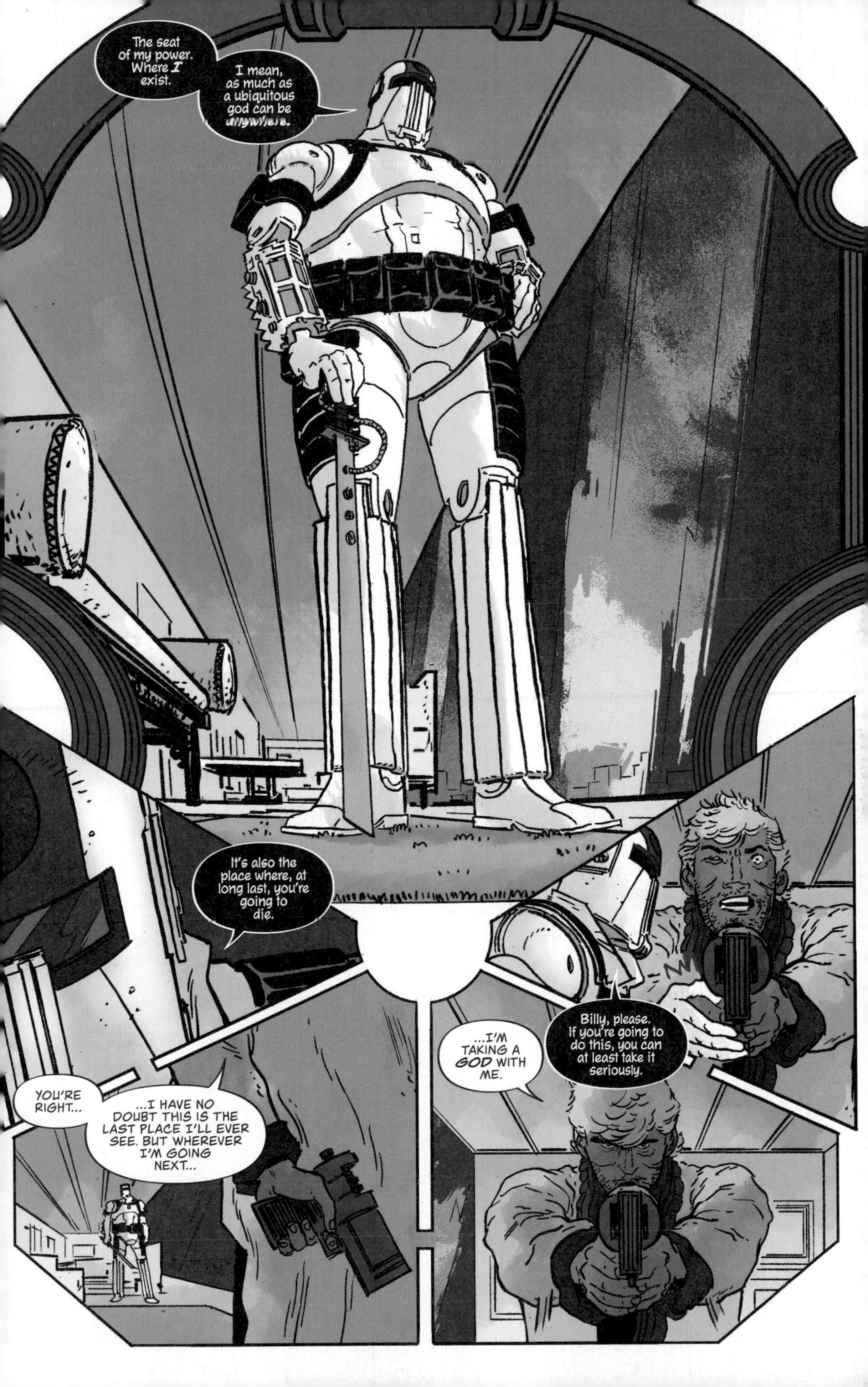

The seat of my power. Where *I* exist.
I mean, as much as a ubiquitous god can be anywhere.
It's also the place where, at long last, you're going to die.
YOU'RE RIGHT...
...I HAVE NO DOUBT THIS IS THE LAST PLACE I'LL EVER SEE. BUT WHEREVER I'M GOING NEXT...
...I'M TAKING A *GOD* WITH ME.
Billy, please. If you're going to do this, you can at least take it seriously.

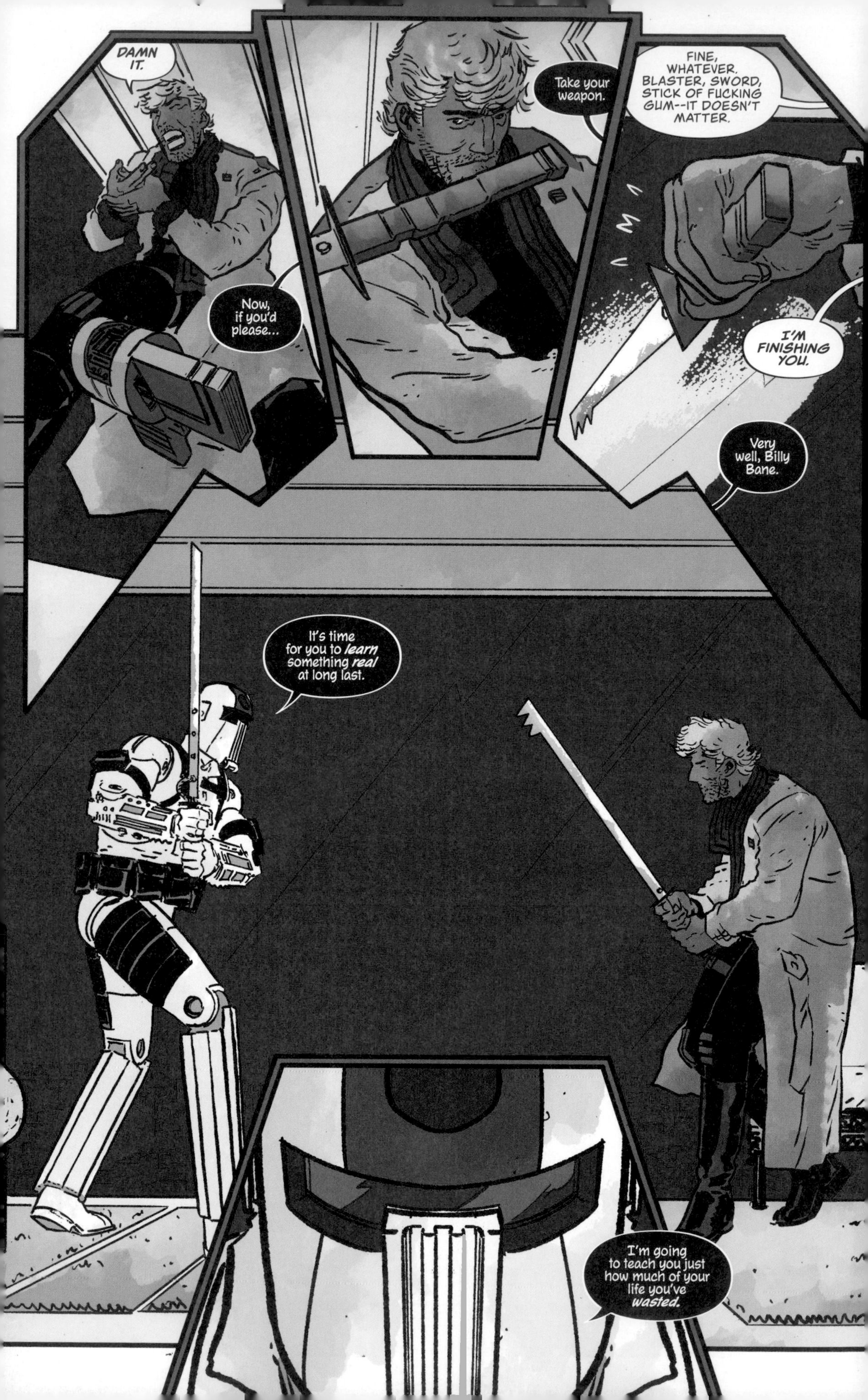
DAMN IT.
Now, if you'd please...
Take your weapon.
FINE, WHATEVER. BLASTER, SWORD, STICK OF FUCKING GUM--IT DOESN'T MATTER.
I'M FINISHING YOU.
Very well, Billy Bane.
It's time for you to *learn* something *real* at long last.
I'm going to teach you just how much of your life you've *wasted*.

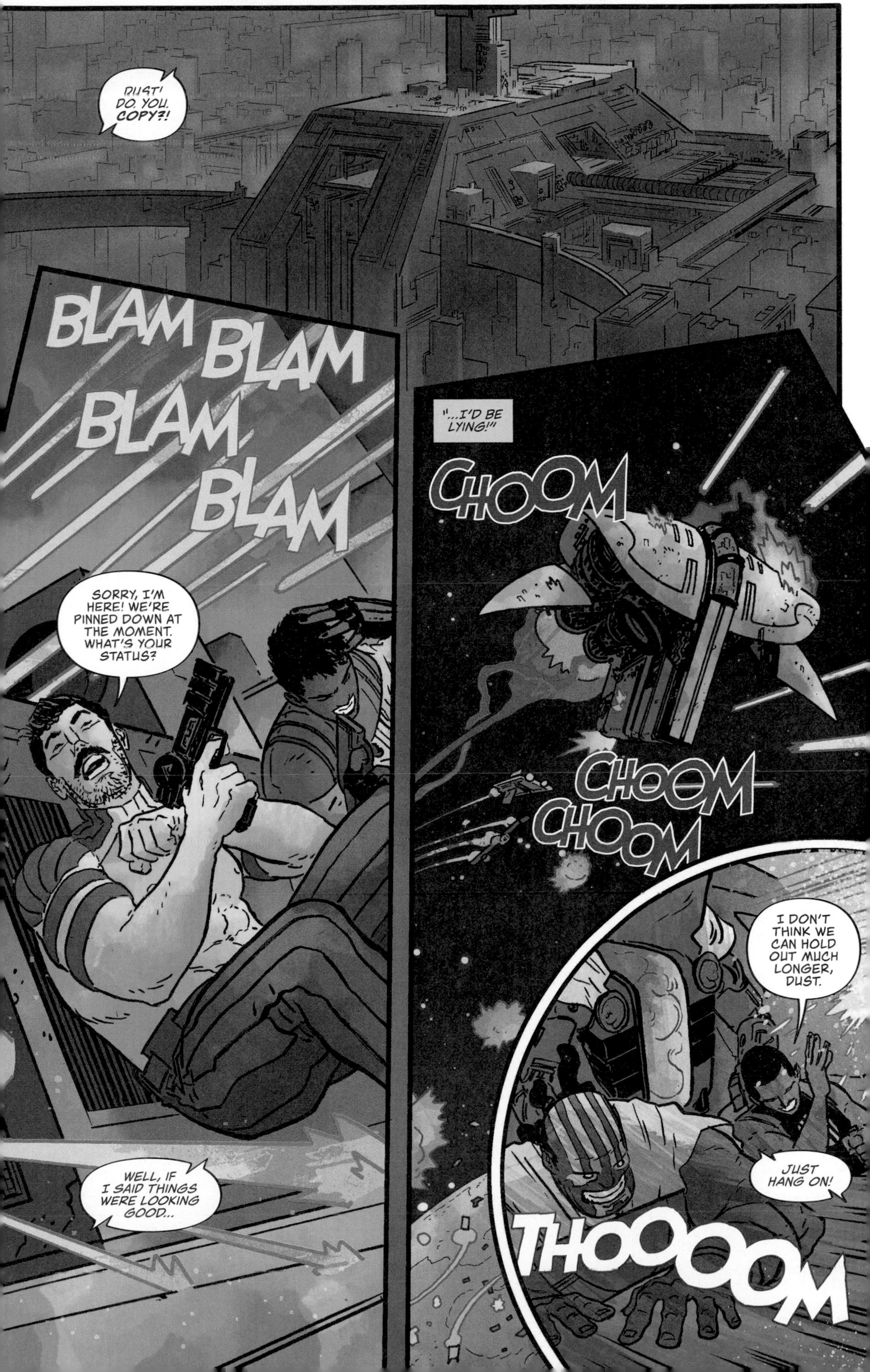
DUST!
DO. YOU.
COPY?!
BLAM BLAM
BLAM
BLAM
SORRY, I'M HERE! WE'RE PINNED DOWN AT THE MOMENT. WHAT'S YOUR STATUS?
WELL, IF I SAID THINGS WERE LOOKING GOOD...
"...I'D BE LYING!"
CHOOM
CHOOM
CHOOM
I DON'T THINK WE CAN HOLD OUT MUCH LONGER, DUST.
JUST HANG ON!
THOOOOM

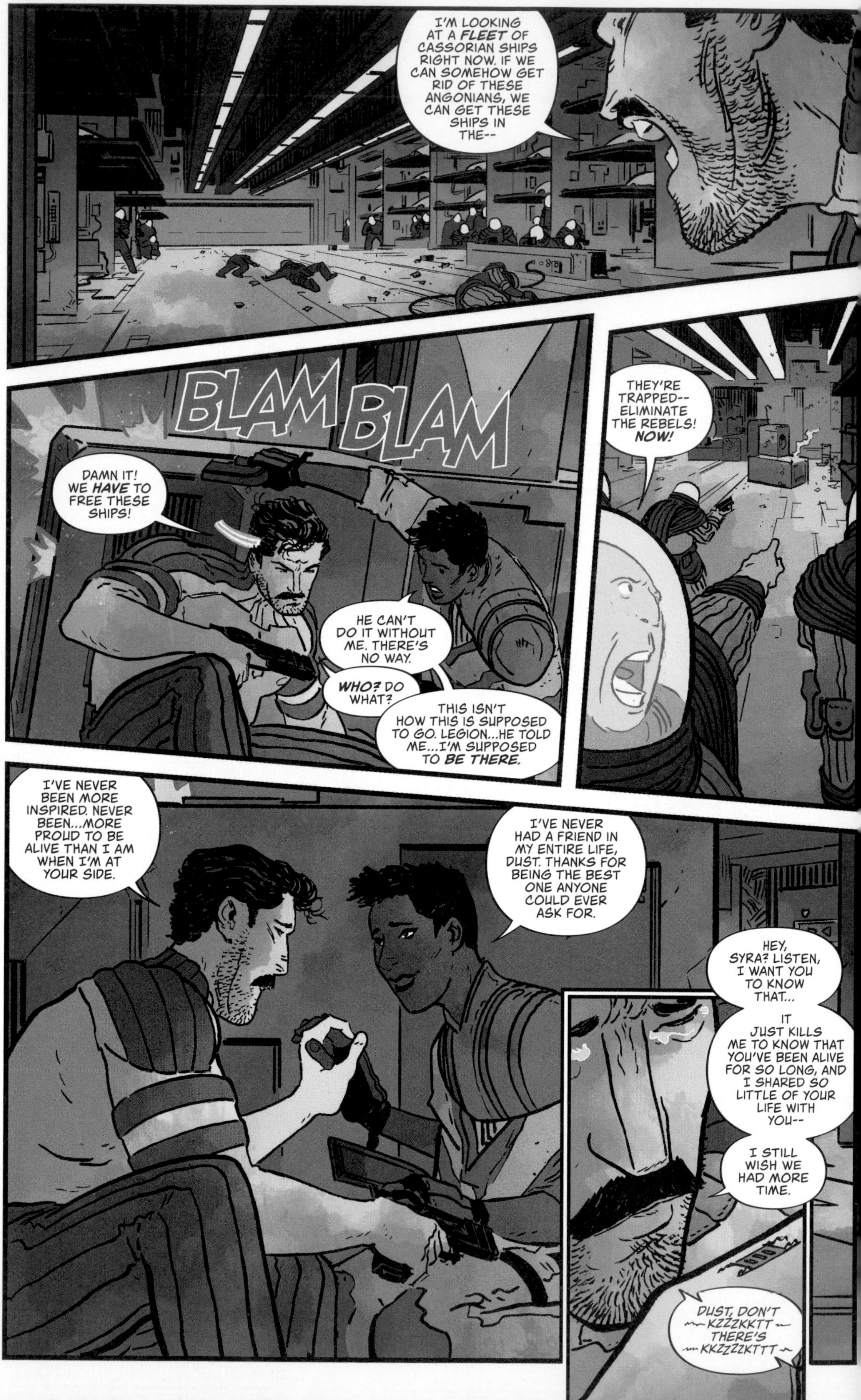
I'M LOOKING AT A FLEET OF CASSORIAN SHIPS RIGHT NOW. IF WE CAN SOMEHOW GET RID OF THESE ANGONIANS, WE CAN GET THESE SHIPS IN THE--
BLAM BLAM
DAMN IT! WE HAVE TO FREE THESE SHIPS!
HE CAN'T DO IT WITHOUT ME. THERE'S NO WAY.
WHO? DO WHAT?
THIS ISN'T HOW THIS IS SUPPOSED TO GO. LEGION...HE TOLD ME...I'M SUPPOSED TO BE THERE.
THEY'RE TRAPPED-- ELIMINATE THE REBELS! NOW!
I'VE NEVER BEEN MORE INSPIRED. NEVER BEEN...MORE PROUD TO BE ALIVE THAN I AM WHEN I'M AT YOUR SIDE.
I'VE NEVER HAD A FRIEND IN MY ENTIRE LIFE, DUST. THANKS FOR BEING THE BEST ONE ANYONE COULD EVER ASK FOR.
HEY, SYRA? LISTEN, I WANT YOU TO KNOW THAT...
IT JUST KILLS ME TO KNOW THAT YOU'VE BEEN ALIVE FOR SO LONG, AND I SHARED SO LITTLE OF YOUR LIFE WITH YOU--
I STILL WISH WE HAD MORE TIME.
DUST, DON'T KZZZKKTT THERE'S KKZZZZKTTT

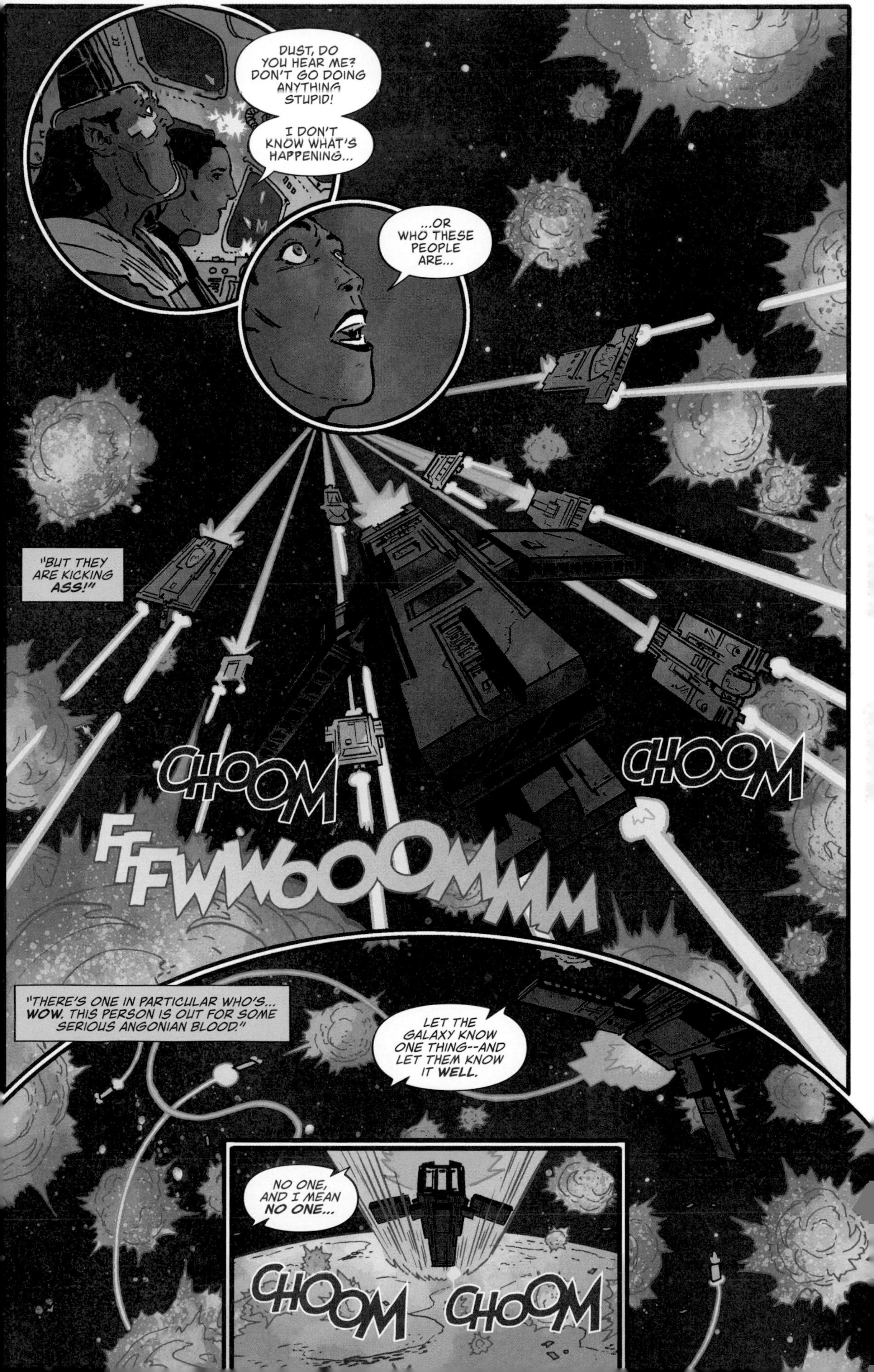
DUST, DO YOU HEAR ME? DON'T GO DOING ANYTHING STUPID!
I DON'T KNOW WHAT'S HAPPENING...
...OR WHO THESE PEOPLE ARE...
"BUT THEY ARE KICKING ASS!"
CHOOM
CHOOM
FFFWHOOOMMMM
"THERE'S ONE IN PARTICULAR WHO'S... WOW. THIS PERSON IS OUT FOR SOME SERIOUS ANGONIAN BLOOD."
LET THE GALAXY KNOW ONE THING--AND LET THEM KNOW IT WELL.
NO ONE, AND I MEAN NO ONE...
CHOOM
CHOOM

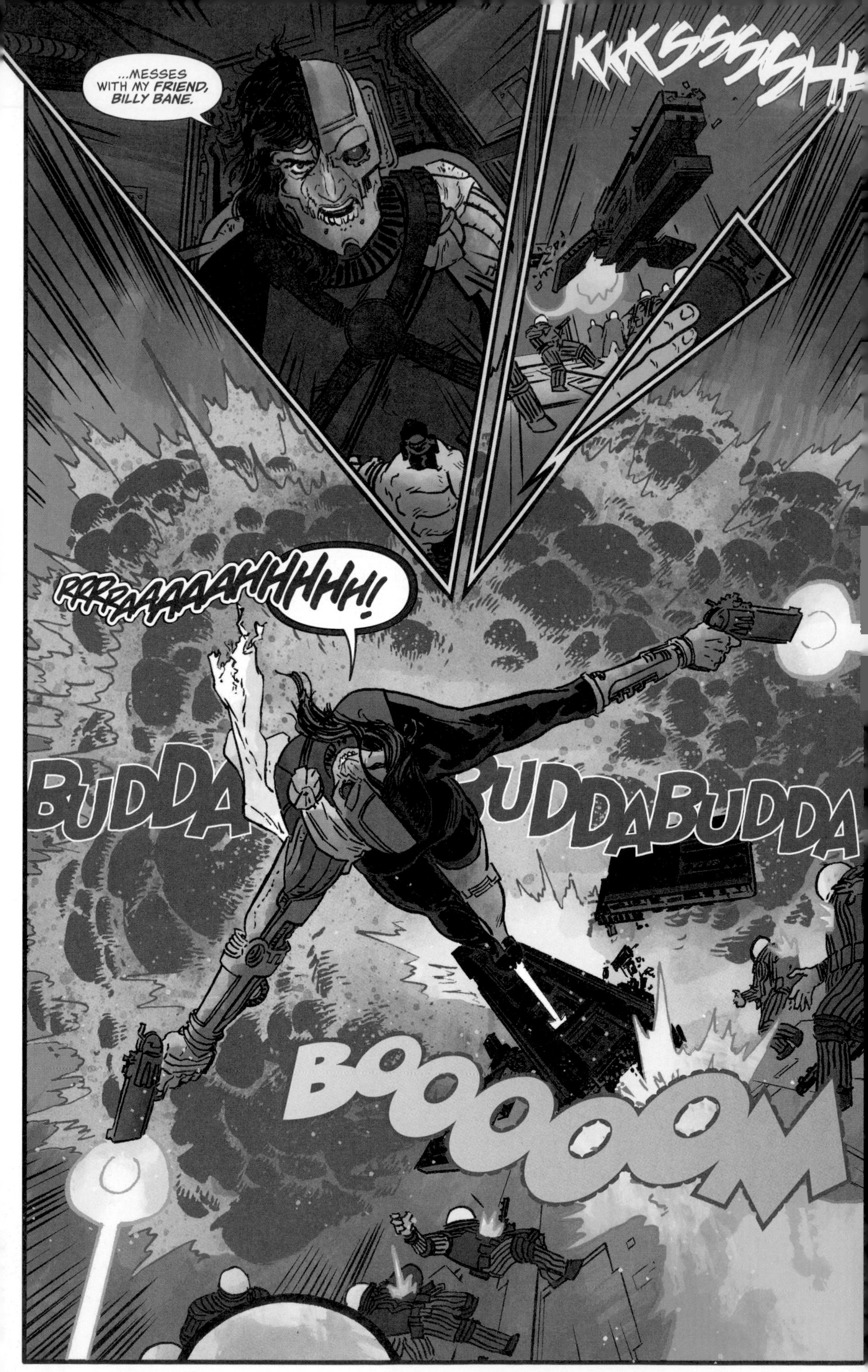
...MESSES WITH MY FRIEND, BILLY BANE.
KKKSSSSSSHH
RRRRAAAAAHHHHH!
BUDDA
BUDDABUDDA
BOOOOOM

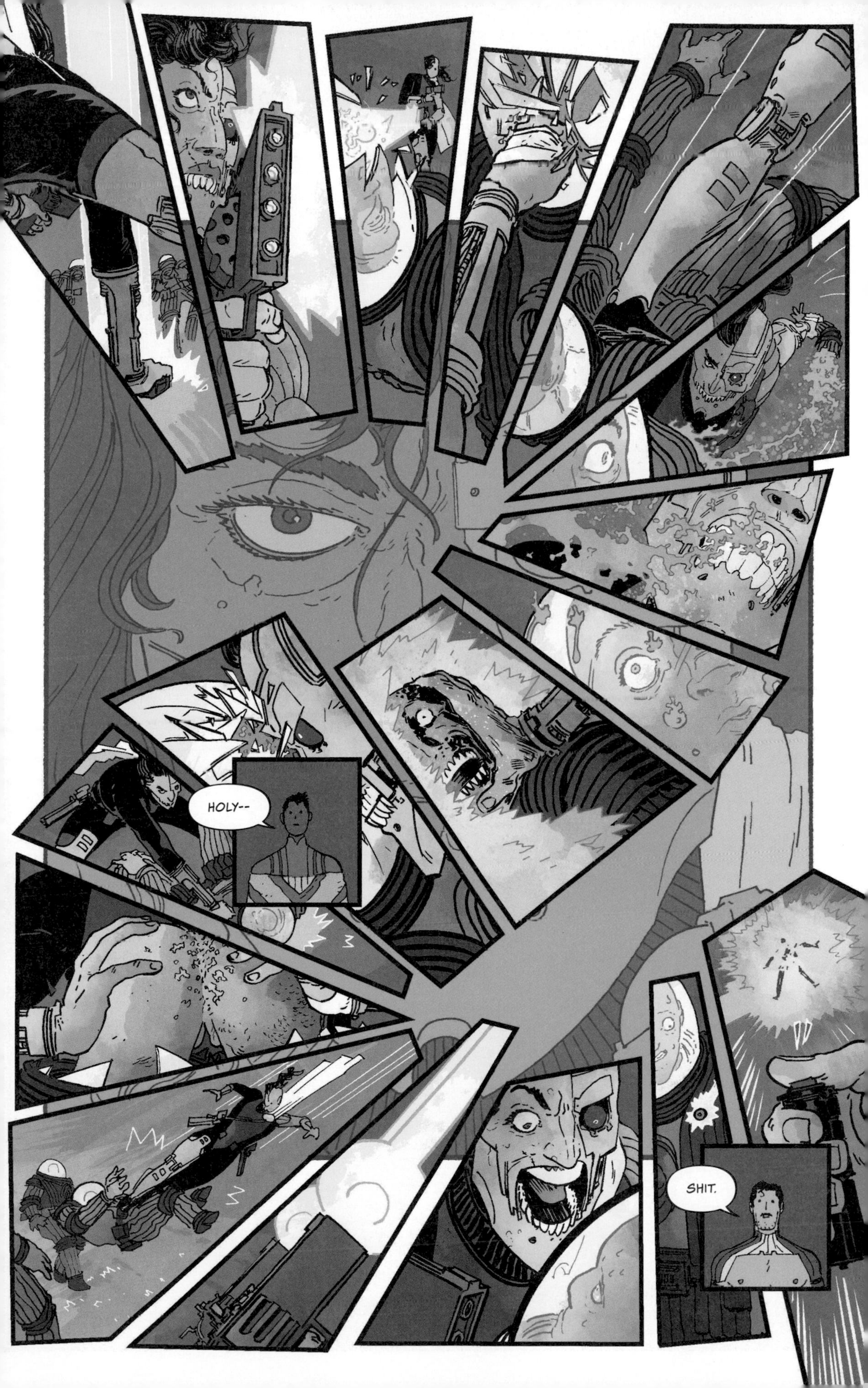
HOLY--
SHIT.

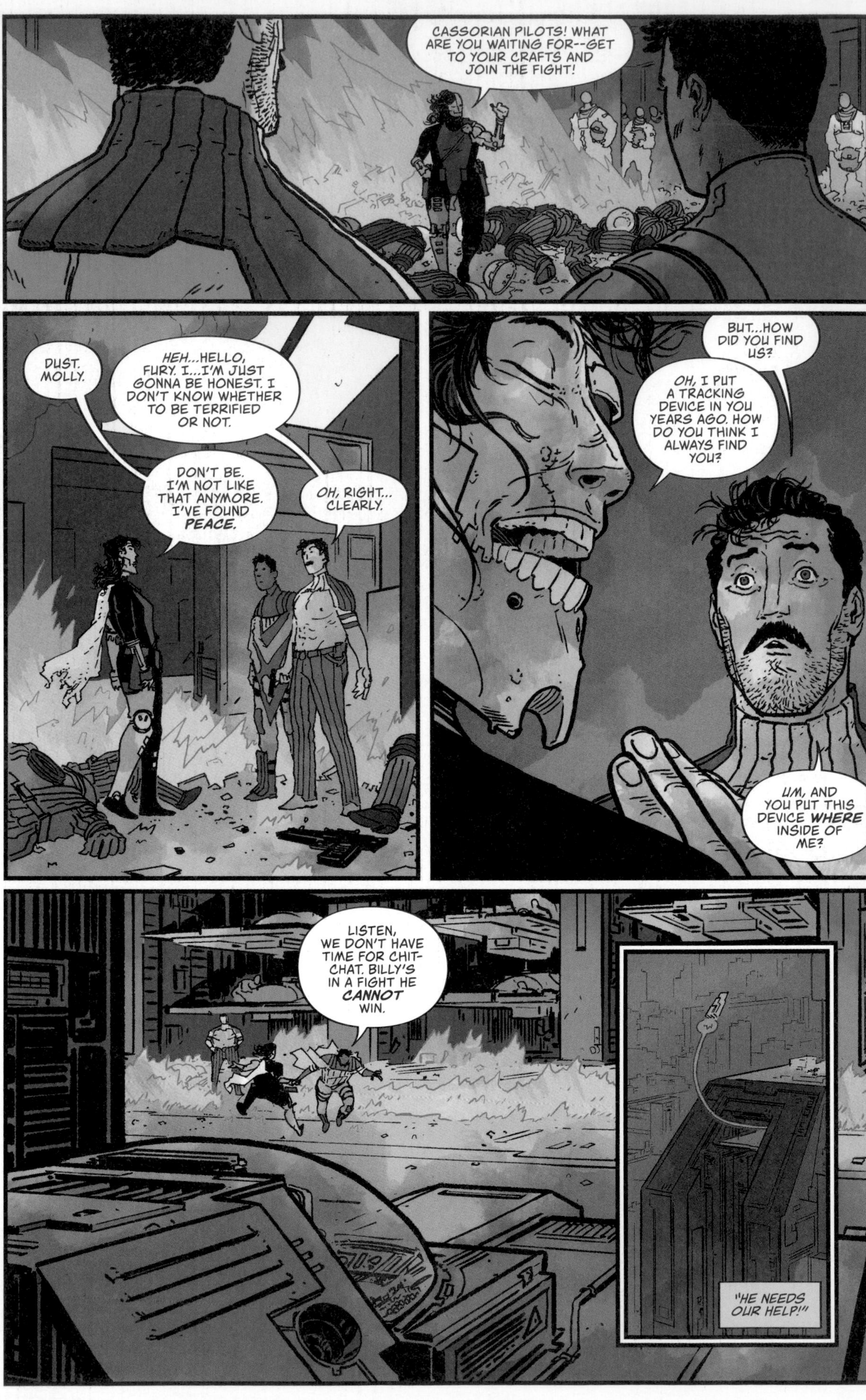
CASSORIAN PILOTS! WHAT ARE YOU WAITING FOR--GET TO YOUR CRAFTS AND JOIN THE FIGHT!
DUST. MOLLY.
HEH...HELLO, FURY. I...I'M JUST GONNA BE HONEST. I DON'T KNOW WHETHER TO BE TERRIFIED OR NOT.
DON'T BE. I'M NOT LIKE THAT ANYMORE. I'VE FOUND PEACE.
OH, RIGHT... CLEARLY.
BUT...HOW DID YOU FIND US?
OH, I PUT A TRACKING DEVICE IN YOU YEARS AGO. HOW DO YOU THINK I ALWAYS FIND YOU?
UM, AND YOU PUT THIS DEVICE WHERE INSIDE OF ME?
LISTEN, WE DON'T HAVE TIME FOR CHIT-CHAT. BILLY'S IN A FIGHT HE CANNOT WIN.
"HE NEEDS OUR HELP!"

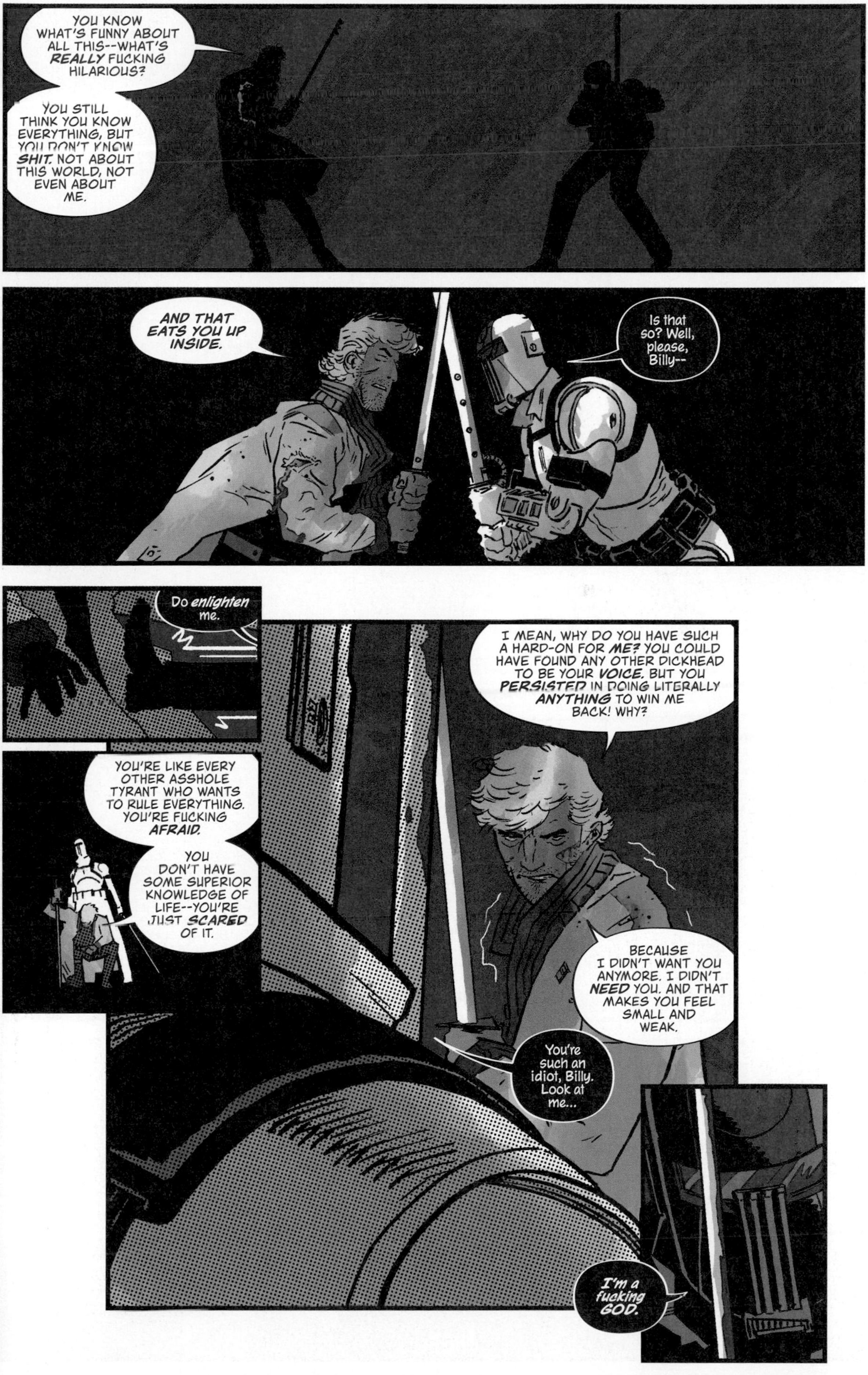
YOU KNOW WHAT'S FUNNY ABOUT ALL THIS--WHAT'S REALLY FUCKING HILARIOUS?
YOU STILL THINK YOU KNOW EVERYTHING, BUT YOU DON'T KNOW SHIT. NOT ABOUT THIS WORLD, NOT EVEN ABOUT ME.
AND THAT EATS YOU UP INSIDE.
Is that so? Well, please, Billy--
Do enlighten me.
I MEAN, WHY DO YOU HAVE SUCH A HARD-ON FOR ME? YOU COULD HAVE FOUND ANY OTHER DICKHEAD TO BE YOUR VOICE. BUT YOU PERSISTED IN DOING LITERALLY ANYTHING TO WIN ME BACK! WHY?
YOU'RE LIKE EVERY OTHER ASSHOLE TYRANT WHO WANTS TO RULE EVERYTHING. YOU'RE FUCKING AFRAID.
YOU DON'T HAVE SOME SUPERIOR KNOWLEDGE OF LIFE--YOU'RE JUST SCARED OF IT.
BECAUSE I DIDN'T WANT YOU ANYMORE. I DIDN'T NEED YOU. AND THAT MAKES YOU FEEL SMALL AND WEAK.
You're such an idiot, Billy. Look at me...
I'm a fucking GOD.

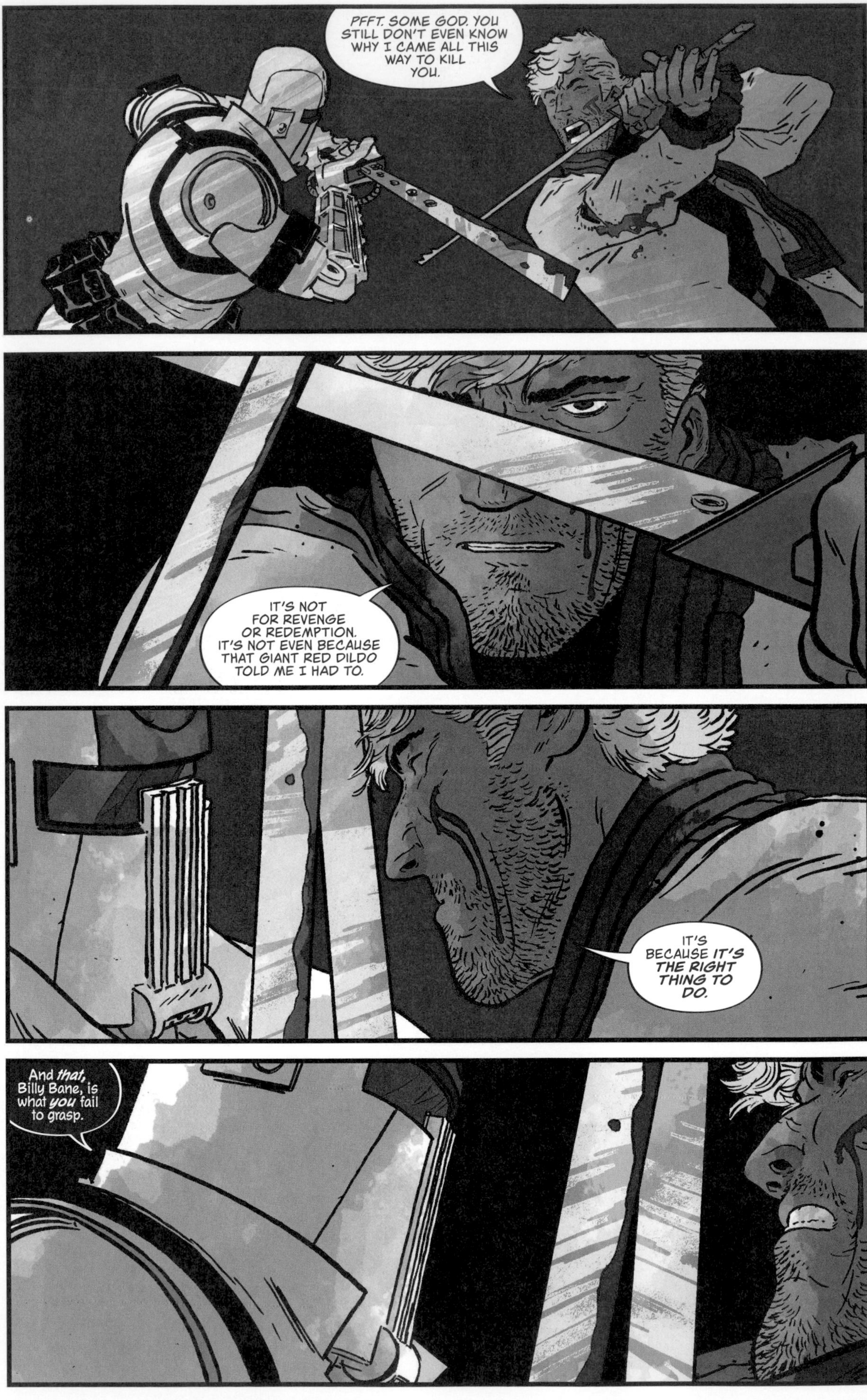
PFFT. SOME GOD. YOU STILL DON'T EVEN KNOW WHY I CAME ALL THIS WAY TO KILL YOU.
IT'S NOT FOR REVENGE OR REDEMPTION. IT'S NOT EVEN BECAUSE THAT GIANT RED DILDO TOLD ME I HAD TO.
IT'S BECAUSE *IT'S THE RIGHT THING TO DO.*
And *that,* Billy Bane, is what *you* fail to grasp.

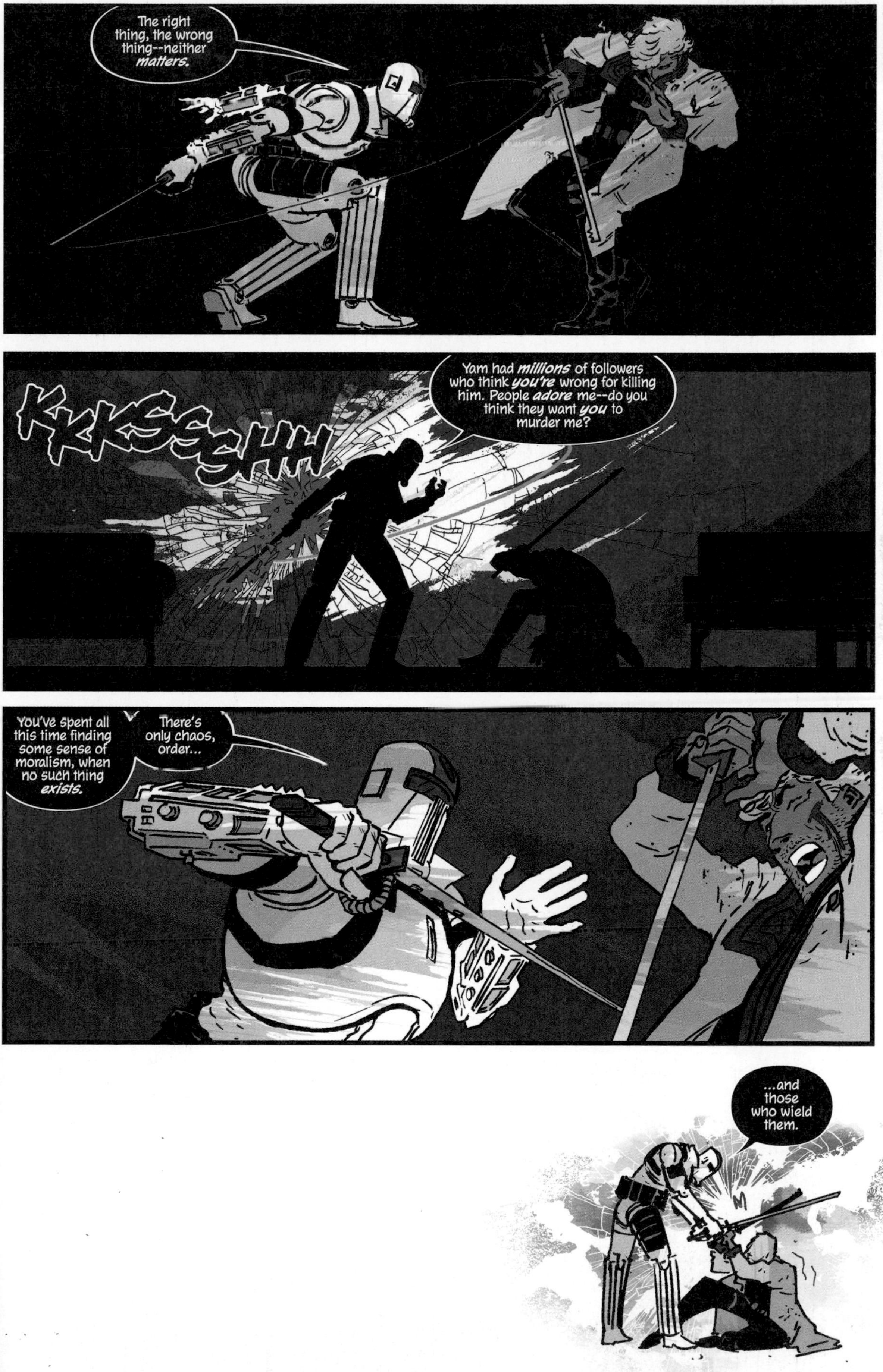
The right thing, the wrong thing--neither *matters.*
KKKSSSHHH
Yam had *millions* of followers who think *you're* wrong for killing him. People *adore* me--do you think they want *you* to murder me?
You've spent all this time finding some sense of moralism, when no such thing *exists.*
There's only chaos, order...
...and those who wield them.

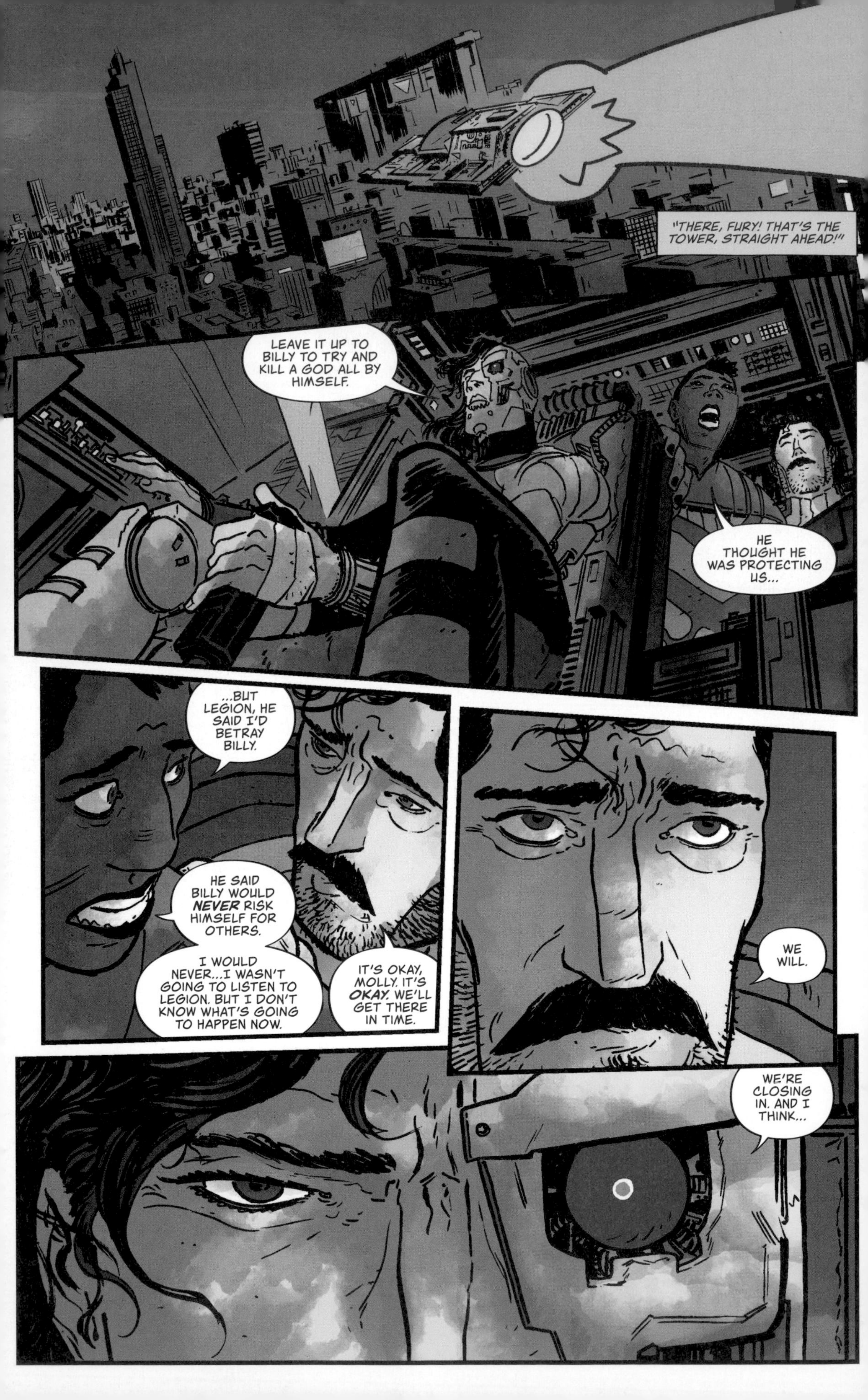
"THERE, FURY! THAT'S THE TOWER, STRAIGHT AHEAD!"
LEAVE IT UP TO BILLY TO TRY AND KILL A GOD ALL BY HIMSELF.
HE THOUGHT HE WAS PROTECTING US...
...BUT LEGION, HE SAID I'D BETRAY BILLY.
HE SAID BILLY WOULD **NEVER** RISK HIMSELF FOR OTHERS.
I WOULD NEVER...I WASN'T GOING TO LISTEN TO LEGION. BUT I DON'T KNOW WHAT'S GOING TO HAPPEN NOW.
IT'S OKAY, MOLLY. IT'S **OKAY.** WE'LL GET THERE IN TIME.
WE WILL.
WE'RE CLOSING IN. AND I THINK...

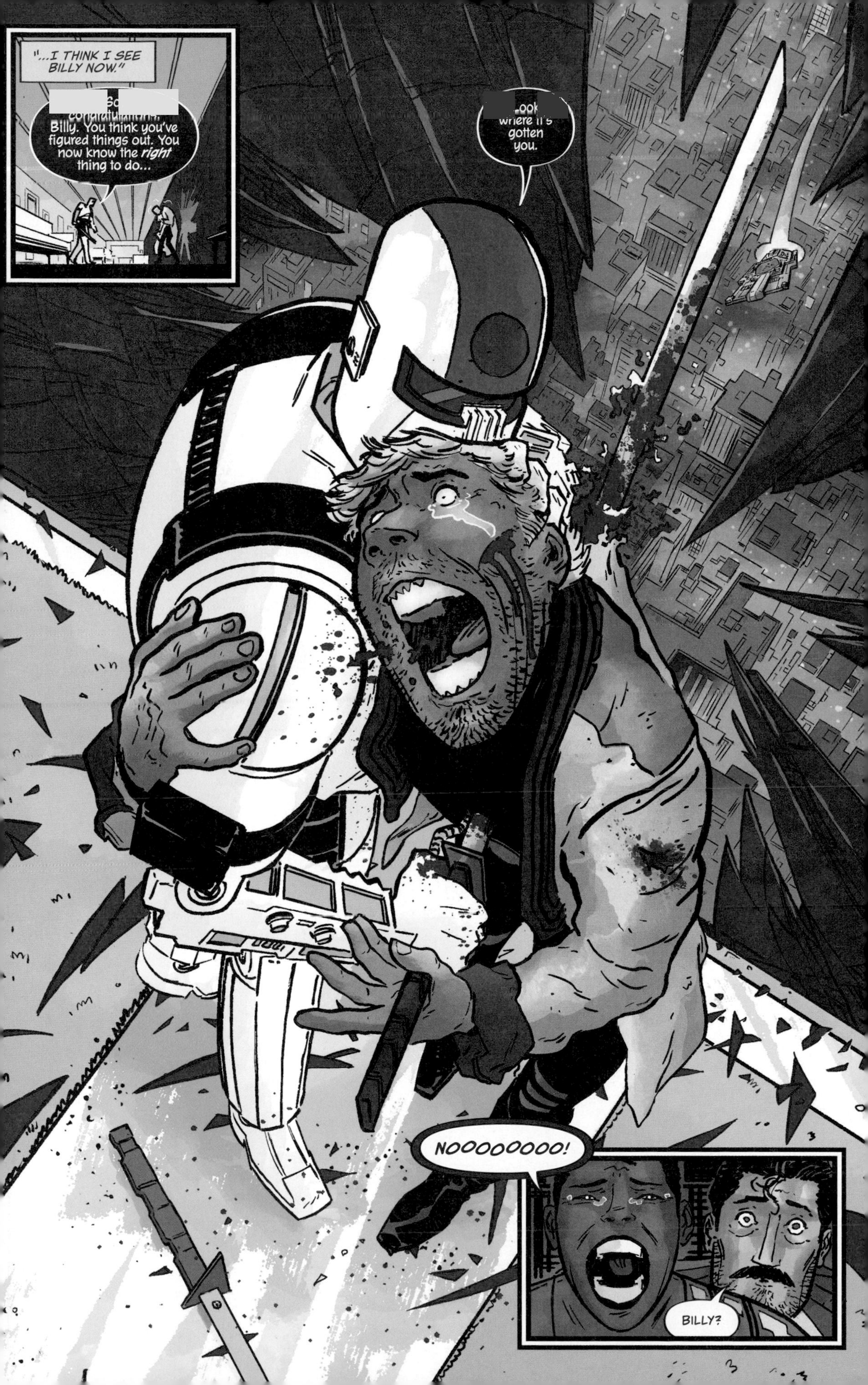
"...I THINK I SEE BILLY NOW."
[redacted] Billy. You think you've figured things out. You now know the *right* thing to do...
[redacted] where it's gotten you.
NOOOOOOOO!
BILLY?

CHAPTER TWENTYFIVE

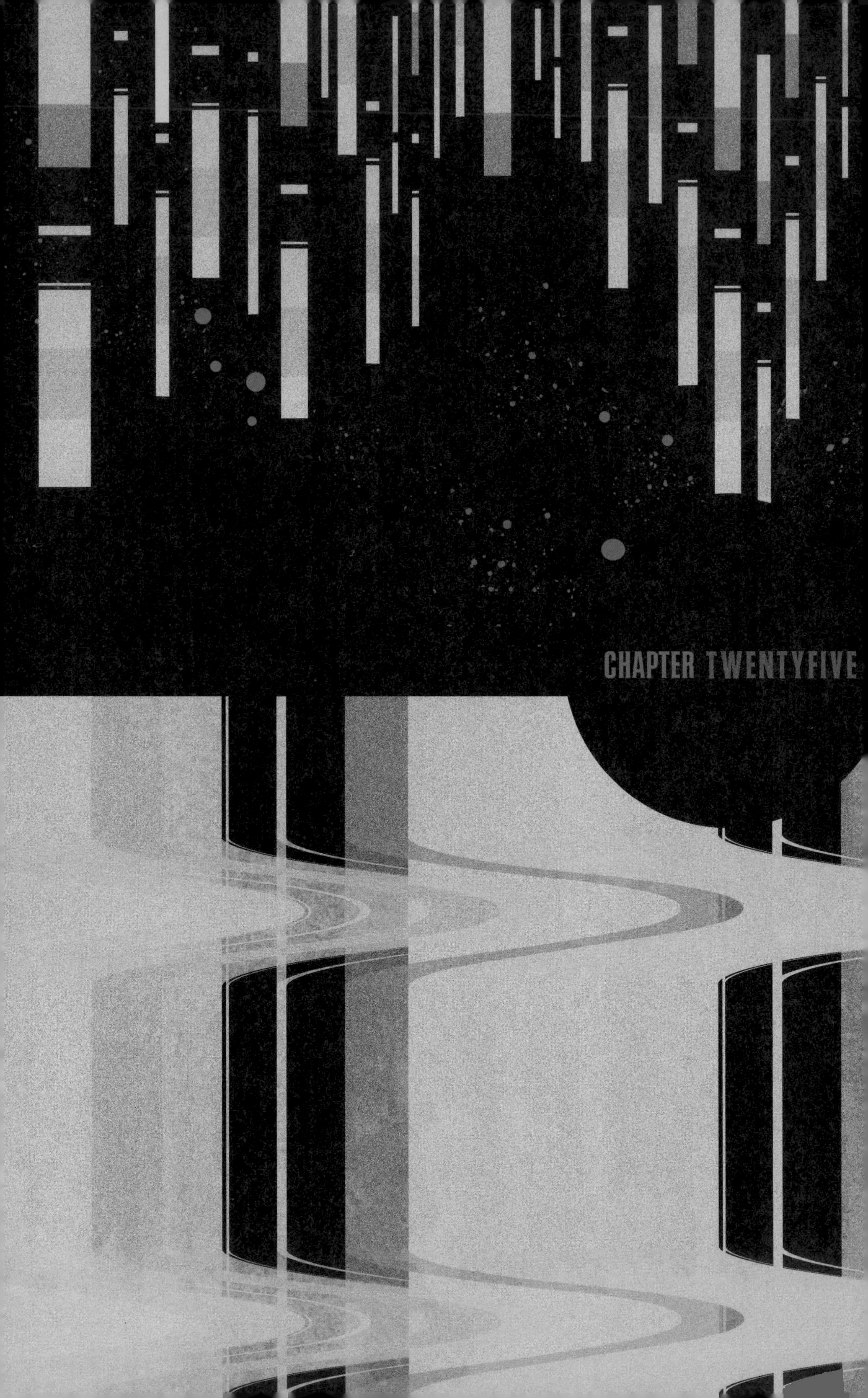

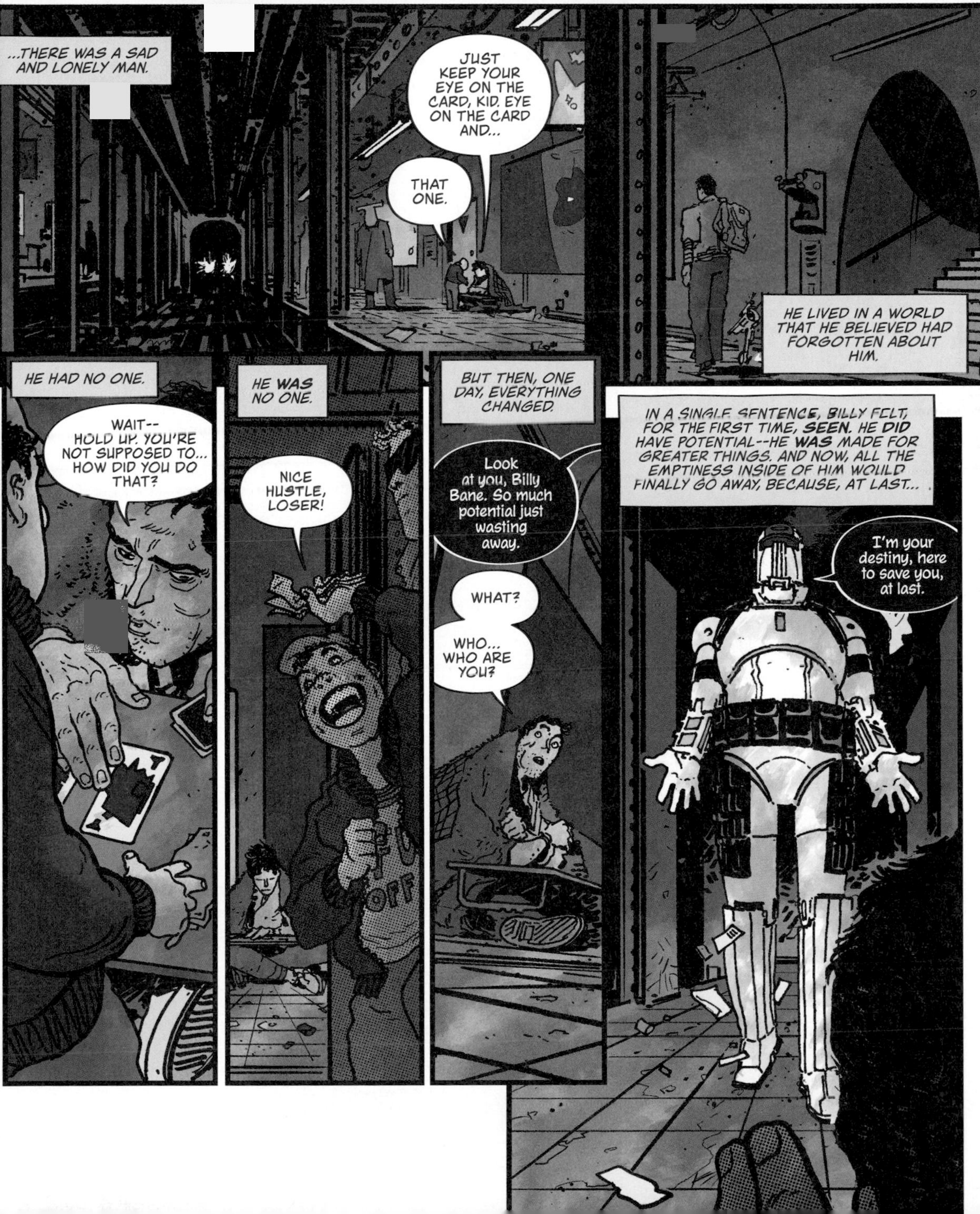
...THERE WAS A SAD AND LONELY MAN.
JUST KEEP YOUR EYE ON THE CARD, KID. EYE ON THE CARD AND...
THAT ONE.
HE LIVED IN A WORLD THAT HE BELIEVED HAD FORGOTTEN ABOUT HIM.
HE HAD NO ONE.
WAIT-- HOLD UP. YOU'RE NOT SUPPOSED TO... HOW DID YOU DO THAT?
HE **WAS** NO ONE.
NICE HUSTLE, LOSER!
BUT THEN, ONE DAY, EVERYTHING CHANGED.
Look at you, Billy Bane. So much potential just wasting away.
WHAT?
WHO... WHO ARE YOU?
IN A SINGLE SENTENCE, BILLY FELT, FOR THE FIRST TIME, **SEEN.** HE **DID** HAVE POTENTIAL--HE **WAS** MADE FOR GREATER THINGS. AND NOW, ALL THE EMPTINESS INSIDE OF HIM WOULD FINALLY GO AWAY, BECAUSE, AT LAST...
I'm your destiny, here to save you, at last.

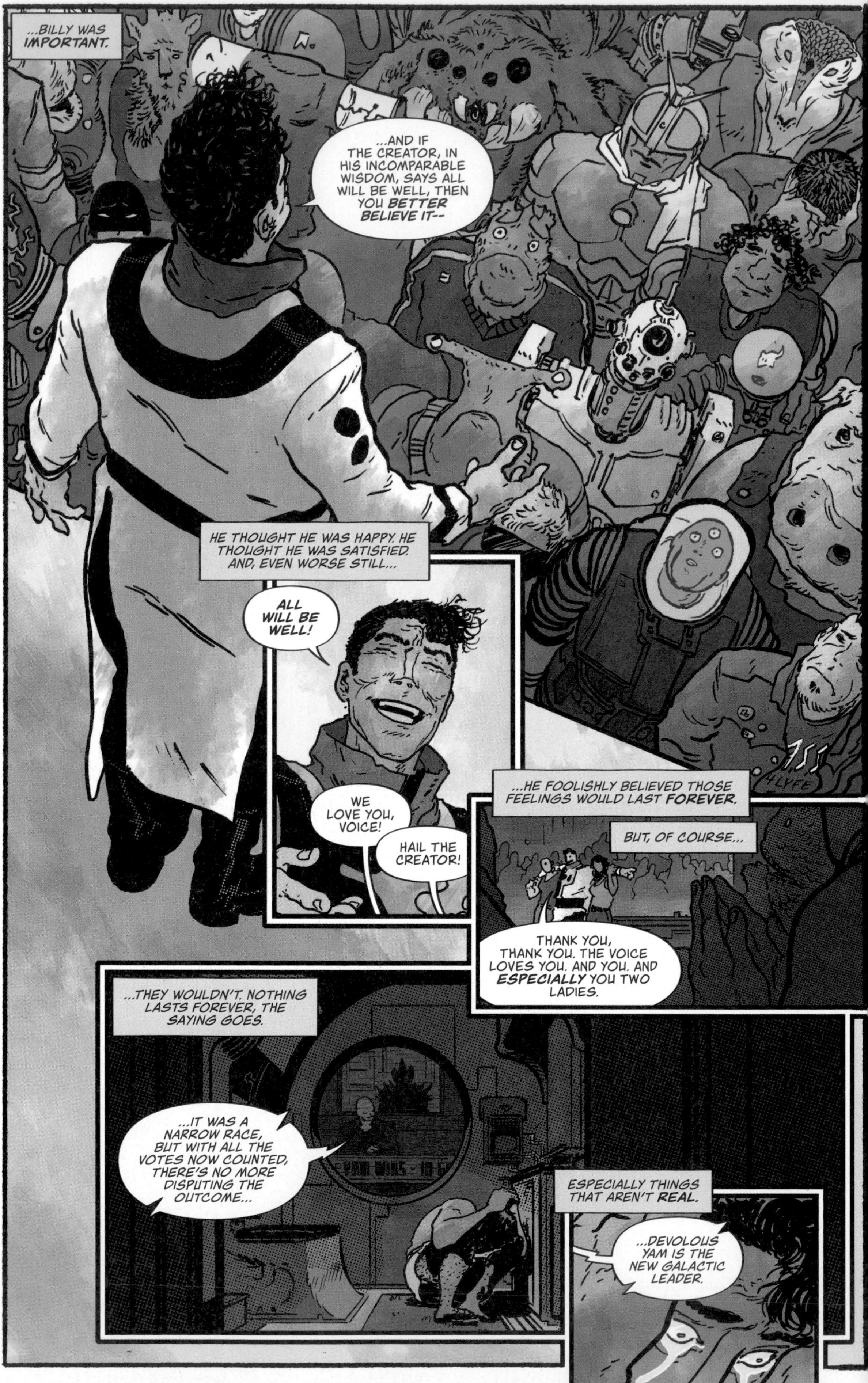
...BILLY WAS IMPORTANT.
...AND IF THE CREATOR, IN HIS INCOMPARABLE WISDOM, SAYS ALL WILL BE WELL, THEN YOU BETTER BELIEVE IT--
HE THOUGHT HE WAS HAPPY. HE THOUGHT HE WAS SATISFIED. AND, EVEN WORSE STILL...
ALL WILL BE WELL!
WE LOVE YOU, VOICE!
HAIL THE CREATOR!
4LYFE
...HE FOOLISHLY BELIEVED THOSE FEELINGS WOULD LAST FOREVER.
BUT, OF COURSE...
THANK YOU, THANK YOU. THE VOICE LOVES YOU. AND YOU. AND ESPECIALLY YOU TWO LADIES.
...THEY WOULDN'T. NOTHING LASTS FOREVER, THE SAYING GOES.
...IT WAS A NARROW RACE, BUT WITH ALL THE VOTES NOW COUNTED, THERE'S NO MORE DISPUTING THE OUTCOME...
ESPECIALLY THINGS THAT AREN'T REAL.
...DEVOLOUS YAM IS THE NEW GALACTIC LEADER.

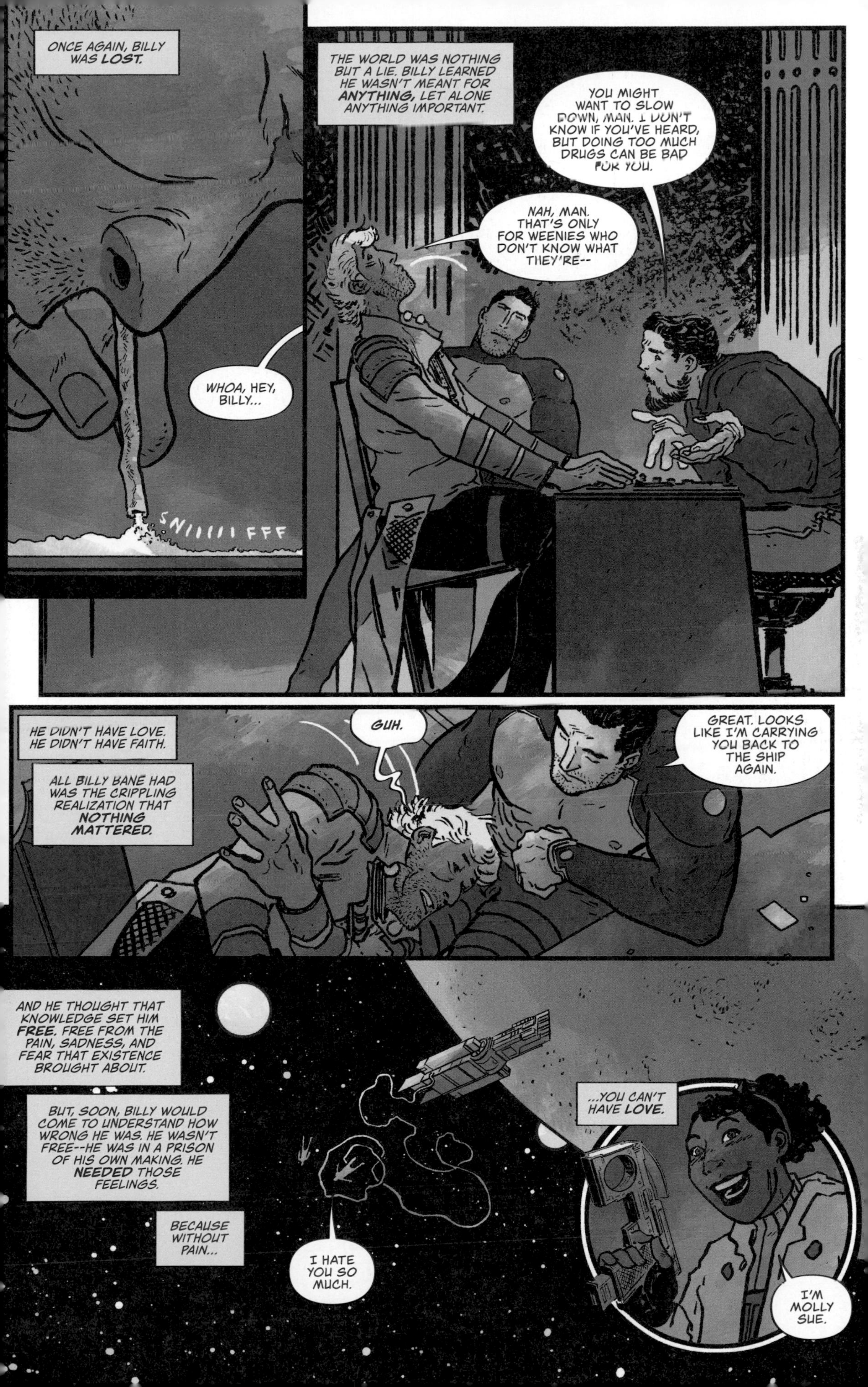
ONCE AGAIN, BILLY WAS LOST.
SNIIIIIFFF
WHOA, HEY, BILLY...
THE WORLD WAS NOTHING BUT A LIE. BILLY LEARNED HE WASN'T MEANT FOR ANYTHING, LET ALONE ANYTHING IMPORTANT.
YOU MIGHT WANT TO SLOW DOWN, MAN. I DON'T KNOW IF YOU'VE HEARD, BUT DOING TOO MUCH DRUGS CAN BE BAD FOR YOU.
NAH, MAN. THAT'S ONLY FOR WEENIES WHO DON'T KNOW WHAT THEY'RE--
HE DIDN'T HAVE LOVE. HE DIDN'T HAVE FAITH.
ALL BILLY BANE HAD WAS THE CRIPPLING REALIZATION THAT NOTHING MATTERED.
GUH.
GREAT. LOOKS LIKE I'M CARRYING YOU BACK TO THE SHIP AGAIN.
AND HE THOUGHT THAT KNOWLEDGE SET HIM FREE. FREE FROM THE PAIN, SADNESS, AND FEAR THAT EXISTENCE BROUGHT ABOUT.
BUT, SOON, BILLY WOULD COME TO UNDERSTAND HOW WRONG HE WAS. HE WASN'T FREE--HE WAS IN A PRISON OF HIS OWN MAKING. HE NEEDED THOSE FEELINGS.
BECAUSE WITHOUT PAIN...
I HATE YOU SO MUCH.
...YOU CAN'T HAVE LOVE.
I'M MOLLY SUE.

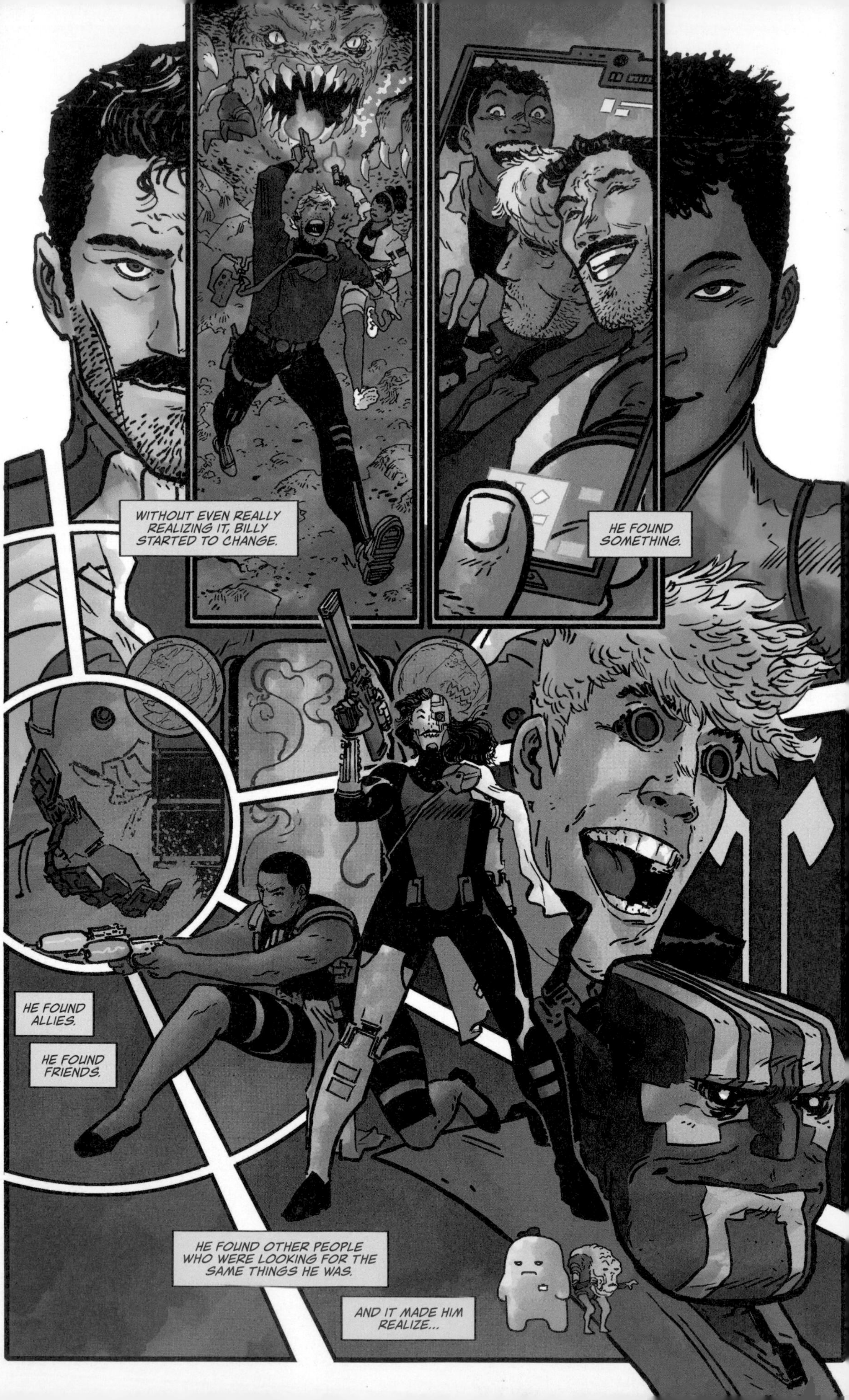
WITHOUT EVEN REALLY REALIZING IT, BILLY STARTED TO CHANGE.
HE FOUND SOMETHING.
HE FOUND ALLIES.
HE FOUND FRIENDS.
HE FOUND OTHER PEOPLE WHO WERE LOOKING FOR THE SAME THINGS HE WAS.
AND IT MADE HIM REALIZE...

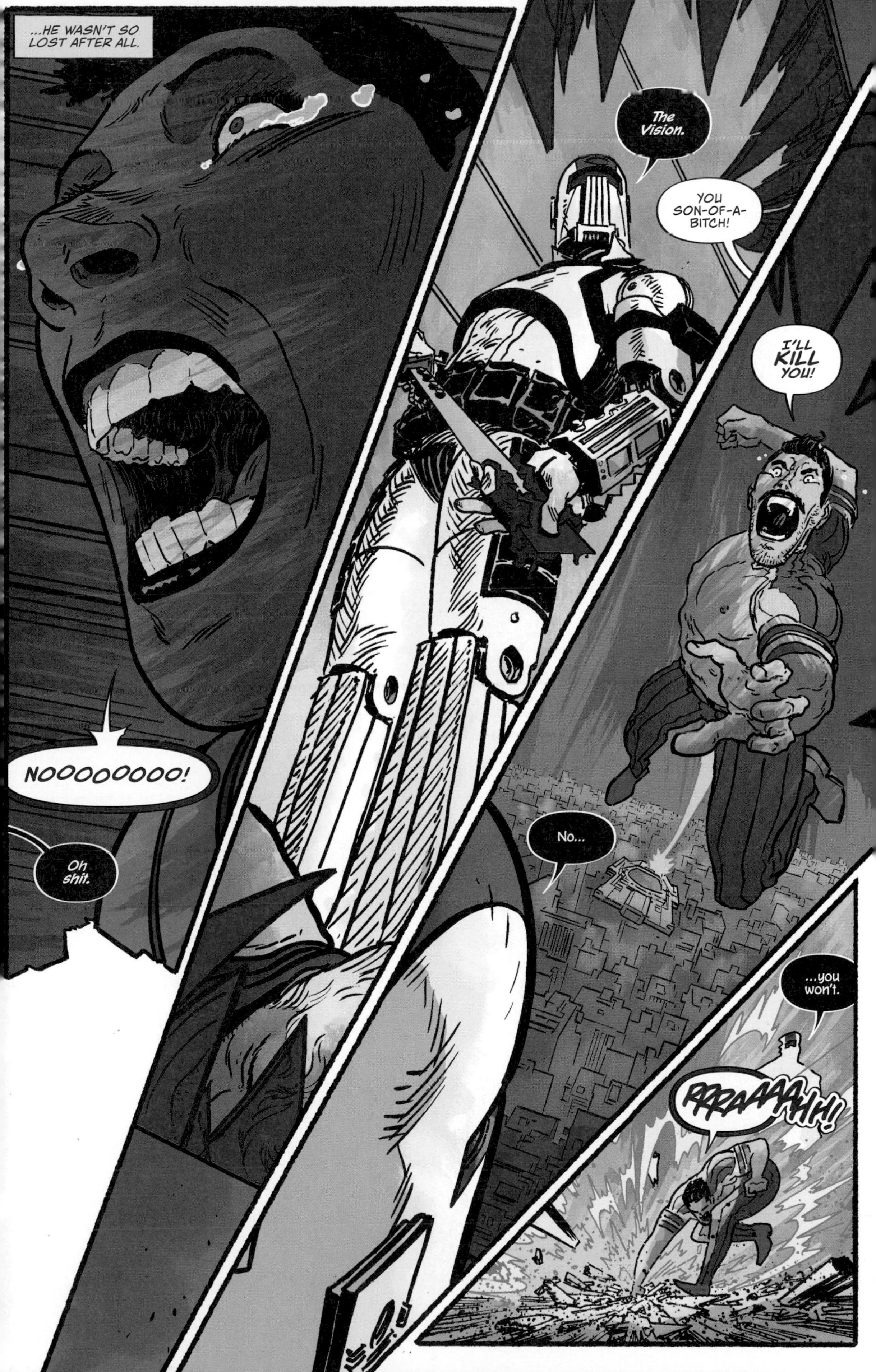
...HE WASN'T SO LOST AFTER ALL.
NOOOOOOOO!
Oh shit.
The Vision.
YOU SON-OF-A-BITCH!
I'LL KILL YOU!
No...
...you won't.
RRRAAAAAHH!!

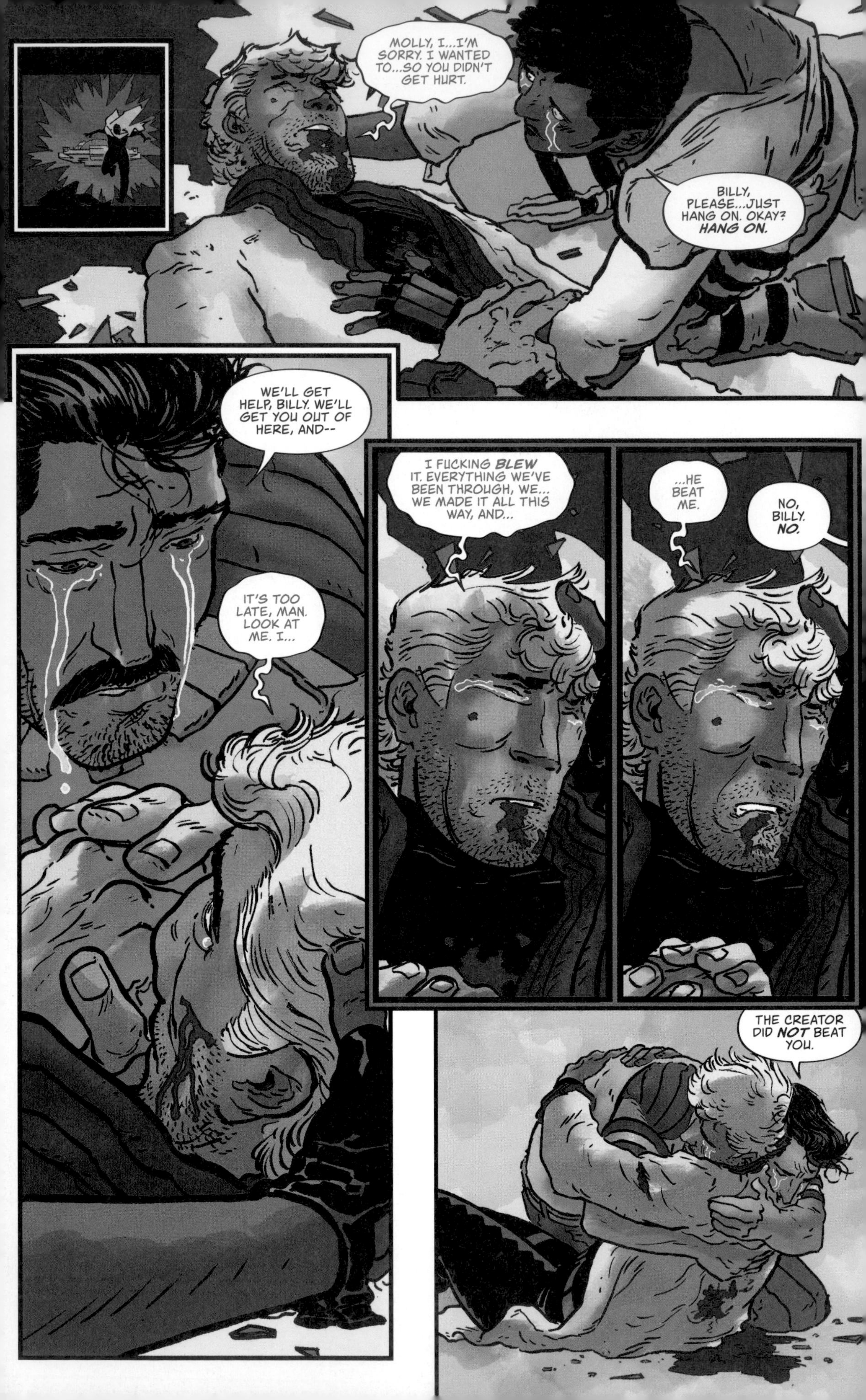
MOLLY, I...I'M SORRY. I WANTED TO...SO YOU DIDN'T GET HURT.
BILLY, PLEASE...JUST HANG ON. OKAY? HANG ON.
WE'LL GET HELP, BILLY. WE'LL GET YOU OUT OF HERE, AND--
IT'S TOO LATE, MAN. LOOK AT ME. I...
I FUCKING BLEW IT. EVERYTHING WE'VE BEEN THROUGH, WE... WE MADE IT ALL THIS WAY, AND...
...HE BEAT ME.
NO, BILLY. NO.
THE CREATOR DID NOT BEAT YOU.

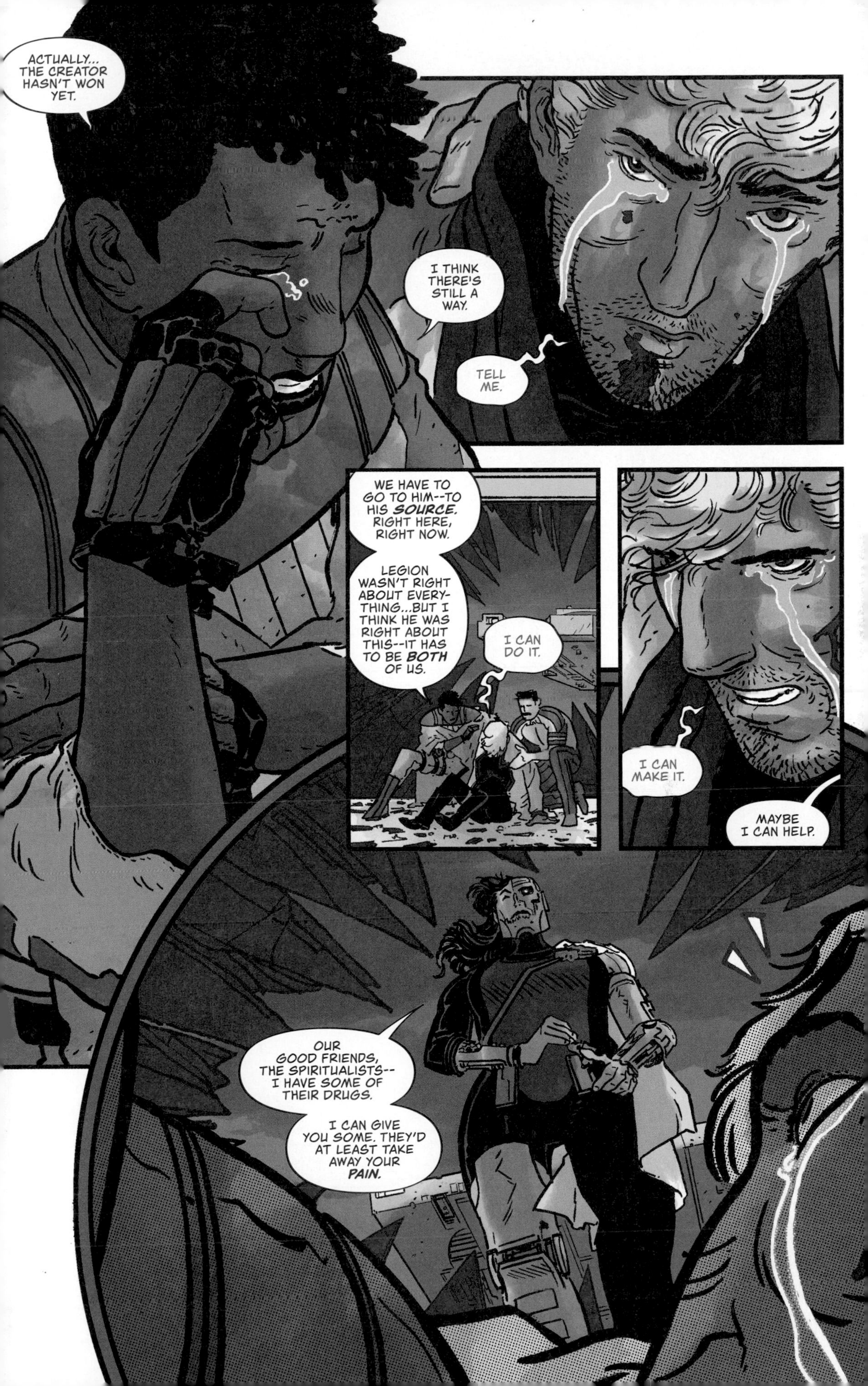
ACTUALLY... THE CREATOR HASN'T WON YET.
I THINK THERE'S STILL A WAY.
TELL ME.
WE HAVE TO GO TO HIM--TO HIS SOURCE. RIGHT HERE, RIGHT NOW.
LEGION WASN'T RIGHT ABOUT EVERY-THING...BUT I THINK HE WAS RIGHT ABOUT THIS--IT HAS TO BE BOTH OF US.
I CAN DO IT.
I CAN MAKE IT.
MAYBE I CAN HELP.
OUR GOOD FRIENDS, THE SPIRITUALISTS-- I HAVE SOME OF THEIR DRUGS.
I CAN GIVE YOU SOME. THEY'D AT LEAST TAKE AWAY YOUR PAIN.

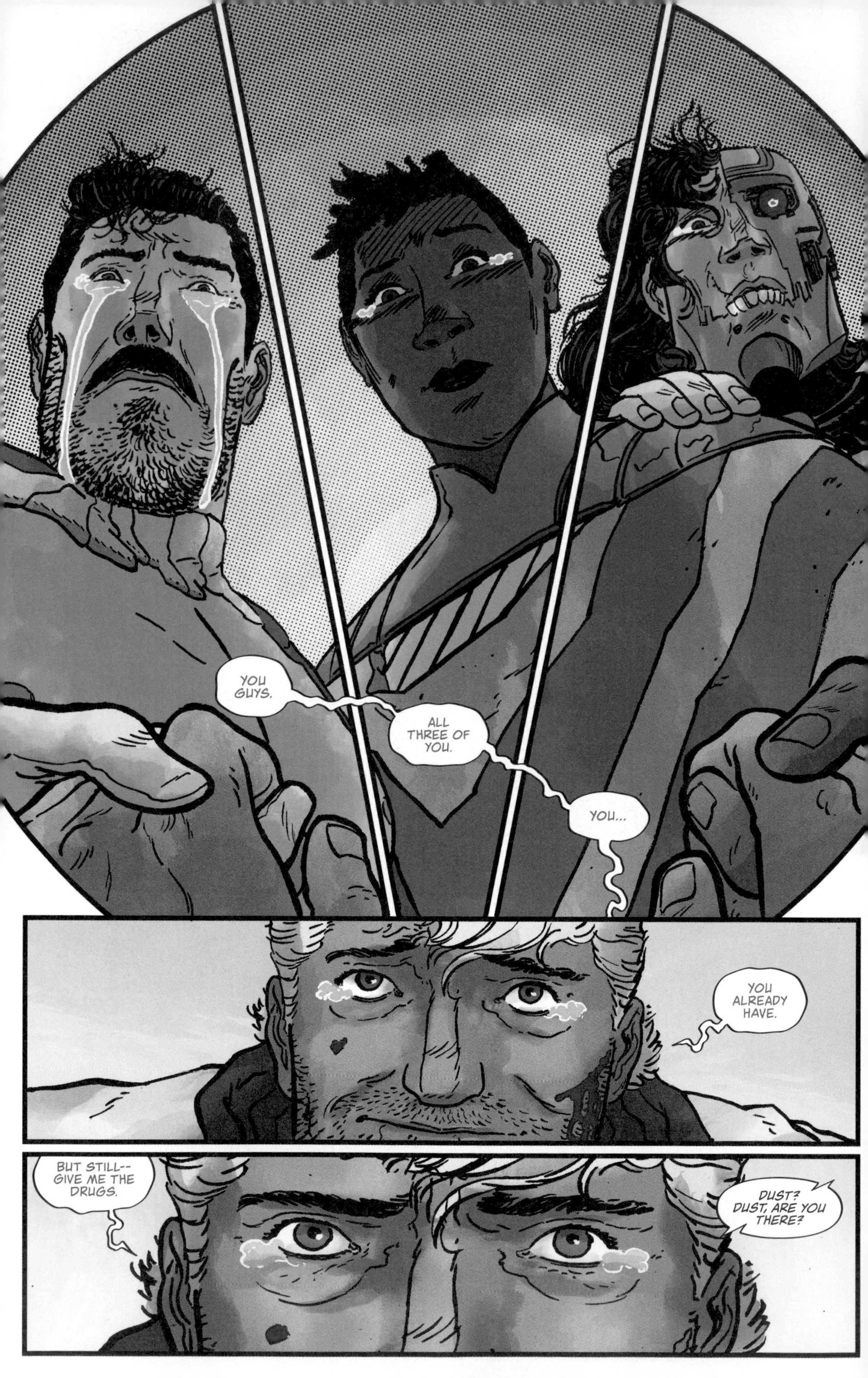
YOU GUYS.
ALL THREE OF YOU.
YOU...
YOU ALREADY HAVE.
BUT STILL-- GIVE ME THE DRUGS.
DUST? DUST, ARE YOU THERE?

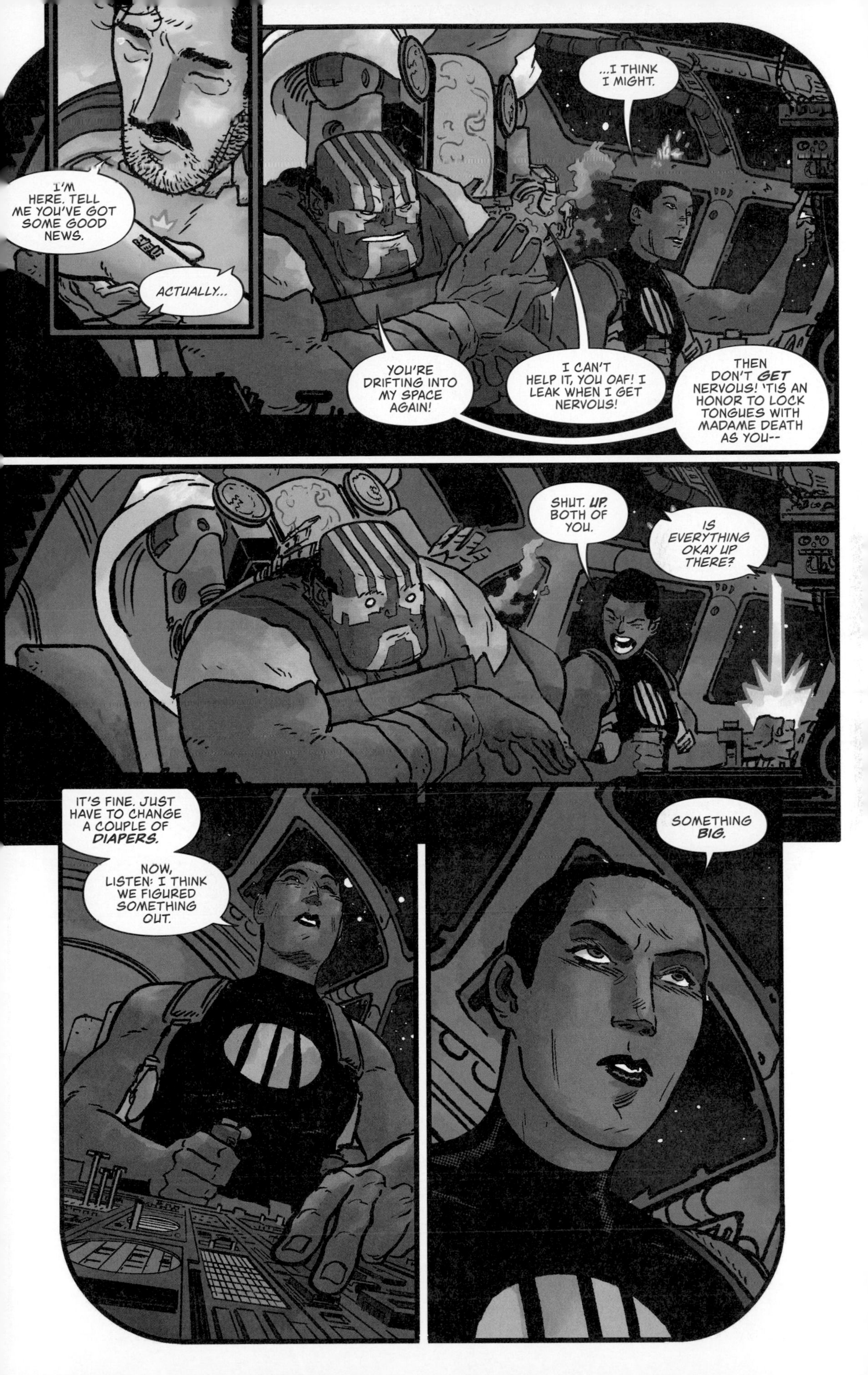
I'M HERE. TELL ME YOU'VE GOT SOME GOOD NEWS.
ACTUALLY...
...I THINK I MIGHT.
YOU'RE DRIFTING INTO MY SPACE AGAIN!
I CAN'T HELP IT, YOU OAF! I LEAK WHEN I GET NERVOUS!
THEN DON'T **GET** NERVOUS! 'TIS AN HONOR TO LOCK TONGUES WITH MADAME DEATH AS YOU--
SHUT. **UP.** BOTH OF YOU.
IS EVERYTHING OKAY UP THERE?
IT'S FINE. JUST HAVE TO CHANGE A COUPLE OF **DIAPERS.**
NOW, LISTEN: I THINK WE FIGURED SOMETHING OUT.
SOMETHING **BIG.**

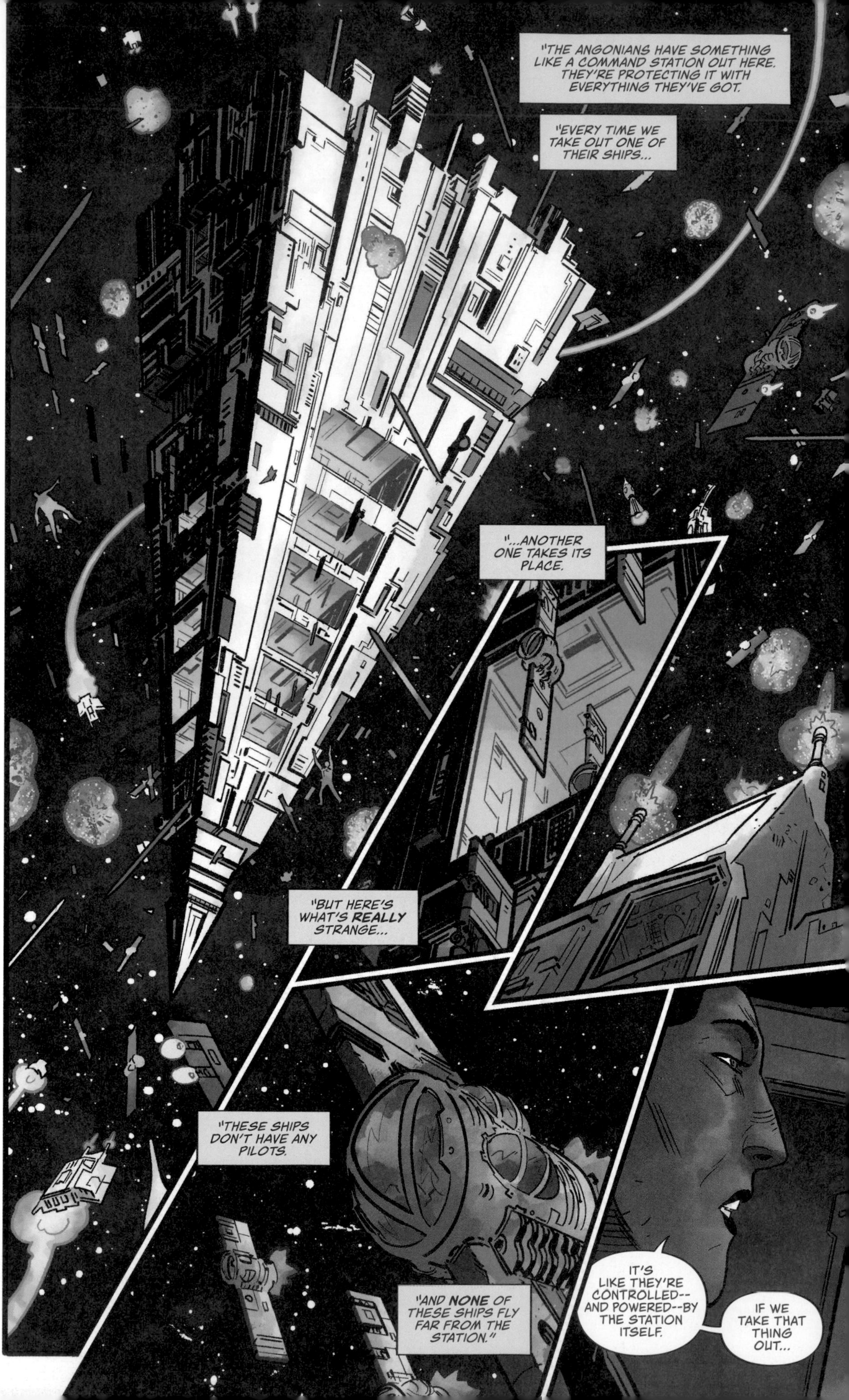
"THE ANGONIANS HAVE SOMETHING LIKE A COMMAND STATION OUT HERE. THEY'RE PROTECTING IT WITH EVERYTHING THEY'VE GOT.
"EVERY TIME WE TAKE OUT ONE OF THEIR SHIPS...
"...ANOTHER ONE TAKES ITS PLACE.
"BUT HERE'S WHAT'S **REALLY** STRANGE...
"THESE SHIPS DON'T HAVE ANY PILOTS.
"AND **NONE** OF THESE SHIPS FLY FAR FROM THE STATION."
IT'S LIKE THEY'RE CONTROLLED-- AND POWERED--BY THE STATION ITSELF.
IF WE TAKE THAT THING OUT...

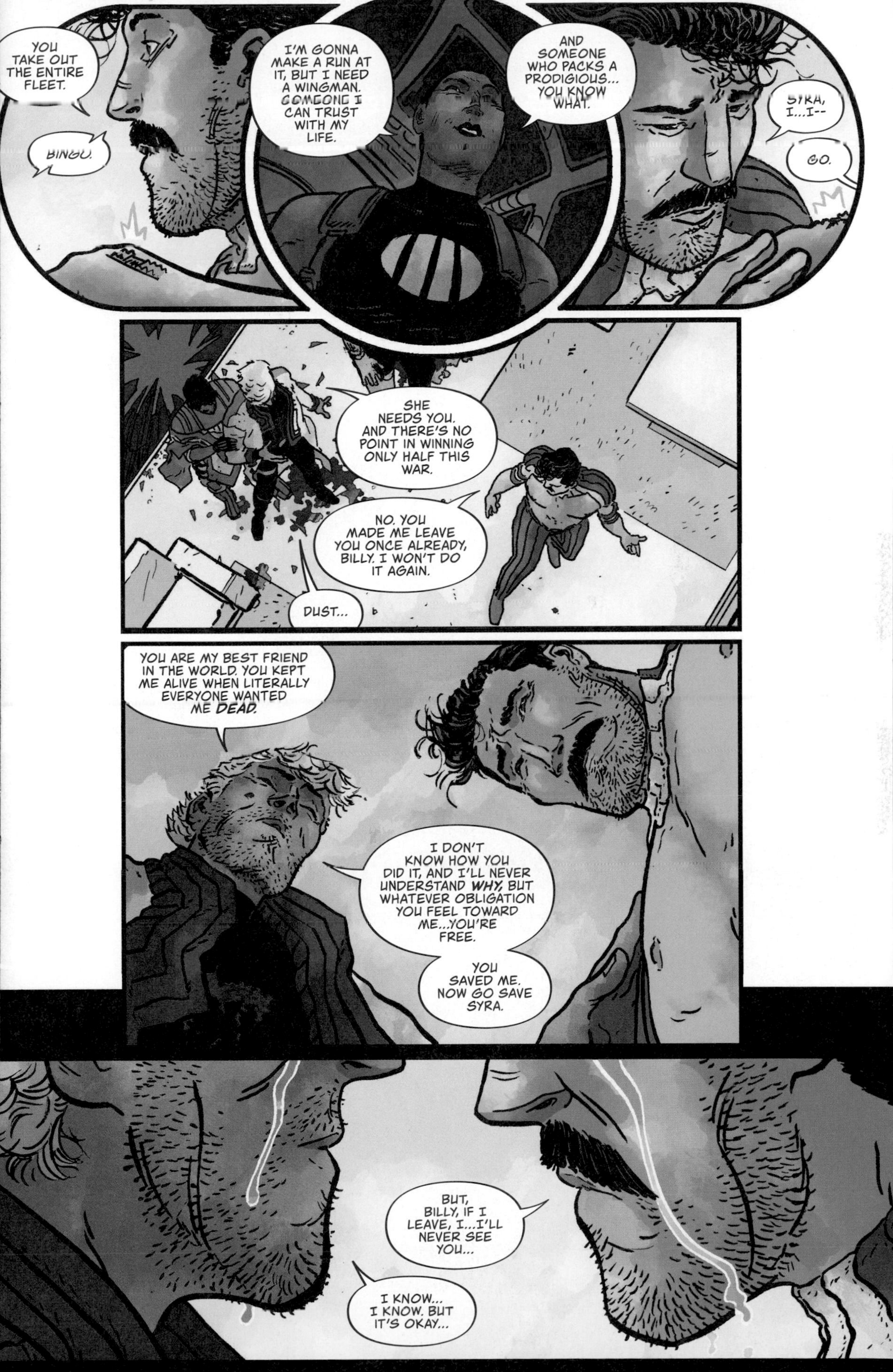
YOU TAKE OUT THE ENTIRE FLEET.
BINGO.
I'M GONNA MAKE A RUN AT IT, BUT I NEED A WINGMAN. SOMEONE I CAN TRUST WITH MY LIFE.
AND SOMEONE WHO PACKS A PRODIGIOUS... YOU KNOW WHAT.
SYRA, I...I--
GO.
SHE NEEDS YOU. AND THERE'S NO POINT IN WINNING ONLY HALF THIS WAR.
NO. YOU MADE ME LEAVE YOU ONCE ALREADY, BILLY. I WON'T DO IT AGAIN.
DUST...
YOU ARE MY BEST FRIEND IN THE WORLD. YOU KEPT ME ALIVE WHEN LITERALLY EVERYONE WANTED ME DEAD.
I DON'T KNOW HOW YOU DID IT, AND I'LL NEVER UNDERSTAND WHY, BUT WHATEVER OBLIGATION YOU FEEL TOWARD ME...YOU'RE FREE.
YOU SAVED ME. NOW GO SAVE SYRA.
BUT, BILLY, IF I LEAVE, I...I'LL NEVER SEE YOU...
I KNOW... I KNOW. BUT IT'S OKAY...

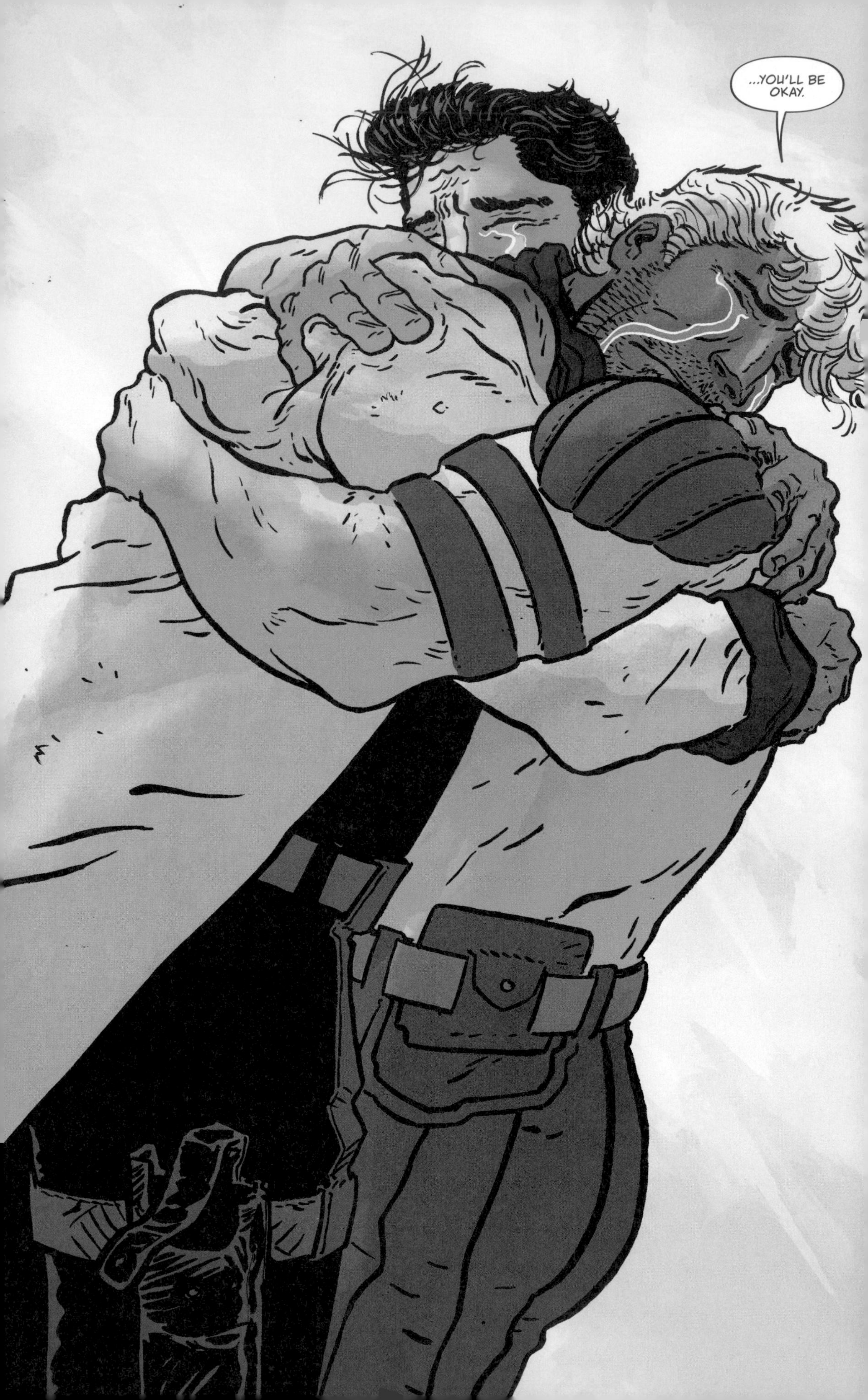
...YOU'LL BE OKAY.

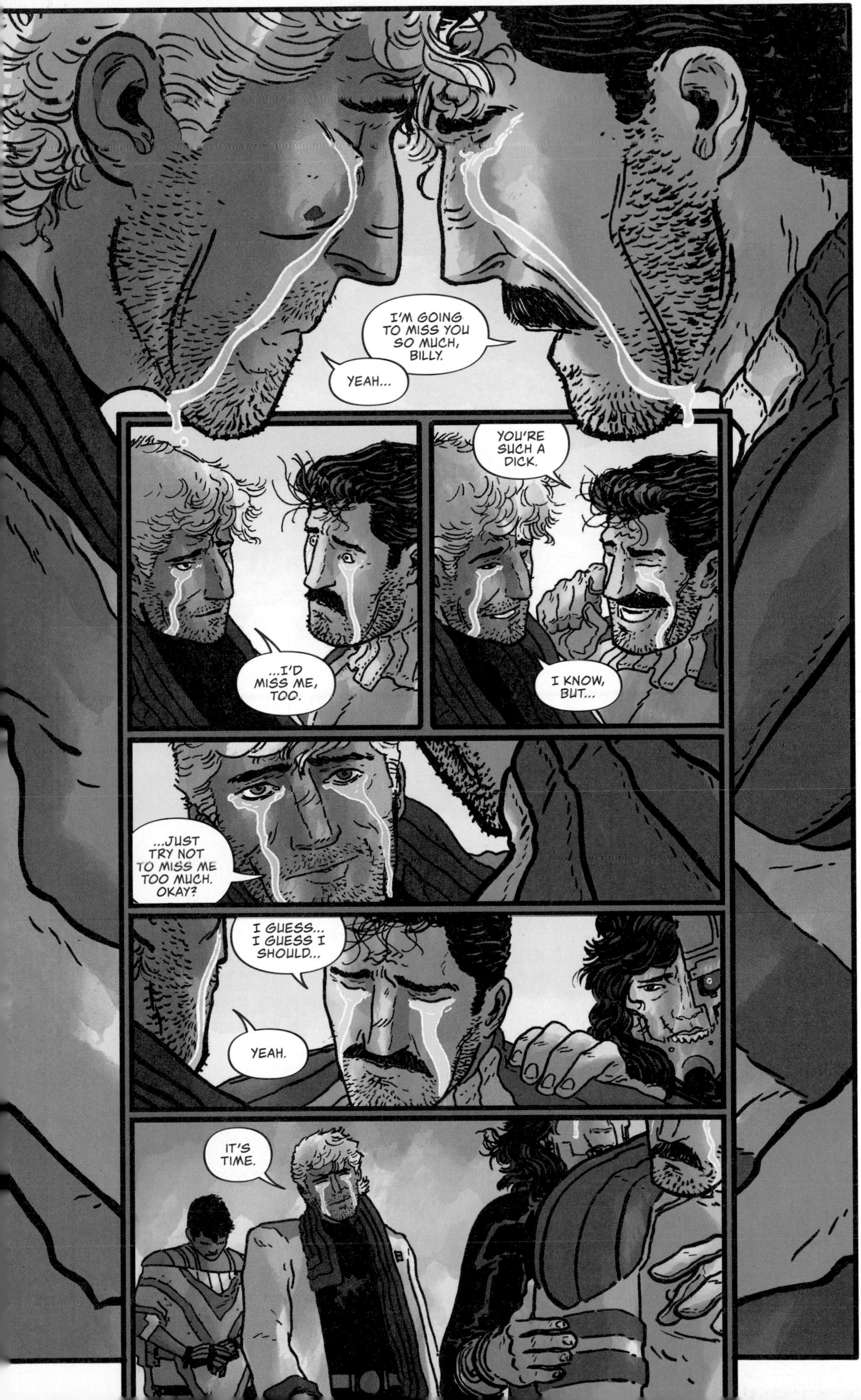
I'M GOING TO MISS YOU SO MUCH, BILLY.
YEAH...
...I'D MISS ME, TOO.
YOU'RE SUCH A DICK.
I KNOW, BUT...
...JUST TRY NOT TO MISS ME TOO MUCH. OKAY?
I GUESS... I GUESS I SHOULD...
YEAH.
IT'S TIME.

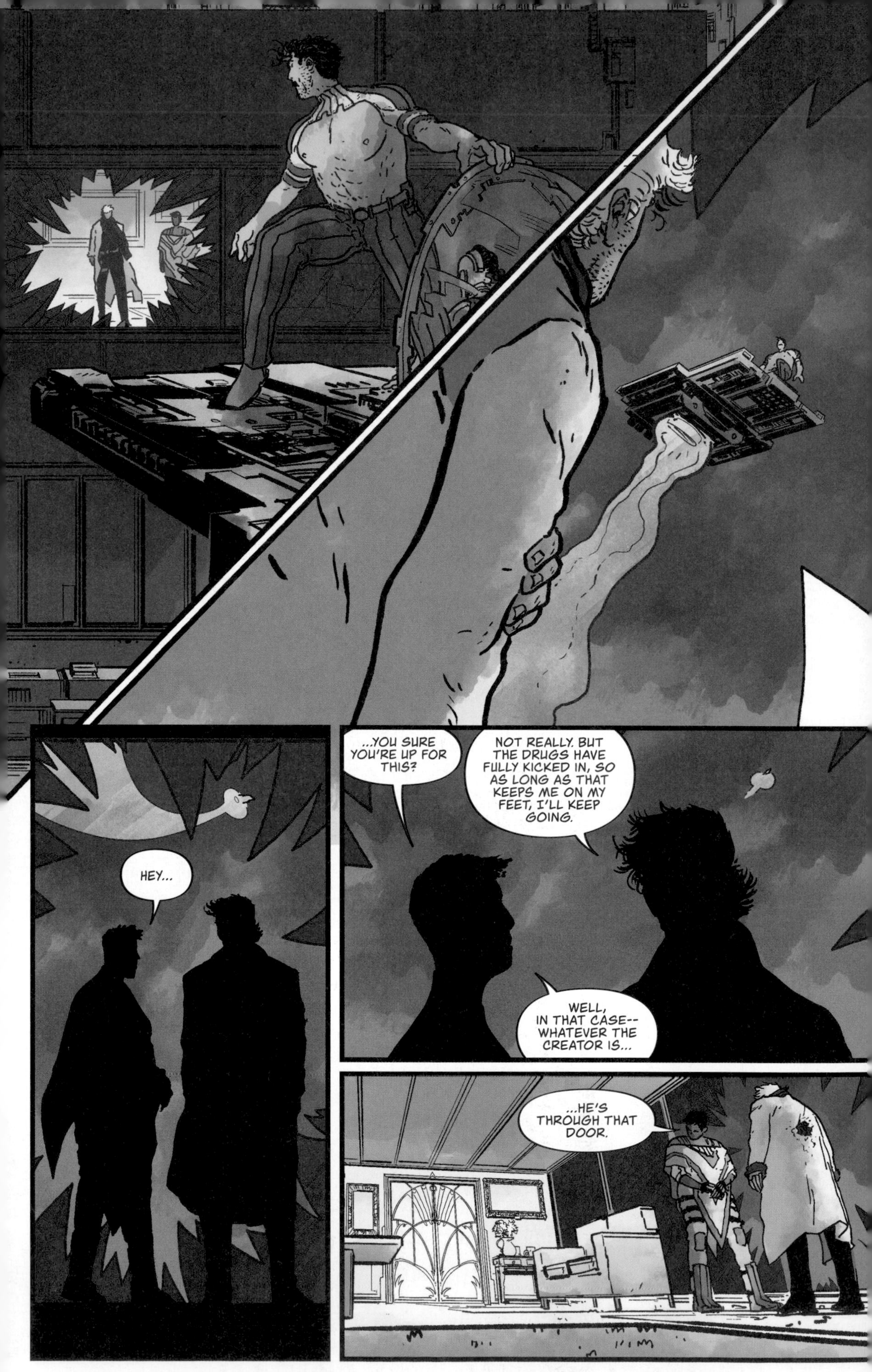
HEY...
...YOU SURE YOU'RE UP FOR THIS?
NOT REALLY. BUT THE DRUGS HAVE FULLY KICKED IN, SO AS LONG AS THAT KEEPS ME ON MY FEET, I'LL KEEP GOING.
WELL, IN THAT CASE-- WHATEVER THE CREATOR IS...
...HE'S THROUGH THAT DOOR.

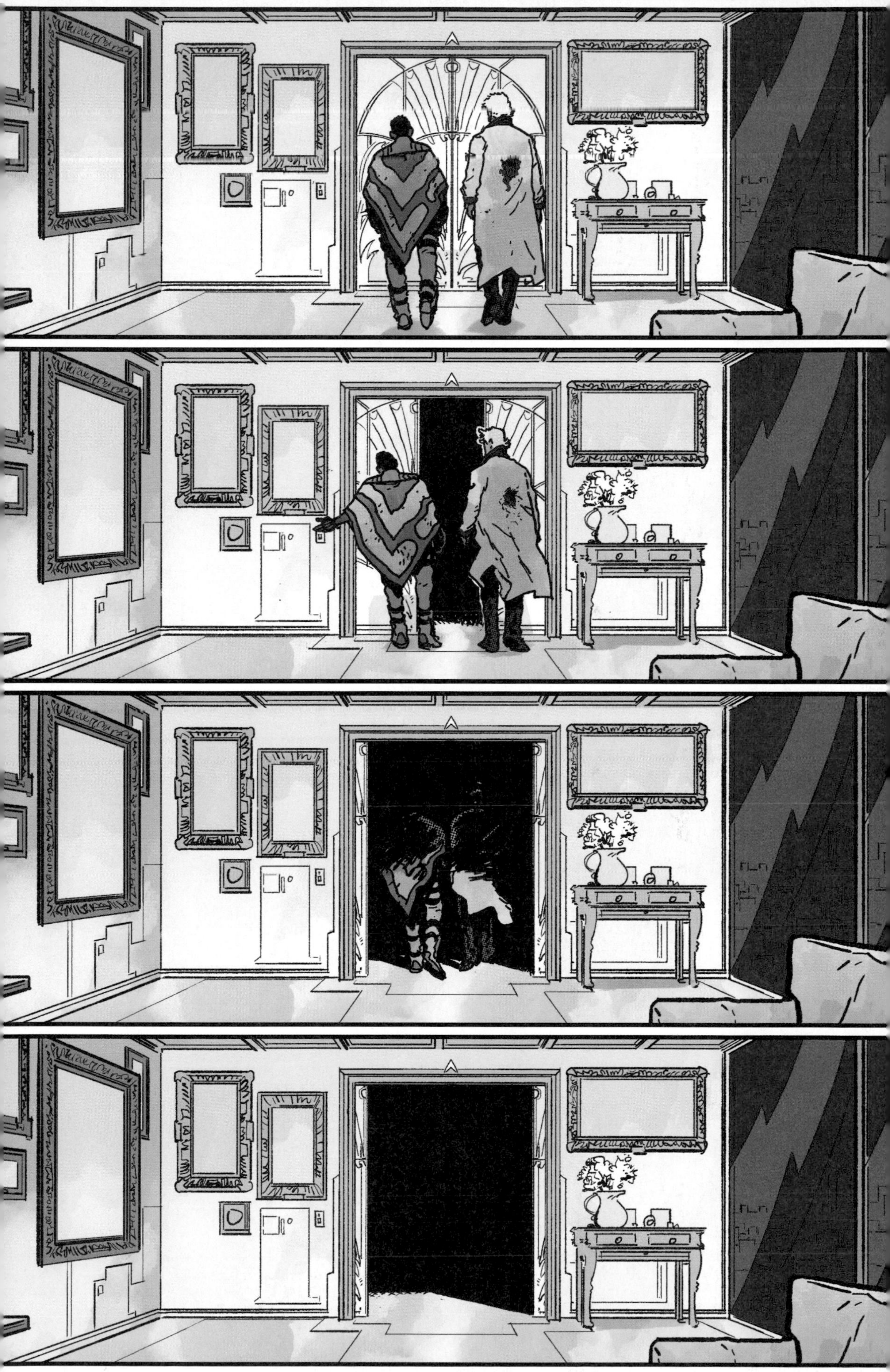

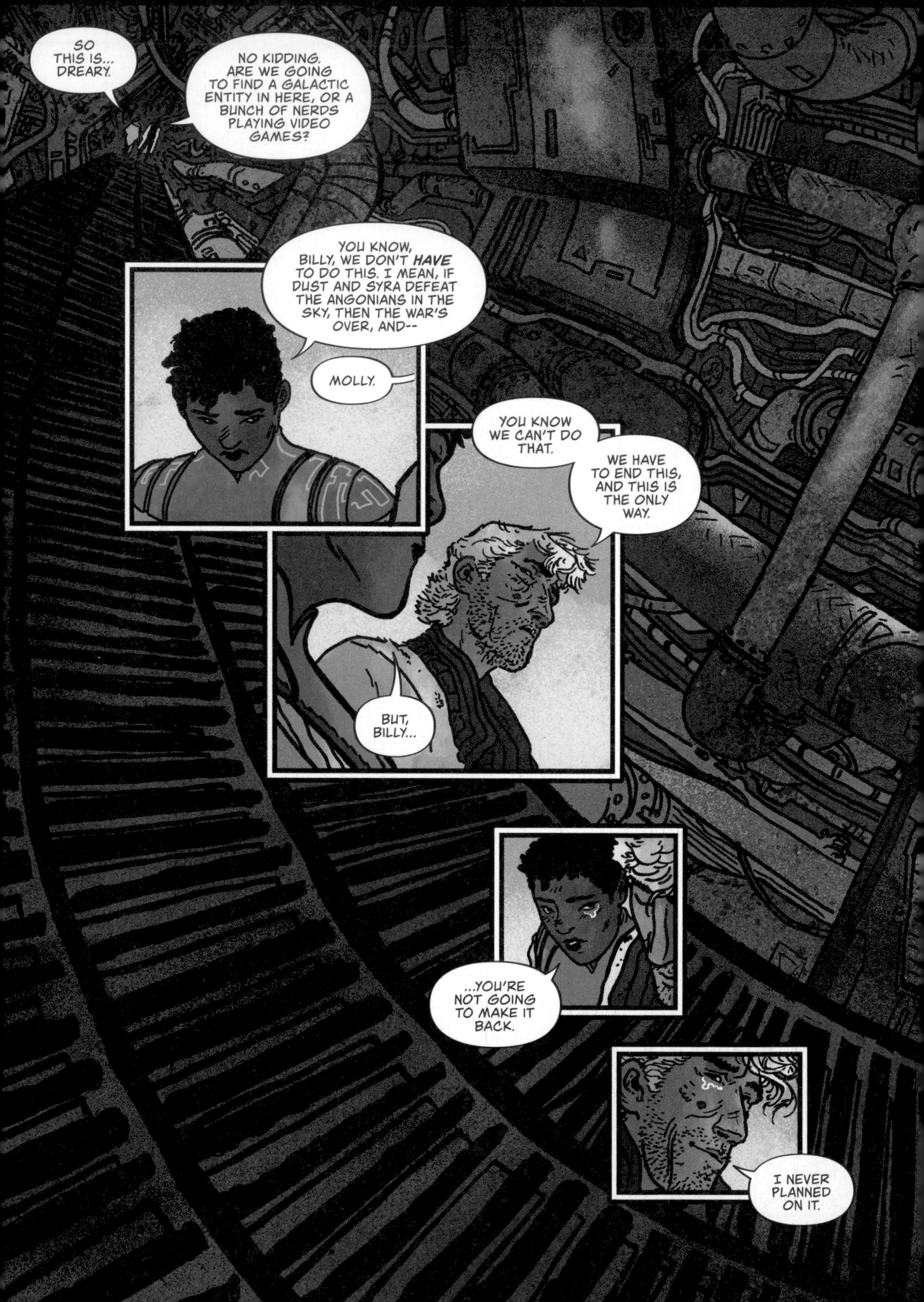
SO THIS IS... DREARY.
NO KIDDING. ARE WE GOING TO FIND A GALACTIC ENTITY IN HERE, OR A BUNCH OF NERDS PLAYING VIDEO GAMES?
YOU KNOW, BILLY, WE DON'T HAVE TO DO THIS. I MEAN, IF DUST AND SYRA DEFEAT THE ANGONIANS IN THE SKY, THEN THE WAR'S OVER, AND--
MOLLY.
YOU KNOW WE CAN'T DO THAT.
WE HAVE TO END THIS, AND THIS IS THE ONLY WAY.
BUT, BILLY...
...YOU'RE NOT GOING TO MAKE IT BACK.
I NEVER PLANNED ON IT.

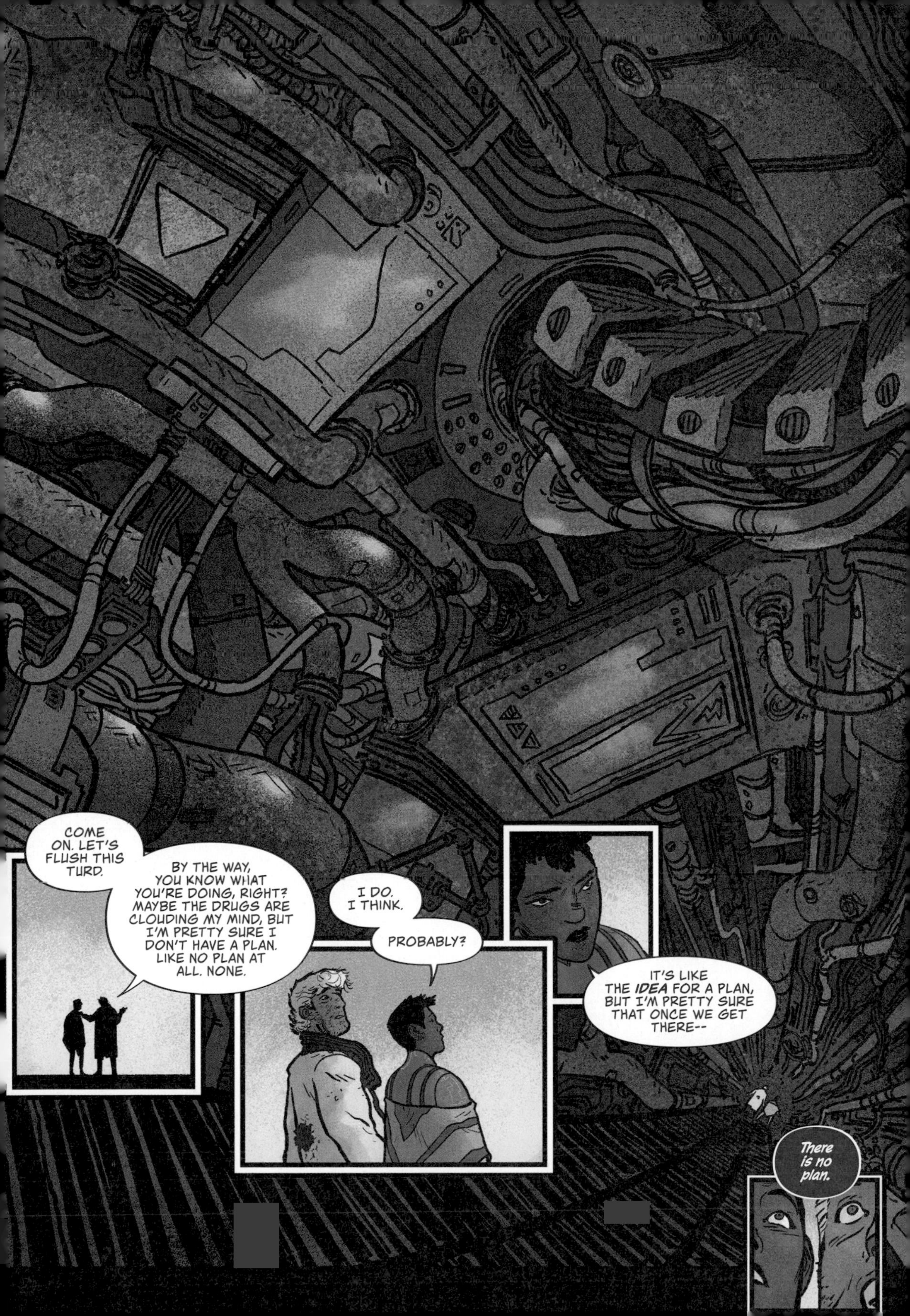
COME ON. LET'S FLUSH THIS TURD.
BY THE WAY, YOU KNOW WHAT YOU'RE DOING, RIGHT? MAYBE THE DRUGS ARE CLOUDING MY MIND, BUT I'M PRETTY SURE I DON'T HAVE A PLAN. LIKE NO PLAN AT ALL. NONE.
I DO. I THINK.
PROBABLY?
IT'S LIKE THE *IDEA* FOR A PLAN, BUT I'M PRETTY SURE THAT ONCE WE GET THERE--
There is no plan.

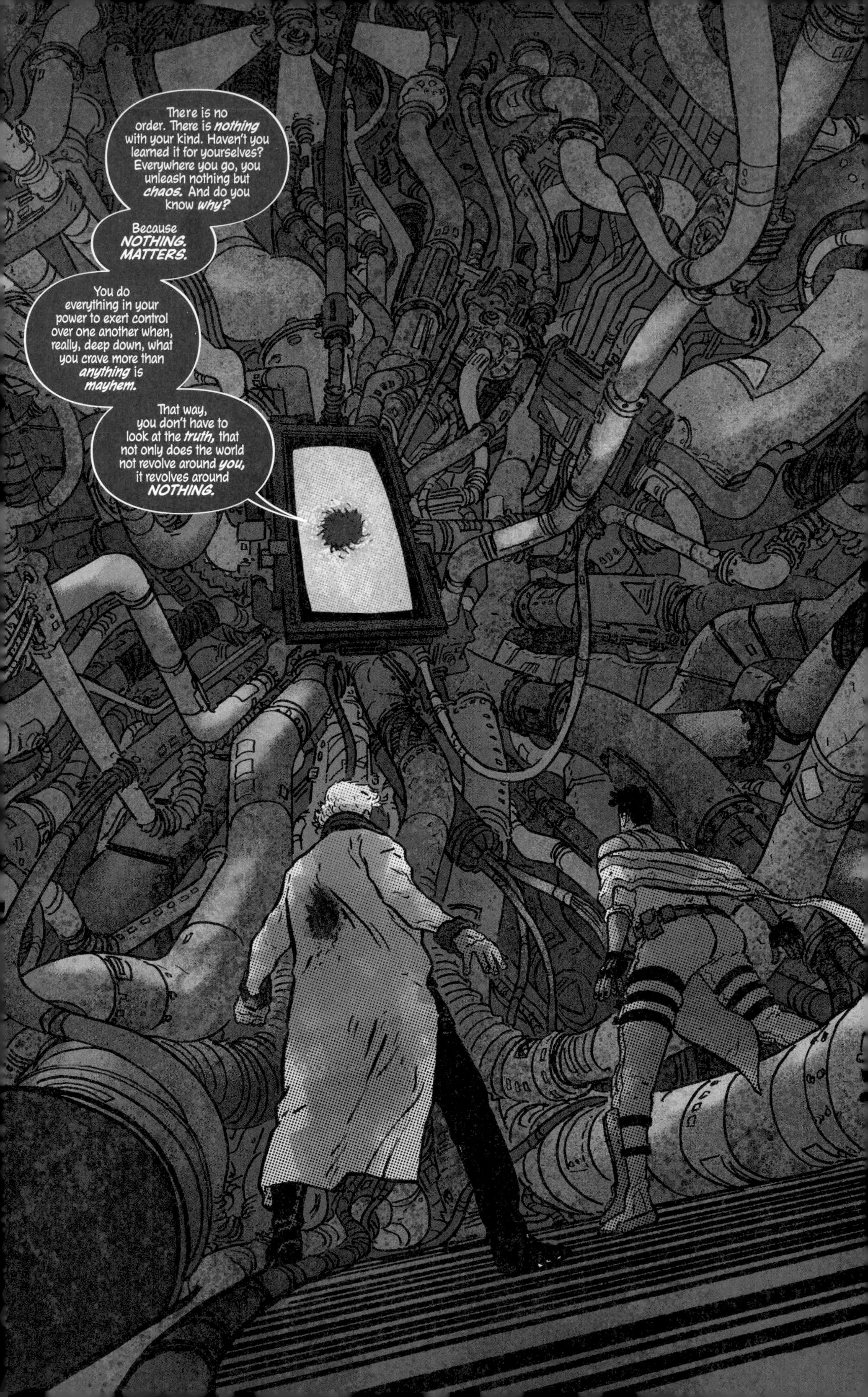
There is no order. There is *nothing* with your kind. Haven't you learned it for yourselves? Everywhere you go, you unleash nothing but *chaos.* And do you know *why?*
Because **NOTHING. MATTERS.**
You do everything in your power to exert control over one another when, really, deep down, what you crave more than *anything* is *mayhem.*
That way, you don't have to look at the *truth,* that not only does the world not revolve around *you,* it revolves around **NOTHING.**

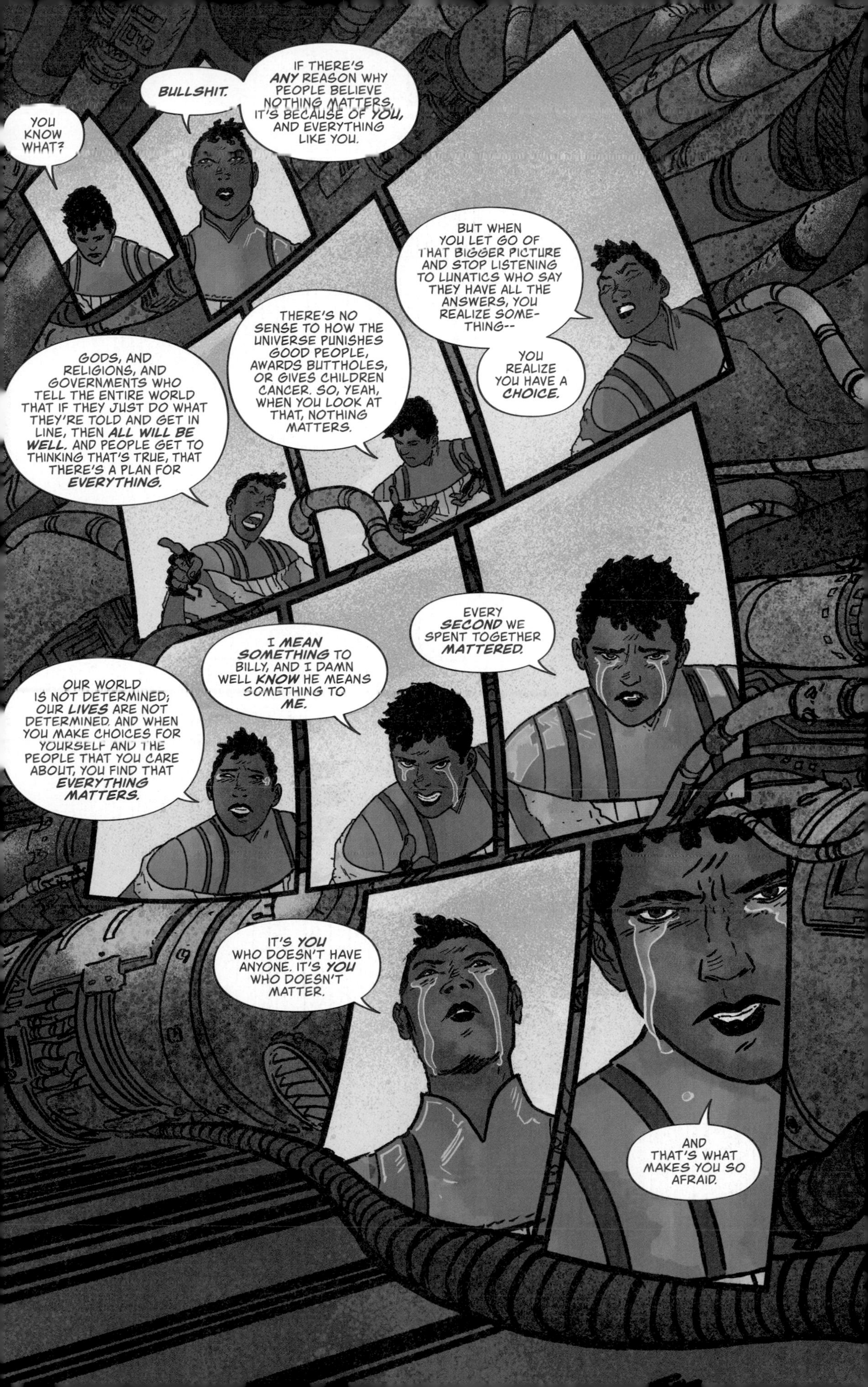
YOU KNOW WHAT?
BULLSHIT.
IF THERE'S ANY REASON WHY PEOPLE BELIEVE NOTHING MATTERS, IT'S BECAUSE OF YOU, AND EVERYTHING LIKE YOU.
BUT WHEN YOU LET GO OF THAT BIGGER PICTURE AND STOP LISTENING TO LUNATICS WHO SAY THEY HAVE ALL THE ANSWERS, YOU REALIZE SOME-THING--
YOU REALIZE YOU HAVE A CHOICE.
GODS, AND RELIGIONS, AND GOVERNMENTS WHO TELL THE ENTIRE WORLD THAT IF THEY JUST DO WHAT THEY'RE TOLD AND GET IN LINE, THEN ALL WILL BE WELL. AND PEOPLE GET TO THINKING THAT'S TRUE, THAT THERE'S A PLAN FOR EVERYTHING.
THERE'S NO SENSE TO HOW THE UNIVERSE PUNISHES GOOD PEOPLE, AWARDS BUTTHOLES, OR GIVES CHILDREN CANCER. SO, YEAH, WHEN YOU LOOK AT THAT, NOTHING MATTERS.
OUR WORLD IS NOT DETERMINED; OUR LIVES ARE NOT DETERMINED. AND WHEN YOU MAKE CHOICES FOR YOURSELF AND THE PEOPLE THAT YOU CARE ABOUT, YOU FIND THAT EVERYTHING MATTERS.
I MEAN SOMETHING TO BILLY, AND I DAMN WELL KNOW HE MEANS SOMETHING TO ME.
EVERY SECOND WE SPENT TOGETHER MATTERED.
IT'S YOU WHO DOESN'T HAVE ANYONE. IT'S YOU WHO DOESN'T MATTER.
AND THAT'S WHAT MAKES YOU SO AFRAID.

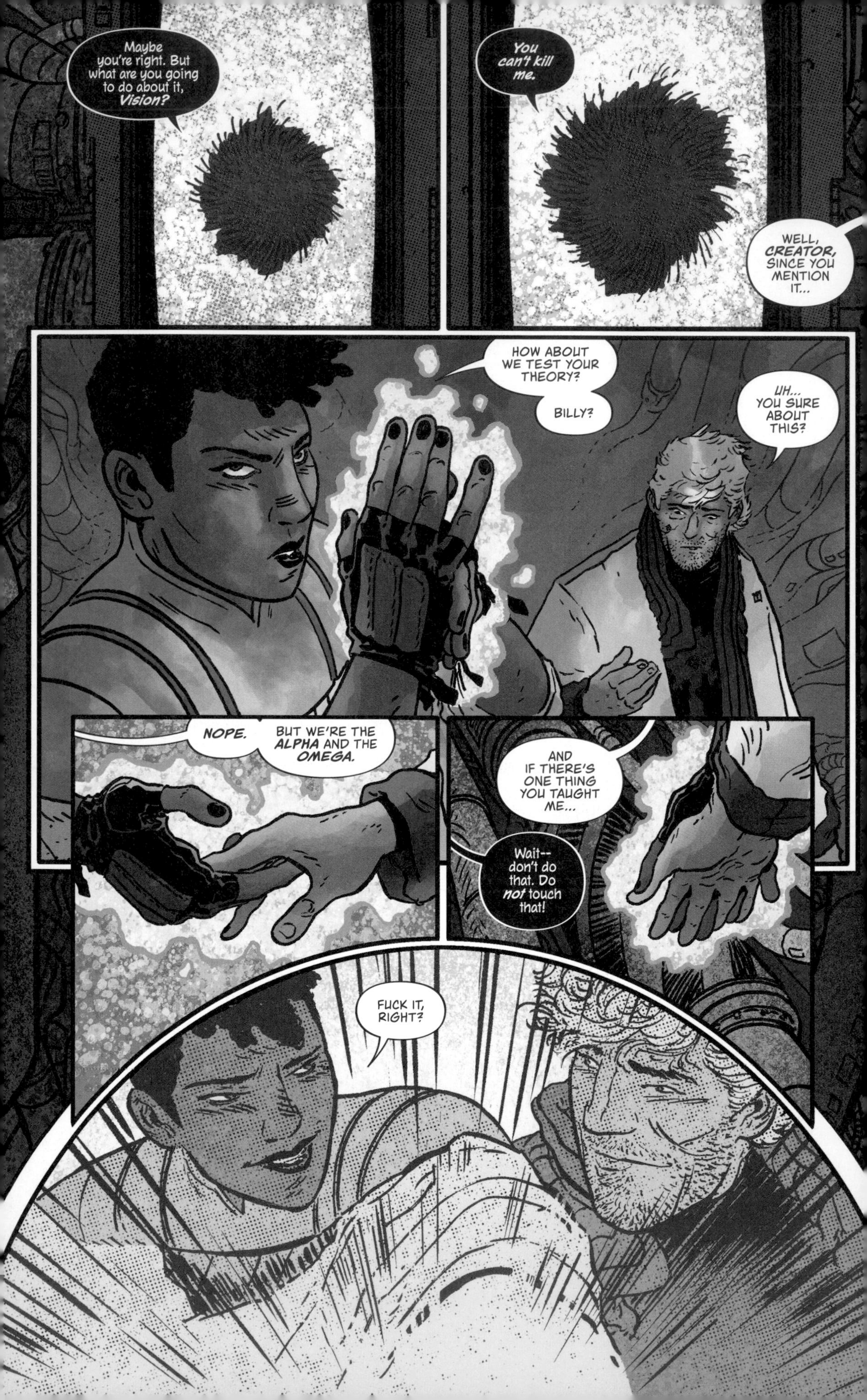
Maybe you're right. But what are you going to do about it, Vision?
You can't kill me.
WELL, CREATOR, SINCE YOU MENTION IT...
HOW ABOUT WE TEST YOUR THEORY?
BILLY?
UH... YOU SURE ABOUT THIS?
NOPE.
BUT WE'RE THE ALPHA AND THE OMEGA.
AND IF THERE'S ONE THING YOU TAUGHT ME...
Wait-- don't do that. Do not touch that!
FUCK IT, RIGHT?

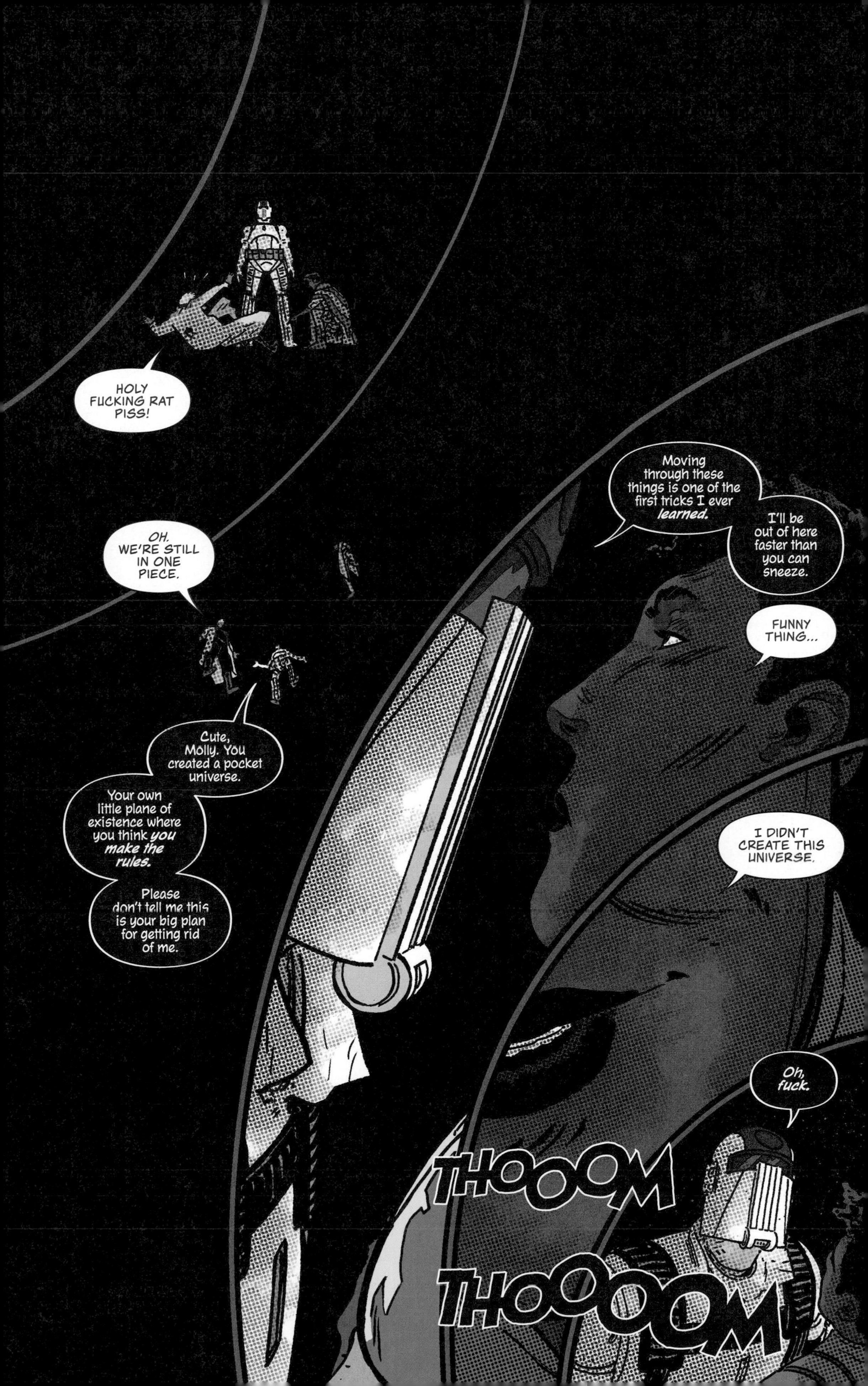
HOLY FUCKING RAT PISS!
OH. WE'RE STILL IN ONE PIECE.
Cute, Molly. You created a pocket universe.
Your own little plane of existence where you think *you make the rules.*
Please don't tell me this is your big plan for getting rid of me.
Moving through these things is one of the first tricks I ever *learned.*
I'll be out of here faster than you can sneeze.
FUNNY THING...
I DIDN'T CREATE THIS UNIVERSE.
Oh, fuck.
THOOOOM
THOOOOOM

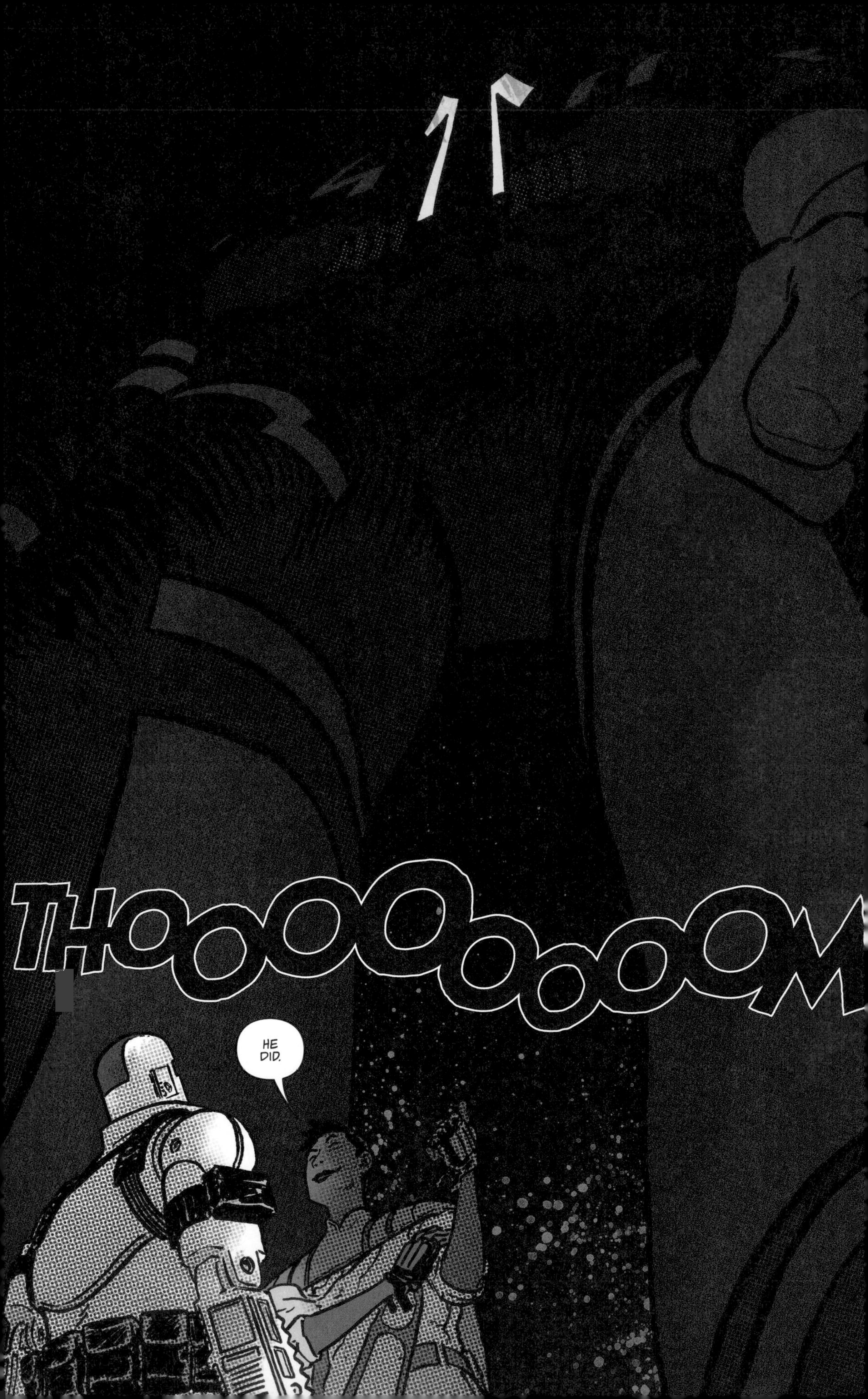
THOOOOOOOOOM
HE DID.

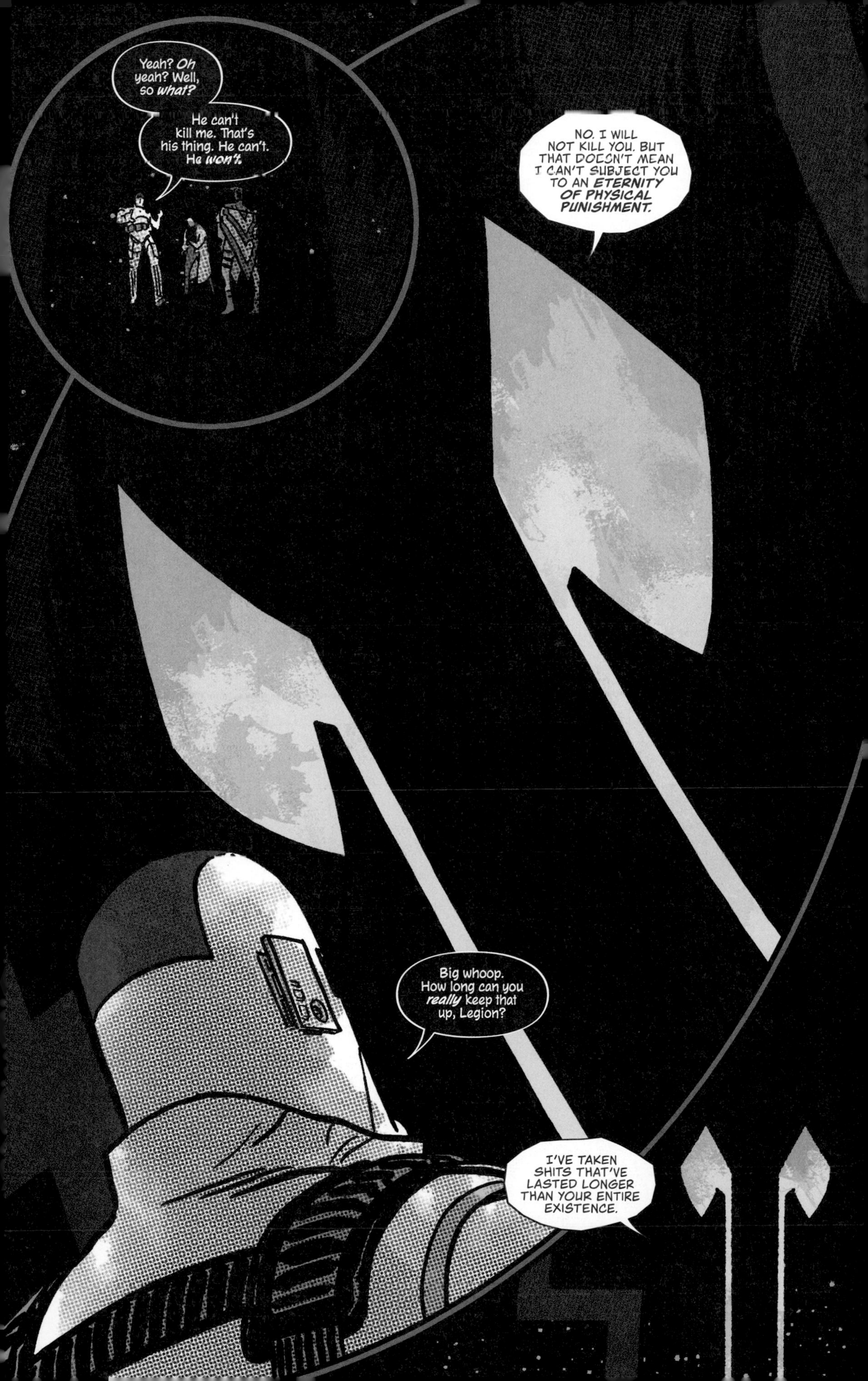
Yeah? *Oh* yeah? Well, so *what?*
He can't kill me. That's his thing. He can't. He *won't.*
NO. I WILL NOT KILL YOU. BUT THAT DOESN'T MEAN I CAN'T SUBJECT YOU TO AN ***ETERNITY OF PHYSICAL PUNISHMENT.***
Big whoop. How long can you ***really*** keep that up, Legion?
I'VE TAKEN SHITS THAT'VE LASTED LONGER THAN YOUR ENTIRE EXISTENCE.

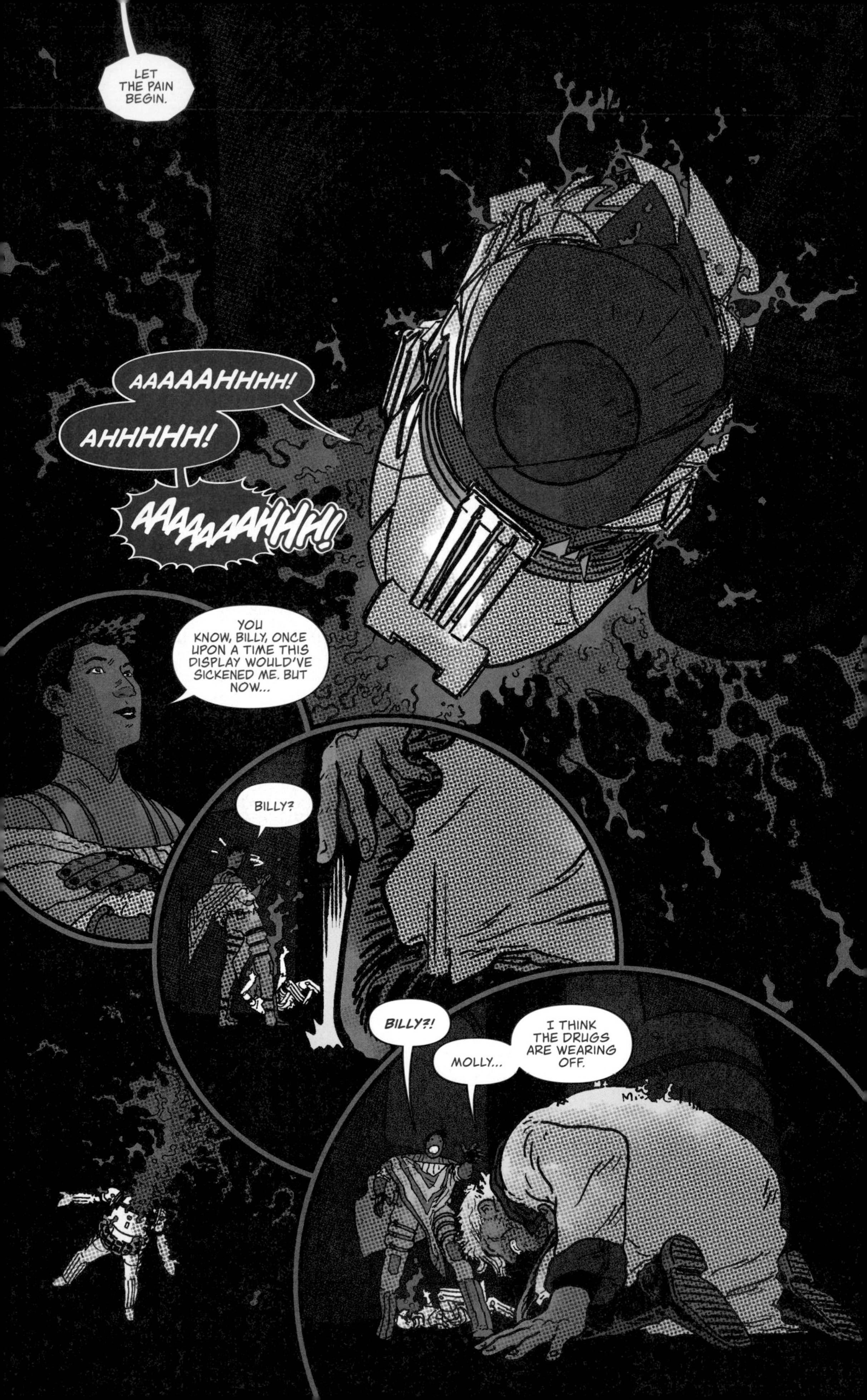
LET THE PAIN BEGIN.
AAAAAHHHH!
AHHHHH!
AAAAAAAHHHH!
YOU KNOW, BILLY, ONCE UPON A TIME THIS DISPLAY WOULD'VE SICKENED ME. BUT NOW...
BILLY?
BILLY?!
MOLLY...
I THINK THE DRUGS ARE WEARING OFF.

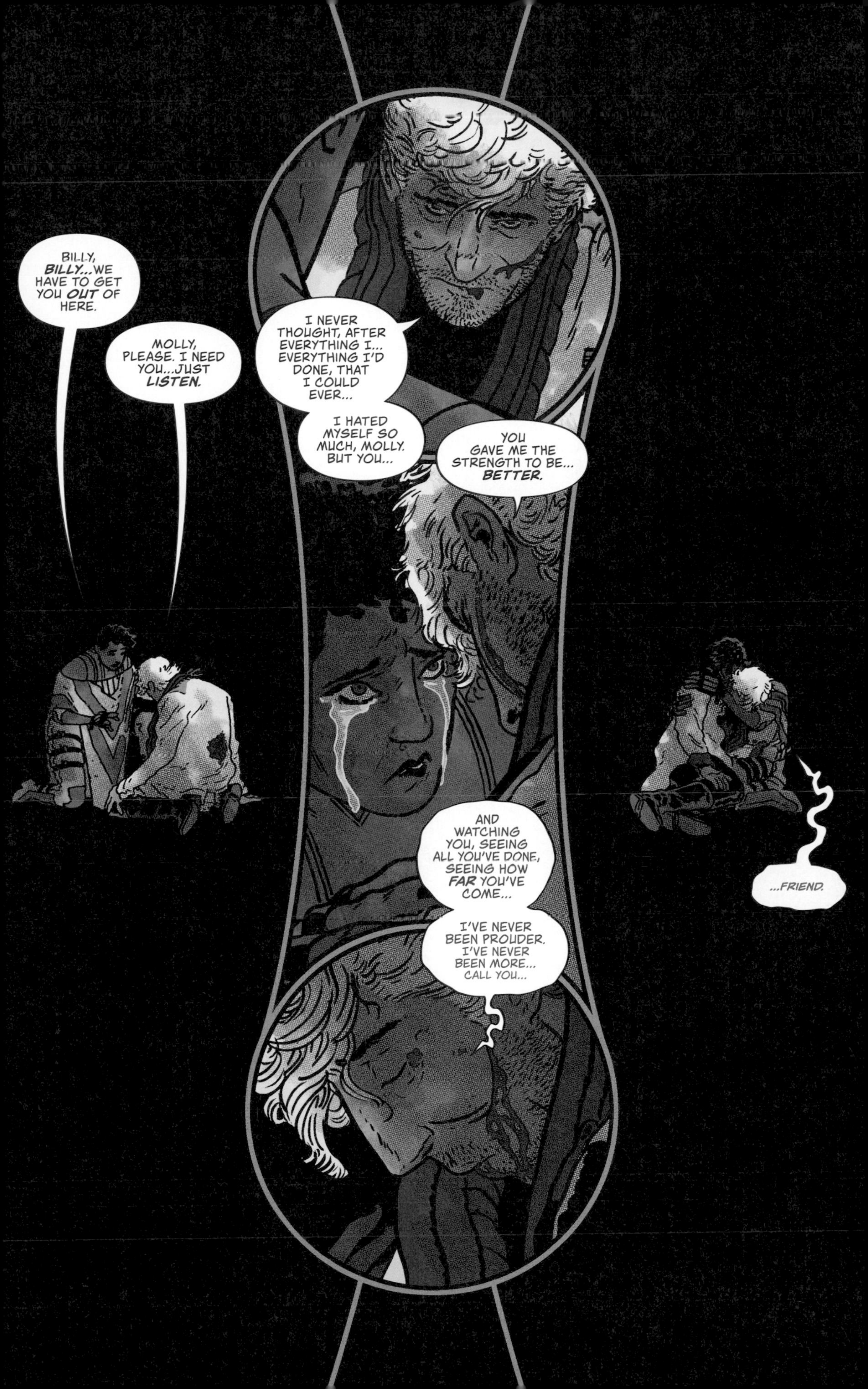
BILLY, *BILLY...* WE HAVE TO GET YOU *OUT* OF HERE.
MOLLY, PLEASE. I NEED YOU...JUST *LISTEN.*
I NEVER THOUGHT, AFTER EVERYTHING I... EVERYTHING I'D DONE, THAT I COULD EVER...
I HATED MYSELF SO MUCH, MOLLY. BUT YOU...
YOU GAVE ME THE STRENGTH TO BE... *BETTER.*
AND WATCHING YOU, SEEING ALL YOU'VE DONE, SEEING HOW *FAR* YOU'VE COME...
I'VE NEVER BEEN PROUDER. I'VE NEVER BEEN MORE... CALL YOU...
...FRIEND.

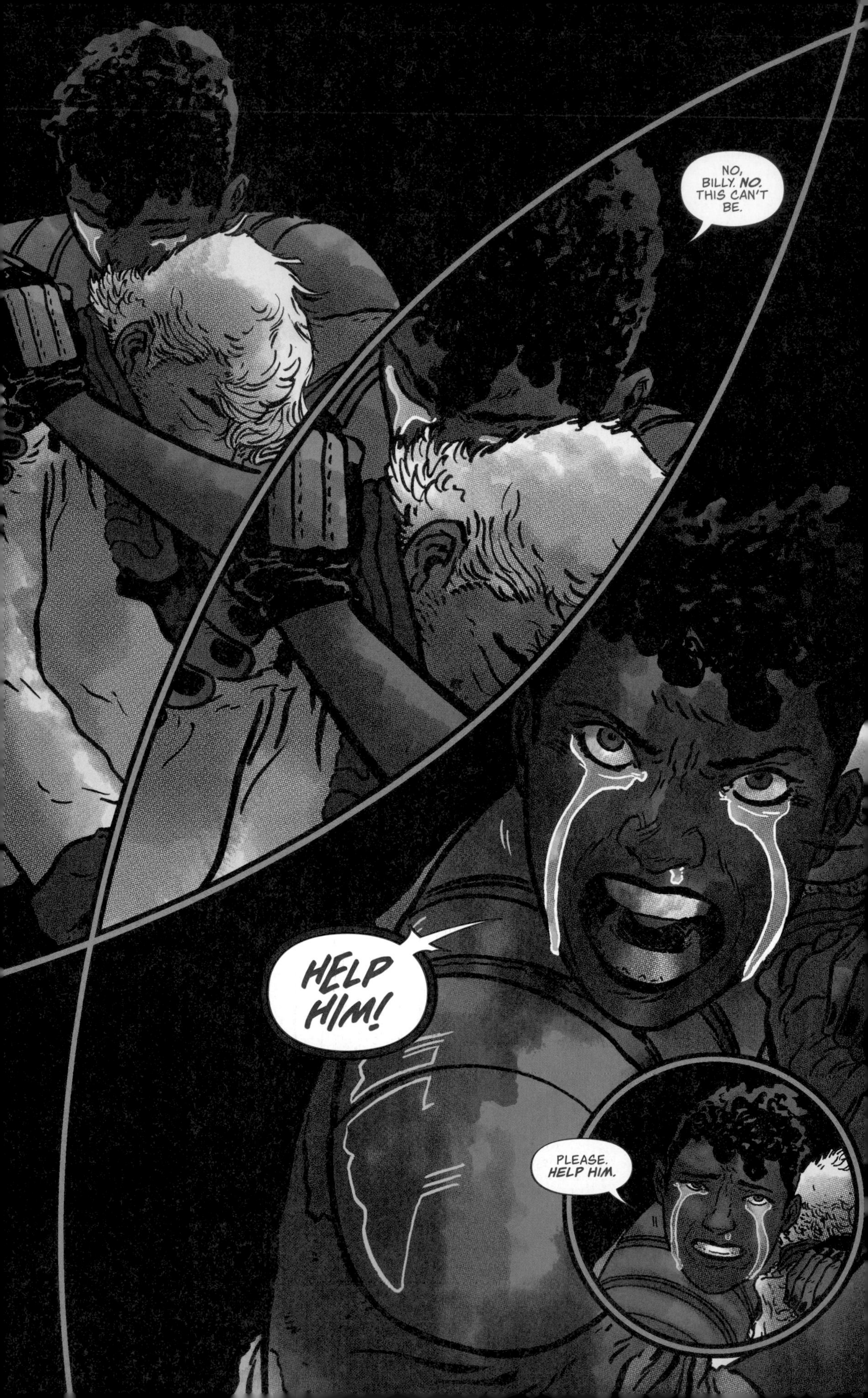
NO, BILLY. NO. THIS CAN'T BE.
HELP HIM!
PLEASE. HELP HIM.

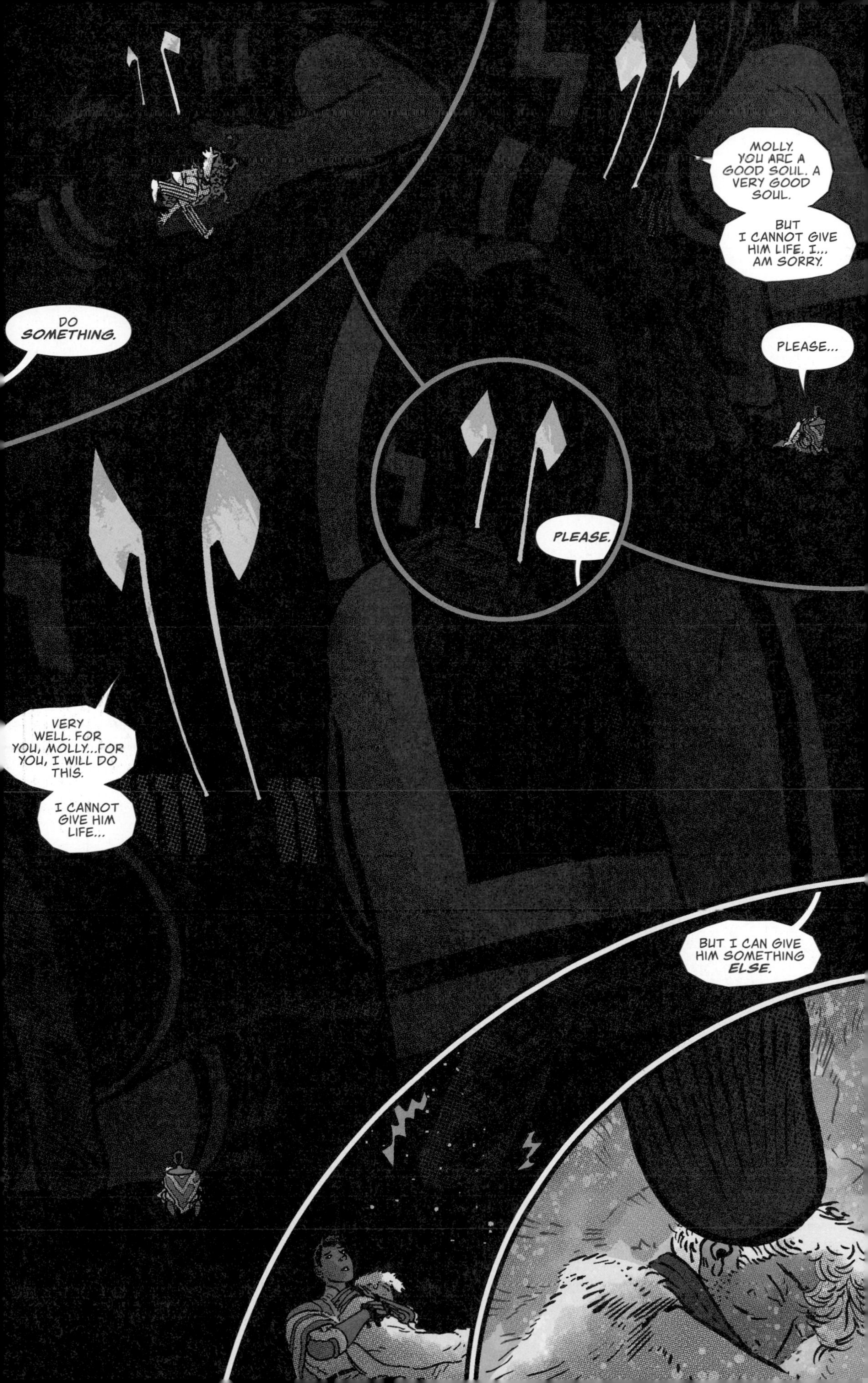
MOLLY. YOU ARE A GOOD SOUL. A VERY GOOD SOUL.
BUT I CANNOT GIVE HIM LIFE. I... AM SORRY.
DO SOMETHING.
PLEASE...
PLEASE.
VERY WELL. FOR YOU, MOLLY...FOR YOU, I WILL DO THIS.
I CANNOT GIVE HIM LIFE...
BUT I CAN GIVE HIM SOMETHING ELSE.

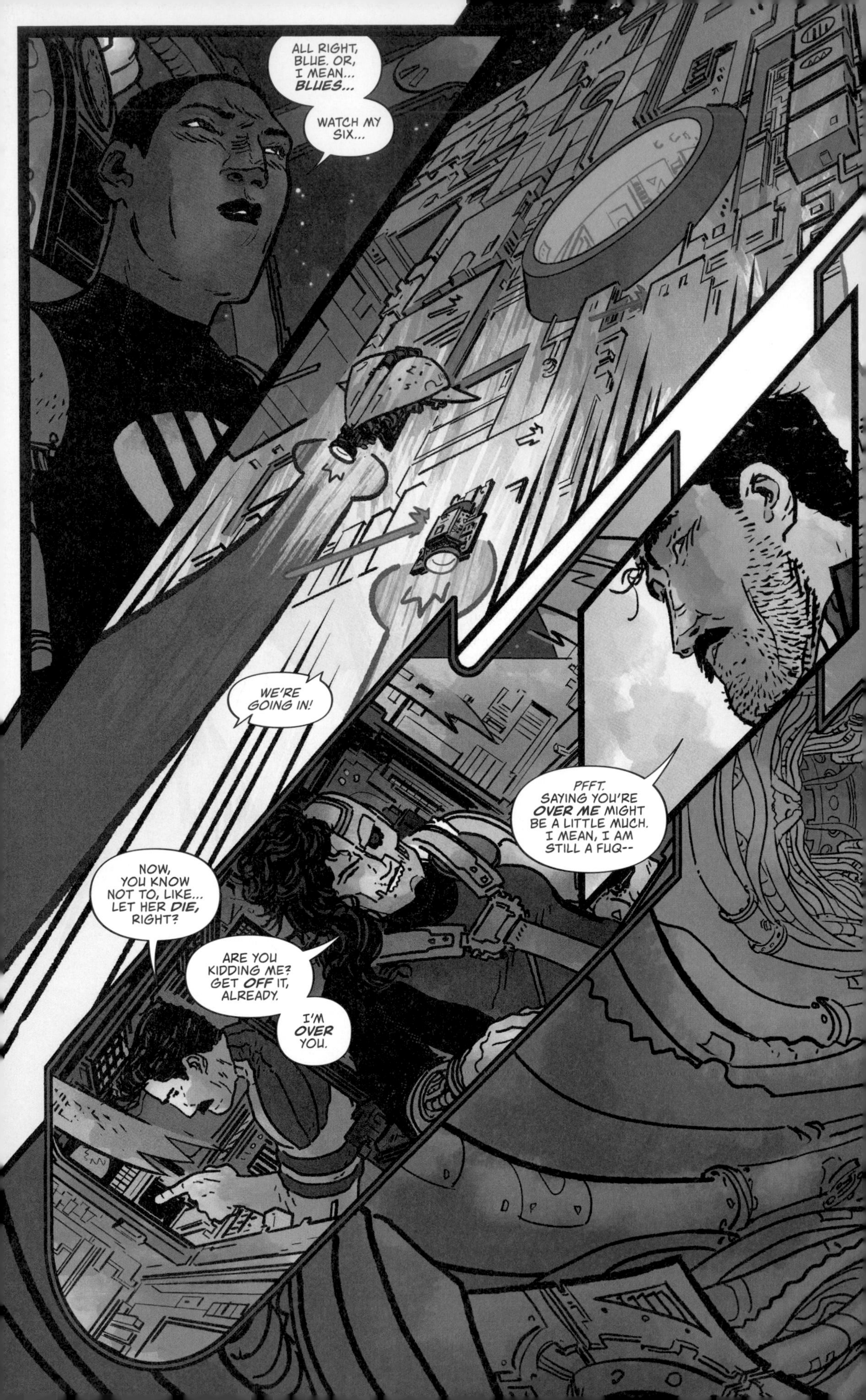
ALL RIGHT, BLUE. OR, I MEAN... BLUES...
WATCH MY SIX...
WE'RE GOING IN!
PFFT. SAYING YOU'RE OVER ME MIGHT BE A LITTLE MUCH. I MEAN, I AM STILL A FUQ--
NOW, YOU KNOW NOT TO, LIKE... LET HER DIE, RIGHT?
ARE YOU KIDDING ME? GET OFF IT, ALREADY.
I'M OVER YOU.

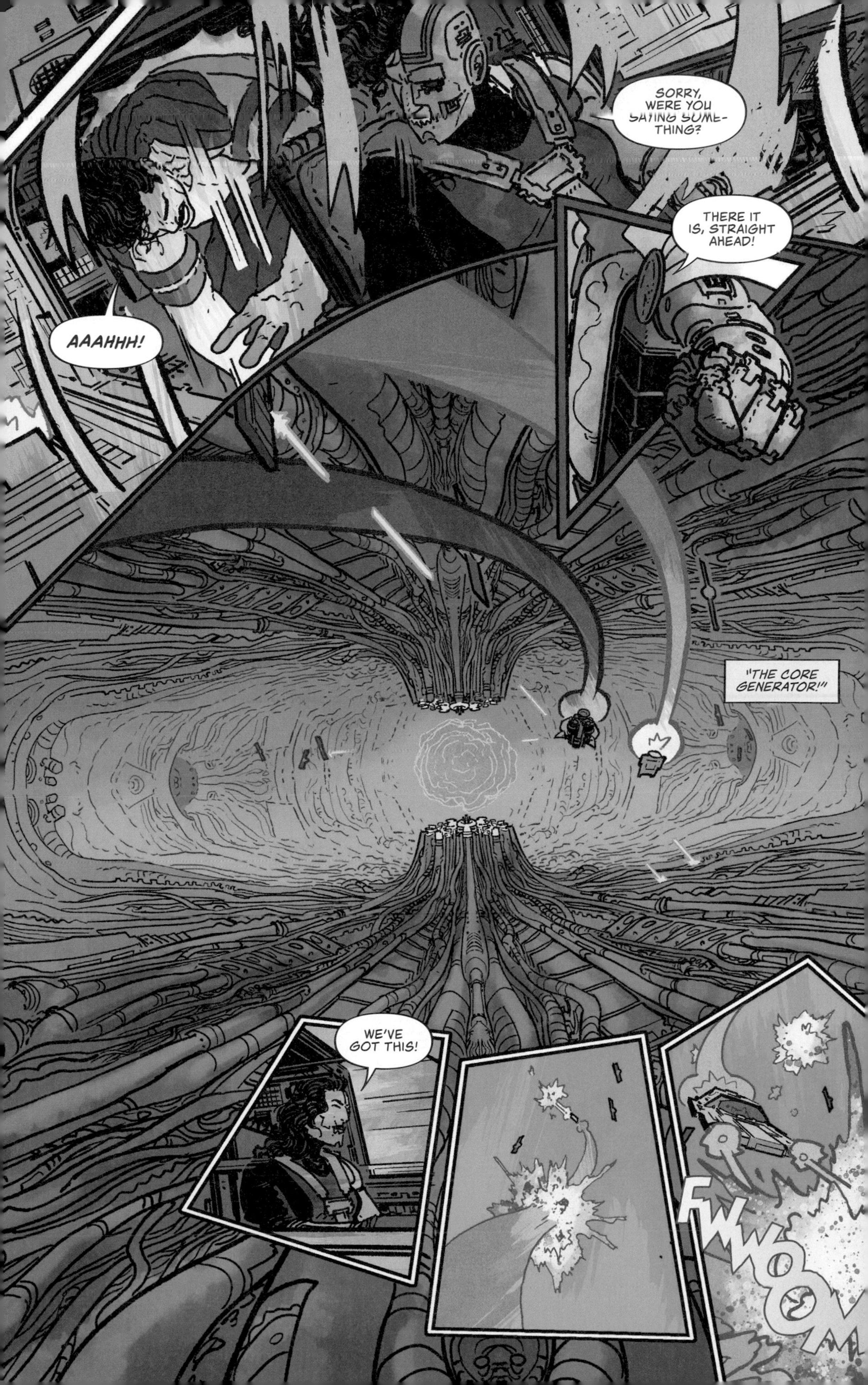
SORRY, WERE YOU SAYING SOME-THING?
AAAHHH!
THERE IT IS, STRAIGHT AHEAD!
"THE CORE GENERATOR!"
WE'VE GOT THIS!
FWWOOOM

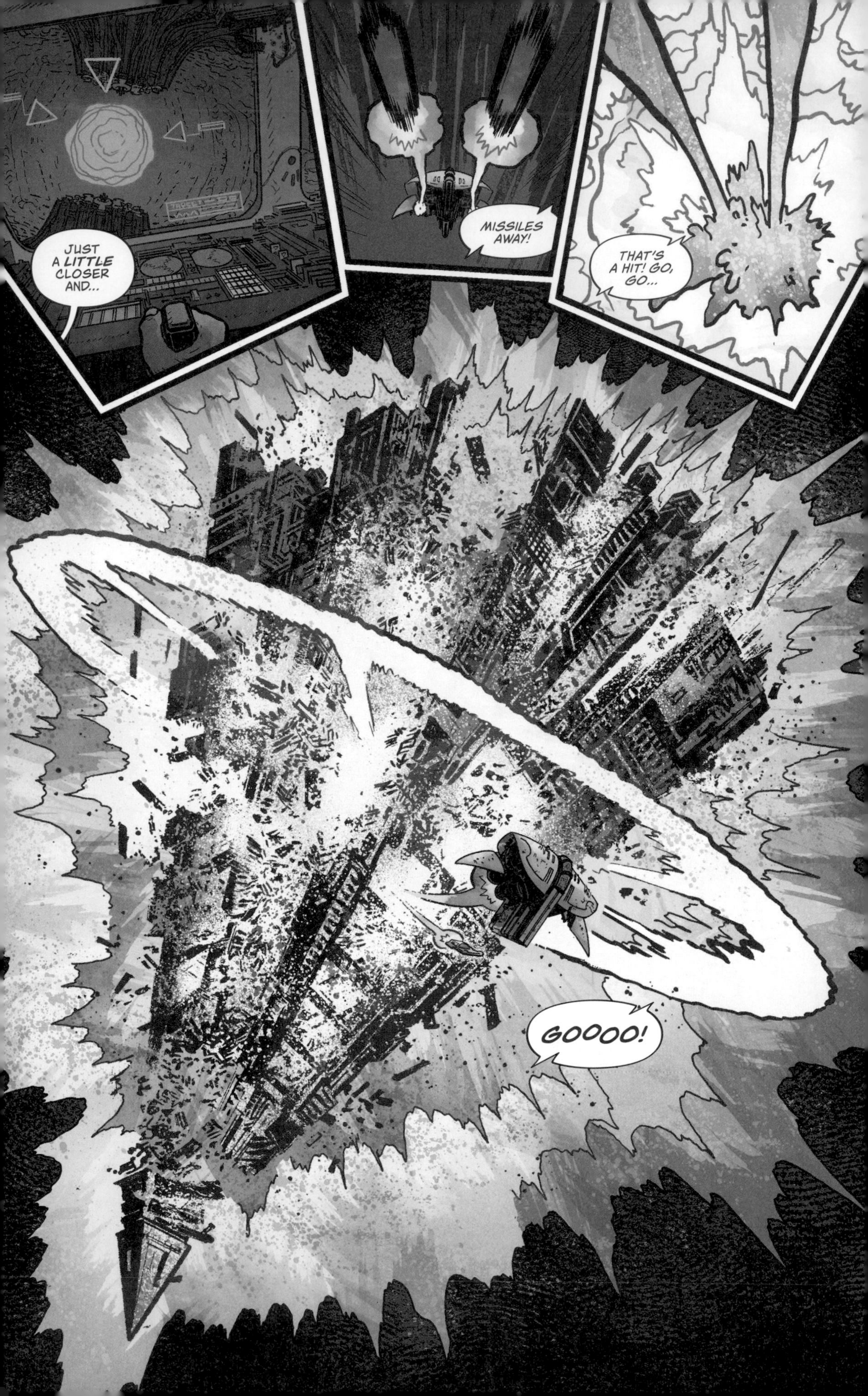
JUST A LITTLE CLOSER AND...
MISSILES AWAY!
THAT'S A HIT! GO, GO...
GOOOO!

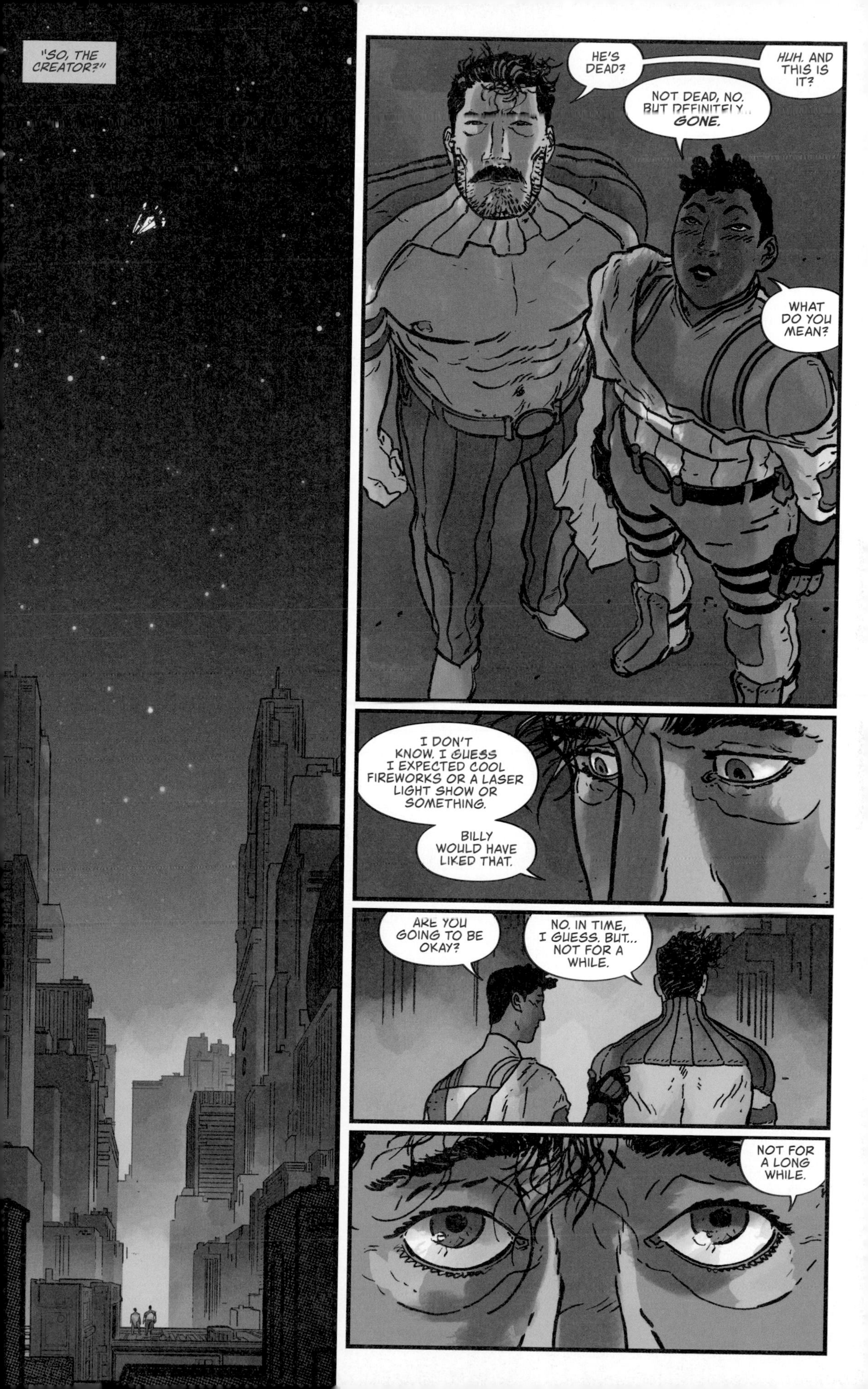
"SO, THE CREATOR?"
HE'S DEAD?
HUH. AND THIS IS IT?
NOT DEAD, NO. BUT DEFINITELY... GONE.
WHAT DO YOU MEAN?
I DON'T KNOW. I GUESS I EXPECTED COOL FIREWORKS OR A LASER LIGHT SHOW OR SOMETHING.
BILLY WOULD HAVE LIKED THAT.
ARE YOU GOING TO BE OKAY?
NO. IN TIME, I GUESS. BUT... NOT FOR A WHILE.
NOT FOR A LONG WHILE.

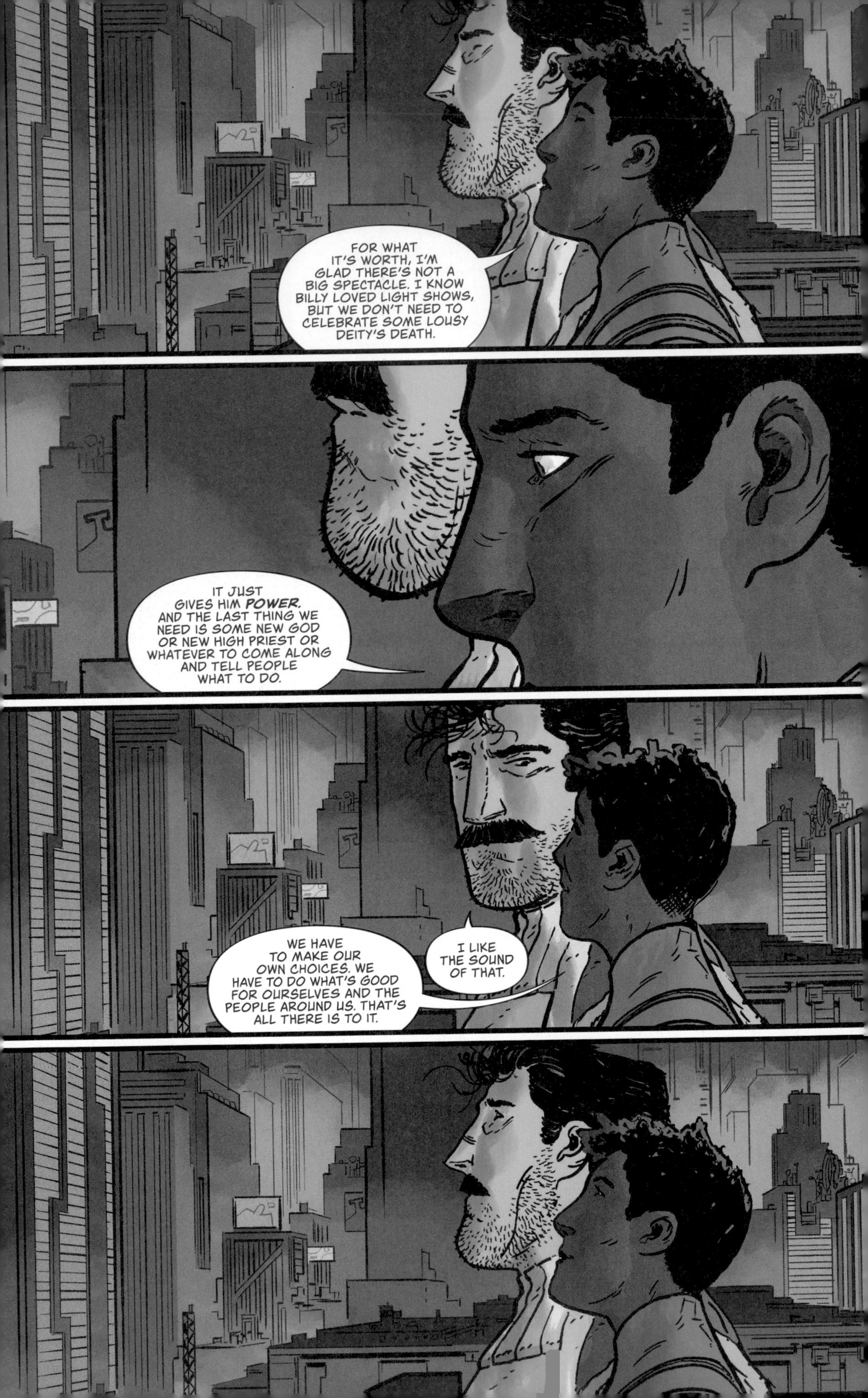

FOR WHAT IT'S WORTH, I'M GLAD THERE'S NOT A BIG SPECTACLE. I KNOW BILLY LOVED LIGHT SHOWS, BUT WE DON'T NEED TO CELEBRATE SOME LOUSY DEITY'S DEATH.
IT JUST GIVES HIM *POWER.* AND THE LAST THING WE NEED IS SOME NEW GOD OR NEW HIGH PRIEST OR WHATEVER TO COME ALONG AND TELL PEOPLE WHAT TO DO.
WE HAVE TO MAKE OUR OWN CHOICES. WE HAVE TO DO WHAT'S GOOD FOR OURSELVES AND THE PEOPLE AROUND US. THAT'S ALL THERE IS TO IT.
I LIKE THE SOUND OF THAT.

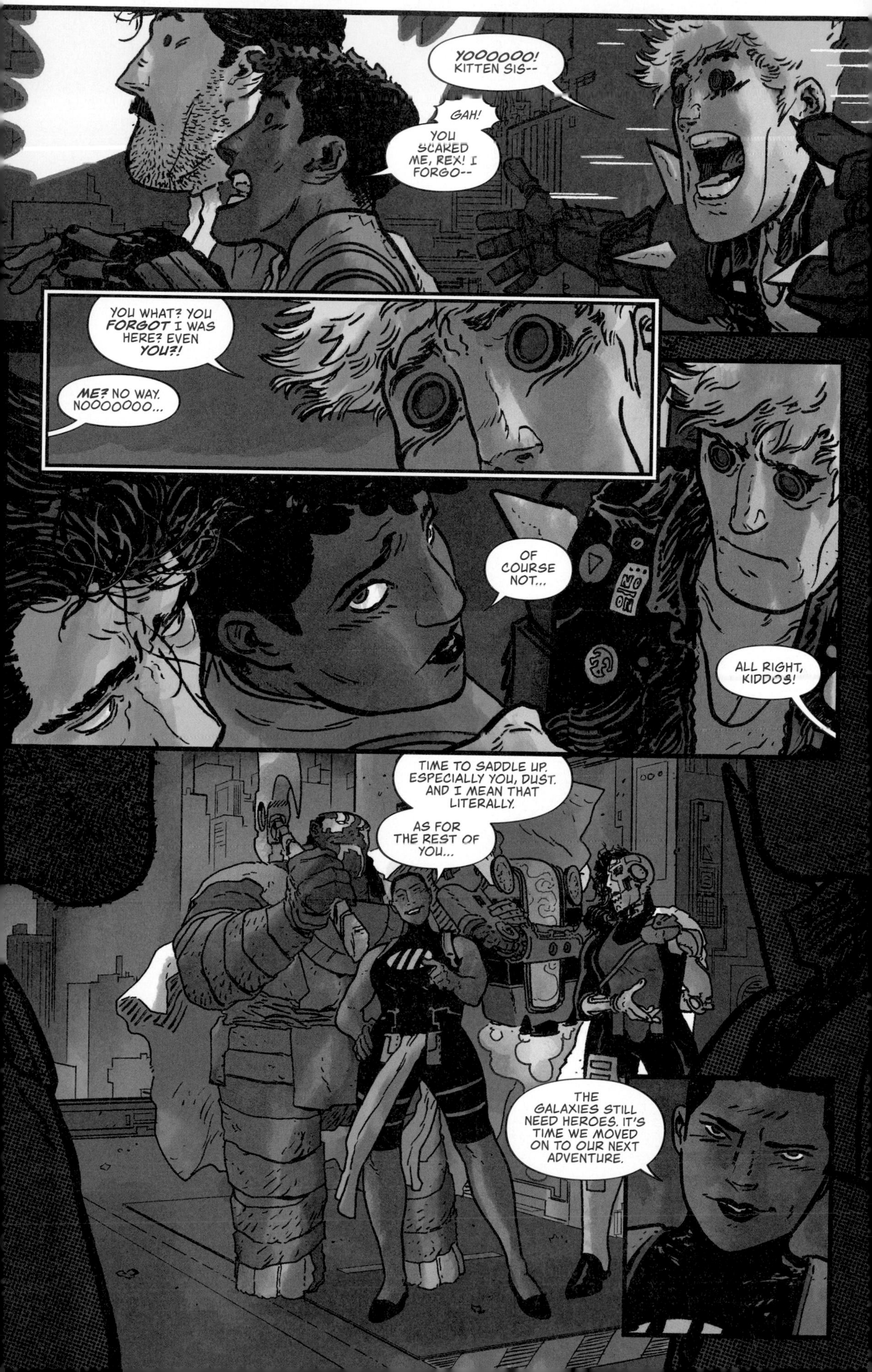
YOOOOOO! KITTEN SIS--
GAH!
YOU SCARED ME, REX! I FORGO--
YOU WHAT? YOU FORGOT I WAS HERE? EVEN YOU?!
ME? NO WAY. NOOOOOOO...
OF COURSE NOT...
ALL RIGHT, KIDDOS!
TIME TO SADDLE UP. ESPECIALLY YOU, DUST. AND I MEAN THAT LITERALLY.
AS FOR THE REST OF YOU...
THE GALAXIES STILL NEED HEROES. IT'S TIME WE MOVED ON TO OUR NEXT ADVENTURE.

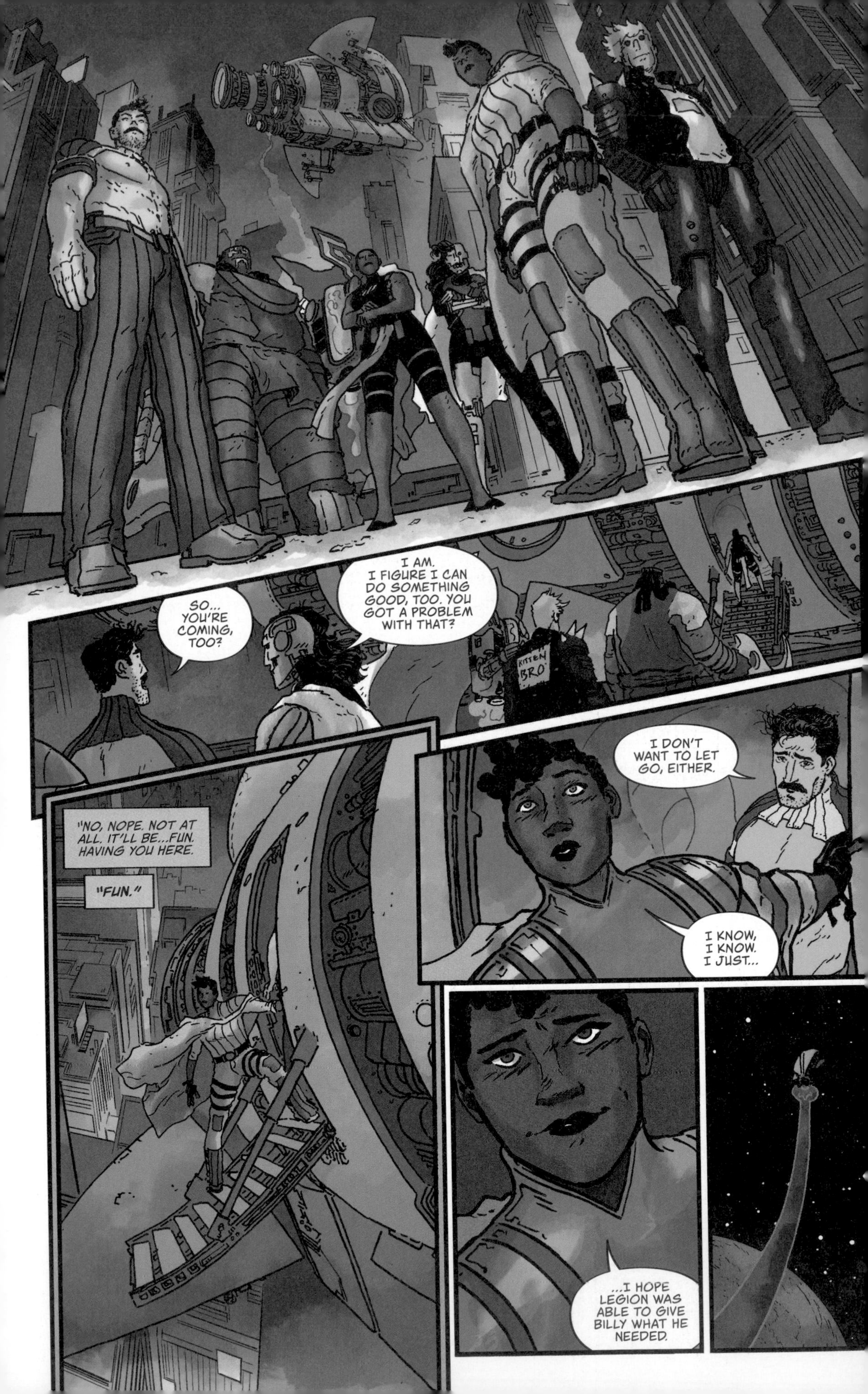
SO... YOU'RE COMING, TOO?
I AM. I FIGURE I CAN DO SOMETHING GOOD, TOO. YOU GOT A PROBLEM WITH THAT?
KITTEN BRO
"NO, NOPE. NOT AT ALL. IT'LL BE...FUN. HAVING YOU HERE.
"FUN."
I DON'T WANT TO LET GO, EITHER.
I KNOW, I KNOW. I JUST...
...I HOPE LEGION WAS ABLE TO GIVE BILLY WHAT HE NEEDED.

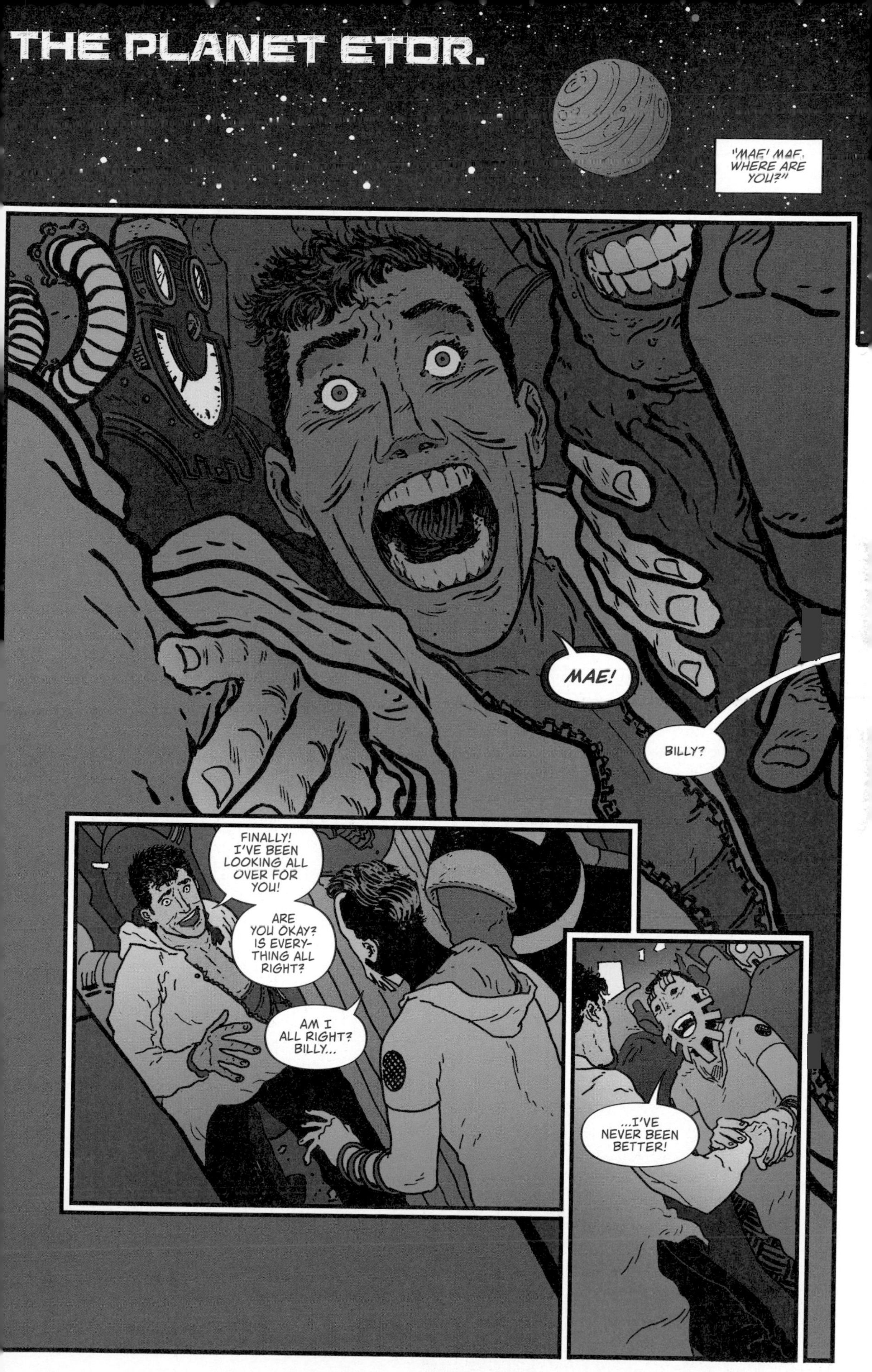
THE PLANET ETOR.
"MAE! MAE, WHERE ARE YOU?"
MAE!
BILLY?
FINALLY! I'VE BEEN LOOKING ALL OVER FOR YOU!
ARE YOU OKAY? IS EVERY-THING ALL RIGHT?
AM I ALL RIGHT? BILLY...
...I'VE NEVER BEEN BETTER!

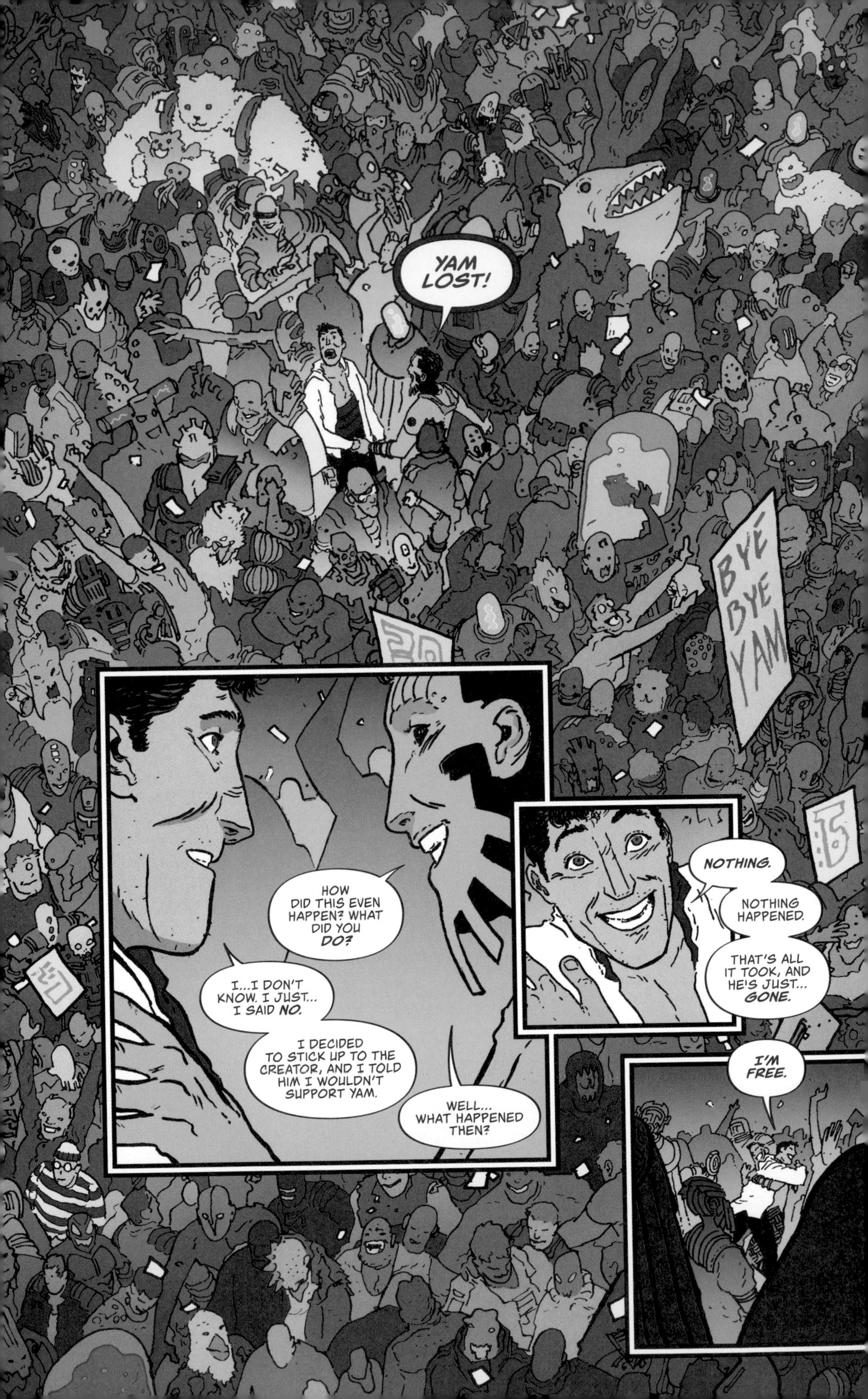
YAM LOST!
BYE BYE YAM
HOW DID THIS EVEN HAPPEN? WHAT DID YOU DO?
I...I DON'T KNOW. I JUST... I SAID NO.
I DECIDED TO STICK UP TO THE CREATOR, AND I TOLD HIM I WOULDN'T SUPPORT YAM.
WELL... WHAT HAPPENED THEN?
NOTHING.
NOTHING HAPPENED.
THAT'S ALL IT TOOK, AND HE'S JUST... GONE.
I'M FREE.

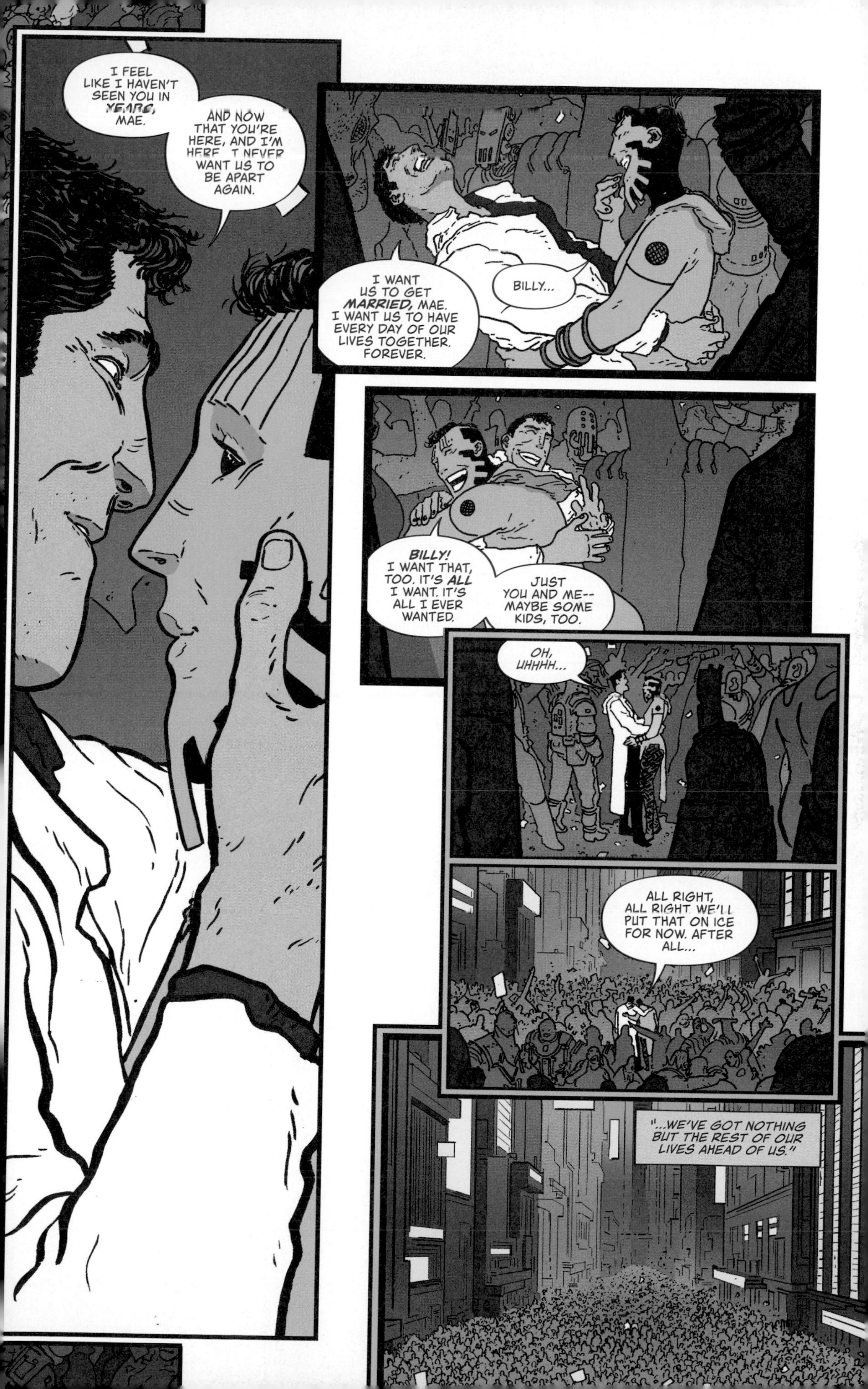
I FEEL LIKE I HAVEN'T SEEN YOU IN YEARS, MAE.
AND NOW THAT YOU'RE HERE, AND I'M HERE, I NEVER WANT US TO BE APART AGAIN.
I WANT US TO GET MARRIED, MAE. I WANT US TO HAVE EVERY DAY OF OUR LIVES TOGETHER. FOREVER.
BILLY...
BILLY! I WANT THAT, TOO. IT'S ALL I WANT. IT'S ALL I EVER WANTED.
JUST YOU AND ME-- MAYBE SOME KIDS, TOO.
OH, UHHHH...
ALL RIGHT, ALL RIGHT. WE'LL PUT THAT ON ICE FOR NOW. AFTER ALL...
"...WE'VE GOT NOTHING BUT THE REST OF OUR LIVES AHEAD OF US."

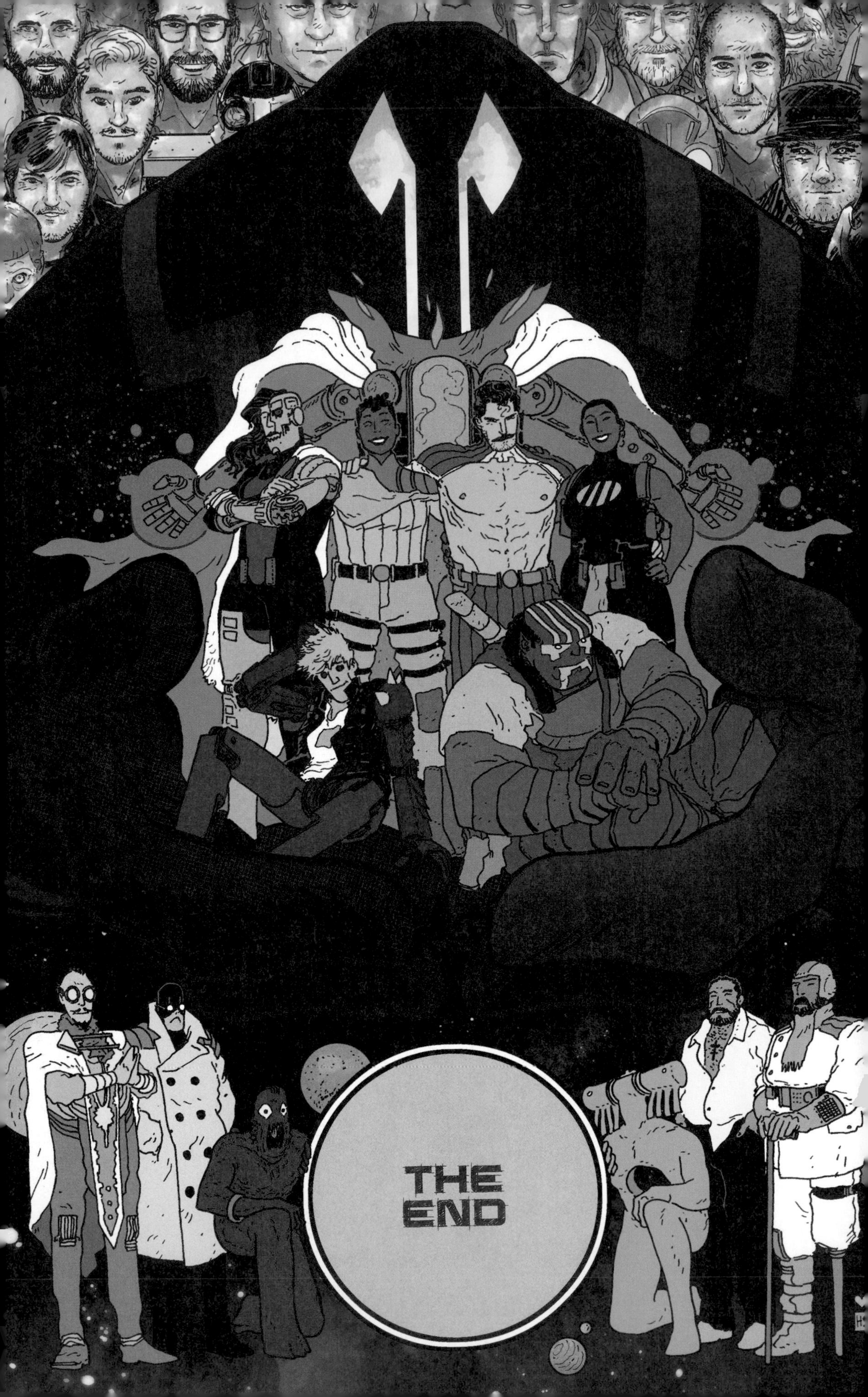
THE
END

COVER GALLERY

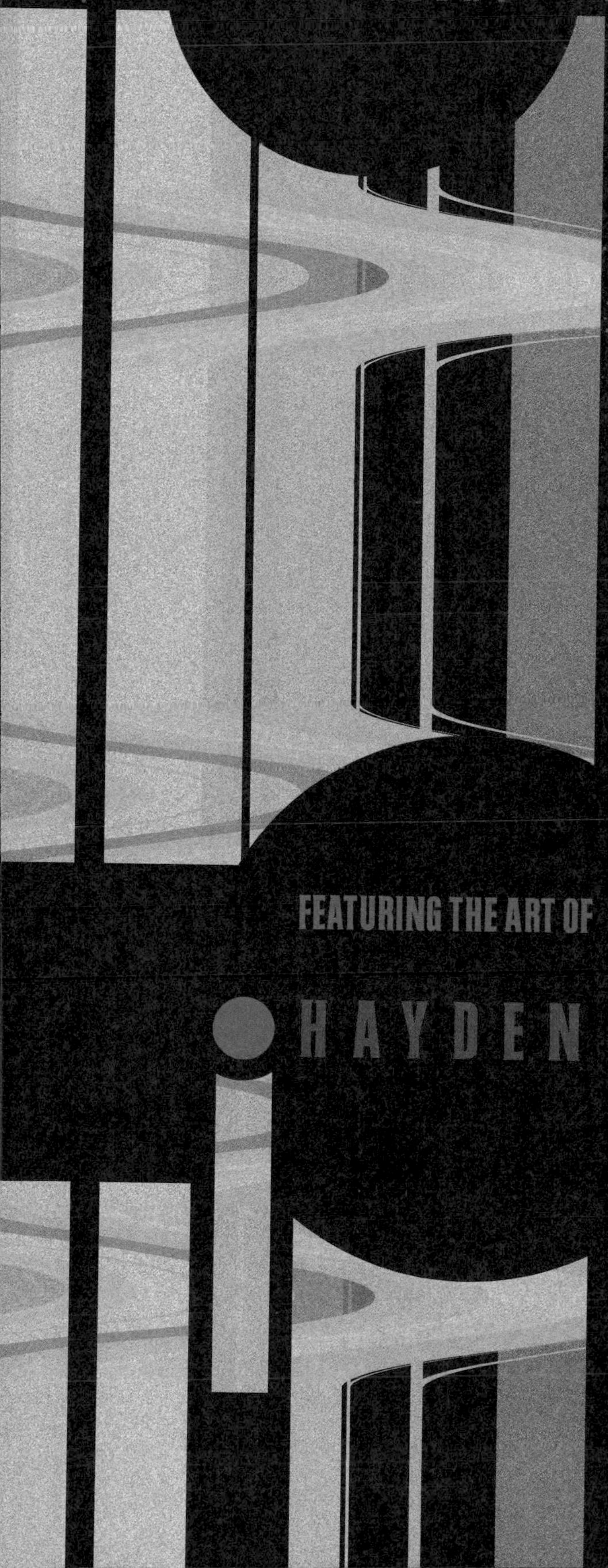

FEATURING THE ART OF

HAYDEN SHERMA

COVER ISSUE 21 // HAYDEN SHERMAN

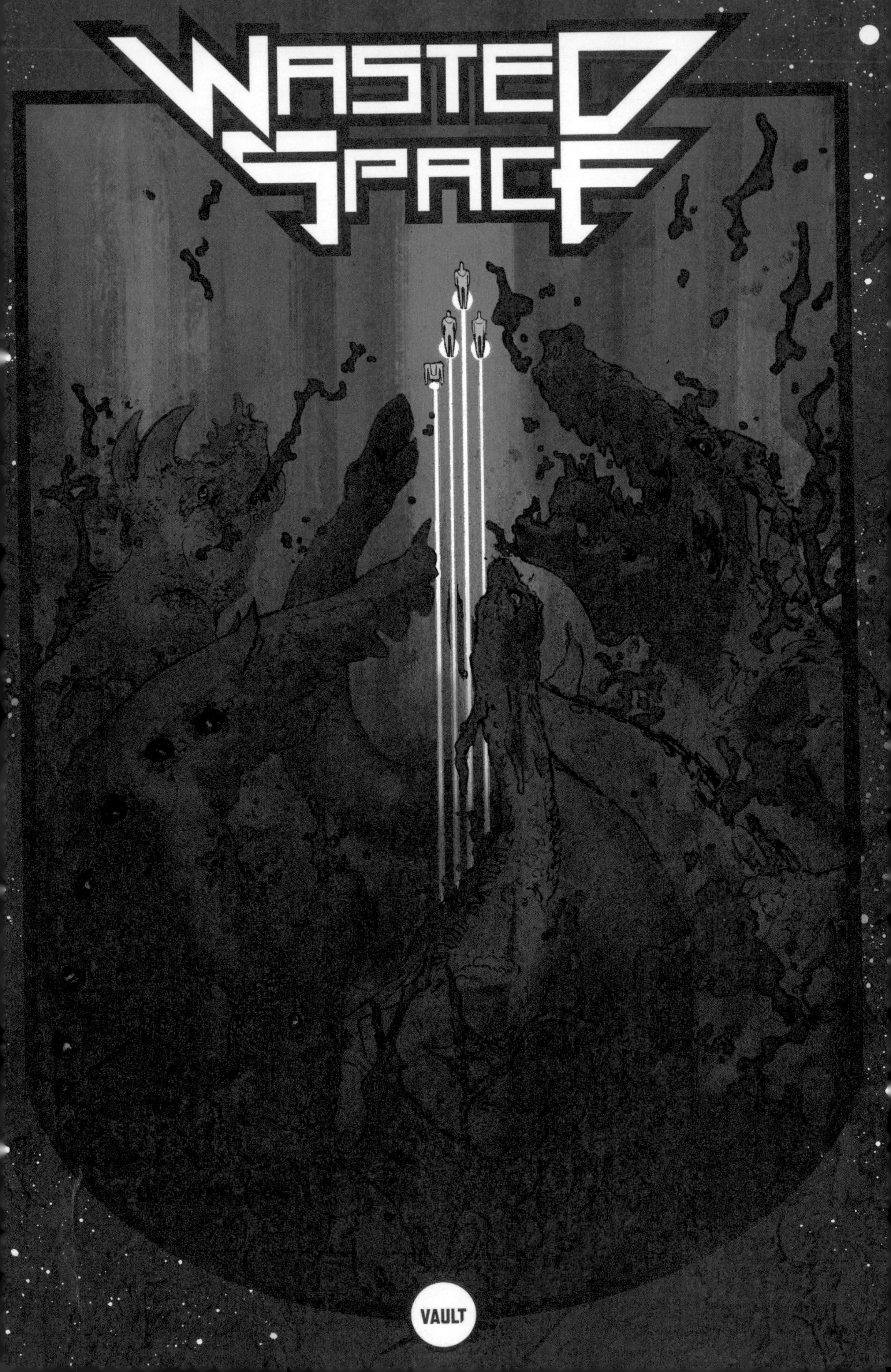

WASTED SPACE
VAULT

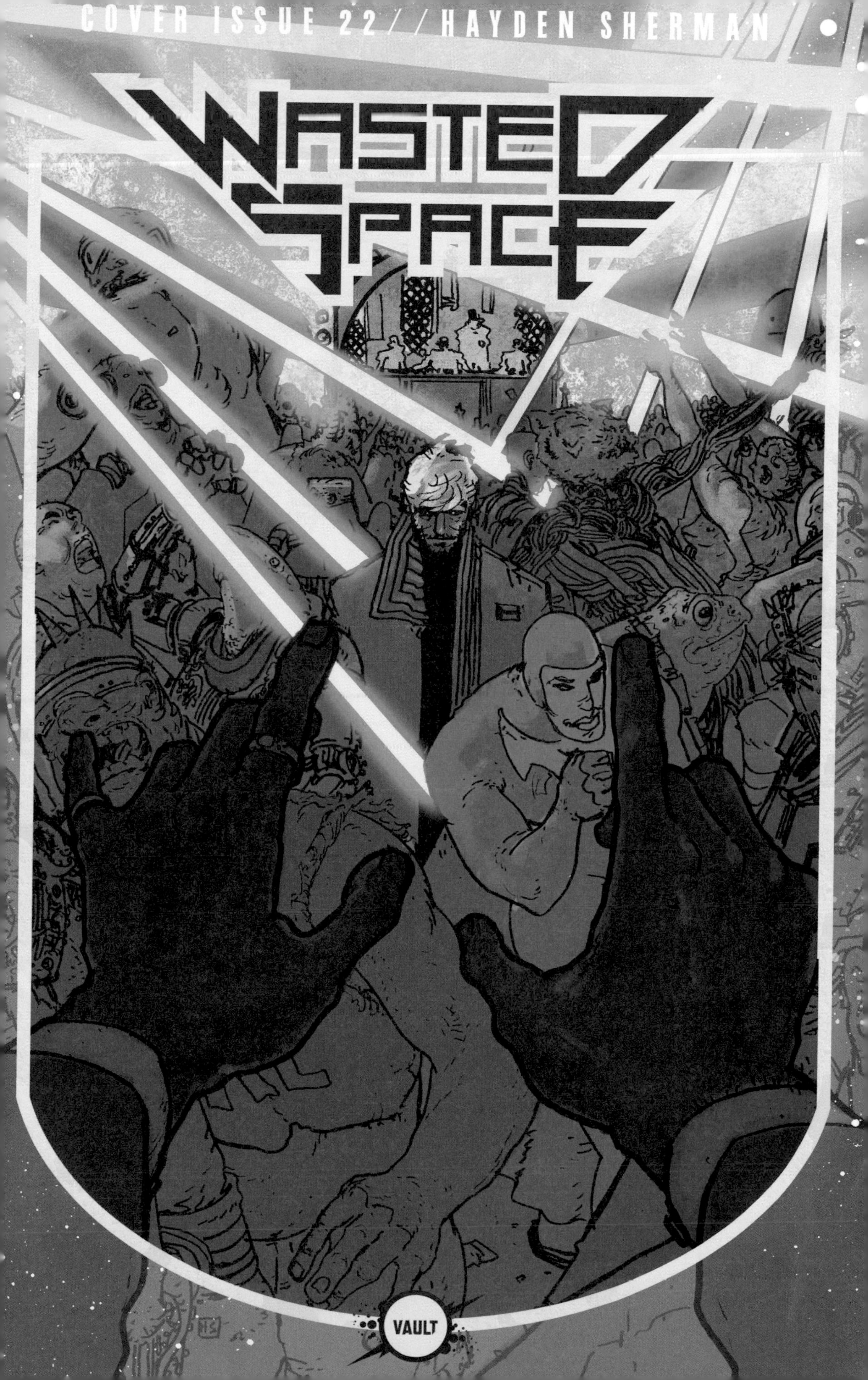
COVER ISSUE 22 / / HAYDEN SHERMAN
WASTED SPACE
VAULT

COVER ISSUE 23 / / HAYDEN SHERMAN

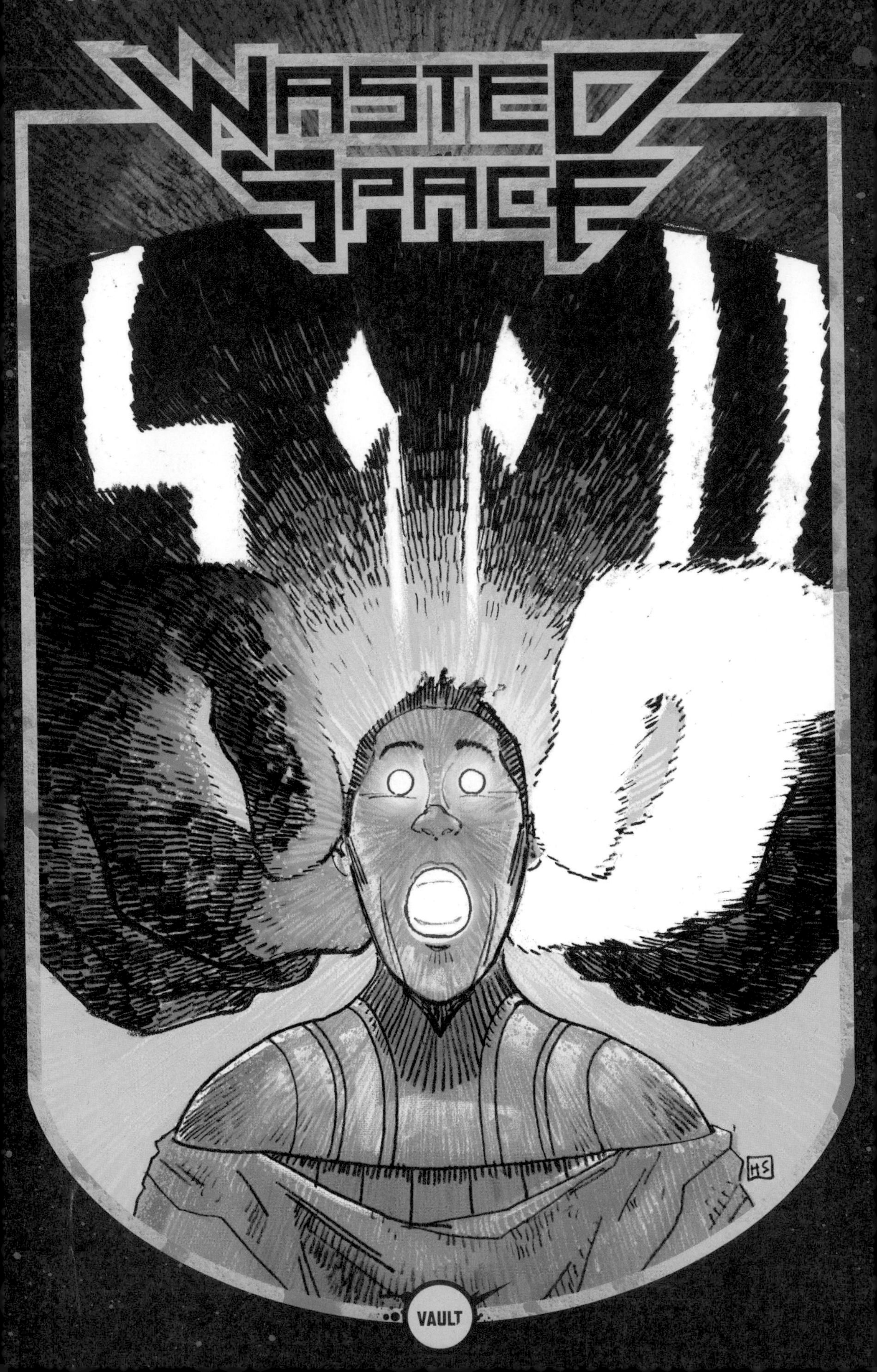
WASTED SPACE
HS
VAULT

COVER ISSUE 24//HAYDEN SHERMAN

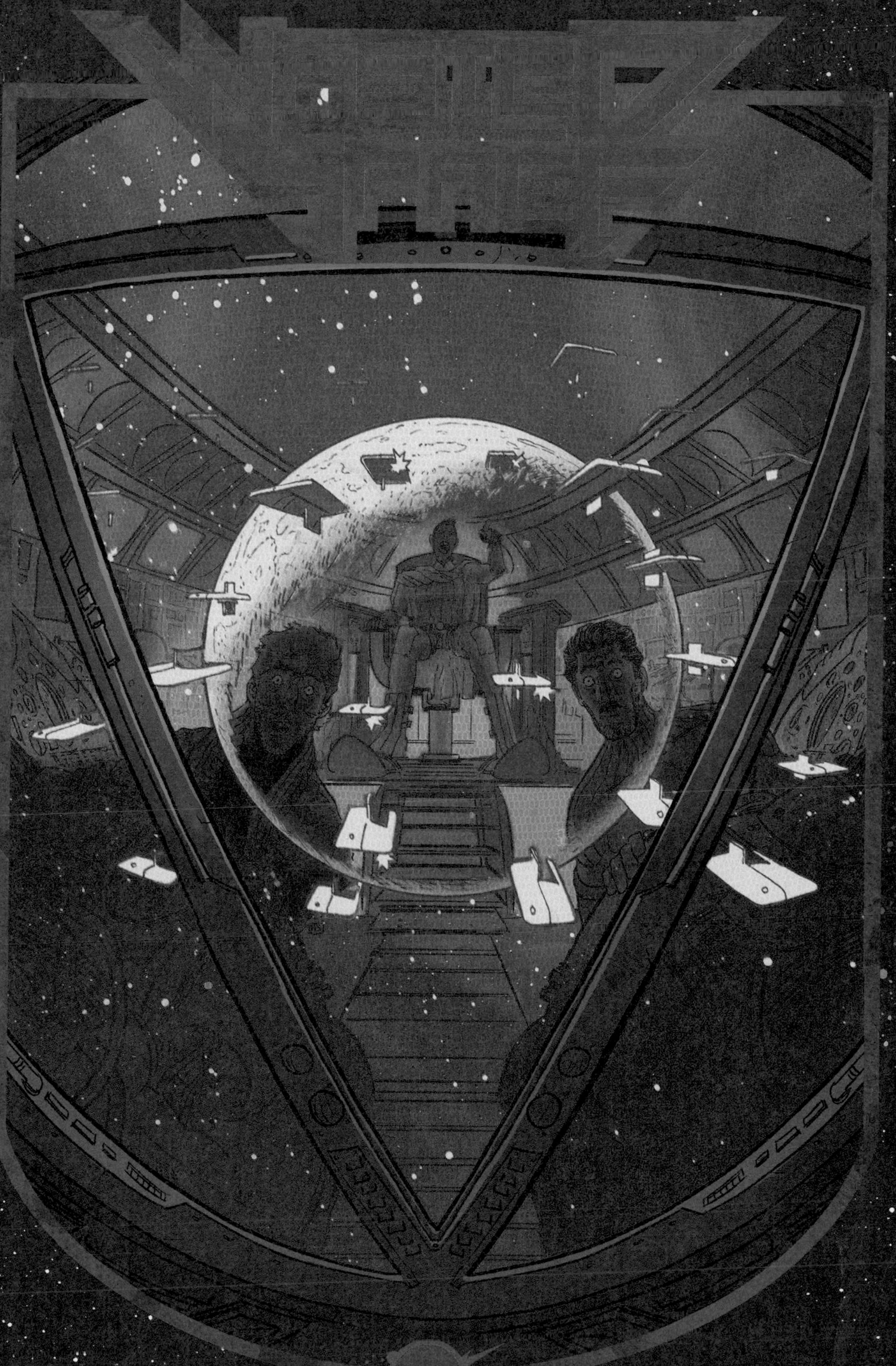

COVER ISSUE 25//HAYDEN SHERMAN

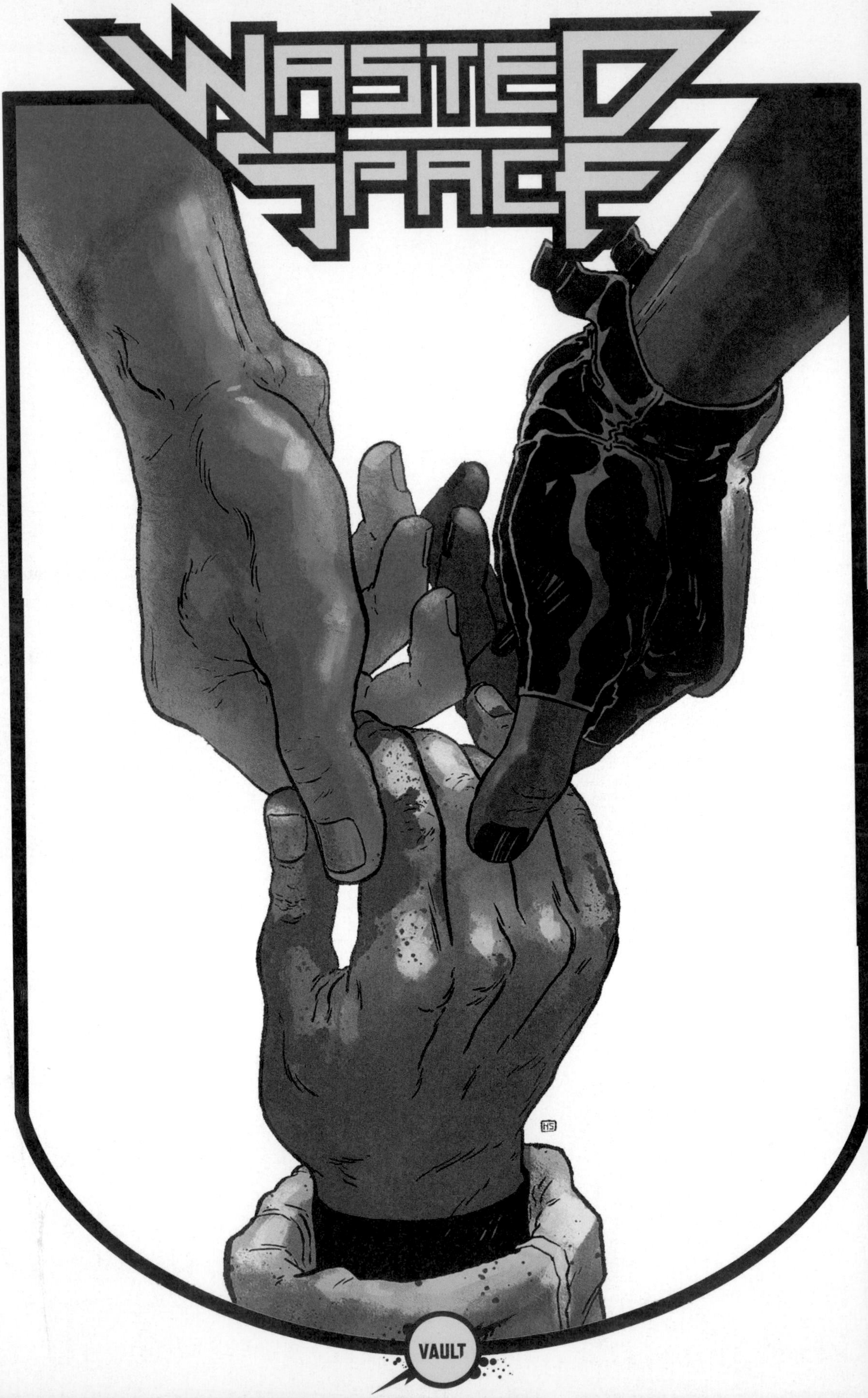

WASTED SPACE
HS
VAULT

TO THE RETAILERS, READERS, AND EVERYONE ELSE
WHO HAS SUPPORTED WASTED SPACE...

WE ARE SO TRULY GRATEFUL THAT YOU
JOINED US ON THIS RIDE.

FROM THE ENTIRE CREATIVE TEAM,

THANK YOU.

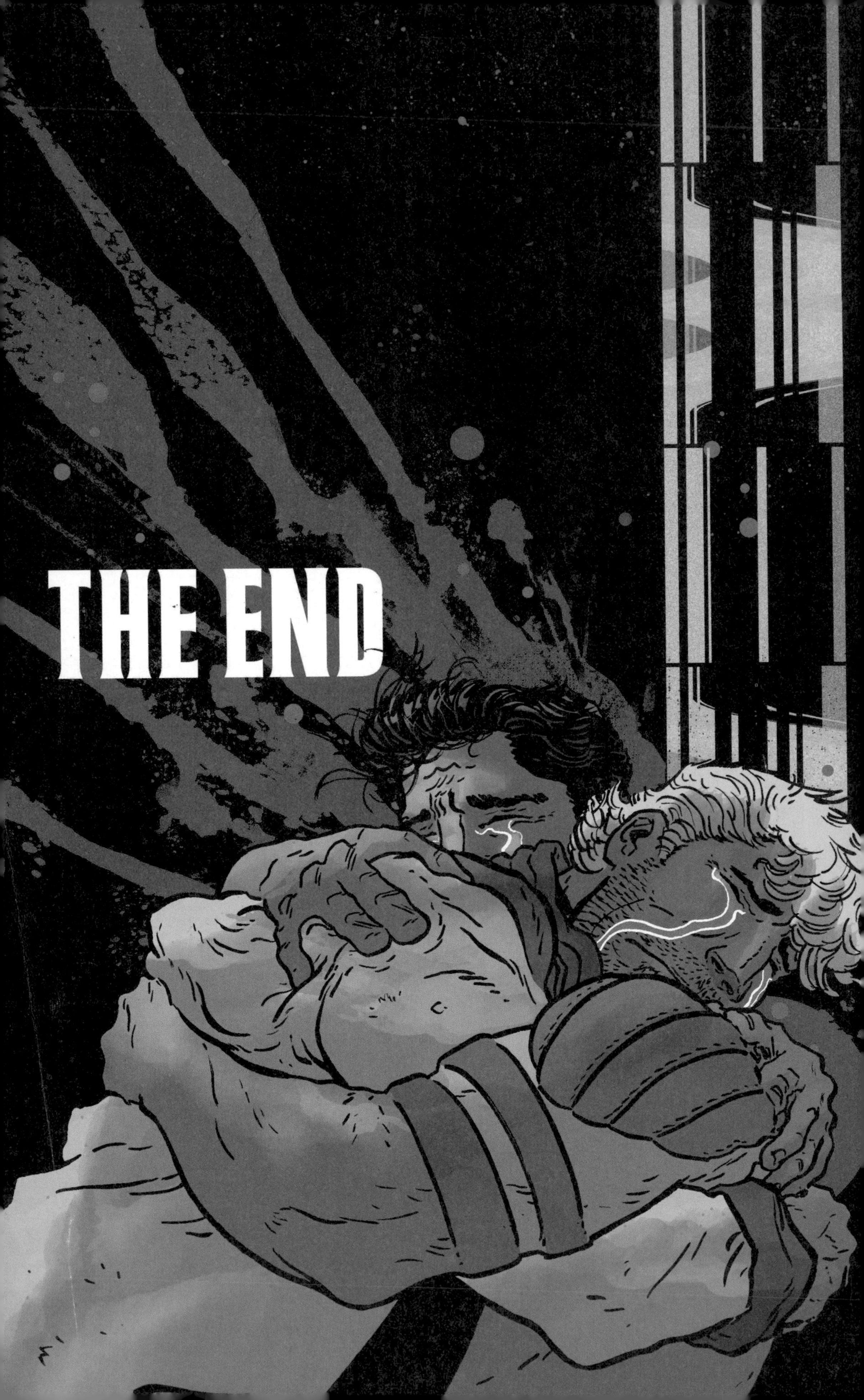
THE END